PRAISE FOR

WONDER WHEN YOU'LL MISS ME

"Amanda Davis writes prose that is precise, elegant, and strong, and she tells a story that is at once harrowing and, strangely, filled with adventure."

— MICHAEL CHABON, author of
Summerland

"Amanda Davis writes gently, even poetically, about extraordinary brutality. She has a distinctively creepy, even noirish, sensibility."

— *New York Times Book Review*

"I couldn't put it down.... I LOVED it. I don't like anything, either. It's brilliant, sad, funny, amazing, original, and a complete and utter page-turner."

— KATE CHRISTENSEN, author of
Jeremy Thrane and *In the Drink*

"[A] wonderful high-wire act." — *Vanity Fair*

"This book is a circus *Pygmalion*—a spectacular tale of injury, heartbreak, and metamorphosis."

— JONATHAN AMES, author of
The Extra Man

"[An] auspicious debut novel. Davis revitalizes the . . . circus motif with her tensely lyrical prose and full-bodied characterizations."

— *Publishers Weekly*

"At the end of this rich and satisfying novel . . . I did not want to leave."
—MICHELLE CHALFOUN, author of
Roustabout and *The Width of the Sea*

"Stunning. . . . This is an astonishing debut: dark, disturbing, and fiercely openhearted."
—*Booklist*

"With a whirl of images, plunges of despair, and leaps of hope, this book is the best sort of literary amusement park ride—a carousel for the senses, and a roller-coaster ride for the heart."
—JUDY BUDNITZ, author of
If I Told You Once and *Flying Leap*

"The real pleasures of this wise and emotionally resonant novel come . . . from the authenticity of its voice."
—*Time Out* (New York)

"Davis has created a lucid, compelling page-turner that defies categorization. This is a stunning novel and Faith's story is uncomfortably tragic, brutally honest, and beautifully rendered. . . . *Wonder When You'll Miss Me* is, quite simply, a great novel."
—Bookreporter.com

Michael Darter

ABOUT THE AUTHOR

AMANDA DAVIS's previous work includes the story collection *Circling the Drain*. A talented, insightful, and
acclaimed young writer, Ms. Davis died in March 2003.
Wonder When You'll Miss Me was her first novel.

Wonder When You'll Miss Me

Also by the Author

Circling the Drain

WONDER WHEN YOU'LL MISS ME

A Novel

AMANDA DAVIS

Perennial
An Imprint of HarperCollins*Publishers*

Grateful acknowledgment is made to reprint the excerpts from:

"Leaving on a Jet Plane," words and music by John Denver. Copyright © 1967; renewed 1995 Cherry Lane Music Publishing Company, Inc. International copyright secured. All rights reserved.

"My Dixie Darling" by A. P. Carter. Copyright © 1957 by Peer International Corporation. Copyright renewed. Used by permission. All rights reserved.

A hardcover edition of this book was published in 2003 by William Morrow, an imprint of HarperCollins Publishers.

HarperCollins books may be purchased for educational, business, or sales promotional use. For information please write: Special Markets Department, HarperCollins Publishers Inc., 10 East 53rd Street, New York, NY 10022.

First Perennial edition published 2004.

Designed by Bernard Klein

The Library of Congress has catalogued the hardcover edition as follows:

Davis, Amanda.
Wonder when you'll miss me / Amanda Davis. — 1st ed.
p. cm.
ISBN 0-688-16781-0
1. Runaway teenagers—Fiction. 2. Teenage girls—Fiction. 3. Rape victims—Fiction. 4. Weight loss—Fiction. 5. Revenge—Fiction. 6. Circus—Fiction. I. Title.

PS3554.A9314 W66 2003
813'.54—dc21   2002024118

ISBN 0-06-053426-5 (pbk.)

04 05 06 07 08 ❖/RRD 10 9 8 7 6 5 4 3 2 1

For my parents,
Jim and Francie Davis

And I was yet aware that this was only a moment, that the world waited outside, as hungry as a tiger, and that trouble stretched above us, longer than the sky.

—James Baldwin

WONDER WHEN YOU'LL MISS ME

ONE

At school I was careful not to look like I watched everything, but I did. The fat girl fell into step beside me. She had a handful of gumdrops and sugar on her chin.

"There are all kinds of anger," she said. "Some kinds are just more useful than others."

A locker slammed behind us. I tried not to speak too loudly, because no one except me saw her. "I'm not angry," I whispered.

"Saying you're not angry is one kind," she said. "Not very useful at all, though."

I ignored her and brushed hair out of my eyes. There were days when she was a comfort and days when she was a nightmare. I had yet to determine what kind of day this would be.

We made our way outside. The fat girl had stringy brown hair and wore a blue blouse that was spotted and stained. She sucked on a Fudgsicle as though the autumn day was blissful and warm, but I was freezing. We pressed ourselves against the courtyard wall to watch the crowd file by. When I turned my head she followed my gaze and patted my shoulder.

"Don't get your hopes up, Faith," she said. "Sweetie, I'm telling you, that is never going to work out."

She was talking about Tony Giobambera, who had dark curly hair all over his body and smiled with his mouth but not with his eyes; who walked slowly, like a man with a secret.

I said, "You never know."

She said, "Actually, I do know." Then she sucked off a big piece of chocolate.

Tony Giobambera settled on his rock and lit a cigarette. I followed the fat girl to a place where we could watch him. He smoked like the cigarette was an extension of his ropey arm and rough hand. When he leaned back and blew a stream into the sky, I watched the pout of his lips, the black curl that fell over one eye. Then Tony Giobambera smiled in our direction and I wanted to disappear.

"Nothing like a little attention to send you over the edge," the fat girl said.

"What would *you* do?" I said. "I mean I don't think you'd do anything different."

"I'd think about getting even," she said. "I'd think about making something happen."

Instead I found a better place on the grass where I could see him but pretend to stare off into space, thinking about more important things than how much I would give up just to have Tony Giobambera run his finger along my cheek and my throat again.

~~~

It was after what I did, the long summer after I'd shed myself completely and was prepared to come back to school like a whole new person, only inside it was still me. It was at an end-of-the-summer party a week before school started. I'd walked there from my house and the Carolina night was humid and heavy. I sang softly to myself, thinking of how different I looked, of what it would be like to walk into a party in normal-person clothes bought from a normal store.

I smoothed the front of my new sleeveless green blouse. I could hear the party behind the big white door. I took a deep breath and rang the bell, but nothing happened.

I leaned over a little and through the windows I saw people draped over couches and moving in the dark. I rang the bell again, then tried the door. It was open.

Inside, Led Zeppelin blasted from the stereo. A guy and a girl curled up together in the corner of the foyer. In the living room, people stood in clumps along the wall or splayed themselves over couches and chairs. The house rang with noise. I walked down a hallway. I put my hands in my pockets, then took them out again.

In the kitchen I found a beer but didn't open it. The smell of pot drifted up the stairs from the basement. A few muscled guys and a pale, fragile-looking girl sat around the kitchen table flipping quarters into a glass. They slurred their words, laughing loudly and hitting each other in the back of the head when a quarter missed the cup. *Drink, drink, drink!* they chanted. The girl smoked a cigarette with a glazed smile. One guy glanced up at me, but looked away quickly. I blushed anyway.

I wandered downstairs to the basement, where I recognized a few people from last year's English class. They sat in a circle around a reedy guy with long blond hair and a red bong, hanging on every word he had to say. He told a complicated story, something involving a car and the police, but I couldn't follow it. Every so often one of the girls shook her head. "Fuck," she said, and ran her tongue over her braces. "Holy fuck."

I went back upstairs and walked from room to room waiting for someone to notice the new me, but no one seemed to. Disappointment pushed me outside. I tripped my way down wooden stairs, away from the bright lights of the house toward the small latticed huddle of a gazebo. Inside there was a bench and I sat, slapping away mosquitoes, with a tightness in my chest that made me want to scream. How could everything change so much and stay exactly the same?

I'd lost forty-eight pounds and my skin had mostly cleared up. I'd missed a whole semester of school and disappeared for seven months. It seemed like no one had even noticed I was gone.

I pulled my knees to my chest and picked at the vines that climbed the trellis overhead, ripping off leaves and stripping them down to their veins. I was wondering how I would possibly survive the whole next year, when Andrea Dutton came stumbling out of the trees. Her clothes were all twisted and covered in pine needles. A minute later, out stepped Tony Giobambera, zipping up his pants and smiling. He caught up to her and threw his arm around her shoulders and they stumbled in my direction.

Andrea Dutton stopped when she saw me and swayed back and forth. Her blond hair had a flat place with a leaf in it and her mascara was smeared in black gashes across her cheeks. She leaned over to peer at me, then straightened up and gave a wheezy little laugh.

"You used to be that really fat chick," she said, her words thick and sloppy. My face burned but I didn't say anything.

Tony Giobambera rolled his eyes. "Andrea, you're a real sweetheart, huh?"

"Shut up, you pig. You don't even recognize her."

"Yeah I do," he said slowly. "You're Faith something, right?" He reached out with one strong hand and traced the outline of my cheek. "You look great," he said, and winked. "Really."

Andrea's eyes were dim. She pointed a finger at me, swaying again. "I heard about what you did."

I pressed against the grid of the gazebo and concentrated on the sounds of crickets, on the dull hum of the party, on the smell of Tony Giobambera, all smoky and male.

Andrea yanked him by the arm so that he lurched towards her. "Let's go."

Tony looked at me, smiled, and all the tightness in me dissolved into warmth. Then he threw his arm around Andrea's shoulders again, and led her away from the gazebo and up the hill towards everyone else.

I'd been holding my breath. When I exhaled the world seemed to settle. It was quieter, the sounds of the party distant and dull. I stayed there until my limbs were stiff and ached from not moving. Still I felt the thin line of his touch.

~~~

In school the fat girl sat behind me in every class.

In American history she sat in Andrea Dutton's old seat because three weeks earlier, right after the party, Andrea Dutton had flipped her car and ended up in the hospital in a coma and everybody said what a tragedy it was.

In math I sat behind Missy Groski. In English it was Jenny Sims. In art, we could sit wherever we wanted, which meant I ended up with the other kids no one wanted to be near: ashy, asthmatic Bobby Thomson, Lester Fine, who was anything but, and Marny Fergus, whose nose never stopped running. The fat girl stood nearby.

"Nice," she said sometimes when I drew something that pleased her. Mostly she whispered about everybody else.

"Simon has a tiny prick," she said. "Elizabeth Martin stuffs her bra. Billy Gustav draws like he's blind."

Art was the only subject I seemed to absorb, the only place I didn't feel myself falling. With most of my homework I turned to the appropriate page and willed myself to become curious, but the words blurred and then puddled, running in rivulets off the paper and onto the floor, leaving behind a damp drained page of nothing.

It all sounded wrong. Instructions I read or heard, things my teachers went over on the board, all of it played at the wrong speed in my head so it sounded jumbled and scratchy. Nothing made sense. In math the numbers dipped and swayed like flirtatious birds, landing within reach then taking off again so I couldn't follow even the simplest line of thought.

It was like I'd left something behind at Berrybrook besides the forty-eight pounds and seven months I'd lost. Some invisible part of my brain forgotten on a shelf somewhere, some key ingredient to navigating the world abandoned in that stupid Tudor building on that stupid green hill. I didn't even know how to look for what was gone, how to recognize it if I found it. How to ask for help.

"They're all morons," the fat girl said about my classmates. She was enormous and rubbery, impossible to ignore. "Losers. You're better than every one of them."

But I didn't want to be better than anyone. I just wanted to be me. And, yes, I wanted to show up, to be noticed. But inside some of me still wanted desperately to disappear. Of course that's what had gotten me to Berry-brook in the first place: trying to disappear.

~~~

I did it on a clear day, just before Christmas. I had thought about it con-stantly and planned a little, but when it came right down to it, I didn't wake up that morning with an idea of what would happen or when I would know. I just knew. The light inside me had flickered and gone out.

I took lots of pills, beautiful pills of all colors. I had saved them for months beforehand, scouring medicine cabinets anywhere I went to add to the stash hidden deep in my closet. After a while I didn't even bother reading labels. What mattered to me was the way they looked together, like colored pebbles, and the slippery way they felt when I reached deep in the jar and let them run through my fingers. I saved up. I waited for just the right moment to swallow so much possibility.

And it came.

I didn't dress up for it. I just took that jar from its hiding place and brought it into bed with me. I had a huge glass of water and I dumped some of the pills into it and swished them around. Others I dry-swallowed one at a time, small and large, white and colored. They made me gag, made my eyes tear, but I washed them down with my cloudy water, more and more and more. I remember the jar nearly half empty. I remember the world oozing and swelling. I remember feeling hopeful.

~~~

I first met the fat girl in the bathroom of a movie theater on the day I heard about Andrea Dutton's car accident. It was the Sunday before school started, four days after the party. I was by myself and two girls I didn't recognize were teasing their hair and talking when I walked in. One girl said to the other, "Did you hear about Andrea Dutton?"

"No," the other girl said. "What?"

"Coma," the first girl said. "Flipped her car and shit. Can you believe it?"

"Jeez," said the second girl, then paused to light a cigarette. "And she was so popular."

By now I was safely in a far stall, but I could smell the smoke. "Who *was* that?" I heard. Maybe she pointed.

"I dunno. Why? You recognize her?"

"I swear that's the fat girl from Homecoming."

"Oh please. I'm so sure."

The old weight settled on my chest. After a few minutes they both left. I stayed in the safety of my stall and tried not to cry. But when I finally pushed open the door to leave, my eyes were red and puffy. I splashed cold water on my face.

"Don't worry about them," someone said from another stall. "Losers. Sheep. Clones. They'll both die in a terrible perming accident, you watch."

I smiled—I couldn't help it—and hiccuped.

The second stall door opened and a girl walked out holding an ice cream sandwich. She was enormous, her face almost squeezed shut with excess flesh, her eyes slits, her cheeks gigantic half-melons. Her fingers were huge and thick.

"Hi," she said. "You must be the Fat Girl from Homecoming."

"Yeah," I said, "but not anymore."

"Bullshit, honey," she said. "Once a fat girl, always a fat girl."

Then she took my arm and led me out of the bathroom.

~~~

I did outpatient therapy. I took the number 4 bus downtown twice a week to see Dr. Fern Hester, who I was supposed to call Fern, and tell how much better everything had become since I'd lost all that weight and decided to live.

Her office was in the Gleryton Hospital Annex, a plain brown building surrounded by shrubs. It was an institutional room with weird homey touches—overstuffed chairs and framed prints and porcelain lamps—

meant to offset the linoleum floor and fluorescent lighting. Fern always sat with her hands clasped lightly and her ankles crossed. Her hair was the color of dirt, and cut in a thin, off-center pageboy. She had big square glasses, which she inched back up her nose by squenching her face together.

I liked her but I didn't trust her, or any of it: the spilling of secrets like so much spoiled milk. I felt that if I whispered any of it, the flow would be unstoppable, bottomless white liquid curdling as it came out, endlessly replenishing itself. And so I choked it all back.

I never told her about the fat girl.

I never talked about Homecoming.

Three weeks earlier, I'd told her, "This girl at school is in a coma." Fern had nodded, concern distorting her face. "And everyone says she was totally drinking and stuff. I didn't really know her."

I shifted in my chair and watched Fern. Her glasses were greasy in the light. They reflected me, brown hair hanging limp, pimple near my nose. Lone figure against a bare rose-papered wall.

Andrea Dutton's absence had torn a gaping hole in the fabric of our school, of the town, even. I pictured her lying in a hospital bed, her blond hair cascading along a pillow, her pale skin smooth and pearly, her lips open just enough for a tube to pass through. Her room must be lined in flowers, I thought, with her parents holding a vigil by her side. There could be no doubt that people wanted her back.

"She goes out with Tony Giobambera," I said softly, then regretted it, because Fern's eyes narrowed and she leaned towards me expectantly.

Silence. What had there been to say about Tony Giobambera? Somehow I think he actually sees me, not just the fat loser I used to be, but me, Faith, a person? I can't breathe properly around him? I want him to save me?

"He's kind of popular," I said. She'd leaned back and scribbled.

~~~

There wasn't a way to talk about some things.

"I know what you mean," the fat girl said, slurping a strawberry milk shake. "You're lucky you have me."

We were sitting on the wall again. Off in the distance, the football field spread in all directions. It looked like a postcard, a painting. It looked as though you could roll it up and cart it away, leaving space for something else to replace it. But that wasn't the case.

Some things were meant to be buried. Collected and washed into a deep pit, with hot, molten tar poured over them to change their shape and substance forever.

Homecoming.

I wore my favorite blue sweater and sang the national anthem with the choir, my breath cloudy in the cold November air. After the game, I walked around until I got winded. While I rested, a group of junior guys offered me punch, red punch that tasted like Popsicles. We drifted towards the bleachers. They were friendly, they made me feel normal. That's the part I could remember clearly.

"Remembering. Yeah, that's a problem," the fat girl agreed, swishing her cup around, trying to find more milk shake. "But there are ways to change things." She turned to me with a scary intensity, as though everything in her had melted into anger. "There are ways to even the score. And there are places we could go."

I closed my eyes. Blood pounded in my ears. I felt her hand move in circles on my back.

~~~

Berrybrook had been what you might expect. A long white hallway. Concerned and pointed questions. Lots of sitting in a circle with other angry teenagers trying to explore our rage.

It was an interminable pale blur.

I was kept on an extended plan, fed a special diet and made to exercise. I'm sure my mom coughed up a lot of money for that, but Daddy had died with good insurance, so weren't we lucky?

I told them what I needed to, but never let on that my head floated like a balloon, far above my body. That from up there I looked down on my exercising self, the nutty group of us talking about our pain. That even my clean white room was seen from somewhere near the ceiling.

There were no mirrors. To relieve us of the eyes of the outside world and add to the illusion that inside Berrybrook we were safe, we were not supposed to see ourselves. I was not shown the removal of my outer layers, though I felt my body become firmer and evaporate, felt whole parts of me fall away.

But after a while, all of that was easy. What was hard was going home. They told us all along it would be difficult, but I wasn't prepared for the sharpness of the outside, the strong smells, the noise, the color.

When my mother drove me home that first day, the world seemed to be made of marshmallows: everything was spongy and bright. She came through a town that was exactly as I'd left it in an ambulance many months before. She relayed little bits of information: *There's a sale on jeans this Thursday. You'll need new clothes. Uncle Harry broke his leg.* I didn't speak.

She pulled into our driveway and our house seemed to quiver. It was a giant stone reproduction of the house I'd imagined for so many months. It didn't seem real.

I waited for her to unlock the door, then bolted to my room. It was extremely clean. I knew, without looking, that it had been pillaged for clues to my unraveling.

While I leaned in the doorway, movement caught my eye. There, in the corner, stood a skinny, stringy-haired girl with huge, terrified eyes. When I moved my hand, she moved hers. I looked to the side, she did the same. I stepped towards her and she grew larger.

When my mother saw me, she smiled and put her hands on her hips. "Dinner is served," she said.

I followed her to the kitchen but I had no appetite. I couldn't remember what an appetite felt like. Food was something I had ceased to want or understand, it was instead an evil obligation, something to be endured if possible, avoided if not.

We were much too careful to talk about anything, and the silence was stifling. Even our chewing seemed to echo against the walls. I wanted to tell her something, anything to make it better, but I couldn't. I kept quiet, nodding and smiling when it seemed appropriate.

"Ground rules," my mother said, her eyes bright. "I think we need some ground rules. What do you think? Spend some time together. Maybe we should eat together every night? That's going to be hard, given my schedule, but if you think that's something you really need, I think I could make some adjustments. At least I can try. Now, I know, these months have been difficult, but look at you! You look terrific, honey, just great! I really can't wait to take you shopping."

I tried to swallow, but the turkey had swelled in my mouth. I chewed and chewed and chewed. I felt my face grow red, tears tumble down my cheeks, but I didn't know what to do. Finally I spit the food into my napkin.

"We can go to Belk's on Friday and pick out some cute outfits together. Won't that be fun? Would you like that?"

I wiped at my eyes to dry them and nodded but she didn't seem to have noticed any of it. "May I be excused?" I said. "Please?"

My mother took a sip of wine, then refilled her glass before answering. She didn't look at me.

"Sure," she'd said, but her voice was soft. "You do whatever you want."

~ ~ ~

After school I threw my hair into a ponytail, changed into running shoes and sweatpants, a sports bra and my favorite T-shirt—a soft green faded one that had belonged to my dad. The fat girl followed me silently to the edge of the driveway and waved at me with a chicken leg when I took off down the road. I hated running: it hurt and I couldn't breathe for the first ten or fifteen minutes, but the rhythmic *slam, slam, slam* of shoe against pavement cleared my head. It was the only time that my body felt like it belonged to me. I rounded a curve and focused only on the road ahead, pushing myself to forget I was running and just float in a blank empty space above the pounding of feet. By the time I got home I was flushed and tired.

I took a quick shower and tried to read the assignment in *Our Great Nation* but got stuck on page 43. I read it over and over, discovering at the end of each loop that I had no idea what it had said. So I flopped on the couch and watched TV instead, letting canned laughter wash away my jagged thoughts and the shrapnel of the day. At dusk my mother came home.

She entered the house quietly and I heard her leave her bag in the hall and kick off her shoes. By the time she came to stand next to me in front of the television in her stocking feet, she had a tumbler of scotch. I sat up and made room for her on the couch, but she didn't sit. I watched her cradle her glass in both hands. They were fine and smooth with long fingers. She twisted her engagement ring so it stood upright, then ran a hand through her hair and cleared her throat.

"Learn anything today?" she said without looking at me, and I saw the dark circles under her eyes, her roots growing in gray. I stared at her feet instead.

"I read that President Johnson got impeached."

"What?" she said. Her feet were tiny, her toenails painted a dark rose color.

"Nothing. Never mind."

The ice clinked against the side of her glass. "Why don't you sit?" I said, and patted the couch beside me. She sank into it but kept her attention on the screen, where a TV dad was teaching a TV son how to fix his bike.

"How was your day, Mom?" I said.

"Fine, sweetheart. It was fine."

I was tired and I wanted something else. I reached out and touched her shoulder. She flinched away, smiling brightly. "I should get going on dinner," she said. "You must be hungry." But she returned her gaze to the television, mesmerized only for as long as it took to swallow her scotch. Then she headed back to the kitchen and I spread out on the couch again.

~~~

We had a quiet dinner of skinless chicken and microwaved green beans. For dessert there were Weight Watchers brownies, but I didn't want one. The future streamed ahead of me: a dark, endless river of days just like this one. I made a halfhearted stab at homework and then climbed into bed. Time to sleep until I had to do it again.

But the fat girl slumped in a chair in the corner of my room, eating popcorn with butter from a large porcelain bowl. Her face was greasy from stuffing handfuls in her mouth. Her flesh rippled and hung. She was so disgusting.

"I think we need to talk," she said.

I stuck my head under a pillow and pushed the fabric of the pillow into my ears.

"Things aren't going anywhere, Faith," she said, kicking the chair. "You know I'm right. Don't even try to ignore it."

Her muffled voice came through loud and clear. I sat up straight. "How could I know that?! How the hell could things go well when you won't leave me alone!?"

She licked her fingers, one by one, and watched me.

"You fucking horrible cow!" I yelled. "You miserable piece of shit!"

In charged Mom, barreling through the door. "Faith!" she said, with concern in her voice—but I saw the truth in the stupid expression she'd worn since I came back. She was afraid of me, her daughter the monster, and she couldn't hide it.

"You should knock!" I sniffled, and bit my lip. When I turned to her it was with a face of stone. "Hello, I'm sixteen and entitled to privacy . . ."

She held the doorknob like she could swing in or out. *Make your choice, Mom,* I whispered deep inside my head, but I knew she wouldn't choose what I secretly hoped.

I was right: she backed out of the room, closing the door quietly, leaving me alone with the fat girl.

11

"Things are just never going to be the same," the fat girl whispered, and I almost heard sympathy, but then she grabbed a handful of M&M's and cupped them near her mouth.

"Hey, Faith," she said, giggling. "Do these remind you of something? Something you swallowed?"

"Fuck you," I said. But she'd been right. The fat girl always spoke the truth. Things were never going to be normal. There was no relief ahead. Each day would be hot and airless, a festival of shame and humiliation just like it was before, only now I'd become invisible.

"Time works wonders," the fat girl said, and I wanted to hit her.

"Sorry," she said. "But it does, I'm just saying."

She was quiet for a moment and then when she spoke her voice was almost tender. "Besides, there are possibilities," she said. "Plenty of possibilities."

~·~·~

The next day the fat girl tackled lunch full of information.

I thought about what she said, about what it would mean to strike back, to get even, but I couldn't imagine it would make me feel better.

"Oh, it would," said the fat girl. "It would feel really *good*." She spoke to me like I was a stupid child. In her lap was a roasting pan with a whole crispy chicken. She severed one wing with a small gold knife. "When someone kicks you," she said slowly, "you get up and kick them back."

"I don't know," I said, and the fat girl shook her head.

"What do you want to remember," she asked me, delicately cutting away at the bird, "doing what you've been told or changing everything?"

"Changing everything," I whispered.

"Right," she said, and gnawed on a drumstick.

"Right," I said, and took the knife she handed me.

~·~·~

A few teachers had taken me aside to mention carefully that they knew how much school I'd missed and they were available if I needed assistance catching up. No one directly mentioned why I'd been gone. Mrs. Lemont, in math, had looked at me strangely and kept her hands close to her body, like I might leave a sticky stain on her palms if she touched me. Mrs. Wilson, the chemistry teacher, had told me there were no favors for people like me and that phrase sang through my head the whole next day, *people like me*. It made me laugh. I wanted to stop her and say, *Excuse me, Mrs.*

Wilson, could you clarify? Would that be just attempted suicides, or anyone who's spent time in a loony bin? I couldn't even imagine the look on her soft squishy face.

Mr. Feldman, my English teacher, was a mousy man, oddly formal, with small rounded shoulders and a terrible balding pattern. Books got him so excited that his high forehead turned red and beady and he took his round wire glasses off and used them to poke the air. Shakespeare practically made him froth at the mouth.

He asked me to stay after the bell rang and I knew what was coming next.

"I'll be late to history," I'd said.

"I'll write you a pass, Miss Duckle, it's okay." Mr. Feldman gestured to a desk near him and came around and sat on the edge of his. He cleared his throat. "Faith," he said. "I know where you've been. I know it must be rough being back here and—"

Then he paused for a long time and I had to concentrate to keep my mind from drifting away.

"—well, I know what it's like to return to school after a . . ." He cleared his throat. ". . . long absence," he said finally.

He looked at the ceiling and then clasped his hands in front of him and shook them at me like a small round tambourine. "All I'm saying is, I don't want you to feel pressured. I want you to feel like you have whatever space you need to . . . adjust."

I blinked and then realized he wanted something from me.

"Thanks, Mr. Feldman," I said. "Thanks a lot."

"Your work is . . ." he trailed off again. I wondered what place he'd been to and where he'd returned but I didn't ask. "If you're having problems . . ." he said. "If you need anything, you can come to me, Faith."

I wanted to leave the room so badly I could taste it. He looked like there was something else he wanted to say. I waited. Then the bell rang again and I stood. He lunged at me and gave me an awkward, stiff hug. "There, there," he said.

~~~

After my last class, I went to use the bathroom. The hallways were deserted, the day was over. The fat girl was nowhere to be found. I wandered through the school looking but didn't see her anywhere. I went outside, to the low wall, but she wasn't there, either.

Then I saw her at the bottom of the hill. She was spinning in loops and arcs in the center of the football field. Her skirt swung over the grass, her body was a giant blue swirl. I got halfway down the hill, then stopped.

Homecoming had been almost a year ago, when I was still huge and lumbering. The bleachers, that night, the whole of it swept up on me then, sudden and hazy.

We stood with our red plastic cups, breath fogging the air. The guys were so friendly and I felt charming. They laughed at everything I said and punched each other's arms, clustering around. We talked about something, our voices colliding, our steamy breath forming tiny clouds that spiraled up and drifted off into the night. A boy with blue eyes whispered, *Where have you been all my life?* I hiccuped, giggled. I couldn't stop grinning. I tossed my hair. They buzzed around me, all smiles.

She's nice, one boy said to another. Everything was rubbery and unreal. The blue-eyed boy put his arm around me and leaned in close. *You're so pretty, Faith, do you have a boyfriend?* he whispered. I flushed, unsteady. *Does someone love you like you deserve to be loved?* No, I thought. *More punch,* someone offered, and I took a long drink. The guys nodded their heads, closing in around me. A tall boy's voice cut the air, loud and clear, *John, you know what they say about fat girls, right?* My head was thick and cloudy, I couldn't really breathe. *What do they say?* answered a boy in a red parka. I didn't know what to do. *Fat girls are hungry,* said another boy with a ratty mustache. *Fat girls are hungry,* an echo. I turned to leave but they had my arms. *C'mon, Faith,* Blue Eyes said, *I thought you liked us.* I don't feel well, I whispered. My heart pounded.

Feed the fat girl! Someone pushed me to my knees. Someone else had my arms, his nails jagged, a striped silver ring on his middle finger. Right in my ear, *You tell anyone and we'll kill you.* I stared at buckles and pockets. He pinched my nose so my mouth fell open. Then the terrible sound of zippers and one after the other they came at me, chanting. *Feed the fat girl!* Over and over I gagged, I couldn't breathe. *We'll tell what a slut you are.* Then I was shoved to all fours. I stared at hands, at sneakers and boots, the cuffs of pants and jeans. *The fatter the berry the sweeter the juice.* And laughter. *The fatter the berry the sweeter the juice.*

~~~

I didn't make it down the hill. I got halfway, and my stomach turned over. I sat hard on the ground and smelled fresh-cut grass, honeysuckle. Far away a lawn mower hummed. The field was utterly empty—the fat girl was nowhere, was gone.

I couldn't breathe right. I closed my eyes, crossed my fingers, and wished desperately for a sign, any sign that things would be okay. Then I felt a hand on my shoulder and yelped.

Tony Giobambera leapt away from me. "Sorry," he mumbled, uneasy. "I saw you sit. You okay?"

"Yeah," I bellowed. I tried to say, "I'm fine," but instead began to cry.

"Here," he said, and helped me to my feet. "Here."

He put an arm around my shoulders and led me to the bleachers. I smelled him: cigarettes, sweat, something musky and male. We sat side by side and I was drowning and floating all at once. I didn't know what to do.

"Um," he said. He shoved his hands in his pockets. "You all right?"

His gravelly voice calmed me. I groped around for an answer. "Sure," I said, my own voice squeaky and weird. We sat quietly like that for a minute. He looked out over the field. I studied his clear blue eyes and bumpy skin. His lips were perfect and full. One big black curl arced over his left brow.

The silence squeezed at me and I felt like I should say something, anything. "I'm real sorry about your girlfriend," I said.

"Oh." He looked at me quizzically. "Yeah . . ." Then he took a deep breath. "Listen, about what happened . . ." His voice trailed off. "That was really fucked up is all," he said.

I wasn't sure what he meant. But my silence held three things: the desire to preserve that perfect, unspoiled moment, and the knowledge that everything in me that hurt wanted a say right then, and how afraid I was of what would happen if I let it.

I looked out over the field. Far away, by the line of trees I saw a large blue shape spin and whirl, then fall down. She stayed like that for a minute, then rose, lurched wildly, and spun again.

Tony Giobambera lit a cigarette and offered me one. I hesitated, then took it and leaned into the flame he cupped.

I dragged and exhaled. My head fluttered lightly off my shoulders. A bug buzzed by. I swatted it away. The fat girl spun and fell.

I felt the air around us charge with energy, atoms bombarding on all sides. "What do you dream?" I asked him, and he squinted at me.

"Dumb things, mostly," he said, like it was the most normal question in the world. "Sometimes dragons or really stupid shit, cars, school . . ."

I took a deep breath and tilted my head towards him. I tapped my cigarette and watched the ash tumble to the ground.

"What about you?"

I felt the fat girl's knife in my pocket, its weight solid and warm. I thought about my most frequent dream, where stars peppered the sky and I stood on a patch of grass, swelling, and rose above everything until I was immense and powerful and threw fear into the hearts of those below. I was an enormous hungry moon, able to swallow the world. I hovered there, swaying back and forth, but I always woke falling.

Tony Giobambera's hands were on his knees. His fingers were long and thin. On his right hand was a silver ring. I focused on it, on the pattern of it, but didn't answer.

I kept it all to myself, as though the power of words could make things come true. In the distance the fat girl spun and fell, spun and fell, a violent scratch of blue in the clear green day. She knew everything that mattered, everything there was.

I inhaled and blew smoke up into the sky where it dissolved and disappeared. "Nothing dangerous," I told him. "Nothing to be alarmed about."

There was a gentle breeze and the knife was warm in my fingers, warm against my leg. In the distance the fat girl fell. Tony finished his cigarette and ground it into the bleachers with the heel of a scuffed black boot. "I oughtta go," he said, looking straight ahead. "You need a ride?"

I felt the knife's smooth shell and tried to think, but my answer came quickly. "Sure," I said.

I followed him up the hill and was careful not to look over my shoulder, though I felt the bleachers behind me like a living, breathing thing. I knew the fat girl was back there too. I knew she would catch up.

TWO

AFTER I swallowed all those pills, I woke in Gleryton Hospital. Later I learned I'd been in a coma for almost two days and only barely survived. My room was a creepy pale green. Sometimes I blinked and it was dark outside, blinked again and the day nurse was taking blood. Sometimes I lay alert for what felt like hours but were only minutes dripping slowly by.

My mother stood by my bed. She had her arms crossed, holding herself and swaying back and forth. It was dark outside and I tried to say something. She leaned towards me and became my dead father looking nervous and worried.

Daddy— I managed before I fell asleep again. Sleep was dark and dense, a syrupy underwater place without dreams.

I don't know how long I was there but one night we left. My mom had help from an orderly loading me into her car and then we drove out of town. I drifted in and out. She talked the whole time, her voice like a black fly, buzzing, buzzing, trying to find the window that would set it free.

I woke to another wheelchair and a big dark house. Everything was dim then. I was dim, the world was dim. And the next thing I knew it was morning in a pale room with a sour smell and a small, red-haired girl, dressed in blue, staring out the window.

I was woozy and thick. I tried to sit up but my body was made of rubber and wouldn't cooperate. I rolled over on my side, grabbed the metal bar rimming the bed, and tried to pull myself up, but my arm was an elastic band: it just stretched and stretched, growing as long as it wanted but doing nothing to hoist me.

"Meds."

I couldn't see her face—her back was to me—but I knew the voice hadn't been mine. "What?" My voice came out as tissue paper, thin and light.

"Meds," she said again. "They have you doped out of your mind." Her words were pinballs flying around my head, repeating and repeating before they made any sense, and then it was one at a time, as though they'd each struck a flipper to be flung back into the room. "Might as well enjoy them," she said. "It just gets worse."

It. Just. Gets. Worse.

She never turned around. I wondered if she had no face, if her bright ratty hair hung all around her head. In my addled state this made sense. My eyelids were heavy and I drifted back into blackness. The last thing I thought about was the sour smell. Urine. Then sleep.

~~~

When I woke, the room was empty. The other side of the room was a mess: the area around the girl's bed and bookcase was plastered in ragged pages from magazines that looked as though they'd been ripped out and taped to the wall in haste. Her bed was unmade but partially covered by an enormous pink blanket that was bunched up where she'd kicked it aside. The edge of the blanket nearest me said STARLING in a shaky markered uppercase. On top of her pillow were three stuffed chickens: a pink, a pale green, and a light blue, all in a row.

My head faced the doorway. A bookcase crouched at the foot of my bed and beyond that was an institutional blue vinyl chair under the other window. Our ceiling was low and hung with spotted white acoustical tile. An oval rag rug in shades of green and blue covered the center of the dark, scuffed, hardwood floor. The sheets smelled like bleach and the building had a deep hum. All my observations exhausted me.

There was a knock at the door and then my mother pushed it open. "I brought you something from home," she said. "To brighten the room."

I nodded and tried to smile, tried to sit up. She had brought me her quilt, folded and clutched close like she was chilly. It had repeating squares of wonderful fabric: jewel-colored satins, bright ginghams, dark velvets.

I wanted to thank her but my mouth was rubbery. I knew the story of the quilt. When she was eighteen, my mother decided to leave home and move to the city rather than attend the local junior college and work in my grandparents' pharmacy. My grandmother was furious at my mother's impending departure and felt very strongly that she should stay. Two weeks before she was supposed to leave, at my grandmother's insistence, my mother went to help out an older cousin who'd just had a baby. While she was away, my grandmother cut all of my mother's good clothes into small squares and sewed them into an angry quilt. I don't know what happened when she returned and found the quilt. I only knew that she left anyway, taking it with her, and that I never met my grandparents.

The room was very quiet. My mother took a step forward and spread the quilt over me, my grandmother's blanket of shame, my mother's blanket of defiance. There was the occasional sound of faraway footsteps, a tiny gentle patter, then nothing. There was the low, distant hum. I drifted back to sleep.

~~~

For a while day and night bled into one another. Then one day a nurse came to get me and I was brought into the fold.

I remember that first walk down the hall. My legs were weak and the floor prickled beneath my feet. The edges of everything wavered. I felt that if I reached out to touch a hard surface it might very well not be there at all, but I kept such thoughts to myself. There were seven or eight people watching TV, none of whom seemed to have any interest in me. One guy had a burned face. Another twitched and tapped nervously. A girl in the corner hid behind her tangled hair. I found their inattention comforting. I tried to smile at the introductions but I really didn't care who any of these people were, and I could tell they didn't care about me either. I stood on gray linoleum in a sterile room. We had all been brought there by fate and fortune, but as far as I knew, no one had chosen to be there and I figured I didn't have to befriend anyone. As if I even knew how.

~~~

Then each morning I woke to the blinding Berrybrook sunlight and thought I was a little girl in my bed at home again, that my father would come and wake me at any minute. And then, slowly, I blinked awake to the ceiling tiles and the scuffed wood floor, the chrome-rimmed bed and the hum of the room, and realized that I'd grown up.

My days had plenty of structure: meals and group therapy, recreation time and nap time, individual therapy and exercise. I was fed pills in little paper cups at regular intervals and I gave myself over to them. I let my mind float free and numbly pushed through the soup of each day, hopeless and confused and alive.

But it was just one more thing. One more way the days would form and even at the bottom of everything I was, I just didn't care that much right then. It was all about *one more day* and *just for now* and every other cliché in the world. It was all about waking and eating and running and sleeping. And it was about getting through to the next day, all of it even, nobody hurt. Me alive, though I still wasn't sure I wanted to be.

I had all sorts of assumptions about Berrybrook. I thought life would be orderly and controlled. I believed there was no future and no past, no identity, only the present. I thought I was among the broken, waiting to be fixed—that hope was something we would earn.

I had private therapy sessions four days a week. "Tell me how you feel, Faith," he said. Dr. Barry Ronnynole. *Very Runnynose*, we called him. "How I feel," I always repeated. How I felt was none of his fucking business. No one's fucking goddamned business but my own. I felt the way I felt and that was mine, belonged only to me.

"I'm okay," I said, blandly. Or: "I'm tired today."

I didn't say what burned inside me: that sometimes I bubbled with something dark. That I was angry and angry and angry.

Because the more I didn't say it, the more I wasn't. The calmer I sounded, the calmer I was. And the more I felt it all fade away, all of it: Homecoming, my empty echoing house. All of it.

"I'm a little restless," I might say. Or, "I'm thinking a lot about home."

In Group some people talked about the stuff that had happened to them, the stuff they'd done. I felt disconnected from all of them. If anything, ending up at Berrybrook further convinced me of what I'd long believed to be true: that if I spoke of even the most innocent thing, the rest would come tumbling out of me, endlessly replenishing itself. That my need was as voracious as it was hideous, and the only sensible thing to do was choke it all back. So I sat on my folding chair, the world a strange sequence of hazy images, the room filled with strangers as sad and demented as I must have been to end up there, and I kept some things to myself.

~~~

But then my roommate, Starling, became the first friend I'd made in years. It had been so long since I'd felt that suck, that energy of drawing out that comes from another person's attentions. After a week or two of

20

quiet indifference, she began to warm to me. It started with small kindnesses—she'd smile at me, or leave the light on if she went to sleep before I came back from the common room—and evolved from there until she'd developed an interest in me that I found suspect until I realized it was sincere. Starling Yates was many things, but she was extremely sincere.

"Tell me what your favorite foods are," she said. Or: "What's the first memory you have and how old were you?" Or: "Have you ever been in love?" And I told her: Artichokes. Waking to a bad dream in the middle of the night and calling out so that my father came and held me until I fell back asleep when I was three. No.

And she told me things too. That she had a gay older brother named Charlie who was her best friend. That her father had a gambling problem and wasn't around much. That her mother had run away with his brother when Starling was four. That she could barely remember her, but what she did remember was a certain sweet perfume, shiny red heels, stockings hanging in the bathroom, being spanked for wetting the bed.

In the daytime Starling was effusive but never talked about herself. In the comfort of darkness she told me long complicated stories and I listened with every pore, afraid somewhere in the back of my mind that if my attention wavered, even for a moment, her interest in me might fade, casting me back into the depths of solitude.

"I started to hear things when I was seven," Starling whispered late one night. "I would wake up and feel myself listening. Sometimes I remembered what had been said, sometimes I didn't. At first I told Charlie about it because I told him everything, but he didn't believe me so I stopped. By the time I was eight I heard this voice all the time. A girl I played with, who lived down the street, invited me to come to church with her family and I went for the first time ever. After that I believed it was Satan talking to me, which meant I was evil." She arranged her chickens on her lap.

"I was very scared. I asked the voice to go away. I begged, but it didn't. It told me things I shouldn't know, told me to do things I shouldn't do. So one night I jumped out of my bedroom window to shut it up. I broke my ankle and my wrist, but the voice didn't leave. My dad and Charlie took me to the hospital and I told them why I did it, that Satan was talking in my head. That was my first psychiatric admission." She gave a short laugh. "The first of many. On and off, I've pretty much been in the system since then."

I couldn't see her face in the moonlight. She didn't sound upset, just matter-of-fact about the whole thing. "Did it ever stop?" I asked. "The voice, I mean."

"No." She was quiet for a few moments. When she turned her face towards the moonlight, she looked pale and small and calm.

"I've tried everything you can imagine," she said. "Taken pills, jumped from moving cars, hung myself . . . Charlie always saved me is the thing. And it never worked. By the time I was eleven I'd even had electroshock therapy—which fucking hurts!—but it never left. And I know now." She paused. "I know now that it's not Satan talking to me."

"So who is it?" I asked, but she just shook her head.

~~~

The days were endless, and they sped by. Starling's life unfurled before me in the wee hours and everyone else's problems were public during the day. She told me that her brother Charlie worked in a restaurant but had a boyfriend in the circus and that he and their father didn't speak, though they shared the same house. I learned that she was eighteen, lactose intolerant, anemic, manic-depressive, and allergic to wheat, dust, mold, and chocolate. She could barely eat anything and what she did eat she often got rid of—evidenced by her raw gums and bad breath.

But the whole ward loved her. People gravitated towards her. There was a radiance she had, a way that her presence made you feel better. I felt chosen by her. I'd never been chosen for anything in my life.

"You watch everyone," Starling said one day when we were sitting in the common room. "I've seen it. You watch everyone and everything that goes on around here, don't you?"

I swallowed and nodded. It wasn't something I'd ever thought about before, but I supposed I did. I had always watched other people, noted their habits and manners. Ever since I was a little kid.

"I like that." She made this declaration as if it meant so much more. And it did.

~~~

So Starling Yates became my friend. She called me Annabelle, after her favorite Poe poem, and everyone else did too. As much as it violated everything I had told myself, and even as it terrified me, I was grateful for her friendship. But I should have known better than to let myself believe in someone. I should have learned how devastating that could be.

Starling inventoried her suicide attempts. She was very frank about trying to kill herself. She spoke openly in Group, and I assumed to her doctors. She didn't seem to think there was anything wrong with wanting to die. But I started to. Slowly, simply, I began to want to live. I don't know what the transformation was, what made the light inside me begin to burn again, but something did. Some infinitesimal grain of hope was born in me in that terrible place. I guarded it fiercely, and kept it tucked away.

I liked to imagine Starling's rescues. Charlie binding her wrists in strips of his shirt and carrying them above his head with one arm, the other lifting and dragging his sister's naked body to the bed to the phone, to the safety of Berrybrook. Charlie stepped in at the last moments. Charlie had found her with a gun, had come home to the garage door shut and a motor running. Charlie had discovered her drifting in a sea of pink. In my mind Charlie was a superhero.

"I tried pulling my boombox in the bath with me," she whispered one night. "What a fucking idiot. It was battery operated. I ruined it." She took a deep breath. "I didn't know it had to be plugged into the wall. I don't think Charlie even knows about that time."

I liked to hear anything Starling had to say, but especially stories about her brother's rescues, the near misses, about this amazing elliptical closeness they shared. I liked to think of people so connected that one could sense when the other was about to self-destruct. And I liked when she talked about him, because her voice became giddy. I knew she trusted him more than herself, and I doubted she trusted anyone else.

"Don't you know how lucky you are?" I asked her once.

"Don't be ridiculous."

"No, I'm serious." I was. It was another evening, the anonymous darkness that gave me the courage to say it. "You have someone who cares about you that much. It must mean that deep down you're never lonely."

She was quiet for a long time and I thought about how different my life would be if I'd had a brother or a sister, someone to take my side, someone to emulate.

"It's not that easy," she said, and her voice was flat. "It doesn't mean the things you think."

She was sitting up; I could see her outlined against the pale wall. "You're going to bust out of there someday," she said, pointing at me. "I wish I'd be around to see it."

"Oh, give me a break," I said. "You're not going anywhere. Why don't you just accept the fact that you're going to live?" Silence. I tried to make light of it. I smiled, but she didn't smile back. "I don't want you to go," I said. "I'd be all alone again."

But she didn't answer, and lay back down, a signal that the conversation was over.

~~~

I liked to hear Starling talk because she had a way of telling stories that made you want to hold your breath. It was something in the way she stacked her words, and it was the stories themselves, but most of all it was Starling's eyes and the way they squinted and got darker when she needed you to believe her.

"Do you think you're really crazy?" I asked her. I knew that what I really meant was, *Am I?* She pushed the chickens off her lap and scooted over and stretched across her bed so her hair dragged on the floor.

"Somewhat," she said. "But all worthwhile people are. I'm not worried about that. I believe that everything happens for a reason. You were put in this room for a reason. You were saved from all your pills for a reason." She paused for a moment and then sat up and faced me. "I know that God speaks to me for a reason."

"God? You think it's God telling you to kill yourself?"

She nodded. "How can I not listen?" she said. There were tears in her eyes. "Since I know who it is, how can I not do whatever he asks?"

~~~

And then there was the week that Disco and Johnny fought over the TV, each running to the lounge as soon as Group was out, trying to get the remote first. It began as a simple disagreement over *Gomer Pyle* but intensified, day by day, until the whole ward had taken sides over control of the remote. Objectively—which no one was—the argument, the contest, was stupid. But it had escalated to a point of no return—beyond the hiding of the remote into the enlistment of others as decoys and obstacles in its pursuit. Beyond even the reason for the fight in the first place (as if there had been a reason other than we were all restless and medicated and in a loony bin). And one day, finally, Group let out and Disco and Johnny, who had been by the door, pacing and muttering, charged into the hall and tore down its smooth sterile length towards the TV.

But one of Johnny's sneakers was untied so he began to trip and threw himself into Disco, who stumbled and shrieked, grabbing Johnny's long blond ponytail on the way down, pulling as they fell and rolled. There were cracks and thumps as their heads and bodies hit the ground, both too wrapped up in the mission of mutual destruction to break their own falls, and they began to pummel each other, rolling in an awful angry mess back and forth, back and forth.

We gathered and stood watching. I was with John Falk; I saw Starling near Nurse Claiborne. Another nurse lumbered up as quickly as she could, yelling *Hey, hey, hey, hey* but it was Nurse Claiborne who grabbed Disco first, his eyes wild and unfocused, and yanked him off of Johnny, whose head he had been banging into the linoleum floor. They were both bleeding and Johnny had a loose lower tooth that he moved back and forth with his finger, while trying to squeeze his nose shut to stop its flow. Disco had a long gash above one eye; another cut was a slice of pink along his dark cheek where the skin had split. They were panting and spent.

"Assholes," Blade said, under his breath. Kate was whimpering quietly. Violence always set her off. Cookie wrapped one arm around her and Hilton pushed by them and headed to the TV room. Gina and Lauren followed. John Falk went, and then I went. Hilton already had the remote.

"Crazy motherfuckers," he muttered, and found an old episode of *Bewitched*, his favorite. We all settled in to our customary places on the various worn couches and chairs. I had learned early on who sat where and how much trouble you made by stealing someone's seat. Everyone except Starling had a customary place. John Falk couldn't hear very well because of his missing left ear, so he always took the red chair nearest the television. Hilton liked the center of the pale green couch. Usually Disco sat on one side of him and Johnny on the other but today the nurses had taken them off for a "discussion," which most likely meant solitary and we wouldn't be seeing them for a while. Cookie and Gina and Lauren liked the blue couch and Blade inevitably sat on the floor. I sat against the pale green wall on a gray couch—the least comfortable, but the one with the most room. Starling sat wherever she wanted because no one minded giving up their seat to her.

But that day Starling didn't come sit with us and I didn't really think about it. Sometimes she got dizzy and went back to our room, or had therapy or a visit with Dr. Stone, the physician. Maybe she was in the bathroom.

By dinner, though, when I still hadn't seen her and the retelling of Disco and Johnny's fight had become unbearable (one of Cookie's obsessive-compulsive habits was to tell a story over and over and over again until you thought your head might explode), I got nervous. I had looked in our room after lunch and not seen her. Now a whisper of unease sent me back again. This time I paced the room slowly, listening for something.

Her bed was empty, except for her chickens—Starling was insane about her chickens. They had been a gift from her brother and she was exceptionally anal about leaving them on her bed and in the room and in a row and in a specific color order—pink, pale green, light blue—but now I noticed there were only two. The pink one was missing.

And then I saw a small blue smear by the foot of her bed and another and another. Something wiped up but not completely.

I found her under the bed. I knew the moment I pulled her out—she had thick blue liquid running down her cheeks and she was an awful pale gray color. I screamed and yelled and people came running and then she was being lifted onto a stretcher and wheeled away.

She drank nearly a gallon of cleaning fluid. After she was taken away I wasn't allowed to see her again. They stripped the room so thoroughly that it was as though she'd never been there at all. But news drifted back to the ward. Starling was in a coma for a day, two days, four days. And then her family turned off the machines.

Our routine never shifted, never changed. Our days lost their color, washed out to gray. And my nights stretched in infinite lonely directions, entirely empty now.

But I was angry with her for leaving. I was angry at her for being crazy enough to listen to that voice and though I fiercely missed her, I didn't forgive her desertion. After that, Berrybrook slid by, month by month, as though time had no viscosity at all. It seemed like minutes between my commitment to the game of getting well and my reentry into the tournament of high school.

THREE

Tony walked fast and I skipped along to keep up. When we reached the parking lot it was mostly empty. Gravel crunched beneath our feet. A few solitary cars waited for someone to finish a makeup test or a yearbook meeting.

"I'm over there," he said, pointing across the lot at the shiny blue MG sparkling in the corner space, but I already knew the car. Everyone did.

My mouth was dry, my cheeks flushed. "That's your car?" I said, and hoped I sounded surprised. Tony seemed to swell with pride the closer we got. When we reached the car he stood for a moment before opening the door, his hand resting lightly on the trunk, moving in slow loving circles.

"Rebuilt her myself," he said, walking around the corner, his fingers tracing it lightly. "Took me almost a year. My cousin Enzo did the paint job. Originally she was, you know, green."

"Does she have a name?"

He jerked his head up like he was angry, but didn't answer. He unlocked his door, climbed in and started the car, then leaned over and unlocked my door. I took a deep breath and sat down, pulling my purple backpack onto my knees. I was acutely aware of how near he was.

Tony lit another cigarette but didn't offer me one. I rolled down my window. The silence made me nervous.

"LilyAnn."

He said it so quietly I wasn't sure I'd heard him correctly.

"What?"

"LilyAnn," he said. "The MG. She's called LilyAnn."

He looked irritated, but I thought that was possibly the sweetest thing in the whole world.

"Can I have a cigarette?"

"Yeah." He handed me one and the lighter and I surprised myself by lighting it on the first try. I put the lighter in the ashtray and we peeled out of the parking lot.

The wind blew through my hair and the noise prohibited any conversation, which was fine, because I had no idea what to say, though a thousand questions fluttered through my blood. Apart from my quick, awkward directions, we didn't speak. When we reached my driveway we sat for a minute with the engine idling.

"Thanks for the ride," I said.

"No big," he said. "Catch you later."

I climbed out of the car, holding my backpack to my chest, and slammed the door. He gunned the motor and drove off. I stood there for a minute on our front lawn surveying the neighborhood. Everything seemed to shimmer in the afternoon sun. I'd been in Tony Giobambera's car! He'd given me cigarettes and driven me home! I'd sat next to him, like a normal person, like someone he wasn't embarrassed to know! I swung the backpack over one shoulder and turned to go inside.

"Not so fast," she said.

The euphoria of the car ride spit out of me like air from a popped balloon. "Shit," I whispered.

"I can't believe you're this stupid." The fat girl sat on the front porch with a big spoon and a jar of chunky peanut butter. "Wake up, Faith," she said, shaking the spoon at me. "Pay attention now." Her voice was low and scary. I didn't move.

"You can't ride with him, okay? You can't talk to him, you can't know him *unless you want to do something about him*, understand. You saw that ring."

"He could be anyone," I said. "Half the guys at school have those rings."

"Well, you better stay away from half the guys at school, then." She was muttering now. "Like that isn't enough reason."

"I'll hang out with whoever I want."

"No," she said. "You'll listen to me."

We stood like that holding each other back with our eyes. Then I pushed past her and went into the house.

~~~

Inside it was cool and dark. There was a note on the table under the hall mirror. *Meeting after work. Dinner in fridge. Lv, M.*

I crumpled the note and stuffed it in my pocket. I hadn't gotten the mail on my way in, and I didn't want to go back down the driveway because I knew the fat girl would be waiting for me. Instead I dragged my feet along the rug in the living room, dumped my backpack by the couch, and left my jacket hanging on the wooden chair by the doorway. I kicked my way into the kitchen and straight to the fridge. Inside, wrapped in tinfoil with a small note in neat letters, was my dinner. *Dinner*, it said in my mother's handwriting. *Enjoy!*

I closed the fridge, turned, and sat on the floor with my back against its door. I knew what it probably was: turkey and peas, my mother's standard leftover package, but I wasn't hungry. Ever since Berrybrook, I only felt hungry in dreams. When I was awake, food made me nauseated or nervous or both.

I stared at the pattern of the linoleum and let myself imagine: what if . . . What if I had asked Tony Giobambera inside and he'd said, *Sure, Faith. Cool*, and followed me up the steps? But then my mind cut off, because I couldn't imagine what I would have done next. I tried to picture myself saying, *Would you like a glass of water, Tony?* I clenched my face to erase the thought.

"Oh, Faith."

I didn't look up. I didn't look at her or say anything, just covered my ears with my hands and squeezed my shut eyes even tighter.

But I could still hear the fat girl. "Look, I realize you're pissed or whatever," she said, chewing loudly. "But hear me out: we have to move on. There's more to look forward to than this."

I tried to blot out her words but they came from all around me and inside.

"How about we do it, hon?" she said softly. "How about we take off?"

I raised my head. "Leave?"

"Leave. Vamoose. Get the hell out of Dodge. Go off and live a little."

She sat at the table, her enormous legs spilling over the edges of the cane chairs. Against the yellow flowered wallpaper, she was a bright blue ball. "You have marshmallow on your chin," I told her.

She wiped it with the back of her hand, a dismissive gesture, then cocked her head to the side. "There are a whole lot of places to go," she said. "And all of them are new to us."

I struggled to stand up. My feet had pins and needles and I shifted from one to the other and back, shaking them out. Just take off? Just leave and run away?

The fat girl had a crafty look that made me nervous. "Go where? I'm only sixteen, remember, what about school? And I don't have any money or anywhere to go." I ticked these things off on my fingers.

"Faith, sit down," she said. I sat.

"Okay, school." She brushed it away like the marshmallow, with a flick of her wrist. "Worry about that later. School sucks, and besides, you're screwing up, right?"

I nodded.

"So you're sixteen. A hundred years ago you'd be married with five kids by now. How are you ever going to grow up here? You have to leave to do that."

She gathered her long straight hair with one hand and pulled it around to the side. Her face was a shining globe of flesh. "Now what was the other thing? Right, money." She sighed and looked concerned. "That is true, we need money." She pursed her lips. "It's easy enough," she said brightly. "You'll get a job."

I stood completely still. Everything she said made perfect sense to me. The idea of leaving was a firecracker in my stomach, fuse burning slowly. A job. Leave.

The fat girl brushed crumbs from the table into her big dimpled hand, then lumbered to the sink and tossed them in. She turned to face me and smiled, her whole face lit up. "Oh, Faith," she said. "Aren't you excited?"

I smiled back and shoved my hands deep in the pockets of my jeans. My fingers closed around the knife. I looked around the kitchen and thought of leaving it again, going off to somewhere else only to dream longingly of its familiarity. Giving up my room and my front door and the comfy green couch in the living room where I could lie on my side and watch TV. Leaving my bed, so perfectly soft and worn in just right.

But then I thought of school. Of dinner with my mom. Of Fern and my great academic record. Of Andrea Dutton. And of driving away in a shiny car, my hair streaming behind me, nothing in my way but the open road and my untarnished future.

It didn't sound so bad, really.

"A job." Already I was thinking about the savings bonds my grandmother had sent me when I was a kid, and of the way my mother sometimes left her wallet on her dresser, and of things I could sell: my father's gold cuff links, for example. The fancy watch I'd gotten for a birthday.

"A job," the fat girl said. The plan was hatched.

~~~

When I was young my mother and father fought a lot behind closed doors. I learned to tell when something was wrong by the meals my mother cooked. If she believed my father had lost an argument, or was absolutely wrong about something, she made Cauliflower Pie. If she was merely angry with him she made Salmon Loaf. I loved both and noted the dinnertime tension only in passing, my main concern being the creamy noodles or smooth pink fluff. These were my father's least favorite dishes, but when she made them and he ate, I knew everything was right with the world, his sad face stiff and resigned, our meal quiet and polite.

Please pass the peas, Faith, he might say, though they rested by my mother's elbow. And I would.

My father was a quiet man, sad and solemn, but equipped with a terrifying temper: all hissed words and cold vows. When he wasn't angry—which was most of the time—he loved me unequivocally and I knew that, not only because he told me frequently, but also because it rose off of him in waves. I was his child and therefore was perfect (except for the occasional mistake). My father thought I was beautiful and sweet. He excused my size, dismissing my mother's critical comments about it with a wave of his hand. He was not a trim man himself and he often said we came from a large family: large in goals, generosity, and girth.

"You have nothing to be ashamed of," he would say with a hand on my plump cheek. "You're my little muffin."

My mother did not agree. She was slender, worked at it, and couldn't bear the sight of her chubby daughter. Beginning when I was in first or second grade she'd put me on diets and clucked her tongue at me when I asked for seconds. She packed me lunches with carrot sticks and no sweets, but still I swelled. Sometimes at home I caught her watching me from across the room, a distant, distracted look on her face, confused, as though she wasn't sure who I was or where I'd come from.

For several summers she lobbied to send me to Fat Camp. I heard hissed references to their disagreement on the subject. My mother thought it was important and my father thought it would give me a horrible complex. The idea of a camp full of fat kids made me uneasy and claustrophobic, but they never asked for my opinion and I had long ago learned not to volunteer it. That was rude, in my father's eyes, and rudeness was one of the few things that would set him off. I had no intention of alienating my only ally.

My father was given to big hugs and emotional pronouncements. At supper out of the blue he might pop up with *I love you both so much*. Or: *I'm so happy*. Or: *Isn't this nice, all of us together?* And it was. We loved him, and when he said these things I felt my heart swell up and outward, filling with light and warmth. Later he'd grow quiet and remote, unable to listen to anything I said, though he'd mumble encouragingly, *mmhmm, mmhmm*, while I groped around the dark world of words trying to become more interesting before his eyes. Trying to rivet his attention to me, *I am here, I am here*, trying to make him care as much as he said he did.

He died unexpectedly when I was eleven. He wasn't sick or anything. One day he just put his head down on his desk and never woke up again. People then explained *aneurysm* to me like it was a bomb, but I thought of it more often as a small timer ticking inside of his brain—inside everyone's brain—that stopped with a loud pop when your time was up.

The funeral was held in the huge old church we'd attended when I was smaller. I had always loved its stained-glass windows and tall brown walls, the dark heavy beams that arched high above the pews. But what I remember most about the funeral are tiny things: the shininess of the casket, reflecting a light from above. Loose petals that fell to the floor. The touch of strangers. The way silence seemed to rise up like a sail, or a cloud, filling with air and smothering everything except the echoes of stifled coughs and throat clearing. The weight of the hymnal that I didn't open. The pastor saying *Richard Duckle, Richard Duckle* and me translating each time: *Daddy, Daddy*.

My father had been a well-respected man. People I didn't know but recognized from the Gleryton community were there along with the familiar family friends. Relatives I couldn't place or had never met and old business partners of my father's flew in. Ladies from church. Clients. Neighbors who had moved away. And afterwards, after the ceremony, our house was thick with people, talking, laughing, clutching at me and pulling me close.

Mrs. Ibarista was there. Apparently my father had stopped by her bakery for a sweet roll every week for twelve years.

"Why don't you work for me, Faithy," she'd said. "I could use a nice girl like you making some cakes and things. I teach you everything."

And I heard her from a great distance, the way I heard everything that day, through a long foggy tunnel. "Okay," I told her. "Sure."

Someone whispered that my mother was lying down, that she'd taken something to help her sleep. I nodded as though I understood. After a while I slipped away to my bedroom where I listened to the muffled sounds of strangers, my stomach raw and empty. And then they left, one by one, and the silence arrived, dense and impenetrable.

Afterwards, things were never the same. I had never thought of our house as large before, but now it seemed to be made of endless rooms, each spilling into the other with a quiet that made me want to hold my breath. My mother slipped inside herself and I learned to spend hours in my room just so I would have a door to shut.

~~~

I loved working at Ibarista's Bakery. I had a knack for making icing flowers, Mrs. Ibarista said. I was a natural. It made me very happy: the delicacy of the icing, the careful way I had to squirt food coloring to mix just the right shade of pink or blue or peach; the smell of the worn back room, all sugar and sweetness that seeped into my clothes when I left. And I loved the flowers themselves, spun on small plastic platforms, dainty and fine.

But I quit when I started my sophomore year of high school. I told her it was because I didn't have enough time for my homework, but really it was because so many high school kids came to Ibarista's when classes let out and I saw how they looked at me, fat as I was, surrounded by cakes and pastries and pies. I saw the pity and disgust that flashed across their faces like sudden pain.

But I couldn't tell Mrs. Ibarista that was the reason. She would have said, *Faith, you gotta not listen to these kids, okay? They don't know you, what do you care what they think?*

She couldn't understand how much I did care. How desperately I wanted to avoid drawing attention to my enormous size. Or, as Mrs. Ibarista liked to say, "my chunkiness." There was little room for pity in Mrs. Ibarista's world. Life was about being tough and accepting whatever gritty hand you'd been dealt by a fierce and vengeful God, then just getting on with things.

When I quit, Mrs. Ibarista was rolling flaky dough for lemon custard tarts. She gave me a long hard look, then wiped her hands on a cloth and pulled me to her and hugged me. She drew her lips together and sighed heavily.

"Faithy," she said. "You do what you gotta do. I will miss you and the customers will miss you."

Then she went back to rolling the dough.

At first I stopped in and visited after school. She had a new girl working there then. A pasty blond girl named Tammy, from the private Catholic school, who didn't quite meet your eyes when you spoke to her.

But after Homecoming I never went in again. I had this sense that Mrs. Ibarista would take one look at my face and know. She'd always known the truth without my telling it and I couldn't bear to have her narrow her eyes the way she did, and put her hands on either side of her floury apron and shake her head in disappointment. Or throw her head back so that her dark hair almost touched her back and shout at God in Italian. I couldn't and I didn't. I never went in again.

~~~

I wanted to leave like an explosion. It was no longer a question of whether or not to go. It was just a question of when and how.

I bought a small blue notebook and began to jot down ideas. Leaving, it seemed to me, was both incredibly simple and heavily complex. Whatever idea for escape I had, I wrote it down: *Train. Bus. Cruise ship.* I felt like the answer was just ahead of me somewhere, but I had no idea what it was. I jotted down ideas for money as well, jobs I could do, skills I had: *clerk, cashier, waitress, baby-sitter.*

Of course, I did not mention any of it to Fern Hester.

The fat girl coached me on the way to Fern's office. "Nothing," she kept saying. "Nothing at all." On the bus, "Faith, I mean it—you watch what you say." And in the elevator up, ". . . because you just let things slip sometimes, Faith, and we can't risk that. Especially if everything goes as planned."

As planned.

As planned meant *striking back*. As planned meant *leaving like you mean it*. As planned meant *something to remember you by*.

We had not yet reached an agreement about what was planned.

~~~

I applied to be a cashier at the SaveLots, at Bandy Drugs, at the local U-Haul, at Mitler's Grocery. I applied to stock inventory at a ball-bearing warehouse, answer phones at a clinic, and sell encyclopedias. I even applied to do absolutely anything at the Gleryton animal shelter.

"You can volunteer," the tired woman who took the application clipboard from me said. "But there's a waiting list for that, too."

No one hired me.

Each application I filled out was drenched in so much hope that it affected my penmanship and infused my answers. I became better at filling out forms. Now under "position" at Ibarista's Bakery, I wrote: *Confectionery Technician*. Under reason for leaving I wrote: *Needed at home*. I was learning that a manipulation of the facts was absolutely in order. No one needed to know anything else factual, for that matter. By the time I applied at the BumperLube to be an "appointment specialist," I had worked myself into a lying lather, inventing jobs and skills and positions and amazing horizons of experience I had never even imagined possible. If I could leave and tackle the world on my own, what did I need with *absolute* truth? Truth was as malleable as time, it seemed to me, or fate. There was no reason to feel limited by the facts.

Amy's After School Care, Tino's Pizzeria, Gino's Pizzeria, Gino's Pizzeria Two, the LeBlanc Restaurant, landscaping, managing the Treasure Chest Arcade—I even tried to get a paper route. My expectations had been low, then high, then desperate and all-encompassing. But I grew tired of smiling while people with jobs looked me up and down and tried to decide what I was worth.

I began to doubt the plan.

"We could go see the guidance counselor," the fat girl said. We were sitting on the low wall watching people change classes. The fat girl had cotton candy. The wind kept blowing her hair into it and she was absorbed by picking pink fluff from her long brown bangs.

"I don't want to see the guidance counselor," I said. I knew I sounded pissy, but I also knew Mrs. Twine would just smile at me in that pitying way she had, and I'd feel even more hopeless and incapable.

"She might know something," the fat girl said.

I ignored her. Across from us I saw a cluster of boys collecting, their backs angled in a huddle. One of them looked over his shoulder at me and then quickly looked away.

"Let's go, Faith," the fat girl said. Her voice was firm but urgent. I couldn't quite breathe.

"Hey!" She yanked my elbow so that I nearly lost my balance. "Up. Now."

"*Okay!*" I shook myself free and stomped off towards my locker. I resisted the urge to see if they watched.

~~~

Clark's was a big fancy restaurant with brightly colored umbrellas hanging from the ceiling. All of the waitresses wore white shirts and identical neckties swimming with green and orange fish. It was a place I'd been taken for birthdays and I figured it would be a good place to work.

I didn't know what to wear, but the fat girl suggested black and white. "Dress like them and they'll hire you," she said. "Works every time."

"Like you've ever even been to a job interview," I said.

But in the end I listened to her and walked the whole way there in a pair of black jeans and one of my dad's old white oxford shirts.

The restaurant sat by itself surrounded by a parking lot. It looked dark inside and there weren't many cars.

"You wait out here," I said, but she just snorted and ignored me, following behind, sucking on a Popsicle.

I pushed through the heavy wooden doors and stood blinking in the sudden darkness, waiting for my eyes to adjust. Near the entrance a perky brunette with inches of makeup watched me from a lectern. She smiled, then looked me up and down.

"Can I help you?" she asked.

Behind her, teams of white-shirted women lit candles all over the restaurant, each bending with a flame, then rising, pivoting, and bending again, like large, clumsy moths. Directly ahead, a tall guy with spiky red hair was wiping glasses with a rag and hanging them from a rack above his head. My courage began to falter.

"Um, I was just wondering . . ."

My voice sounded thin and high. I cleared my throat. *Buck up*, I told myself, *buck up*. But inside I felt a creeping sense of shame. They were never going to hire me. All these people were beautiful, fresh faced, and perky. Not the kind of people who'd want me around.

"I was wondering if you're hiring," I blurted.

The woman gave me a warm smile. "Well, not right now, but things turn over quickly around here and we may be looking soon. What's your name?"

"Faith Duckle."

"And, Faith, how old are you?"

"Sixteen," I said, shifting from one foot to the other.

"Sixteen," she repeated, and I saw her thinking. "Well, you can't serve alcohol unless you're eighteen," she said finally. "So waiting tables is out, you have a little time there, but are you willing to work hard? We may have an opening for a busboy . . . busgirl soon. Do you want to fill out an application?"

"Sure," I said. I wasn't sure what a busgirl was but it sounded fine. She led me to one of the tables and gave me a black pen and a sheet of paper littered with questions.

When I had finished, I brought it back and stood awkwardly, trying to figure out what to do with my hands. "Thank you," I said, overly bright, and smiled as wide as I could, baring my teeth and willing myself to look as shiny and fresh as someone who deserved to be there. Then the fat girl scooped up a handful of mints and I followed her out the door.

~~~

I walked home from Clark's thinking grand thoughts. I would work hard and then we would take off, abandoning school and the terrible claustrophobic familiarity of Gleryton.

"I bet they'll hire me," I said, talking as fast as the words could come. "I'll work really hard and I bet I'll make a lot of money. They must make a lot of money, huh? How much do you think we need?"

The fat girl kicked along beside me with her hands behind her back. She didn't say anything. Finally I couldn't take it. I stopped by the side of the road.

"What?" I said.

She sighed and looked beyond my shoulder to the field that bordered the road. "You are still going to have to *do* something to strike back. You can't just leave like nothing happened. You have to make a point."

"Oh please," I said. "Be serious. There's nothing for me to do. I mean what *point* could I possibly make before we leave?"

"You *know*, Faith," she said. "You know what you have to do."

I pushed past her and began to run as fast as I could in the direction of my house. My head pounded in time with my feet, asphalt crunched beneath me. My face was warm and sweat began to stream down my back, soaking my father's shirt. I only looked over my shoulder once. The fat girl was a blue dot in the distance.

~~~

The next day I was supposed to go see Fern Hester. The fat girl walked ahead of me eating a string of licorice, and the sun filtered through the pine trees and played over the top of her head so that her hair, dancing with light, looked shiny and smooth. Her sleeves were pushed up and the skin at her elbows dimpled where the fat gathered. She wasn't speaking to me. All day she'd been following me around like a petulant shadow, sighing and snorting, but didn't answer when I asked what her problem was.

We shifted in the sun and ignored each other until the bus pulled up. Then I slung my backpack over my shoulder and climbed on board. I slid my coins into the slot and walked back without looking at the driver.

The fat girl rode for free.

The bus was mostly empty. I walked halfway back, took a window seat, and leaned my head against the cool glass. Through the window the world looked distant and manageable.

Soon we zoomed down the highway, heading downtown, and the fat girl, who still hadn't spoken, began to hum beside me.

> Leaving on a jet plane
> Don't know when I'll be back again . . .

"All right, already," I said as quietly as I could. "I get it."

She stopped humming and looked at me. "Do you, Faith? Because I hate to think I've been wasting my time."

I didn't answer. Ahead of me an old lady whose hair was so thin her pink scalp shone through sat next to a guy in an army jacket leaning forward, reading something in his lap. The bus smelled like exhaust. I was tired, so tired.

It was three forty-five. I had fifteen minutes before my appointment with Fern and I didn't want to go. I didn't want to talk about how I felt or what I thought or my father or my mother or any of it at all. I didn't want to say anything.

We got off at our stop and the bus lurched away, leaving a small cloud of gray smoke and a quiet space where its noise had been. I whipped around. Behind me ugly apartment buildings punched the wide sky. Even the trees lining the sidewalk seemed sharp and hostile. I stepped off the curb and onto mulch and made my way to a weathered wooden bench, where I sat.

I put my head in my hands and looked at my feet, tucked in their dirty suede sneakers. It was all so outrageously boring, all this talking. Where was the part of me that was angry? The part that made me want to claw the sky?

"I'm right here," the fat girl said. "Faith, I'm here."

She put her arm around me and pulled me to her, whispering all sorts of things. "We're going to leave," she was saying. "Honey, I believe in you. We're going to survive and we're going to have fun. You just watch. You just sit back and watch."

~ ~ ~

I skipped my appointment. I was surprised that the fat girl didn't try to talk me out of it, just looked over her shoulder at the Annex building for a minute, then nodded quietly and rubbed my arm.

"Maybe it is time for a break," she said. "Let's walk around. Let's go look at the pawnshops. Or . . . what do you want to do?"

"That's fine," I said. But that wasn't what I wanted to do. The roads were mostly empty of people. Cars whizzed by, one after the other, but except for the occasional drooping old man on a bench, there weren't many people on this stretch of Gleryton Road Extension. Then we came to regular Gleryton Road. Here was a band of old shops, many of which were now vacant. They had once been the center of everything, before the strip malls and shopping malls began to cluster outside the Yander section of Gleryton. I liked this part of town, its old-fashioned architecture and empty streets. The shops here were small and dusty or boarded up. They all had family names in faded letters: WALKER'S SHOE REPAIR, THOMPSON'S DRY CLEANING, J. LIPSKY FURNITURE. All the chain stores had opened in the malls. My favorite thing for a while had been to wander down South Cherry Road and stop in the three pawnshops there, just looking at the things people traded away.

"We're near South Cherry and the pawns," I said. We'd stopped at the intersection and the fat girl nodded from the curb.

I took a deep breath. "But I want to go to the hospital."

She jerked her head like I'd spit and stared at me with narrowed eyes. "You want to skip Fern to go to the fucking hospital? Why?"

I wanted to see Andrea Dutton. I didn't know why. It had something to do with the way I thought everyone missed her. With the enormous get well card that the cheerleaders had posted in the lobby so that the whole school could sign it. With the way that no one had noticed I'd been gone. She was who Tony Giobambera loved. I couldn't explain it, didn't want to explain it, but I needed to see her.

I started walking again. The fat girl called after me, but I just put my hands over my ears and walked faster, listening to the sound of my blood and my breath and the cars that sped past. It all kept time. I didn't turn around or even look over my shoulder to see if she was following. I didn't care. I was going to push through the double doors of Gleryton Hospital and find my way to Andrea Dutton's room.

After a while I took my hands from my ears and stuffed them in the pockets of my coat. And I kept going.

It took almost forty minutes to reach the main entrance and the closer I got the more I doubted my plan. I didn't want anyone to see me visiting Andrea Dutton, most of all Andrea Dutton herself. What if she pointed that accusatory finger again, *I know what you did.*

What if I ran into folks from school—cheerleaders, football players, all those people who Andrea knew, who she talked to and whispered with in the hall? Or what if her church group or her parents were there? What would I say to her parents?

All at once I wanted the fat girl. I stopped and turned around, but she wasn't trailing behind me as I'd thought. I couldn't even see her big blue form off in the distance. It was just me and the empty day, sky clear, sun sinking. Afternoon fading away.

And I was there. I was at the hospital. The world was made of a million tiny choices and I held one of them in my palm.

~~~

When they pumped my stomach it was in Gleryton Hospital, though I didn't remember it. The coma vigil was there and my first few days in a psych ward. Those few days I remembered, though only vaguely, in sudden shadowy images that it took a while to place. But when I pushed through those doors the smell brought it all back, fiercer and more immediate than I could ever have imagined. Gleryton Hospital smelled of ammonia and stale air and illness. It smelled of fluorescent light and color-coded pathways through the building's bowels, and it smelled of hope and desperation, of midnight anxiety and catnaps and pain.

I stood in the entrance and inhaled. Things washed over me faster than I could track them. I floated and plummeted all at once. And then I turned and saw the fat girl behind me, a blue flash beyond the glass, watching me from the other side.

I went to the front desk. There were flyers under the glass on the countertop. *Winston's Grief Counseling,* one read, *Helping Time Do Its Job, Helping You Move On.*

"Room twelve sixteen," the nurse said, and pointed towards a bank of elevators.

~·~·~

The twelfth floor had the wide hallways and cold bright lights I remembered. My stint at Gleryton swept up on me, but I shook it off. That was over, I told myself. All that had happened long ago, nearly a year ago, no one would recognize me. It was a closed chapter, a done deal. Still the speckled linoleum floors and the ceiling tiles and the rounded gray Formica nurses' station were uncomfortably familiar.

A calm disembodied voice flooded the corridor at regular intervals. *Kchshhskksh. Dr. Samuels to Radiology. Dr. Samuels to Radiology.* Even this was like a newly remembered dream.

I found 1216 easily but instead of going in, I walked around the floor trying to appear inconspicuous and peeking in other rooms. There were lots of legs and feet and ends of beds. Lots of IV stands and the clattering sound of curtains being pulled back, skittering along their metal tracks. There were a few people: the occasional bored or distracted patient in a pale, flapping gown walking slowly or being pushed in a wheelchair down the hall, or just sitting there, not even taking it in anymore, their faces all the same, blank and tired. I kept going, strolling as though I knew where I was headed, my face warm, my head pounding. I wasn't quite ready to face Andrea Dutton.

I found a rest room and went in, leaning into the mirror to study my face. I looked more like me now. Which is not to say that I looked so different from the girl my mother had brought home from Berrybrook those months ago, only that now I knew she was supposed to be me.

I took a deep breath. If I was going to be brave, then I'd better be brave. I threw my shoulders back and swallowed. "Hi!" I said to the mirror. Too cheerful. "Hello there," I said with more tragedy in my voice.

~·~·~

The nurses' station hummed and bustled behind me and ahead there was an empty gurney in the hall. Men and women in pale blue scrubs sauntered by. I didn't look at them, just straight ahead, as though I knew exactly what I was doing.

Then I reached 1216. It had a plain brown door with a high small window. I peeked in and through the crosshatched glass I could make out the foot of a hospital bed with a dark green curtain partially drawn, and beyond that, by the window, another bed. So Andrea Dutton didn't have a private room. There were flowers on a table by the window, ordinary cheerful bouquets of bright carnations and baby's breath with small stiff cards peeking from between their petals.

A face stared back at me, eyes even with mine. I jumped back and froze. A blond woman in a pale yellow sweater opened the door. She had bags under her eyes and a brittle smile. "Are you a friend of Andie's?" she said. Her voice was breathy.

I wasn't sure how to answer. I smiled and gave a half-nod while trying to peer around her and into the room. The green curtain moved and a nurse walked out, stepping past me into the hall.

"They were just taking blood," the woman said. She looked like Andrea, but grown up. "Did you want to come in?"

I nodded and she stepped aside to let me pass.

Andrea Dutton lay small and limp, arms by her side, hooked to machines that beeped and hummed. Without the customary veil of makeup, she looked as though she were made of porcelain, except that a yellowish bruise covered part of her cheek, neck, and the collarbone that peeked through her pale gown. Her head had been shaved; her skull was bandaged.

"It's nice that you're visiting," Mrs. Dutton said. "She was awake for a while today." She sat on a chair near the bed and her small reddish hands rubbed themselves up and down on her denim thighs. "What's your name, so I can tell Andie you stopped by?"

The air in the room was dizzying, so bright and stale. All the energy came from the voice of machines. Over where the curtain around the next bed ended, feet, covered by a thin white sheet, poked out. I didn't know what to say. Andrea Dutton. When I spoke my voice sounded too loud for the room.

"Annabelle. Tell her Annabelle visited." Mrs. Dutton nodded.

"She's feeling better?"

Mrs. Dutton took her daughter's limp right hand in hers. "Yes," she said cheerily. "Maybe you heard that she got out of the ICU a week ago? The doctors say we're right on schedule." She smiled at me for just a moment and then her eyes focused on something behind me, high up the wall. I resisted the urge to turn around. "It just takes a long time," she said, but now she sounded like she was talking to herself.

"I really hope she feels better."

"I come every day." Mrs. Dutton leaned forward and fluffed Andrea's pillows. "And her brothers come after school. Her father comes when he can but I think it's the school friends that do her the most good."

I looked at Andrea, who hadn't moved at all, not even to blink or wiggle, and wondered how Mrs. Dutton could tell.

"I know everyone's worried about her."

"I'm sorry, Annabelle," she said, smiling and wiping at one eye. She laughed. "I don't know why I'm so wound up. Sometimes this even feels normal." She gave a short laugh. Her eyes were incredibly sad.

I backed towards the door. I wanted to run out of that room.

"Come back soon," she said. "If you see Missy or Jenny at school, tell them to come and see her. Andie loves visitors. They don't have to stay long."

"I will," I said, nodding. "I'll do that." And then I took off down the hall as fast as I could.

~~~~

By the time I got home it was late. The hall light was on and my mother had pinned a note beneath the vase on the table. *F,* it said. *No Fern? What happened this afternoon? Am at GHFA mtg. Home by 8, then we talk! Lv, M.*

"Shit," I said.

The fat girl plopped down on the living room couch. "What did you expect?"

I walked past her and into the kitchen. I took an apple from a bowl on the table and bit hard as I sat down, but it was mealy so I got up and tossed it in the garbage. In the fridge there was a pint of skim milk, half a bottle of white wine, something brown in a Tupperware container, a package of Weight Watcher's lasagna with a yellow Post-it on it (*Faith*), and some white cheese.

The night seemed incredibly quiet. I sat there with my feet on the table, telling myself lasagna was fine, but then my mind drifted to the hospital and Andrea Dutton, to her mother's bright voice, and then to the "talk" with my mother, which I could almost map out word for word before she even got home. All about my *need to take responsibility* and my *incredible insensitivity and selfishness* . . . There were only a few variations on how self-centered I was and how much my mother sacrificed to do well by me since my father's departure. Even *departure,* a word she often used when yelling at me, made it sound like he'd left her on purpose, not keeled over. I sat in the growing darkness, waiting for her to return.

"Let's have a glass of wine," the fat girl said. "One little glass."

I closed my eyes and sighed.

"Come on," she said. "You want to sit here and wait to get into trouble?"

No. I rose and went to the fridge again and got out the lasagna. I took a cold bite, standing at the counter, but it seemed to grow in my mouth. I forced myself to chew and swallow and took another, and a third, then dumped the rest down the garbage disposal and switched it on.

The fat girl was watching me. "Well?" she said.

"I haven't had anything to drink since a certain red punch. I thought you were supposed to look after me."

"Says who?" The fat girl winked. "Come on. We're practicing for the real world."

I grabbed the bottle by the neck and followed her out the door.

When I returned home for the second time that evening I was cold and drunk. The fat girl and I had wandered around drinking from the bottle and sneaking through the darkness until the damp ground and icy air got to be too much.

My mother was asleep on the couch in the living room with an empty glass on the floor by her head and a magazine by her feet. I closed the front door carefully and tiptoed up the stairs holding my breath to be as silent as possible.

"Faith?"

I froze.

"Faith?"

"Yes." My lips were rubbery and thick. I concentrated on sounding normal. "I'm really tired. I'm going to bed."

"I want to talk to you." Her drowsy voice still came from the living room and I weighed the idea of running up the stairs and locking my door but thought better of it. Reason was nearly always the best approach to my mother.

"Can we do it in the morning?" I took a deep breath. "Mom, it was an accident about Fern. I should have called."

Wrong thing to say. I heard her rise and thump down the hall.

"You're damn right you should have called! You think money is free? I have to pay for your therapy even if you don't show up, and you wasted Fern's *time*, Faith. That's a very *arrogant* thing to do."

I didn't say anything. My back was still to her, my hand on the banister heading up. My cheeks were hot.

"Turn around and answer me, young lady."

"I'm sorry, Mom." I turned around but kept my eyes lowered, staring at the brown carpet and my mother's stocking feet, the tiny black seam across her toes. "I stayed after for help in chemistry and . . ." I tried to control my voice, but my words were blurry and I felt myself sway. My mother didn't seem to notice.

"This is a warning, Faith," she said. "I want you to think about your actions. Understand?"

I stifled a sigh.

"Yes, ma'am," I said.

She seemed satisfied and turned to go. "Oh, by the way," she said over her shoulder, "some woman from Clark's restaurant called and left a phone number. Didn't say what it was about."

She hovered for a minute, her back to me. She seemed to be waiting for something.

"Job," I said. "I applied for a job."

"Oh." She straightened a picture on the wall. "I see. You don't have time to go to Fern, but you have time to run across town? Is this *job* going to interfere with your schoolwork? With your therapy?"

"No. I promise."

"We'll see," she said, and left.

Gratefully I made my way to bed.

~~~

In the morning I stumbled to the bathroom and drank glass after glass of water, head pounding, mouth full of sand. My skin smelled sour, like wine. A shower helped immensely, and by the time I'd made it downstairs, dressed and ready to go, the evening before had diminished to a dull throb and some wooziness. Not entirely pleasant, but manageable.

On the kitchen table was a note: *Emily—Clark's*, and a phone number. I folded it, tucked it in my pocket, drank a glass of skim milk, and left for school. The fat girl met me at the corner of Darby Road.

"Ugh," she said. She looked awful. She was wearing an enormous gray coat over her shapeless blue dress. Her hair was matted on one side and she had dark bags under her eyes.

"You look terrible," I said, but she just glared at me and lumbered along. Each car that passed seemed to fill her with pain. "Ugh," she said. "Oh."

"What's wrong with you?"

She didn't speak. I fingered the note in my pocket. "I'll call after school," I said.

She stopped short and swayed a little. Her face was shiny and pale. "You okay?" I reached out to touch her but she backed away, then turned and walked in the opposite direction of school. I waited for a minute, watching her. After a few more steps she turned and bent double, vomiting into the ditch by the road. I dropped my bag and ran over. I pulled her hair back and ran my hand in circles on her back. When her heaving finally stopped she straightened slowly and wiped her mouth with the back of her sleeve.

"You're going to be late," she said.

I stood uncertainly and then walked ahead, scooped my bag up, and headed towards school. I checked over my shoulder. She was still standing there in her gray coat but I went ahead anyway.

~~~

Jenny Sims was a cheerleader like Andrea. She had big pouty lips and a way of listening with her head tilted gently. Today she wore jeans so faded they were almost white and a gray zip-up sweatshirt over a pale pink T-shirt. Her streaked blond hair was pulled back in a ponytail that hung with just the right amount of bounce. Her heavy bangs brushed her eyes, which were clear and lashy and so blue they were almost violet. She was endearingly shy and very smart. All the guys were in love with her. Everything about her was feminine—she even walked in a quiet, girly way. Everyone wanted to be near her. Though I'd been in classes with her since elementary school, I had never actually spoken to her, but she was best friends with Andrea Dutton, so she must have been who Mrs. Dutton meant.

After third period American history I followed Jenny Sims into the hall. I wanted to say something, but I didn't know what. All around us people called to each other and slammed lockers. I couldn't tear my eyes from the back of Jenny Sims's tiny head or her swinging ponytail. The fat girl stood by my side.

Jenny reached her locker and fumbled with her combination. I shifted from one foot to the other, unsure of what I wanted to say. Someone walked past and bumped me so that I banged against the lockers. Jenny Sims looked up.

"Hi," I said. My mouth was dry. I was acutely aware of the fat girl humming beside me.

Jenny focused on her locker and the business of exchanging books. I tried to remind myself that she was shy. "I'm Faith," I said.

Silence, then a small "I know."

I cleared my throat and took a deep breath. "I was at the hospital yesterday. I mean I had to visit someone, so . . . my uncle, I had to visit him and so I was in Gleryton Hospital, you know . . ."

She faced me, hands crossed over her textbooks, a patient, slightly bored look on her face. I could tell she was watching people pass by to see if they noticed us talking.

". . . and so I just happened to be near the twelfth floor and so I stopped in to see Andrea Dutton—"

"What?" She gave me her full attention now. "You did what?"

"I visited Andrea and her mother—"

Jenny Sims shook her head, turned around, and walked away. I followed. I had to dodge people to keep up with her. "Hey," I called. "Hey!" But she just kept going, slipping up the stairs towards the library.

"She wants you to visit," I yelled after her retreating figure. "That's all."

People in a hurry jostled past me so that I bounced to one side, then the other. Jenny Sims disappeared through the library doors. I just stood there, my whole body loose and confused.

"Smoke," the fat girl said.

Tony Giobambera could have finished his cigarette by now, but I hadn't the heart to hurry. Who was I to care whether Andrea Dutton got visitors if her best friend didn't even care? We pushed outside and plopped down on the cold ground.

"I can't take much more of this," the fat girl muttered. I saw frosting on her cheek. She had her head back as though sunbathing, but the day was gray, the light was thin.

I lay back and closed my eyes and tried, like her, to feel the sun.

FOUR

I CALLED Clark's restaurant and was told to report for training that afternoon. I hung up the phone and leapt around the room whooping and shouting. *Job! Job! Job!* I didn't care how hard it would be as long as I could make some money, stash it away, and go somewhere else, somewhere it was possible to start over. The fat girl watched me from the couch, a pint of mint ice cream in her lap. She didn't say anything, just shook her head and licked the back of her spoon.

I arrived at the restaurant wearing the white oxford shirt and black pants I'd had on when I applied. Emily introduced herself as the night manager and then presented me to Chuck, a tall stringy guy with spiky red hair and tattoos that wound up his arms, disappearing under his rolled-up sleeves and reappearing at the edge of his neck. He didn't look directly at me but handed me an apron and showed me how to tie it, then pointed things out to me—bus buckets, bar mops, lowboys—I thought that even the lingo was exciting.

I had a dull flicker I couldn't place. I recognized him as the guy who'd been wiping glasses when I came in to apply, but I also had the sense that I knew him from somewhere. I expected this feeling to diminish over the course of the evening, but it didn't. While Chuck showed me how to set a table, where the utensils were kept, how to pour water from the side of a pitcher, it grew, slow and steady, like a subtle warmth. I knew that I knew him.

We were halfway through the shift when I figured it out.

"You have to empty the trash periodically," Chuck was saying. "Otherwise the wait staff can't scrape for the dishwasher and he'll get mad and call you a son of a bitch and the chefs can't toss their shit and they get mad and you don't eat, right? So here's the fresh bags and out there's the Dumpster."

He had a way of talking and moving at the same time, illustrating things with his hands by slicing the air in big circles or, now, hoisting a huge garbage bag over one shoulder.

I followed him to the Dumpster. "We can smoke out here," he said. "Provided it's not too busy. If it's busy they'll kill you. Or if they're just in a bad mood." He laughed. "Whichever."

"Are they too busy now?" I asked, but he ignored me.

"Make no mistake. You're the fall guy around here. Someone needs a scapegoat, you're it. It's always the bus. Waitress gets a bad tip, her first re-action is *Chuck, did you take money off twenty-six?*"

He said this in a high squeaky voice with a hand on either hip, his lips squeezed like he tasted something sour. He shook a finger at me. "*Because they were nice people and I know for a FACT they wouldn't leave me such a shit-ass tip.*"

He fished a pack of cigarettes from his pocket and offered me one, then leaned back against the Dumpster. "Now you listen to me, girl. Every-one'll leave a shit-ass tip now and again. Some more than others, but everyone's capable, and"—he hit his chest—"Charlie Yates doesn't swipe tips." He grinned, then struck a match and inhaled. He leaned his head back and blew smoke at the sky while handing me the matches on his open palm.

But I didn't take them, or even hear what he said next, because I was too busy hearing what he'd just said: Yates. Charlie Yates was Starling's twenty-year-old brother, I was almost positive. He was from Yander and he'd visited her in the hospital once, though I'd only seen him from a dis-tance. She'd told me so much about him. I didn't know what to say.

"—fucking dishes, too. I mean it isn't like they don't break a glass here or there through the course of the night, right, but who do they look to when the count is low? Bus. That's your answer—"

The door opened and a pissed-looking blonde stuck her head outside. It seemed like it pained her to speak to us.

"Hel-*lo*, Chuck," she said. "I need water on four, twelve, and sixteen, and Marcy has *two* tables that need to be cleared."

She turned and went back inside.

Charlie sighed, dropped his cigarette, and ground it into the pavement. He mumbled something under his breath and shook his head. I still couldn't think of what to say, only that this was Charlie who Starling had whispered about; Charlie who had a boyfriend in the circus; Charlie who she'd thought could save her. This was Charlie who'd done all those things she'd told me and here I was set to work with him every night.

I dropped my unlit cigarette and tried to grind it like he had. Then I followed him back inside.

~~~

We refilled water and cleared dirty dishes. We brought clean forks and warm bread to people who didn't even notice us. All the while we were careful to keep our white aprons pristine and our expressions polite. We emptied garbage. We fetched clean napkins. And at the end of the evening we sat down to eat.

For the first time in almost a year I was starving.

We had chicken and corn bread, black-eyed peas and greens. When Emily, the night manager, wasn't looking, Charlie poured half of his beer into a glass and stuck a straw in it for me. "Your ginger ale," he said loudly when he set it down in front of me. I thought I saw a waitress roll her eyes but kept myself from double-checking.

Instead, I watched Charlie.

He ate quickly and with great concentration—gusto, even. He used the corn bread to sop up the gravy on his plate and every so often he gave a satisfied grunt. "Mmmhmmm," he said, and washed it all down with beer.

He ate all of his and half of mine, which was okay with me, as it hadn't taken much to fill me up. The beer and the sounds of the empty restaurant made me drowsy. It echoed with our movements and those of the wait staff in the booth behind us. Even the kitchen was quiet. The chef and the dishwasher sat at the bar nursing drinks.

"It ain't a bad place to be," Charlie said, looking at me with the sleepy eyes of a big meal finished quickly. "I've worked here a while and don't have many complaints, you know. I don't mind it so much and they're good about letting me go when I need to." He closed his eyes and let out a huge resounding belch that prompted groans, snorts, and giggles from the table behind us.

"Chuck, you are so nasty," someone said.

He grinned and tipped the last of his beer at me. "Hey, you were good tonight. You'll work out just fine."

"Thanks," I said. It was the first he'd really addressed me, instead of just talking or teaching, and I warmed at his words.

"I'm real happy to have a job," I said.

And something washed over me then, something warm and comfortable. I found myself wanting to tell him things, wanting to explain about leaving and ask his advice. But I kept quiet.

"You'll do fine," he said again. "Just fine." And then he looked at me strangely, almost like he was seeing me for the first time. He shook his head and got up to clear our plates.

~~~

Outside Clark's, the fat girl was perched on a wide concrete planter, smoking a cigarette. "Since when do you smoke?" I said. My head still spun from the night. I was deeply and thoroughly exhausted—even my bones felt heavy. The fat girl sneered, narrowed her eyes, and fell into step beside me.

The evening was nippy and I wished I'd worn a coat, but I was too satisfied with the way things had gone to worry much about it. The voices of the restaurant swam through my head—laughter, orders, music, the clinking of glasses and scraping of forks against plates. I found myself grinning at things I'd overheard, and at Charlie's praise.

"Hello," the fat girl said.

"What?" It came out harsher than I'd meant it. I kept walking. There were crickets chirping and from one of the small houses off in the distance I heard the laughter of a television. The fat girl's hands were free and swung by her side. She marched along, not looking in my direction. Her voice was nasty and sharp.

"So you don't feel like filling me in on your evening?"

"What do you want to know?"

"What do you think I might want to know?" She gave an angry grunt. "Why are you playing games with me? You know very well what I would want to know."

She stopped and grabbed me by the arm so that I jerked back.

"Ow."

I didn't meet her eyes. Instead I watched the street and looked at the quiet houses streaming up the road, lit only by porch lights. I thought of all the people sleeping peacefully inside them. Dreaming dense, lovely, unworried things. My evening's elation evaporated slowly, floating away on the chilly breeze.

"Listen," I said, finally. "There's not much to tell. You could have come inside if you were so interested."

"Would you have liked that, Faith?" She jerked my arm again, and I saw that her teeth were clenched. There were tears in her eyes.

"What do you think I do for you, Faith?" She pounded her chest. "I protect you. I keep you as safe as I can. You can't shut me out." She wrapped her arms around me and pulled me to her. I was stiff and wooden but she hugged me just the same. "You need me," she crooned, rocking back and forth. "You do. Remember that, okay? You need me."

~~~

The next morning, when I turned into the driveway of school, I saw Tony Giobambera locking up LilyAnn in the parking lot. I didn't know whether to wait or not, but I slowed my gait enough that I arrived at the walkway almost the same time he did.

"Hey," I said. It escaped before I had time to obsess over speaking or not speaking, and Tony, who I suppose was accustomed to people speaking to him at school, nodded in my direction, lifted a hand, and then held the door open for me.

I felt everyone looking. I passed by him and it was as though the world had slowed to turn and watch as we walked in, him just a little behind but unarguably *next* to me, close enough to establish that we were walking *together*, through school. And then, like thunder, it all crashed back to normal speed, lockers slamming, people calling to each other, books falling and sliding along the linoleum, the click of locks opened and shut. And there, in our path, stood Jenny Sims, books balanced on one perfect hip, head a little to the side so that her white-gold ponytail tickled one shoulder.

"Hey babe," Tony said, and reached down and kissed her full and long on the mouth.

I couldn't breathe. She gave me a look, part smile, part ice, linked her arm through his, and pulled him along. I stood still, frozen to my spot on the floor. Tony looked over his shoulder at me and nodded good-bye.

And, just a hair too late, I nodded back and the bell rang.

~~~

"What did you expect, Faith?"

I ignored the fat girl, outside on the wall—left her to her mountain of crab legs and what was left of the cocktail sauce. I watched my breath clouding in the morning cool. We had to get to English. I was supposed to have read *The Scarlet Letter,* but I hadn't. I hadn't read much of anything, but I knew Mr. Feldman would leave me alone.

In the hall I tried to get my bearings. Here was the school I knew as I knew life itself: the goods and bads, the things I understood and things I never would. And then there was Clark's, where I'd felt myself evaluated purely on the basis of how I carried trash or replaced a dropped spoon. I was useful, needed, but without context.

I liked it.

I didn't have to see Fern for another few days and as I walked towards my locker I thought about what I might say, the things she'd want to hear, that would prevent her from trying to climb inside my head: *taking responsibility, learning acceptance, trying my best.*

~~~

Clark's quickly became routine and familiar. My ability to escape detection was an asset—no one wants to see the busgirl—and somehow I was able to refill water, replace silverware, and wipe tables without anyone really focusing on me. I loved the mindlessness of it—pure energy, physical response without thought. I liked the surge of chatter, the music of crockery, of glass and utensil. I liked following Charlie around and the careful conversations we had out back while sneaking cigarettes.

I waited to tell him about Starling. Not intentionally, but I hadn't told him when I first figured it out, and now it felt weird to say anything. I didn't know how to bring it up or how he would react. In the four shifts I'd worked with him, he still hadn't mentioned her, or even his family. All he talked about so far was circuses and sideshows and his tattoos. He dreamed of becoming a fully illustrated man.

A huge, fierce tiger crouched across his left shoulder. It was red and orange and yellow and black. There was a brown-and-red falcon flying along his forearm. On one of his hands, above the knuckles, small dark letters spelled PRINCE, and on the other, FLAME. A colorful, complicated band of dancing Gypsies circled his right wrist, and on the side of his neck, just under one ear, a finely scaled snake curled in loops. And though I hadn't seen it, I knew what was inked over his heart: three chickens—one pink, one pale green, one light blue.

But I'd begun to fixate on how to confess all I knew about him, that I'd seen Starling sleeping night after night, that she'd told me how their mother had left when she was a toddler, about their spaced-out father and raising themselves.

Then one night Charlie said, "You're funny. You listen really hard." We were out back, leaning against the enormous Dumpster and watching through the large windows as the staff set up for dinner.

"Why is that funny?" I asked. I was very tired. The fat girl had kept me up the night before, bothering me endlessly while I tried to study and then shaking me awake to ask me when we should go, where we should go. North? West? What about New Orleans? All day I'd felt like my head was full of syrup.

"I don't know," he said, thoughtfully. "I guess people aren't usually interested in other people the way you are . . . but that's cool."

Off in the distance a train whistled and then a car alarm began to bleat. We were still for a long time. I took a deep breath.

"How'd you come to be so into the circus?" I asked. I couldn't look at his face.

"It's a long story," he said. "I'll tell you some other time," and then we went inside.

~~~~~

"I knew her," I said later while he hoisted garbage from the dishwasher's trash can. "Your sister, Starling. I knew her. At Berrybrook."

~~~~~

Later we sat outside under the stars in the parking lot and I told him how Starling used to laugh and make us all laugh. How, in her manic periods, she could convince us to do anything that occurred to her. Dance, play Truth or Dare. Or, one time, gather all the toilet paper on the ward and use it to bowl down the hall. How when she was gone we barely spoke to each other anymore. How still those halls became without her wild energy, her all-encompassing madness.

While I spoke and he listened, I was calm. It felt right, like he was a part of Starling and she was with us.

Charlie smoked cigarette after cigarette, his jaw clenched, fingers trembling. It was very late, nearly midnight. The restaurant had closed at nine and everyone had left by ten.

"I miss her," he said. "So damn much."

I reached out and touched his arm, lightly put my fingers on the falcon. Only for a second. Then my hand felt heavy and awkward. Out of the corner of my eye I saw a blur of blue and turned. The fat girl leaned against the side of the building. She looked angry and mean.

"What do you see?" He sounded curious and turned to look over his shoulder one way, and then the other. "Is it a ghost?" he asked, but I could tell he wasn't making fun. I shook my head and closed my eyes. I felt the fat girl watching and couldn't breathe. I bit my bottom lip and dug my fin-

gernails into the soft underside of my wrist as deep as I could, and it hurt.
I blinked the tears back.

"I see things sometimes," he said. "It's okay."

"I'm going to leave here," I blurted, and felt the fat girl's fury like a laser
beam but I didn't care, not at all, it was so good to get it out. "I'm going to
get out of here and go somewhere else."

"Where?"

I wished that I knew. "Maybe New Orleans," I said. "Or San Francisco.
Or somewhere north, you know. Like New York City."

"When?"

I shrugged. "I don't know."

"Hmmmm." He didn't seem surprised or alarmed. It was really quiet
then. Not even a car in the distance, no moon to get the crickets going.

Charlie lit another cigarette, then pointed to his falcon. "I got this one
at this place called Mike's in Nashville. It wasn't my first." He touched his
heart, where I knew the chickens were. "I got something else first. But I
knew I wanted more after that. Tattoos are weird, you know. They're, like,
addictive. You fall in love with them and then you want to cover yourself.
It's like you're reclaiming your body or something. Marking it up just for
yourself."

He blew a smoke ring and I leaned over and took a cigarette without
asking.

"The thing is I always wanted to be in the circus, ever since I was little. Well, Starling must have told you that. But, see, I didn't have anything I could do. I'm not the clowning type, right. I'm not a juggler or an
aerialist or a tumbler or whatever. So it wasn't until I met Marco—" He
jerked his head up suddenly. "Starling probably told you that too, right?
About me?"

"He's your boyfriend?"

Charlie nodded. "Yeah. And he's in the sideshow. I never thought it
could be possible until I met him."

He shook his head. "But anyway, Nashville, right? I'd left town and was
living there for a while. I was trying to find a place . . . I don't know. I liked
it and all, I mean I sort of connected with some of the folks I met, but . . .
The thing is, the only place I've ever felt like I wasn't all the time getting
judged for some bullshit or other was when I've been with a show."

I waited for him to go on but he didn't. After a minute or so, he said,
"Sometime—I mean not tonight, okay—but sometime you should tell me
why you're going."

I nodded.

He put out the cigarette and stood up.

I stood also and then Starling's big brother wrapped his long arms around me, and I couldn't fight it back anymore, I began to sob, all of it tumbling out of me like an avalanche. He held me tight and rocked a little. "It's okay," he said.

~~~

Oh, the freedom in that. The freedom in letting even some of the bats out of the attic, the rats out of the dungeon. Charlie drove me home and I left his car feeling light and giddy. When I got upstairs, the fat girl was sitting on my bed.

"Move," I said. It was odd how strong I felt. Without saying a word she rose slowly and walked to the chair. I threw my bag down and pulled my pajamas from under my pillow.

"Tomorrow's Fern," the fat girl said.

"I know."

"I hope you won't be sharing anything inappropriate with *her*."

I changed out of my clothes completely before answering. I turned but she was staring out the window into the night. I shook my head. "No," I said quietly.

~~~

First period. Art. Tiny, chipper Ms. Winters wasn't there. Instead we had a substitute, a huge, barrel-chested man in a crisp white shirt and a camouflage tie.

"I am Mr. Goffelnowski," he said, and wrote it on the board at the same time in huge loopy letters. His handwriting was girly, but he looked like a marine.

He leaned against the blackboard and ran one hand through his silvery crew cut. "I'm your substitute today, and I will not put up with funny business, am I understood?!" He had the voice of a drill sergeant. Everyone exchanged looks. Across the table from me, wheezy Bobby Thomson raised an eyebrow. No one was in the mood to argue at eight-fifteen. We all nodded.

"Take out some paper," Mr. Goffelnowski commanded. We didn't move. This was confusing: did he mean notebook paper or the drawing paper that Ms. Winters kept in the cabinet by her desk? "I SAID TAKE OUT SOME PAPER!"

Out came the notebooks. The room filled with the clatter of binders opening and closing, the zip of paper torn from spirals.

Mr. Goffelnowski paced the room now, depositing a small pile of number-two pencils on each table. "Don't touch these until I tell you to!" he said, pointing at the pencils and warning us with his eyes. "Okay. Now, *everyone take a pencil.*"

We did.

"And . . ." he raised one arm above his head and pointed a finger at the ceiling tiles. "GET READY . . . *get set* . . ." He lunged forward and lowered his arm as if we were to clear the starting gate. "DRAW!"

Again confusion kept us from moving. We were used to Ms. Winters, who was in her mid-twenties and liked to play music and tell us to choose a color for the way we felt that day.

"DOES ANYONE IN THIS ROOM WANT TO DO *PUSH-UPS*? HUH? IN FRONT OF THE WHOLE G.D. CLASS?!"

Silence.

"WELL THEN YOU BETTER GET TO IT, UNDERSTAND?"

We did. We spent the rest of the period scribbling, doodling, and shading, in consecrated silence.

~~~

When the bell rang, the fat girl was waiting by my locker with a corn dog that she swirled in a small cup of ketchup.

"Hi," I said. I was sleepy and my hand, which was covered in graphite from the number-two pencil, ached from all the drawing. "You missed a hell of a sub," I told her, but she was deep into the corn dog. We walked to the bathroom. I saw Jenny Sims down the hall and wondered if she'd visited Andrea Dutton yet.

"Doubt it," the fat girl said. She had ketchup on her chin and down the front of her blue shirt. I pointed at it. "Shit," she said.

Ahead of us Jenny pushed through the bathroom doors and we followed. There was a cluster of five or six girls in there, so I had to wait for a sink. The fat girl stood in the corner dabbing at her chest with paper towels. Finally a sink opened up. In the mirror I could see that the bathroom had emptied out and I squirted my palms with stinky pink soap from the dispenser.

"Great," said the fat girl. "Now you're going to smell like a dentist's office all day."

"Shut up. Like you smell so great yourself," I said, just as Jenny Sims walked out of a stall.

I froze. She raised her eyebrows and gave a little laugh. "Excuse me?" She looked around. "Who were you talking to?"

"No one."

She opened her eyes wide. "Riiiiiiight," she said slowly, then washed her hands and left.

"Hey," the fat girl said.

I looked down; the water was still running and my hands were red. I turned it off and wiped them on my jeans. I had the dizzying feeling that the world had just tumbled away from me again.

"Oh shit," I said, and we headed to English.

~~~

By fourth period I was convinced that everyone was laughing at me.

"You need to relax," the fat girl said, but I kept my mouth shut, afraid to answer. We passed Tony Giobambera in the hall and he didn't look at me. I stopped and turned to follow him, but the fat girl hooked my arm and dragged me to math.

Missy Groski smiled creepily when I walked in.

When I sat down she turned around. "Talk to yourself much, freak?" She shook her head and wrinkled her nose in disgust.

My face burned. Jenny was friends with Missy. I felt sick.

"Page two seventy-six," Mrs. Lemont said.

~~~

By gym, I was a sweaty wreck. All of a sudden I'd been noticed, but in the wrong way, in an awful way. I told Coach Ford that I didn't feel well and he let me sit on the bleachers even though I didn't have a note—more proof that I was an acknowledged crazy person.

"You're really paranoid," the fat girl said.

The class was playing volleyball, split into four teams, rotating serves. The room was incredibly loud and echoed as balls slammed off the ceiling and walls and gym floor, and people yelled things back and forth to each other. I felt it might be safe to talk.

"Okay," I said, trying to move my lips as little as possible. "How are we going to leave?"

"You want to get them back, Faith. To send a message, you have to make a move."

"I don't even know who they are," I said, and my voice was small.

"I think you do."

But I didn't, did I? Everything seemed insurmountable. I stared at her until she met my gaze. "I really don't know who they are," I said. "Really."

She sighed and shook her head. "Unbelievable."

"But you know?"

She nodded.

I looked back at the game as a tall, muscled boy lunged at the net and missed a return. I bit my lip. "What exactly did you mean by make a move?" I said.

She watched me for a minute and then she smiled.

"All right," she said. "Good."

~~~

I was nervous to see Charlie again. I hadn't worked since that late, confessional evening and I worried that he might behave as though nothing at all had happened. But I was wrong.

"Faith!" Charlie called from across the restaurant. "How's my gal?" He was grinning. My whole body through to my bones relaxed and I smiled back at him. "Look at this," he said when I got close enough. He unbuttoned and unrolled his sleeve to show me a huge white bandage with a dark stain, covering the middle of his forearm.

"What happened?"

"New tattoo," he said.

I made a face. "I didn't know they bled."

"Totally normal." But he winced as he carefully peeled the bandage back. On his arm was a carousel, very colorful and scabby.

"It's beautiful," I said. It was so detailed and intricate I could almost see it moving.

"Look carefully . . . what's missing?"

I concentrated but I wasn't sure. I blinked up at him and he smiled.

~~~

"It's the brass ring," I said half an hour later when we had both donned our aprons and were drying the silverware with bar mops.

"Huh?"

"That's what's missing, right?"

"You're good," he said, and smiled.

"Did your boyfriend get the brass ring on his arm?"

Charlie dropped a fork and clamped a hand over my mouth, his eyes wide with alarm. He hissed, "*SHHHHHHHHHHH*," and looked over his shoulder, but the chef was downstairs; the wait staff had only just begun to arrive and were chattering away in the dining room.

"Sorry," I mumbled through his palm. And when he released me: "What's wrong?"

"Look . . . no one knows about me here and I like it that way, okay?"

I nodded. All secrets were safe with me.

~~~

At school I was a robot, a Martian, a ghost. I floated through the halls with my mouth closed and my eyes open. I was stealthy, like a busgirl, but I was watching.

~~~

"Can you cover for me?" Charlie whispered. I had a tray of waters and the dining room was full.

"Whatever you need."

"I'm just running to the bathroom."

"No problem, Charlie. Go."

He was gone twenty or thirty minutes. I cleared dishes so fast that Jerry, the dishwasher, gave me a dirty look. Finally Charlie returned, drowsy-eyed and amiable. He thanked me.

"It's nothing," I said. "Anytime."

He gave me the thumbs-up.

~~~

After chemistry, which I was barely passing, I walked home. Instead of Yander's small houses and the neighborhoods beyond them, instead of the housing projects and then the lovely gates of our street, I saw city streets and skyscrapers. I saw the Eiffel Tower and the Mississippi River. I saw California hills and the Hollywood sign. I saw anything else I could conjure besides Gleryton.

~~~

By the Dumpster Charlie smoked with his thumb and forefinger. He exhaled upwards. I watched carefully and tried my hardest to copy him exactly. When he dropped a cigarette on the pavement, he ground it to nothing with one delicate twist of his right toe. I did the same. If we were very busy and very tired, sometimes we'd squat while we smoked, the relief in our tired legs making up for the discomfort. When he stood, he stretched his arms and twisted his back until it popped. I did the same, and followed him inside with the closest imitation of his cocky step that I could muster.

~~~

The fat girl had a banana muffin and was humming to herself as we walked along Darby Road. The morning air was chilly. I took mittens out of my pockets and watched my breath drift up and away from us like cigarette smoke. "What do you think of tattoos?" I asked.

She narrowed her eyes. "I don't like his influence on you."

"You're just jealous because I have a friend."

"Ha!" Then: "Faith, are you sure you can trust him?"

I turned sharply and examined her big soft face for some trace of guile, but she just stared back at me, all unblinking innocence. I looked away and we kept walking. "I trust him," I said.

"Really," she said. "Because I don't."

~~~

Boys moved through the halls like packs of wild dogs. The fat girl watched me watch them. They were all different sizes, all different heights, but their limbs were somehow uniform, equalized by the similarity in their strides. They were loose and dangerous.

"They need to pay," she whispered.

My stomach clenched and I scowled at her.

But I knew she was right.

~~~

My mother was waiting for me at home after my shift. "We don't talk," she said when I sat opposite her at the kitchen table. "I don't see you anymore."

It sounded rehearsed. I was tired, but I'd been expecting this. I'd been expecting something from her.

"What do you want to talk about?"

Silence. She had an empty glass in front of her and she put it to her mouth as though to take a drink, then put it down again. She rubbed both eyes with one hand. "I don't know," she said finally, her voice low.

I waited for something else, but it didn't come and the minutes just kept ticking by. I was going to leave her alone in this house. I'd been convinced that it would be easier for her, that secretly she wanted me gone as much as I wanted to go, but now I wondered at that. She looked ragged, my mother. Stretched thin and taut. It had never occurred to me that she could be as lonely as me in this house. I licked my lips and groped around for a way to talk to her. "Are you okay?" I said.

"Of course."

She sounded cold, which was enough of a warning signal that I had misjudged her mood. "I think I'll go to bed," I said. "I'm exhausted. It was busy tonight."

She tucked her hair behind her ear and picked up the glass again, studying it as though it hid some secret small world in its recesses. Then she cleared her throat.

"I know that you've been smoking, Faith. That is unacceptable."

A snort escaped and I spoke without thinking. "Since when have I ever been acceptable to you?"

She looked like she'd been slapped. "You will not speak to me like that, young lady." Her gray eyes were hard and angry and her voice was low. "You are my goddamn daughter and as long as you live under this roof there are rules. You do not smoke. When you're grown up you can act like a low-class heathen, but until then you will do as I say. Am I understood?" She was standing now, leaning forward.

"Yes," I said, staring at her hands balled into fists, her knuckles white against the table. I waited until she rose to refill her glass before slipping upstairs to the sanctuary of my room.

~～～

Jenny Sims giggled at me in the hall. They all did. Everyone laughed at me or averted their eyes. *That's that girl who talks to herself,* their gesturing eyebrows seemed to say. *The one from Homecoming—you've heard about her.*

I walked without seeing anything, my vision blurry, but I felt the sea of gawkers part, felt heads turn as I passed. And I left a whispering wake.

~～～

Another evening. Charlie leaned against the Dumpster when I came outside. He appeared to be falling asleep. His head floated down to his chest and then bobbed up again.

"Charlie?"

His expression was dopey. He gave me a lazy smile.

"You get any sleep last night?"

He didn't answer. Then shook his head and closed his eyes again. I went back inside and set up by myself. When Emily asked where Chuck was I said he'd gone downstairs for ice. About an hour after the dinner rush started, Charlie was on the floor, refilling waters and clearing dishes. I was moving too fast to watch him. I'd been doing the work of two as furiously as I could by then, hoping to keep such order that Charlie's absence would go unregistered.

"Thanks, doll," he whispered when he passed me on my way out of the kitchen. His words made my whole evening shimmer.

~~~

"I bet he has one," the fat girl said, and gestured towards Tony Giobambera with a corn muffin. It was smoking time. Tony Giobambera took another drag and we watched, leaning against the low wall and shivering in the nippy air.

"I bet he has a tattoo," she said again.

"Where do you think it is?"

"I'd say right below his belly button."

I giggled, but she didn't. "Okay, what do you think it is?" I asked, and nudged her in the arm. She was staring at him intently.

"Maybe . . ." she began, and then was quiet.

"Maybe what?"

"Nothing," she said, and took a big bite of the muffin.

"What?" I said again, but she ignored me and all of a sudden I was uneasy. "You really *do* think he has a tattoo?"

"Faith." She was warning me. Why was she warning me?

"Come on," I said. "A tattoo below his belly button, what do you think it is?"

"I think it's a fat girl," she said, and I filled with icy water. "A fat girl on her knees."

"Him?" I asked with my eyes closed. The world shifted slightly on its axis. I was cold and hot all at once.

She took a gulp of coffee. She gave a slight but definitive nod.

"I'm not ready," I said. "I'm not ready," but I felt something hard and cold growing in my belly, like a rigid little stone, solid and uncompromising.

"Tony Giobambera." I was floating above us, held to the world by my angry little rock.

The fat girl shrugged. "One," she said.

64

~ ~ ~

"Faith, you seem distracted," Fern said. "Is there something on your mind?"

"No." I shook my head for emphasis. "Not at all. I'm just fine."

"Do you feel healthy?" she asked. "Are you still running?"

"Sure," I said. "But maybe not as fast."

She looked up but I didn't care. I was calm. I was strong.

I met her gaze.

She scribbled away.

~ ~ ~

"Two and Three," the fat girl said softly, and I followed her eyes. They were laughing at their lockers.

"Four," she said later. "Five. Six." They walked easily along the same halls as me. My pebble became a stone became a boulder. I was solid from the inside out.

"Seven," she whispered. The bell rang.

~ ~ ~

We were behind the restaurant a few days later and it was late.

"I want to meet your boyfriend sometime," I said.

Charlie lit a joint.

"Well," he said, and took a deep drag. I had to wait a minute for the rest of the sentence. ". . . that can be arranged. You'd like him. Marco can be inspirational."

He grinned at me. I reached for the joint. I had never smoked pot before and told Charlie this. "It's up to you," he said. I took the paper between my fingers and held it to my lips and inhaled.

"Hold it," he said.

I blew the smoke out. I felt entirely normal. What on earth was the big deal?

"It takes a while," he said. "You'll see."

I shivered. It was cold to be out here like this, but beautiful also. The night was clear; the stars were spilled salt on a black table. I took another drag and my lungs felt open and enormous. We sat quietly for a moment. Then Charlie produced a chocolate bar from the pocket of his coat and unwrapped it slowly. I watched the way his fingers worked and marveled at how lovely they were, how fine and thin and delicate.

"Now you gotta try this," Charlie said.

"Your hands," I said. "Beautiful." It was all I could manage. The air was sharp in my lungs. Words seemed difficult, heavy and thick. "Wow," I said. The inadequacy of language floated before me in all its complex magnitude.

Charlie laughed and held out a piece of chocolate. I took it and its sweetness filled my mouth like a rich, gorgeous song. It was the most amazing thing I had ever tasted.

"You, my sweet friend, are stoned."

I smiled and felt my entire face spring alive.

We let the chocolate melt in our mouths. I was full to overflowing, things were fighting their way out. I took a deep breath and it all swam in me, everything pushing itself up, howling to be heard.

"You wanted to know why we're leaving," I said.

Charlie nodded. "Who's we?"

So I told him about the fat girl.

"Is she here right now?" he asked.

She wasn't. Once she'd seen the joint and heard me start speaking she'd shaken her head. The look she gave me. She knew. And she left quickly, arms crossed over her chest, eyes lowered to watch her feet. She'd set out into the night. But she'd be back.

I shook my head. "She doesn't like you," I said. "She doesn't trust you." My mouth was dry.

"Well, why should she? I'm not sure I would if I were her."

I looked into his pale blue eyes and they confused me. "Would you if you were me?"

"Doesn't matter," he said. "You do. That's what matters. You do or you wouldn't tell me about her or leaving."

He was right. My skin felt like marshmallows.

"Or why," he said.

His face was a little uneven, a little off center. His spiky red hair was tucked up in a gray ski cap that covered his ears. His eyes were big and lashy. They looked like marbles, like azure coins.

"I haven't told anyone," I said, and took a deep breath. I tried to choke it down a little but I couldn't help it, I began to cry, silently, tears that fell in warm lines down my cheeks.

"Aw, Faith," he said and put his arm around me. The canvas of his jacket was rough and smelled like stale smoke and restaurant. I leaned against him and felt small and very tired.

Homecoming.

Homecoming.

Homecoming.

I told him. It was strange how calm I was saying it, how the words arrived one after the other in long perfect sentences, and as they did I could see it vividly, the night cold like this, the red punch that had warmed me, the plastic cups. The hands, the dirt beneath the bleachers.

There were nine in total. Nine guys who'd done it. Eight who made me gag and one who'd held me down for the others. One who'd pinned my arms and pinched my nose so my mouth fell open. One who'd squeezed my body with his knees to hold me while they came at me one after the other, unzipped and laughing. He'd worn a ring. It's what I saw while they approached, that and their belts, their jeans.

I could see the frozen ground and I could taste the saltiness of them, each of them, but I couldn't see any of their faces except Tony's. He'd held me down and made it happen.

I felt their weight against me, one after the other. And I heard the deep silence after, the descent of the darkness that covered me until dawn, when I'd stumbled home, step by step.

When I was done Charlie's arm was tight around me and we were quiet like that. Then I told him that's why I was leaving, that and everything else wrong just added up to too much.

He listened closely and then he said, "Before you go, you should fuck them up good. Maybe with the cops. Or maybe some other way."

"How?" I said. "I'm open to suggestions."

He laughed. "How the hell should I know," he said. "But they shouldn't be allowed to get away with that shit."

No. I agreed. They shouldn't.

~~~

That night I slept the sleep of inanimate objects. When I woke Saturday morning, every bone cracked as it shifted into place.

"Sleep well?" the fat girl said. She stood over me, edgy and alert.

"Hardly."

By the time I'd dressed and made my way to the kitchen, there was a note from my mom on the table.

Errands, Lv. M

I crumpled it up and threw it out. The fat girl had her arms crossed over her chest. "I'm ready to get down to business," she said. "You should be too."

So I spent the morning brainstorming. The fat girl had an endless reservoir of awful ideas, each worse than the next. "You could bake him poisonous brownies," she said. "And then stand there and watch him eat them." Or: "You could borrow a car and run him over." Or: "You could get a gun and shoot off his thing."

I doodled on a piece of paper. Firecrackers and severed limbs. I couldn't believe myself. What would Starling have thought, I wondered. But I'd really never know.

"You could get battery acid," the fat girl said. "That would be easy enough."

~ ~ ~

When my mom came home I was reading the paper. "Hi, honey," she said. "Are you going to go running today? It's not too cold."

I nodded and made myself smile.

"Good."

She put the mail on the table. The phone rang and she answered it. I looked up when I heard her *oh*. She watched me with a conspiratorial raise of the eyebrows. "Sure," she said, and called *Faith* as though I weren't sitting right in front of her. She covered the mouthpiece with her hand. "It's a boy," she said, excited.

My stomach bounced but I made myself smile again and took the receiver. "Hello?"

It was Charlie.

"I'm taking you to the circus, doll," he said. "It's time to meet Marco. I'll pick you up in half an hour."

When I hung up, my mother sat facing me with her hands on her knees. "So . . . ?" she said suggestively.

"It's nothing, Mom. Just a friend from work."

"Okay," she said. "I won't pry." Then a few minutes later, "He sounded cute . . ."

"Mom!"

"Okay!" She threw her palms in the air.

I walked outside and sat on the porch swing, swaying gently. The air was chilly but I didn't mind. I twisted from side to side on the swing, my head crowded with ten thousand horrible images, courtesy of the fat girl. What did it say about me that I'd had a crush on someone who did something so awful to me? My throat was tight.

Down the street I saw someone raking leaves. Everything was familiar, but it was astonishing how much had changed in one short year.

And how much hadn't.

I closed my eyes and tried to refocus my thoughts to the circus, to Marco. When I tried to picture him all I got was Charlie with more tattoos, with a brass ring on his cheek. On his forehead. On his bicep.

A horn honked and I jumped, but it was just a neighbor warning a cat out of the road.

When would I know what it was like to have someone hold my hand?

The fat girl rubbed my back.

"That's not what's important," she said. "That's not what matters most right now, okay?"

Then Charlie arrived in his beat-up little monster of a car, ignoring the driveway to park on the street in front of the house. He unfolded himself from the driver's seat and walked up the lawn, a bright flash of copper hair and gray coat against the lush green of the neighborhood. "Hey there," he said, standing on the steps. In the daylight he looked pale and freckly, skinny and unshaven. His vibrant hair was harsh against his milky skin.

"Come on, doll. We're off to see the wizard."

~ ~ ~

We parked on a side street near the fairgrounds and hiked up the hill, along the highway, against traffic. Cars whipped by and I caught my breath each time a vehicle passed.

"Have you been before? To a circus, I mean?" Charlie fumbled in his pockets for a cigarette but couldn't find one.

"I think Ringling Brothers. When I was little."

"Do you remember it?"

I thought back. I remembered noise. I remembered three rings and peanuts and a man shot out of a cannon and a guy locked in a cage with a tiger. I remembered a car full of clowns and my father's big hand on my head, on my shoulder pulling me towards him.

"Fartlesworth is small," Charlie said. "Not such a commercial show. You ever been down a midway? Seen a sideshow?"

I shook my head.

"Well, that's Marco's gig."

"What does he do?"

"He eats things. Anything, really: wood, lightbulbs, nails." He laughed. "Sometimes it's like kissing a hardware store."

I'd never seen two men kiss. Somehow, knowing Charlie was gay had always been theoretical. Now I had a weird image of him leaning towards a big blurry man with a beard. I shook my head.

We crossed the street and continued along a chain-link fence, woven with strips of green plastic so you couldn't see inside. When we came to a place where it was bent back, a hole torn into it, Charlie ducked under and I followed.

We were standing behind a huge red-and-white-striped tent with a few grimy white trailers and pickup trucks parked in the dirt. "That's the main tent," Charlie said, "the big top. Wanna see?"

I nodded and he led me to a back door (actually a place where the tent hung funny) so we could duck inside. In the darkness it took me a minute to notice that my vision was slatted. We had entered under bleachers. My stomach dropped, but then Charlie reached out and grabbed my elbow and I followed him, ducking support beams, until we came to an aisle and could climb out. We faced a ring made of huge red and blue blocks and filled with sawdust. I shook my head to clear it and saw the amazing web of rigging high above us.

Then I noticed the way Charlie looked. It wasn't just that he stood straighter, his shoulders thrown back, or that he was walking differently— less stompy and more bouncy. It was that light seemed to spill from him.

He wore a small private smile that I couldn't read. He shook his head, as though rousing himself, then waved me along and I followed him to a connecting tent. He lifted the flap and I winced at the deep, unforgiving stench of something—a combination of feet and strong cheese magnified a thousandfold.

"Jesus!"

"It's the tigers," Charlie said, out of the corner of his mouth. "They stink."

We passed behind a wooden wall and I heard scratching and shuffling but couldn't see the cages. I imagined them crouching on the other side.

Then we came to a tented tunnel and emerged, blinking in the sudden daylight. So this was the midway. Carnival game trucks and more trailers were set up in two lines on either side, creating a pavement aisle down the middle. Wooden banners yelled for attention but it was really the flags for the sideshow that interested me. SEE THE WORLD'S SMALLEST TAP DANCING BROTHER AND SISTER, TINA AND TIM! one sign said. And another: GODZUKIA! HALF MAN/HALF MONSTER! There was AMOS RUBLE, TALLEST LIVING MAN IN THE ENTIRE UNIVERSE! and LILY VONGERT, THE WORLD'S ONLY THREE-LEGGED BEARDED LADY, and THE AMAZING RUBBERBOY. And at the end, there was GERMANIA LOUDON, THE FATTEST WOMAN ALIVE!

"Germania Loudon," I said out loud, staring at the trailer.

"Yeah, Gerry's cool," Charlie said, popping with energy and pointing to our right. "Come on, Marco's in here."

And he gestured towards a tented trailer that said only THE DIGESTIVORE!

~~~

We entered through a makeshift room extended from the front of the dirty white trailer. Its roof was tarp and its entrance was made of overlapping fabric walls. Inside there was a small platform and a few chairs, and behind the platform, painted in huge red and orange letters on the inside of the trailer, it said again DIGESTIVORE!

Charlie walked straight up to the platform and stepped over it, then disappeared through the door to the trailer. I followed him.

Inside Charlie tackled a big man with a shaved head and a huge smile. "Hi there," Marco said, laughing, and pushed Charlie off him enough to extend a hand to me.

"Hi."

He was older than I'd thought. He had smile lines around his eyes. An adult. A man who Charlie had sex with. I wasn't quite sure what to do with that.

"Faith."

I nodded and looked around. As if on cue, the elements of the trailer had begun to assert themselves from the background. There was a tiny bed to the left and a tiny kitchen to the right, but the trailer was basically one small room. The floor was a checkerboard of green and black tiles. Red-fringed curtains masked the windows behind Marco and above the bed. A huge, ancient-looking wooden trunk squatted in the corner and the little table where Marco had been sitting was supported by one leg and hinged to the wall. There were black-and-white circus photographs everywhere—a woman balanced on a tightrope; a skinny young man with an elephant standing on its back legs; another woman peddling a unicycle on what looked like a high wire, plates stacked precariously on her head; and lots of different, ancient-looking clowns, their faces painted in shades of gray. Some photographs were framed, some were not. They hung and leaned against walls and on the shallow counters and cabinets. With three of us in it, the trailer was crowded.

"Nice to meet you," I mumbled, aware of silence and of being watched.

"Sit." Marco gestured across Charlie, who sat on his lap, and towards a folding chair opposite him. "Make yourself comfortable."

71

I sat.

"Off me, kitten," Marco said, and Charlie extracted himself and pushed his way past us to the bed, where he flopped dramatically onto his back and gave a huge sigh. I watched his movements, but Marco watched me.

"So I hear you wanted to meet me," he said.

I nodded and swallowed. He sounded grave. It occurred to me that Marco's entire life was packed into this small, mobile space. "How long have you been with the circus?" I asked.

"With this show? Two seasons. Before that I was with Wittman's down in Louisiana, and before that in Arkansas, and before that . . . well, all in all"—he grinned—"I've been on the road about eleven years."

I blinked. So he was old.

"Would you like some ice cream, Faith? Kitten, here, tells me you want to run away from home."

I opened my mouth and closed it again. I looked at Charlie but he lay on his back focused with great concentration on trying to balance a pillow on his foot. He seemed unaware that there was anything wrong with spilling my secrets.

"I . . ." I swallowed. "Sure, I'd love some ice cream."

"It's all right, honey," Marco said. "Don't look so worried. I'm not going to call your parents or anything. Now, tell me: what kind of ice cream do you like?"

I tried to smile, but my face seemed to have frozen. What kind of ice cream did I like? It was a simple question but I didn't know what to say.

"What kind do you have?" I asked.

"Oh, now that's cheating," Marco said. "What I want to know is what you *like*, not what you prefer."

I was definitely out of my element. Did I like the right thing? Flavors spun through my mind. Finally one occurred to me.

"Coffee," I said.

"Are you sure?" Marco stared intently and I had the distinct feeling that he was somehow looking through my head and deep into me.

"Yes," I said. "Coffee."

"That's your favorite?"

"Actually Coffee Heath Bar Crunch," I said. "That's even better."

At this Marco's face erupted into a huge smile. He popped up and walked around to the small refrigerator behind me. "Look," he said.

I turned around. Behind the tiny freezer door he held open were two pints of ice cream. Both were Coffee Heath Bar Crunch.

My mouth hung open. "How did you know . . . ?"

Marco just laughed.

"It's his favorite trick," Charlie said from the corner. "The only magic the poor bastard is truly good at . . . *ice cream magic!*"

I turned to Charlie, who had abandoned the pillow to face us, his body propped up on one elbow. Out of his freckly throat came a barker's voice:

"Faith Duckle, may I introduce you, formally, to the great Marco Klie-boski, aka the *Digestivore!* aka the *Ice Cream Wizard. A man who can swal-low anything, ladies and gentlemen, who can take anything all the way doooooooown his throat and bring it back whoooohooop, right back up, a stomach of iron, a belly of steel! AND an instinct for ice cream that will make you blush!"*

By now Marco was laughing, big deep wheezy laughs.

"Seriously," I said, feeling left out of the joke. "How did you know Cof-fee Heath Bar Crunch was my favorite?"

"He didn't," Charlie said, and swung his legs over the edge of the bed and sat up. "It's just my favorite, too."

~~~

After we'd each had a bowl Marco left us at the table and sat cross-legged on the bed rolling a cigarette. His thick fingers were oddly graceful. I found myself unable to stop watching him. He wore black jeans and a tight gray T-shirt and his body was sleek but powerful. He moved like a panther, quick and graceful. Concentrating like this he seemed scary, but when he smiled his entire face transformed. The brass ring tattooed on his forearm was the only tattoo I could see.

"We can stay for the matinee if you want," Charlie said.

"There are two shows today," Marco said without looking up. "Two-thirty and eight."

"He can get us into the two-thirty," Charlie said. "And if we haul ass and miss the finale we can be at work by five." His eyes urged me to say yes.

"Sure."

"Excellent!"

Marco lit his cigarette and smiled. "You ever think of running away with the circus?"

I blushed. "I don't know," I said. "I'll figure something out."

~~~

We walked along the pavement of the midway. I was overwhelmed by everything and I wondered how much Charlie had told Marco, how he'd talked about me. I pinched myself hard and tried to watch the chaos. The midway had transformed in the brief hour or two since we'd shown up at Marco's. Now there were children and adults everywhere, with balloons and enormous stuffed animals, with cotton candy and popcorn and cheap flashing toys. The place was crowded with movement and color in every direction.

Charlie wouldn't let me go in any of the sideshow tents, just as he hadn't wanted me to stay for Marco's show. "Another time," he said. "Not today."

Charlie stopped outside a trailer that proclaimed the psychic talents of THE GREAT ANDRE SARTINI—HE KNOWS YOUR EVERY THOUGHT! "Wait here," he said, and took a small envelope out of his pocket.

"Can't I come with you?"

"No." His voice was firm.

He disappeared and I watched this strange new world. At first I saw only the crowds of parents and kids, but soon I began to notice the other people. The people who seemed to belong to the chaos, who weren't wearing a mask of excitement or delight. Who looked as though this was a typical afternoon for them.

I pulled my hat down farther so that it covered my ears. It was not too warm. Across the way a boy was trying to hit a row of moving ducks with a ball or a beanbag. "Come on, Paul!" his father kept shouting.

"You ready, doll?" Charlie grabbed my elbow and steered me towards the big top, but stopped when we were almost there. I followed his gaze and saw a girl with curly brown hair wearing a pair of overalls duck behind the tent. "Shit," he said.

"What is it?"

He dug in his pockets and pulled out one of the tickets Marco had given us. "I'll meet you up there."

He disappeared around the side of the tent, but instead of going straight in, I waited a minute and then followed slowly in his tracks. I peered around the side of the tent. Charlie and the girl stood close together. Her arms were crossed and he was pointing at her and yelling, his face all red, but I couldn't hear what he said.

Then she slapped him. Hard.

I retreated quickly and scurried into the tent, handing over my ticket and making my way to our seats. We were high up in the bleachers. I watched the crowd but didn't see Charlie approach. Just as the lights were beginning to dim, he sat down beside me and handed me a box of popcorn. There was no trace of agitation, and in the low light I couldn't even see if his cheek was red, but he certainly didn't act like anything had happened.

Then the show began, clowns and animals and all.

So many things happened so quickly: women rode show horses, then a man and a woman led elephants into the ring. A trio of boys flipped and then balanced on each other's shoulders. Clowns tumbled from a tiny car and spilled onto the sawdust floor. All of it hollered to me, everything robbing my attention from everything else.

Soon Charlie was so beside himself that he seemed like a little kid, a whole other person than the wise adult who'd taught me to bus tables. His instant happiness was contagious.

But it was the aerial act that got me. A trapeze artist—THE TALENTED MISS MINA BALLERINA DANCES THROUGH THE AIR!—stood perched atop a high platform in a sparkly gold-and-purple leotard, her black hair pulled tightly back from her face. She clutched a rope with one hand, which she used to swing through the air to a trapeze that hung from the center of the tent. She flew lightly, gracefully, as though it were perfectly natural to trust her entire body to this single thread. When she grabbed the bar of the trapeze and let go of the rope, her body jerked, leaving her hanging by her other hand, and the entire crowd gasped.

She held the weight of her whole body with that one arm, legs in an elegant leap, head back, spinning this way and that, and then slowly she lowered her other arm and in another abrupt move she was hanging upside down from the trapeze by one knee instead, and again the crowd gasped. Now people leaned forward in their seats. She kicked her other leg over and pulled herself into a sitting position. She began to swing the trapeze back and forth lightly, back and forth, until she'd built up momentum and was moving quickly, hanging and swinging. Then with a dainty flourish, she let go and began to fall, catching herself with only the tops of her feet.

My heart pounded. Below her there was no net, just sawdust over hard ground. Charlie leaned close and I almost jumped out of my skin; I had forgotten he was there. I had forgotten there was anything else in the world besides the talented Mina Ballerina.

"She's pretty good," he whispered.

I realized I'd been holding my breath. "She's fantastic," I whispered back. "I mean just *amazing!*"

Mina swung up and instantly was standing on the trapeze, leaning backwards, so that it began to really move. She wrapped herself in the ropes, she suspended herself horizontally in a twist, this way and that, and the whole time she swung nearly the length of the tent, back and forth, high above the sawdust floor.

She slid to a sitting position again, then spun backwards, around and around the narrow trapeze, then forwards. The lights caught her leotard so that she was a sparkly blur. When she stopped spinning she pushed herself up on her arms slowly until she was in a perfect handstand. By now the trapeze wasn't swinging quite as much, but it was moving and she balanced perfectly still and straight, adjusting with the trapeze, as though being upside down was natural. And then she flipped around the bar some more, a windmill, a propeller, a whirling flash of gold and purple high above the rest of us.

A dark-haired man in red tights hung by his knees from another trapeze that swung down towards Mina and away. The whole crowd murmured. Mina came out of her spin and let go of the trapeze altogether, plummeting in a rapid somersault so she was just a moving ball plunging towards the earth.

But he caught her.

Just at the last minute, she extended her arms and he caught her.

~~~

We were late for work.

"Hey, Chiquita," Charlie said to Angelique, the sous chef, when we walked in. She glared after him, then turned to raise an eyebrow at me. Charlie's heavy footsteps thumped down the stairs and we could hear him whistling.

"You guys are in for it," she said under her breath, but I heard her.

I tied on an apron. I hadn't ever been late to work and I was nervous. I didn't have to wait long.

"*Faith!*" Emily's voice crackled over the intercom from the manager's office.

I jumped, then put down the trash bag I was trying to open and made my way through the kitchen, past the tiny door marked PRIVATE, and up the narrow stairs. Emily sat at her desk. I knocked on the open door to the office and she swung around with crossed arms and narrowed eyes, and launched into a tirade without taking a breath.

"I took a chance on you," she said. "And you've been doing a good job, I'll give you that, but when you're late you throw everything into chaos.

Then *you* don't have time to set up, to restock, so the wait staff isn't well attended to, which means the customers get spottier service, which means *we* make a less than perfect impression, so that people don't come back and we go out of business." There were pink spots high up on her chalky cheeks; her eyes bored a hole through me.

"You are *never, ever* to be late again. Am I understood?!"

I nodded meekly, burning with the shame of letting her down.

"Good." She turned back to the papers on her desk. "Send Chuck up here immediately."

I backed out of the office and tore down the stairs and through the kitchen, determined to set up in half the time, to do a spectacular job so Emily would forgive me.

Charlie had changed into his white oxford and apron and was drying the silverware.

"Emily wants to see you," I said.

"*Yates!*" the intercom crackled again.

"Shit," he said, and headed for the office.

By the time he returned, I'd set up the entire bus station myself. He looked paler than normal, shaken.

"Well . . . ?"

He motioned towards the back of the restaurant and I followed him until we were out of earshot. "They are really fucking mad at me," he said in a low voice. "I tried to talk my way out of it, but I can feel it."

"For what? For being late?"

"Never mind," he said. "Listen, I can't . . ." he looked around then shook his head and walked back towards the kitchen. Then we got busy, but unlike usual, we didn't talk.

"I'm sorry, doll," he said a little later that evening when we took the trash out back after the first rush had died down. "I just have a bad feeling about this place. And you don't want them deciding they don't like you just because they don't like me, so we just have to be careful about hanging out for now."

I didn't say anything, just listened and nodded.

"Hey," he said. "That you knew Starling . . ." He gestured at the sky and the surrounding darkness. "I mean, this has been really great to have met you, you know. Fate and everything. It's like the ice cream." He smiled and thrust a piece of paper at me. It had a phone number on it. "I don't know what's going to happen," he said. "But, listen, if it comes to it, fuck these people with their small minds. You come find me."

I folded it and tucked it away.

"We can talk more on Tuesday," he said. Then he put his finger to his lips and slipped back inside.

~~~

Walking home I kept asking myself why, after a day like this day, when he had taken me to see Marco, when he'd found me at my house and taken me to see the circus, to show me something that made him so happy, why did it feel like good-bye?

Halfway home the fat girl blocked my path. She was in a mean mood. "Let me see what he gave you," she said.

"It's just his phone number."

She began to skip ahead, taunting, *"Faithy has a new best friend . . ."*

"Jealous?" I called.

"Ha!"

"Where were you all day?"

She wouldn't answer, just gave me an evil look and fell into step beside me.

"Fine," I said. "Fuck you if you won't talk to me."

I wanted to tell her about the woman on the trapeze. How I'd held my breath and how my heart had pounded. How I'd seen a whole world up there in the air, and the one down here had disappeared. But I didn't say a thing.

FIVE

At school on Monday I passed Tony Giobambera and Number Three having a laugh by a locker. I couldn't breathe. Fuckheads. Assholes. Laughing. Three's name was Jim, the fat girl whispered. There was no air. There was no place to go. I thought about skipping my next class and calling Charlie, leaving school to go hang out at Marco's if Charlie would come get me, but I dug around in my bag and realized I'd left his number at home. I had an appointment with Fern after school. By the time I got home he'd be at Clark's.

I didn't call.

Then on Tuesday, when I next showed up for work, there was a new guy named Frederico with soft brown eyes who didn't speak much English.

I hung my coat up downstairs but Charlie's coat wasn't there. "Where's Chuck?" I asked Angelique, but she pretended not to hear me. No one in the kitchen said anything and I didn't see Emily anywhere, though I wasn't sure it would be wise to ask her anyway. I headed back out to the dining room. The wait staff had started to arrive. They intimidated me, and I didn't usually talk to them, but everything had changed. Now I didn't care. I charged towards the front of the house.

"Where's Charlie?" I asked a redhead named Meg who had just come in the door. Frederico trailed me like an eager shadow.

She looked blank. "Who?" she asked, taking off her coat.

"*Chuck Yates.*" It came out sounding more annoyed than I meant. She raised an eyebrow.

"He walked out in the middle of a shift, the bastard," Marybeth called from across the room. She slammed down a pepper shaker and the girl to her right refilling the salts laughed.

"When?" I said, but they ignored me, folding back into themselves, engaged in their own chatter, the cluster of other wait staff.

I turned around. Frederico stood watching me, expectant. I showed him how to wipe down the tables and then left him to do it himself and went out back.

Light was fading. The sky was pale. I leaned against the Dumpster. There were cigarette butts on the ground, most likely at least some of them Charlie's. I kicked at them with the toe of my shoe. I told myself it was silly—we didn't have to work together to remain friends, we would see each other outside the restaurant like Charlie said, but something felt wrong. In my gut I just knew it.

When I walked back in the restaurant, Frederico had finished the tables and seemed to want another assignment. I found him a clean bar mop and showed him where the utensils were, then closed myself in the old wooden phone booth. I held my breath while I dialed. Something told me that I wasn't going to find Charlie on the other end of the line and I didn't. The phone just rang and rang.

~~~

I heard it all eventually, in bits and pieces that fit together. Some from Angelique, from Meg and Marybeth, from Ernie, another sous chef.

On Saturday, Emily had told Charlie he'd better watch his expendable ass. They thought he was a negative influence, that he was overstepping the boundaries of his profession, not aware of *his place*. They'd thought he was too casual about his duties, about his timeliness, that he was disrespectful to the staff. And more importantly, there was money missing and she had a hunch that he was responsible.

Sunday was a slow night, slow enough to require only one busperson, but not slow enough for none. In the middle of the first rush, Charlie took off his apron and walked out. The wait staff was still pissed, which was what he had probably wanted. "*What's the point of leaving if no one notices?*" I could hear him say.

Towards the end of the evening Emily called me to the office to make sure I understood *how much they trusted me* and *how confident they were in my abilities.* They might need me to pick up a few extra shifts here or there. I nodded and smiled.

But without the magic of Charlie the evening took hours and hours. The job was drudgery; there was nothing to redeem it. Even the pleasure I'd taken in my own invisibility disappeared without Charlie there to see me. Waitresses barked their orders at Frederico and me, and we hopped around, doing their bidding. It wasn't fun anymore. It was hard, nasty work.

~~~

The next day the fat girl was watching Tony smoke. "How can you?" I asked, but she just shook her head like I didn't know what she had up her sleeve and left me to my mission.

I made my way past the swarming crowds to the three pay phones in the lobby. There was a line for each of them and I waited, shifting from foot to foot. I had to pee. The bell was about to ring. Who the hell were these people talking to?

I was next on the middle pay phone. I watched a pimply girl to my left whisper fierce things into the handset. She kept looking over her shoulder at the line and wincing apologetically. Then I glanced at the phone on my right and recognized the caller. I didn't know his name but I knew him. Seven. As soon as the fat girl had pointed him out, I'd remembered him. *Fat girls are hungry.*

My fingers were ice, my body so cold that my heart stopped beating.

"Yo, you're up," someone said from behind me, and the phone was free. I stumbled forward and dug around in my pocket for Charlie's number.

Seven slammed the phone down, ran a hand through his blond hair, and walked off. He hadn't even noticed me.

I dialed and it rang. And rang. I made a wish and waited.

On the sixth ring a man answered. He sounded confused, like I'd just woken him from a deep sleep.

"Hello, may I please speak to Charlie Yates?"

There was a long pause and then, "Who's this?"

"This is . . . I'm a friend from work."

He snorted. "Charlie's gone," he said. "Sorry." But he didn't sound it.

"Excuse me, sir, but I really need to—"

He hung up.

I stood holding the phone to my ear for what felt like a long time. Then I hung it up slowly and walked away in a fog, everything cloudy.

The bell rang, and the hall emptied quickly. I stood for a minute, then made my way towards math, my footsteps echoing, but when I looked through the tiny window in the classroom door and saw Mrs. Lemont's arm and Missy Groski sneering in her seat, I knew I wasn't going in.

I just kept walking. I went from hall to hall, towards the back of the school. The echo of the second bell seemed to linger in the air long after it had stopped ringing. I walked slowly, methodically, though I didn't really know where I was going. I made my way to a small bathroom on the second floor and stayed there. I peed, then sat on the radiator under the screened glass window and tried to figure out what to do.

When the bell rang for lunch, I left. I didn't worry about getting stopped. Nothing mattered. Outside the cold air felt like freedom.

The fat girl fell into step beside me.

We headed to the fairgrounds. We caught a bus and through its smoky windows I watched the world pass. We drove past the projects and then crossed the river into Yander, where each pastel house seemed to whisper. Any of them could have been Charlie's. And Starling's. I never knew exactly where they lived, but with each home we passed, I could see Starling standing in all her tiny madness on the small square lawn, eyes shining bright at me. But Starling was gone too.

"Maybe it's enough to just leave this place," I said, but the fat girl didn't answer.

We passed a park and a playground, stores I had never seen before, or hadn't noticed. The world had a sharp quality that made me want to memorize it, like everything was made of hard angles and primary colors. We stopped so often that by the time we began to climb Dawford Hill, I'd almost forgotten where I was going. The Gleryton Fairgrounds were at the top, on the very edge of town.

We got off the bus and I tried to get my bearings. Pretty quickly I realized where we were, but it didn't matter. Where the green strips of plastic had been torn away, I could see through the chain-link fence that they were gone. The Fartlesworth Circus was gone. In place of the tents and trailers was a shabby flea market. FRIDAY BARGAINS! a sign said.

My heart was so heavy that my chest could barely hold it; I felt it falling, tumbling down inside of me. I pressed myself against the fence and closed my eyes, willing the flea market to disappear, but when I opened them again it was still there, small and sad. I sank down to sit where I was, on the cold sidewalk, and leaned back against the fence.

Gleryton spread down the hill, streets of houses and stores, churches and trees that had defined my entire life so far. Everything so familiar. Everything I knew.

Besides Berrybrook.

The fat girl stood by the fence, hands in her pockets, looking down at me. "I'm here," she said. "I didn't go anywhere."

~~~

I went to work. I smiled and didn't talk. I went home. Again and again. For a whole week. Then Thursday was Thanksgiving.

"I want us to spend some time together," my mother said. "Ever since you started working at Clark's, I never see you."

I set the table. We would eat in the dining room instead of the kitchen. How special.

I spread a white tablecloth, as instructed, got the china from its dusty cabinet, the good silver. "If you like," my mother called from the kitchen in the strange singsong voice she'd taken to lately, "you can have a glass of wine this evening. I don't mind, since it's a special occasion. It'll be a treat."

Silence. I knew I was supposed to be grateful. To say something grateful or excited.

"Only one, though," she called again; her disembodied voice was tinny. "Because, you know, *those are empty calories, honey!*"

Dinner was skinless breast of turkey. No gravy. Fresh cranberries. Microwaved sweet potatoes (four ounces each). Steamed spinach. And one cup of rice.

For a special treat, my mother had made a fat-free pie of some unidentifiable flavor.

She had three scotches while I sipped my wine.

"Isn't this nice?" she said. "Just the two of us."

Like it was unusual. Like we were bombarded with dinner guests, flustered with social engagements. I blinked. The sound of our utensils scratching the plates was excruciating.

Mom tried again. "Aren't you hungry? You're awfully quiet tonight, honey."

I swallowed. What the hell was there to say? I haven't been hungry in months? That cheerful voice you're using freaks me out? I miss Daddy and you don't have any idea who I am? I'm sick of tasteless diet food?

"Mmmmm," I said. "It's delicious, Mom."

~~~

That night I lay awake in the dark and saw a tiny woman flipping through the air, flipping and flying and being caught by strong ready arms. I saw her hang by one foot and whip around, touch nothing for a moment, fall for a moment, then catch herself with one hand.

To be able to fly like that. To float and flip through the air, trusting your body to keep you from falling? What must that be like? Or to trust your body to fall when you wanted to. To trust your body at all.

I wanted to fly. I wanted to fly and be caught like that.

"We should be going."

The fat girl's voice was soft. Half her face was in shadow, half in the cold blue moonlight that tumbled through my bedroom window so she looked like a creepy blue snowman.

I sat up and kicked the covers off. I scooted backwards to lean against the wall and crossed my legs. We faced each other.

"We should," I said. In an inventory of my life what was left?

"What do you want to do?"

"I want to find Charlie and the circus."

Everything was silent. The crickets. The street. My head. Could it really be this simple? One day you're here, the next you're gone? I looked at my room, this room, whose every crack and crevice I had always known. I thought about the words: *Running. Away. From. Home.*

"If I could hold one of them down for you, who would you want it to be?"

I knew who she meant. I said it without thinking. "Tony Giobambera."

"And what would you want to do?"

I let it out slowly. My words were wooden. "Make him sorry. Make sure he never forgets."

She nodded. "Good," she said. "How?"

I pictured Tony Giobambera, his full lips, his lashy eyes. No matter how hard I concentrated I couldn't make him look like he regretted anything. "Couldn't we just leave? Couldn't we mean to do something, but just leave instead?" I said. But I saw his hands, his ring, those long thin fingers that must have held my arms. And I wanted it so badly then, to make him remember what I wanted to forget.

"Let's cut them off." She leaned forward so the lines of the blinds striped her face. She didn't blink. "Each finger," she said. "Slice them off one by one until what he has left are paws."

"They're *fingers*, for Chrissake," I said. "I can't cut off someone's *finger*!"

"You'd be surprised," she said. "Rage can make you awfully gruesome, awfully brave."

"Is that bravery?"

"Whatever. You wouldn't let us both down, would you?"

But the magnitude of the conversation slammed in from all sides. "This is insane."

"And holding you down so other guys could use you wasn't?"

I didn't answer. She took my hand and led me down the dark stairs and into the quiet kitchen. She opened the freezer and began to rummage. My heart hammered away.

She took out a frozen chicken breast and unwrapped it, then dumped it in the sink and ran the hot water over it. I concentrated on the splashing of the sink, the hum of the refrigerator, but nothing could drown out my heart, *Boom! Boom! Boom!*

The fat girl turned to me and leaned back against the sink. "Open the drawer, Faith," she said.

I obeyed. I knew what she was doing. They were all there, all my mother's best weapons, sharp and ready. I wrapped my fingers around the smooth black handle of a big chef's knife, but the fat girl shook her head. She pointed.

I picked up my mother's cleaver.

"Here," she said, and spread the pink chicken out on the butcher block.

I didn't move.

"Fat girls are hungry, Faith."

Wham!

The flesh resisted, but my cleaver sliced right through. My cleaver did its job, cleaved the meat in two.

Fat girls are hungry.

Again.

And she was right. It felt good. It felt really good.

~ ~ ~

American history. Heart hammering. Jenny Sims's ponytail dripped down her back, all honey and highlights.

"Cut it off. Take a buck knife and shave the back of her head."

"Missy Groski would be better off with her mouth stapled shut, with your initials in her cheek."

"And what about the guys . . . *Knife to face, blade splitting flesh. Think of how smooth that would feel . . .*"

The fat girl whispered all of these things to me. Whispered and whistled inside my head.

"If I go find them—the circus—" I said over my shoulder. "Will you come?"

"You think you can leave me behind?" Her eyes squinted to nothing beneath their enormous folds of flesh. She spat a watermelon seed and it bounced off the concrete wall and lay shiny on the floor in the corner of the classroom. Juice dripped down her chin.

"I'm coming," she whispered. "You need me like you wouldn't believe."

My heart was so goddamn loud. In her hand she held the cleaver, its blade newly sharpened, gleaming.

"Another present," she said.

I felt dizzy.

But I took the knife from her.

~~~

And I found myself in the middle of the hallway, people streaming around me like I was a rock in their river, with that cleaver in my hand. And I held its handle so tightly that my knuckles were white, all bone. The tiny gold knife from before wasn't nearly as heavy. Wouldn't have done the job. This knife had substance to it, weight. This knife was angry, it wanted to celebrate its sharpness against something soft and giving, to split flesh from bone. The knife wanted to find them and make them cry. The knife ached, burned to make something happen. And it needed me to do it. It was warm and smooth in my palm.

The fat girl whispered small things, soothing things. Her words burned a path through my head.

My heart stomped and thudded, loud enough to extinguish the noise of the people around me. I had stopped breathing. I didn't need to breathe. I had an angry knife and a mission, a purpose. I had something that needed to be done. I pushed through the crowd, seeing none of them, shoving my way towards the courtyard, where Tony Giobambera sat on his customary bench enjoying his very last ten-fingered cigarette.

SIX

SHE led me to him, to where he smoked on the rock, leaning back on that hand, its fingers spread perfectly, the ring shiny in the morning light. Classes were changing, there was so much noise. A fight broke out across the courtyard and Tony turned to look. He didn't see me coming. I stood there, frozen, and then I swung at him.

The knife passed through his face, through one edge of those beautiful lips and the whole of his rough cheek and clean through. Blood poured from the enormous gash and I dropped the cleaver and ran.

I heard it clatter and I heard screams and I didn't know if they came from me or the fight or from him. From the torn mouth of Tony Giobambera. I didn't look back, just ran as fast as I could, as if that was what I'd been training for all these months. Through the trees behind school, past the old binder factory warehouse, to the abandoned service station with an unlocked bathroom. The fat girl knew what she was doing, where to go, I saw her up ahead.

Blood had poured out of him.

We threw out my T-shirt, my jeans. My purple backpack had a change of clothes, a few necessities. The fat girl murmured softly as she cut my hair short and spiky, then slathered on peroxide and held my hand. She whispered calm soothing things she thought I'd want to hear. It burned my scalp, but I didn't say a thing, didn't cry, didn't even wince. After she rinsed my hair in the rusty water, I got sick in the toilet and along the side of the dirty wall. The smell was unbearable, but neither of us complained. We heard sirens go by.

"Look, Faith," the fat girl said, and pulled a finger from her pocket.

I had to look away. It was impossible, that pale white thing. I had only sliced his cheek. I had only cut his face. It was impossible and unreal, and proof all at the same time. When I turned back it was gone, she'd tucked it away somewhere.

Outside, we had changed the world forever.

"We have to go when it gets dark," she said. And then she whispered the things she thought I'd need to know in order to become a new person. In order to leave Faith behind.

Later, I don't know when, we made our way through the dense woods to the highway, where I stood on uncertain legs in my new persona and stuck my thumb out. They would be looking for us. They would be looking for me. It was time to leave. All that planning, all that preparation and here we were on the side of the road, my thumb stuck out and my life forever different.

Tony Giobambera's face swam before my eyes. I saw his fingers splayed on the rock and the cleaver. I saw myself pull back and begin to swing and then the fat girl snapped her fingers and pointed towards the car that had passed us.

"Stay with me, Faith," she said. "Stay here."

I managed enough of a smile to tell her that I understood.

~~~

I got us a ride from a college kid named Monty who was sadder than me and a talker. He was so sad and he talked so much that nothing was required of me except staring out the window, and the occasional *Uh-huh*.

He was headed home, to Memphis, Tennessee, where his mother was dying; he'd just received the call and had been driving all night from D.C. He was grateful for my company. So grateful that west of Statesville he thrust his hand between my legs.

Faith would have been paralyzed but Annabelle was not.

I slapped him hard on the side of the head and punched him in the arm. He swerved, but apologized profusely.

In the backseat, the fat girl smiled.

~~~

In Asheville, the fat girl showed me how to shoplift. We took makeup and a shiny magazine from a drugstore and then experimented with our loot in the bathroom of a pool hall across the street. Annabelle was a girl on

TV, in magazines. Annabelle knew how to line her lips and wear a push-up bra. I walked out calmly, eyes lashy and blue-lidded, lips shiny and pink, blush streaking its way up my cheeks.

I looked good. And right now that was the important thing. That was going to get us wherever we needed to go.

~~~

We found a bus station and bought a ticket to Nashville. "Keep to the cities," the fat girl advised. "We need to disappear, not show up uninvited." The ticket was expensive and I protested, thinking we should hitchhike again, but she talked me out of it.

"Soon enough," she said. "Might as well get as far as we can before we go attracting attention."

While we waited for the bus to leave, we found a Goodwill and bought me a short denim skirt, scuffed black cowboy boots, a long underwear shirt, and a tight yellow sweater. The fat girl kept uncrossing my arms from over my chest.

"There is nothing wrong with your breasts," she said, making me blush. "Show them off, for Chrissake, it'll distract people from your face." We ditched my old blue parka for a worn black leather jacket. The fat girl produced a pair of tights. I considered myself in the dusty mirror. I was pretty sure I looked at least nineteen.

"The key to looking older," the fat girl said, "is to try and look younger." I turned to the right and then the left, examining.

I walked out of there a whole other person. No more Faith. Faith was tucked away in my backpack along with almost six hundred dollars, most of which I'd earned.

I was Annabelle and I was going to be okay.

We walked a few blocks to a diner. I wasn't so hungry but the fat girl was. She had all of my pancakes and half my bowl of fruit. Several people around us were reading newspapers.

"Do you think . . . ?" But I didn't have to finish. The fat girl shook her head and took a huge bite of pancake.

"Soon," she said with her mouth full.

~~~

The bus was slow and steady, lurching to a stop in every small town along the way. I slept almost the whole way there. It was dusk when we left and I couldn't see much as we passed through the mountains. Sleep was a heavy black blanket that wrapped itself around me and I didn't struggle and I didn't dream. Outside Knoxville the fat girl prodded me to get out and stretch my legs, but I was tired, so tired. She huffed and went herself.

I woke a few more times to the hazy dawn outlines of indistinguishable small towns. Sometime later I felt fingers move lightly over my nipples, move in circles, and then a hand gripped my arm and I lurched awake, unsure of where I was.

A man was staring at me, his face inches from mine. His eyes were black and bottomless and he had a mean little black goatee.

"You dropped something," he whispered with sour breath.

I tried to shake him free but he had me tightly. He bent down and picked up my tattered magazine and thrust it towards me. "Here," he said. I felt the ghosts of his hands on my chest.

"Let go of me." It came out loud and strong. I saw some of the other passengers stir. He smiled and released my arm but stayed where he was, settled in the fat girl's seat.

I didn't know what to do. Outside we passed pine trees and churches, field after empty field soon to be planted again. I reached down for my backpack and pushed past him into the aisle, stumbling over his long legs. I expected him to grab me but he didn't. I tugged my skirt down and glared at him. There was an empty seat farther back, next to an old woman the color of cinnamon who was snoring with her mouth open and her head against the window. I sat next to her, stiff and violently awake, bag in my lap. Ahead of us, his close-cropped black hair poked above the seat back. My skin still crawled with the feeling of fingers.

~~~

When we arrived in Nashville the man rose and exited the bus without looking back at me. I sat for a minute to let as much distance grow between us as I could, but the lady next to me stood and told me to move.

"Don't you *want* to go?" She clucked and shook her head in wonder. "Been on this bus all *night*."

Once outside, I didn't know what to do except walk quickly. I saw a donut shop and headed for it, my backpack slung over one shoulder. Inside, the fat girl stood nibbling the sprinkles off a glazed jelly donut.

"Where the hell have you been?"

She shrugged and licked her fingers one by one. "Get yourself some coffee, Faith."

"Annabelle."

"Whatever."

We sat at a small orange-and-pink table in the corner. Outside there were just buildings, low commercial sprawl, one store after the other. It felt so different than Gleryton. I took a long drink of the sweet milky coffee. Down the street I saw a man in a shaggy blue bathrobe walking a goat.

The fat girl sighed and put her palms flat on the table. "Shall we check the papers?" she said.

I had almost forgotten. I nodded and dug around for some change to buy us one.

We spread it flat on the table. I looked for a picture of the rock where Tony had always sat smoking, of our own low wall. I looked for a picture of my face or a headline—TERRIBLE INCIDENT AT LOCAL HIGH SCHOOL or SEARCH FOR VIOLENT GIRL CONTINUES, but I found nothing.

Were they after us? Had men in uniform sifted through the contents of my room while my mom stood in the doorway, arms crossed over her chest, shaking her head? After all the messy trouble I'd caused, was she relieved to have me gone? Did she miss me?

"We should probably stay here a day or two," the fat girl said. "Unless you want to head to Atlanta tonight." The fat girl had a map in front of her and rested her big soft chin on her fist, her elbow on the table.

"I guess. Whatever you think."

"Look, it's Sunday, we can move pretty undetected on a Sunday. Monday and Tuesday we'll have to be more careful. But I'm thinking we could stay here a few days anyway, until the middle of next week, maybe. Try and figure things out. Figure out what to do."

I nodded. I didn't care, but I didn't tell her that. I was trying to remember the name of the tattoo shop where Charlie had gotten his falcon when he lived here. It was a one word name, I thought. How many tattoo shops could there be?

~~~

Many.

I thought it was a guy's name: Fred's or Lou's or something like that. There turned out to be six tattoo shops with guy's names. We got directions and walked long enough that my feet began to ache, but we were lucky right off the bat.

The first one was boarded up. But we found Mike's Tattoos and that sounded just about right to me. I didn't quite know what I was going to ask, but the fat girl whispered her encouragement.

"Annabelle," she said.

A short, bored-looking guy was behind the counter. His neck was cir-cled in black-ink barbed wire. I looked at the designs on the wall, sketches of things to etch into your skin and photographs of customers' tattoos. The room was small but crammed with images and the photographs were un-settling in their anonymity: fragments of bodies served up for scrutiny, without the faces that belonged to them. I was stuck on the Chinese char-acters for a while, their bold strokes on people's wrists and the backs of necks. If you inscribed something on your body that didn't mean what you thought it meant—the character for misery mislabeled "happiness," for ex-ample—would you doom yourself to whatever you asked for?

"Look," the fat girl pointed out a smutty cartoon barnyard scene com-plete with farmer, milkmaid, and livestock. I found the Statue of Liberty holding a beer above her head. She was in a section of cartoony tattoos: big-boobed girls in tight T-shirts in various suggestive poses on motorcy-cles. Some of them were sort of cute in an embarrassing way.

I walked the circumference of the room, trailing my hand behind me along the plastic-covered wall. I stopped at a photograph of angel's wings outlined across the broad canvas of a man's back. You could see the skin was puffy and red, there was a little blood in the picture, the tattoo must have been fresh. And then something else caught my eye. Three photo-graphs in a row: a brown-and-red falcon. A band of Gypsies. A chest with three chickens tattooed on it: a light blue, a pale green, and a pink.

Holy shit.

The fat girl noticed me riveted and came to see what had my attention.

"You see something you like?" the guy called.

The fat girl kicked me. "No," I said. It was difficult to focus. "Actually, I'm looking for a guy named Charlie," I said. "These are his tattoos."

The counter guy came out from behind the counter to see what I was pointing at. Color streamed over his skin. Oceans and mountains climbed his arms. "Do you know him?" I asked. "He used to live in Nashville. He's with the Fartlesworth Circus. I want to find them."

The guy scratched at the black-ink barbed wire drawn around his neck. "No," he said. "But I've only been in Nashville about eight months. Ben Dixon's the one you ought to talk to," he said. "He'll be in here in about an hour. He does a lot of circus people. He did everything on this wall."

~~~

While we waited, a couple of skinny redneck girls pushed through the front door and bells tinkled. They wore lots of makeup and were dressed alike: skintight acid-wash jeans and white sweatshirts. They both had stiff blond hair that stood up in a claw in the front. Counter Guy came out to help the girls. One wanted a heart but couldn't decide if it should have a name inside or just initials. The other wanted a motorcycle.

"I know what I want, I want a motorcycle," she said about six times until her friend finally told her to shut up.

And then this guy walked in, tall and skinny, roped in tattoos with a shaved head and small silver hoop earrings—about ten on each ear. "She's been waiting for you," Counter Guy said, pointing at me over the tall hair of the rednecks.

Ben had the sleepy expression of someone who'd just woken up. "Hey," he said. "Let me put my coat away and I'll be right back. Did you already pick out a design?"

I didn't know what to say. The fat girl pinched my calf.

"Ow, yes." I nodded as he disappeared into the back.

"Why'd you do that?" I whispered, but she shook her head.

Ben came back out in a ratty white T-shirt with a gray sweater tied around the waist of his army pants. I stood up.

"Which one is it?"

I pointed at the three chickens and he raised his eyebrows but his expression didn't really change. He nodded, then led me into the back.

~~~

There were rooms back there, small sterile cubicles with doors. He opened one and gestured me onto a doctor's-examining-table-type thing, black vinyl with a few rips through which I could see the frame underneath. I sat.

"Where do you want it?" he asked, pulling thin translucent paper from a roll.

I held my breath. I pointed to my arm, then changed my mind and pointed to my ankle.

"Ankles hurt," he said matter-of-factly. He flipped a switch and something began to hum. He selected a few tiny pots from a shelf—red, blue, white, yellow, black—and put them on a small metal tray stand. Then he sat on an office chair, took the paper, lay it over the photograph, and began to roughly trace the chickens. The fat girl stood beside him, looking over his shoulder. When he took another piece of the paper and traced the chickens from the drawing so that they looked smooth and perfect, she gave me the thumbs-up. I scowled.

"Right or left," he said. "You'll have to take off your boot."

"I don't want it," I blurted.

Ben Dixon stopped what he was doing and looked annoyed. "Okay."

"I just wanted to talk to you."

He put the drawing down on the tray of tiny pots, scooted backwards on his chair, his wheels screeching a little, and studied me. "What do you want?" he said.

"Do you know Charlie Yates?"

He crossed his arms and squinted at me; his mouth squeezed itself into a tiny pucker. "Who are you?"

"I'm a friend," I said. I swallowed. "Annabelle. I'm Annabelle. I need to find him. I need to find the Fartlesworth Circus."

Ben Dixon rose and shut the door. Yes, he knew Charlie. He'd tattooed Charlie. Yes, he'd help me find the circus but I couldn't tell Charlie that I'd met him.

"Why?" I asked, but he just shook his head and got a dark, faraway look. And though the fat girl was making faces at me from her place in the corner behind him, I didn't press it.

He wanted to know how I knew Charlie. I didn't tell him much, beyond knowing Starling and Clark's. I didn't even say why I was looking, though I'd prepared myself to say something cryptic and cliché, something about needing to leave town because things had gotten hairy. But he didn't ask. He told me to head south. Their route, he didn't know exactly but he knew how to figure it out.

"They go through Georgia at some point after North Carolina," he said. "It's a pattern, South Carolina, North Carolina, a minute in Tennessee, then Georgia. They spend a lot of time in Georgia and Alabama, I know."

It all seemed simple to him. Simple that a stranger would show up and simple that no questions be asked. There was a strange kind of trust in that, a tentative agreement that I recognized had nothing to do with me but was implied by something else, something larger. Like he would've helped out anyone that showed up with those two words: circus, Charlie.

He looked me up and down. "You can crash at my place tonight if you need to," he said. "Whatever."

~ ~ ~

We wandered around Nashville until Ben Dixon got off his shift and then followed him home. He lived with some roommates in a peeling brown house, with blankets hanging in the windows. Inside it smelled like years of stale smoke. Ben flicked a switch and flooded a fairly large room with the harsh light of a bare bulb that hung from the ceiling. Against one wall a brown couch spewed stuffing. "You can sleep there," Ben said.

I put my bag down next to it and he disappeared down the hall. I started to follow him but the fat girl blocked my path.

"Let him go," she said. The room was incredibly bright. I sat on the couch and my butt sank down. I could feel the springs, but I didn't care. Even my bones felt heavy. I lay down and used my backpack for a pillow. It had never felt this good to be horizontal, I was so tired. Even though the room was freezing, it didn't take long for me to fall asleep.

I half woke a few hours later to the smell of pot and cigarettes. Someone had turned out the light and put a blanket over me. There was a conversation going on in the next room, but I couldn't make out the words, and I drifted off again.

When I woke for good I had no idea where I was. I sat up, light-headed, and looked around the strange, dark room. I could tell it was daytime by the light peeking through the blankets covering the windows. My mouth tasted foul and furry. Next to the couch I was on, there was a small grubby-looking metal table covered in junk mail and cigarette butts and trash. In the corner, a worn armchair held an open pizza box. Apart from some pencil sketches of gravestones and monuments, there was nothing on the dirty walls. A filthy red rug hid most of the floor, but what peeked out was peeling gray linoleum. The fat girl was asleep in a heap in the corner.

I heard the distant sounds of traffic, and it all came back to me quickly: The tattoo shop, the man on the bus to Nashville, the drugstore in Asheville. The gas station bathroom in Gleryton.

Tony Giobambera and all his blood.

My heart pounded. I reached up and touched my short hair. My blond hair. Where were we? How had this happened? How had things gone this far?

I looked at the fat girl, sleeping so peacefully, all curled up like a big bloated muffin. I walked over and watched her breathing softly, her mouth slightly open, and I hauled off and gave her a good swift kick in the kidneys.

She lurched awake, eyes wide, and stumbled to all fours. I kicked her again, hard, this time in the side. She collapsed with a squawking groan and curled up tight. I was crying and shaking, tears running off my face, but I kicked her again and again, for everything, everything, until I couldn't anymore.

And then I knelt beside her and took her in my arms, wrapping them as far around her as I could, shaking and sobbing.

"You ungrateful cunt," she whispered. But I held on tight, rocking back and forth, so very sorry for everything.

~~~

She forgave me later and she calmed me down. I couldn't stop crying and she sat on the couch with me and held my hand, rubbed my back.

When I was breathing almost normally, she rumpled my short hair and told me she was disappointed. "In what?"

"That you didn't get that tattoo," she said. It made me laugh, which in turn made her laugh, but I had wanted it. In the shop I'd had this fleeting thought that by scratching their secret language on my body, I could belong to that closeness Starling and Charlie had shared.

The whole thing was no more ridiculous than sitting in this dirty living room, than me having run away. "I do sort of want it," I said.

"What?"

"The tattoo."

I stood up then and crossed the room, pulling one of the blankets aside with an idle hand as I went. A bright column of dusty light flooded in, then disappeared. I opened the front door and a gust of fresh, chilly air swept through. There wasn't much to see out there. Just houses, a street. A town. People's uninterrupted lives.

I took a deep breath. The air was delicious. So everything had happened. I had to keep my focus. I had to find Charlie. He would know what to do.

"We could stay," the fat girl said, rubbing her back. "Or we could leave tonight. It's really up to you."

I turned back to her. I didn't want to stay. "Let's go," I said.

"They're probably looking for you by now."

"Yeah."

Then there were footsteps behind me and I glanced over my shoulder, expecting to find Ben Dixon. Instead I met his roommate, Oliver. He jerked his head in the direction of the hallway. "I made some coffee, Annabelle," he said. "You drink coffee?"

I nodded and followed him down the dark hall to a bright filthy kitchen. He motioned for me to sit at a small table and I did. The fat girl crept behind him, making faces at me, but I managed not to laugh.

He poured himself a coffee and one for me. There wasn't any milk, but he handed me a box with a solid brick of sugar inside and after banging it on the table a few times, I poured the sugar and promised myself that the coffee would kill whatever germs were living in the mug he'd given me. It had lots of rings, stains of previous beverages around the rim. When I brushed my thumb along its edge, some of the gunk cleared away. I made a lip-sized space and drank from there.

Despite that, the coffee was tasty and it sharpened the edges of things a little. The dismal fog began to clear from my head. "Where's Ben?" I asked.

"He's running errands. You were sleeping pretty hard. There were people over last night after Dan's show and you didn't even wake up." Oliver stretched his legs out in front of him and took a long sip. "We thought we should just let you sleep, you know."

"Thanks."

He smiled, and his face became less gloomy and long, almost handsome. "No big," he said, and took a cigarette from a pack on the table. He leaned back and lit it. "So Ben wouldn't tell," he said, studying me. "How'd you guys meet?"

"Old friends," the fat girl whispered.

"Old friends," I said.

"From North Carolina?"

Alarm must have registered on my face because his expression was instantly more curious. I had to be careful, I reminded myself. "Yeah. My cousin. Ben knew her."

"I thought it was Chuck Yates," Oliver said. He tapped his cigarette on the edge of the table and I watched the ash fall to the floor. I looked to the fat girl for guidance. She was leaning against the doorway chewing on a Slim Jim. She shrugged.

"Yeah, I guess him too," I said. "You know him?"

"Sure," Oliver said. "He lived here for a while, you know. With us. That was before War Banshee. Back when Terrorist Scum was part of Snot Refugee. I played drums for Snot Refugee."

"Oh. So," I started. "Were Charlie and Ben—"

The fat girl drew her hand across her throat, her eyes wide.

"Huh?"

And Ben Dixon walked in. He had a grocery bag, which he set down on the table and began to unload. He offered me a carton of milk, but my coffee was almost cold.

"How'd you sleep?"

"Great." Oliver still stared at me. I felt my face heat, my cheeks flush.

"How old are you anyway?" It was Ben, not looking at me, just putting something frozen in the freezer.

"How old do you think I am?"

Oliver considered me for a minute, then looked over his shoulder at Ben. "Twenty?"

"Not more than eighteen," Ben said.

"Huh." I stood and took the coffee to the sink. It was full of moldy dishes. I didn't see a sponge or detergent. I turned on the water, which sputtered and choked, then rained out a steady brown stream. I rinsed the cup and set it down.

"So?" Ben was waiting for an answer. I saw the clock behind him and realized it was afternoon, not morning.

The fat girl batted her eyelids from the doorway. "I'll take either of those answers," I said. They exchanged looks but didn't push it.

"I have to go to work," Ben said. "But we can stop by the diner on the way there if you're hungry." My stomach rumbled loudly at the thought.

"Okay," he said. "Get your stuff."

~~~

Over eggs and pancakes he told me to head to Atlanta, to find a tattoo shop called Wenger's. To ask for a guy named Lex.

"As in Luthor?" I said. He smiled.

The diner was mostly empty, just a few weathered old men in baseball caps and a skinny couple sipping coffee with their heads close together. Our waitress had a lazy eye.

"You should check out the Lemon Drop when you're there," he said. "If you like Marilyn Monroe."

"Sure," I said. I wasn't sure how I felt about Marilyn Monroe. It was all flooding back to me again, that unhinged feeling of floating through the world. The incredible dreaminess of it: the lightness in my stomach, the sense that my limbs did not belong to me. I had done something awful and run away. I *was* running away. I looked at my hands holding a coffee cup and couldn't be sure they were mine. If made to pick my hands out of a lineup, what would distinguish them? I was undercover, not myself. I touched my hair. It was very short. Short enough to not be mine. Everything was too bright again. Too loud and sharp. Even in that quiet restaurant. I could hear every plate shift, the groan of the griddle as it strained to cook some meat. The clink of each utensil sounded like a drum crescendo.

Ben Dixon moved an empty sugar packet back and forth across his plate. And then I asked him, "How *do* you know Charlie?"

He watched his hand, the waving sugar, and didn't answer for so long that I began to think he hadn't heard me. But when I went to ask him again, made brave by my imminent departure, the fat girl put her hand on my arm and silenced me.

"Let me give you something to take with you," he said, finally, carefully. And that was all.

I could tell he thought it was weird that I chose the chickens, but he didn't question it. He carved them really tiny on my ankle, like I asked. "A parting gift," he said. "For Charlie."

"And you can give him this for me too," he said just as I was about to leave, backpack slung over one arm, coat in the other, ankle wrapped in cellophane and masking tape. He leaned over and kissed me full on the mouth, his tongue slipping between my lips. I jumped back, tasting him. I backed away. And nodded.

~~~

"That was weird," the fat girl said later as we walked alongside the early evening traffic. I was still floating somewhere in my head, lost in a thick soup of random thoughts.

"Hey," she said, "space girl."

"Sorry." My ankle throbbed a little, a warm dull hum, but the pain was oddly nice. Even while Ben was cutting into me with those tiny whirring needles, it had felt good somehow, brave, the pain more real than anything else. Permanent. And a thought had flashed across my mind for a minute like a translucent message pulled by a prop plane: *Starling would never believe this*.

Ben had loaded me up with antibiotic ointment and bandages. "Keep it clean," he'd said. "Seriously. And don't pick the scab off, whatever you do."

My boots were good for this, protective.

"The kiss and everything, you know?" The fat girl was working on a giant roll of SweeTarts.

"Yeah." I could still feel his mouth on mine. My first kiss, really. Even if it was intended for someone else, it was still at least partially mine.

"Whatever," the fat girl said, and rolled her eyes.

We didn't exactly have a plan to get to Atlanta, though we still had $532. We decided to wait a few hours to hitchhike, to wait until the world was sleeping.

We found a graveyard and climbed over its high stone wall to sit in a dark corner and rest. It felt like the center of night. We sat on the damp grass with our backs against the stones and our legs out in front of us and we looked at the sky arching overhead. I wished for a cigarette, but I hadn't taken any, even though Counter Guy had offered as we left the shop. I was oddly happy though, under the dim stars in this graveyard in this strange city with the fat girl. I wasn't thinking of Fern or my mother or Starling or Andrea Dutton. Or Tony Giobambera. Any of it.

SEVEN

A crazy hippie lady with lots of wild gray hair picked us up hours later in a rusting Chevy Nova and gave us a ride out of Nashville. She said, "I'm only pulling over because I'm sleepy. I'll take you as far as Chattanooga if you keep me awake. I want you to sing, not chitchat." I was relieved not to have to make small talk. I sang camp songs, "Oh Sinner Man," "She'll Be Coming 'Round the Mountain," and the Beatles whenever it looked like she was nodding off. The fat girl dozed in the back.

She left us at a truck stop and there was such a chill in the air that I barely felt my fingers and toes. A big trucker named Willie found us there, standing outside the restaurant and stomping our feet to keep the blood moving, and gave us a lift all the way to Atlanta. I was wary of him, but the fat girl didn't seem concerned. I stared out the window and watched all the towns slip through the darkness along the highway. Mostly my eye caught the neon of chain stores and gas stations, but occasionally I saw a tract of houses or a strip of neighborhood.

He left us at a gas station and I tried to clean myself up in the bathroom. Old makeup smudged in half-moons beneath my eyes. My hair was an awful yellow-orange and stuck up all over. I did what I could in that fluorescent room, even taking off my sweater and swabbing at my armpits with paper towels and shiny pink soap.

When we were ready, I tugged my skirt into place, brushed my teeth with my finger, and put on shimmery lipstick the color of cotton candy.

~~~

It was warmer than Chattanooga had been the night before, but still chilly. More than anything, I wanted to curl up somewhere and sleep, but the fat girl wouldn't let me. "Come on," she said. "Suck it up."

We walked along a stretch of empty road towards the lights we'd seen from the highway and came to a strip of small tired storefronts and a donut shop. Her eyes lit up. Frosting in the morning made her happy all day.

Inside we sat at a bright semicircular counter and I had a coffee and a cruller. It was delicious. It made me realize how hungry I was, wonder how long since I'd eaten, but I was too tired to worry about it. I slurped the coffee instead, and tried to concentrate on clearing the rumble from my skull.

And then, at the fat girl's insistence, we checked the paper and there was a story. Not front page—not that it mattered—but there. It mentioned Tony Giobambera by name, said that he had been in critical condition but was expected to recover. And I learned that it wasn't just his cheek I'd hacked out when I missed his fingers, but a good deal of his tongue.

I saw it fly through the air, landing in the dirt like a wet fish, like a piece of liver.

"Faith?" The fat girl snapped her fingers.

"They recovered the weapon," I said.

"Of course they did," she said. "You left it there."

I looked back at the article. I was not mentioned by name of course, but described: *a history of mental disorder* and *a suicide attempt less than a year ago*. I shoved the paper back to the fat girl and folded the edge of my Styrofoam coffee cup back and forth until it broke off. I folded that piece and the pieces it made, until I'd made a mountain of little white shards.

"Let's check out Hot-lanta," she said. "It's a real city. Lots of cool stuff to do."

"Can't we just find the tattoo shop and get on with it? They probably are looking for me."

"Oh, so suddenly you're not adventurous anymore?" She had that old familiar mean look in her eye and I shook my head, resisting the urge to bury it in my arms. The rhythmic pulse of traffic made my eyes heavy. I fought sleep, gritting my teeth against it.

She pinched me hard and hustled us out, yanking me along by the elbow until we were in the sharp air outside. She slapped me once on each cheek, and I batted her away.

"Walk!"

I stumbled forward and she prodded me in the back.

"March, Faith!"

I did what she said. And soon I was awake. Blurry, vacant, but awake.

~~~

By the time we figured out how to get to Little Five Points, the day had bloomed into a beautiful afternoon. The sky was clear and the streets were teaming with kids my age. The fat girl was oblivious. She had one goal in mind: the Lemon Drop. I didn't see what the big deal was, but Ben Dixon had captured the fat girl's attention and I wasn't up to an argument.

We walked in. Off to the side was a small room full of Marilyn Monroe. The fat girl was transfixed. Any bit of Marilyn memorabilia you could imagine was set up behind glass like an enormous diorama. Letters. Photos. Shoes, dresses, records. A souvenir mirror.

The bartender waved a greeting from behind the scuffed wooden bar. He was a huge man in overalls and no shirt, wiping down glasses. He had a straw-colored mustache and vivid Dr. Seuss tattoos that splattered his freckly arms. *Green Eggs and Ham, The Cat in the Hat, One Fish Two Fish.*

A bumper sticker: MY INNER CHILD IS AN HONOR STUDENT AT THE LEMON DROP.

"Order a drink," the fat girl urged, but I didn't want a drink. I asked for a glass of water and was obliged by the big bartender.

"I'm Tommy," he told me. "What's your name?"

"Annabelle," I said, and then he asked about my cowboy boots, which he liked, he said; they were just like some his girlfriend had and did I know that there were more than sixty thousand kinds of cowboy boots and what the best ones were and when they were invented and why some cowboys preferred a rounded toe to a pointed one and . . .

We'd found ourselves another talker.

"You in school?" he said finally, and I shook my head. "Drop out?"

I nodded. "Me too. After freshman year. My folks never forgave me for not finishing college," he said. "But I never regretted it. Just 'cause everyone else does it doesn't mean you got to."

I was amazed that he thought I was in college. I asked about his tattoos and heard a half-hour monologue on the brilliance of Dr. Seuss. By then the bar had begun to fill up with a mix of hippie and honky-tonk, yuppies and college kids.

"You gonna stay for the band?" he asked. "Sweatblossom. They're real good." I thought we should be going, but the fat girl kicked me in the shins and we stayed.

~~~

Tommy's shift ended around ten and Sweatblossom was still going strong. By then he'd been slipping me free beers for a while. He introduced me to his girlfriend, Lucia, who had a fringe of inky hair around a pale, heart-shaped face and the greenest eyes I'd ever seen. Something about her made me think *dumpling*, though I didn't know what. It wasn't her shape—she was tall and slender. Certainly not her pierced nose, or the spiderweb tattooed around her left arm, or the elaborate sword drawn along her clavicle.

When Tommy and Lucia heard my mumbled (by now, slurry) and convoluted story of how my friend hadn't shown up to fetch me at the bus stop, a look passed between them, something I couldn't decipher. Then they offered their couch for the night and, with the fat girl's nod of approval, I gratefully accepted.

We drove there in Tommy's pickup. It didn't take very long, so it must not have been far, but after a few rights and lefts I had no idea where we were. The landscape had quickly become more rural and wooded. We pulled into the long driveway of a peeling yellow house tucked deep into the forest.

"No neighbors behind us," Tommy said proudly. "Across the street is it. The houses on either side are empty right now and we have all the land out there." He pointed into the woods but I couldn't see much, just night and the trees illuminated by his headlights, which he then shut off.

We climbed out of the truck and I felt woozy, beer sloshing in my stomach. Lucia put out a hand to steady me and I tried to smile my thanks.

Inside, their house was crumbling and filthy, a true punk-rock crash pad, but I was so tired and grateful, I didn't care. Tommy made us all towering sandwiches and I gobbled mine so fast I could barely breathe. And then Lucia lent me a towel and in their grimy mildewed bathroom, I took the best shower of my life, standing under the hottest water I could bear, scrubbing away all the Nashville and Asheville and Gleryton I could find, to emerge clean and pink and new.

~~~

Where was the fat girl?

I pulled the towel tighter around my body and wished I had something other than my old nasty clothes to put back on.

Lucia was waiting for me on the couch. "Annabelle," she said with a slow smile, "you like to party?"

I wasn't sure what to say. My skin glowed where it poked out from the towel, still warm from the shower, and I wanted to curl up somewhere until the last of the beer left my body.

But Lucia was watching me, expectantly. "I guess . . ." I said.

"We do, me and Tommy." She looked straight at me, through me. The light of a Christmas tree in the corner blinked on and off, red and blue against her pale skin. Something in her eyes made me freeze there in my towel in the middle of the room.

"We like you," she said, and patted the place beside her on the couch. I told myself I was misunderstanding everything. I was just tired, I whispered to myself, my perceptions were unreliable.

But I felt very, very awake.

Lucia patted the couch again. She blew a few strands of black hair from her eyes and slowly I went and sat down. She began to rub my back in slow circles. "You like us?"

I nodded and swallowed, afraid of where this was going. Then she slipped her hand around my back and stroked my breast lightly through the towel with her fingertips.

I stiffened, paralyzed by competing impulses, but I didn't move. And then Lucia leaned forward, my whole breast cupped in her hand now, and kissed the back of my neck.

And the side of my neck.

And my ear, softly, her breath in it, my heart pounding, pounding, my own breath heavy and hard.

And then she pushed me back on the couch a little, and kissed me on the mouth, deep and warm and slow, and slipped her hand between my legs.

The whole world slid away, in a heap somewhere. There was only the weight of her on me, and the stroke of her hand between my legs.

I had stopped breathing, or moving, though everything seemed to shudder, and then she moved down, slowly, my towel loose now, piled around us on the couch, she moved down my body, licking me lightly, my breasts, my belly, all the time her hand moved in circles between my legs until her face was there too, and she pushed her way in.

My head was back, my body absorbed by Lucia. I closed my eyes and saw nothing, felt everything, a rainstorm, hard and bright, pounding away at me, coursing along my body.

And then I heard her gasp and I looked up to see Tommy standing over her, naked and enormous, touching her, and suddenly it all came crashing down and I pulled myself away, scrambling to the other side of the couch where I curled up as tight as I could and pulled the wayward towel around me.

"What's wrong, baby?" It was Lucia's voice, slow and syrupy, but I didn't open my eyes, just willed them away, all of it, willed time to rewind by half an hour, an hour, to the point where I'd come from the bathroom feeling utterly renewed. I gulped air and realized I'd been holding my breath. I opened one eye and saw Lucia crawling towards me, her skirt hiked up, her mouth wet, and I buried my head beneath the towel and pulled myself even tighter into a knot.

I stayed like that while they had a whispered conversation, then they moved away, went into their bedroom, and closed the door. And I stayed like that longer, my heart thumping hard, through the creaking and thumping and moaning that came from their room, and later through the silence of the night, with my eyes wide open.

When the whole world was still, I dressed in my dirty clothes and collected my bag and whatever stray clothing I could find so I'd have something else to wear. I found a T-shirt that had been lying on a chair in the corner, a University of Georgia sweatshirt, and a wool hat near the Christmas tree. In the kitchen I took a jar of peanut butter, some bread, a knife, and an apple.

And I let myself out.

~~~

I walked for what seemed like hours, and it grew lighter and warmer. I hadn't known which way to go once the driveway hit the road, so I just picked a direction and walked. The sun still wasn't up but I could tell it would be soon and every bone in my body felt like it had been dipped in lead. I alternated between shame and wonder, shaking my head every once in a while to free it of the images of the previous night. I just wanted to rest. More than anything, more than anything, to sleep.

Eventually I came to a park. I climbed a hill and passed a jungle gym, picnic tables. Where to curl up out of sight? It was all in the open, in full view of the rest of the park and of the road. But eventually I had to give in to my body. I had to lie down. And there was this stone bench that looked incredibly soft and comfortable. And I stretched out on to it, pushing every thought from my head, and the world went dark.

EIGHT

I woke to the fat girl shaking me. Sun in my eyes. Where the hell was I? And then, past her wide hip, I saw Lucia climbing the hill, Tommy in his red truck on the road, and I was up and running before I even fully remembered why.

"Annabelle!"

I ran, knowing the fat girl couldn't keep up. Knowing I had to get away. My backpack thumped against my back but I charged into the woods, oblivious, and crashed ahead.

I could hear Lucia crashing after me.

And then I tripped, and my ankle made a strange sound.

I tried to stand but pain shot through me and I fell back. I couldn't get up.

Lucia was there almost immediately, her eyes wild, reflecting the green of the piney forest. "Annabelle," she said softly. She didn't even seem out of breath, though I was still panting.

"You didn't have to leave us like that. That wasn't polite. After we took you in. After we fed you and gave you a place to sleep." Her hands were on her hips. She didn't sound angry, just firm, but something in the way she spoke kept me from meeting her eyes. "We like you," she said, her voice soft now, coaxing. "We want you to come back with us. To stay for a while."

I shook my head. I tried to say something, but I couldn't think of what. I willed my ankle to feel better.

"You need to come back with us."

"I just have to go," I said, finally. "Last night—"

She waved it away. "That doesn't have to happen again," she said, her words dripping with honey. "If that's what upset you then forget it. We like to party." She ran a hand through her short dark hair. "You said you did. If you don't, that's fine."

I searched her face for some kind of guile, but she met my gaze. Still, I didn't trust her or what she said, any of it. I didn't want to go back. But I couldn't walk. Where was I going to go when I couldn't walk?

I nodded slowly. "Okay," I said.

"I'm going back for Tommy," Lucia said. "He can carry you out of here so you don't have to put weight on that ankle. You stay here."

I nodded again. As soon as she'd left I tried again to stand.

"You need to wrap it," the fat girl said, appearing beside me with a bottle of aspirin.

"Where the hell were you?"

She ignored me and put the aspirin in my bag. She fished around in there and pulled out the T-shirt I'd stolen. "Nice," she said, and ripped it into strips, then bound my ankle tightly.

"At least it wasn't the one with the tattoo," I said. She slung my arm around her shoulder and helped me hobble quickly, as fast as we could, farther into the woods.

~~~

We hid in the dark valley behind two trees that had fallen over each other. We could see Tommy and Lucia far off and could hear their argument. Not the words, just the raised voices, the angry arms pointing this way and that. The shaking of heads. The hands on hips.

They tromped around in circles for a while, darting off in this direction or that. Then Tommy's footsteps approached. I heard them get louder and louder, slower and slower until he stood close enough that I could see his pant leg clearly from where I crouched, curled up into myself like a snail. It was dark and damp where I was, but it was better than being found. I held my breath and closed my eyes and willed myself to be utterly still. After a moment he walked off, kicking leaves and cracking twigs. He was so loud in that quiet place, so very loud. I breathed as silently as I could.

After a while I didn't hear him. And I didn't hear Lucia calling to him. I raised my head carefully and made eye contact with the fat girl, who sat like a sentry with her back against a tree. I raised my eyebrows and she nodded, so I uncurled my stiff body and crawled out from under my hiding place.

The forest was still and cold. My heartbeat slowed. I stood carefully and stretched but my ankle throbbed. The fat girl told me to sleep.

"They could be waiting for you," she said. "Jesus Christ."

And so I lay down and slept, dreaming only dark distant things that I couldn't reach even when I woke. In the woods in the late afternoon the sun filtered through only a little. It took a minute but I knew where I was this time. I made two huge peanut butter sandwiches and ate them quickly, one after the other. The fat girl had a whole Boston Cream Pie.

"Very practical," I said.

"You have to honor your cravings." She winked at me. I thought maybe that would be all, but later she asked about it.

"Did you *like* it? What did it feel like?"

I didn't answer. I didn't know what to say. Even though the whole evening had frightened me, there was something about it that was mine. Something scary and private and strange. I didn't know if I liked it. I just knew that I didn't have to share everything.

~~~

We stayed in the woods through the night and for the whole next day. I was afraid to come out, afraid they'd be waiting, and besides, my ankle ached and I thought it best not to put any weight on it. I crawled a couple of trees over to pee and then back, but that was about it. I was grateful for the sweatshirt and the hat, but even with the added layers and my leather jacket, it was cold. I rationed the jar of water I had, but it ran out the morning of the second day and the fat girl had to do a lot of convincing to get me to head to the water fountain in the park. As it was, I still waited until after dark. But after the second dark night in the woods I was ready to get the hell out of there and go find Lex and the circus and have the whole business be over with already.

Just after sunrise we walked slowly down the road away from Tommy and Lucia's until we came to another road and took that, and so on. It was late afternoon before we found Wenger's.

The shop looked somewhat like the shop in Nashville, with pictures on all the walls (in a quick sweep, I saw no band of Gypsies, no line of chickens, no falcon), a grubby carpet, and a counter. Lex happened to be behind that counter and he was short and thick and generous with his attention. When I told him why I was there, he looked me up and down, winked, and asked to see my tattoo. He seemed disappointed that it was so easy to reveal, but he admired Ben Dixon's handiwork and told me he knew just the person who could help us, an ex-carny named Stretch who was an old man now and owned a junk shop in Athens.

So we took a bus to Athens and found Stretch, up the street from a tattoo shop called Pain and Wonder, just where Lex had said he'd be. And for fifteen dollars and a few hours of looking at old photos of Stretch's career as a contortionist (AINSLEY PRESENTS! THE RUBBER AL-PHABET BOY . . . BORN IN A THOUSAND SHAPES, HE CAN SPELL ANY WORD IN ANY LANGUAGE WITH HIS ELASTIC BODY!), and hearing his endless tales, I was given a worn brochure for the Fartlesworth Circus that listed its route and tour dates.

"It's a few years old," Stretch said. "But it'll probably get you to them. Shows tend to take the same route, keep the audience expecting, you know? You should find them just about where this says."

~~~

Outside in the dusky evening, the fat girl waited on a wooden bench. She punched me in the arm when I told her about the schedule. "Excellent work, girl," she said. I couldn't stop smiling.

We found a restaurant and I ordered rice and beans and corn bread and a huge iced tea, because somehow, as Annabelle, I'd become a girl with an appetite, and I sat in the window watching the lights of the city, certain that finally everything was going to work out. "You know," I said when I'd had my fill, "I'm surprised you don't mind about Charlie anymore."

She was quiet at that, and shook her head without looking at me.

"What?"

"Listen, Faith," she said, her voice low. "Just because I think finding Fartlesworth is okay doesn't mean I trust Charlie. Don't make that mistake, okay?"

"Okay," I mumbled back, sorry I'd brought it up. I didn't feel like fighting or getting a lecture, or having my bright mood tarnished. I wanted us to get along, to move quickly and have some fun for a change. Hadn't we earned some fun?

"What about we go see a movie?" I said. The fat girl shook her head. I sighed, but knew better than to argue. I took our trays and dumped our trash. Then I followed her out into the night.

~~~

We walked for a long while without the fat girl telling me where we were headed. My shoulders ached from the backpack and my ankle throbbed, and by the time she dragged us into an unnecessarily bright diner, I was in a lot of pain. We claimed a booth and the fat girl sat beside me and spread a map out in front of us. I traced our route backwards with my finger. The hours of Athens to Atlanta to Chattanooga to Nashville, the overnight drive to Nashville from Asheville. And then I traced backwards from Asheville to Gleryton.

I pictured my mom all alone in our house. How very empty it must seem now without my dad, without me. Just her glass of scotch and her clean clean rooms and her skinless chicken breasts. I saw her all by herself on the couch staring at the television, and just like that, it was as if a place under my ribs had been rubbed raw and salted. I missed my mother fiercely. I wanted to run to her and throw my arms around her and confess it all, wanted her to stroke my head and tell me everything was going to be okay, everything would be just fine, I should trust her, she would see to it.

The map blurred. I swallowed.

"Oh Christ," the fat girl said. "Jesus, Faith!"

But I couldn't stop the tears from coming, the sobs from bubbling up. She rubbed my back and said things she thought were soothing, but I shook her off. How could she understand? She didn't understand. I wanted my mom.

"Faith," the fat girl said, her voice heavy with reason. "She's not going to make everything better if you go back to her, she's just going to turn you over to the cops because she thinks you're nuts."

This just made me cry harder and the fat girl looked around to see if anyone noticed.

"Listen," she hissed. "Why don't you call her, okay? Quickly so it can't be traced if they try. From a pay phone somewhere safe, somewhere we can get away. Would that make you feel better?"

I nodded. She patted me on the back again and handed me a napkin. I blew my nose and she dug around in the backpack and left two wrinkled dollars on the table to pay for my coffee. We grabbed the bag and the map and left the bright diner for the comfort of darkness.

~~~

I got change at a Laundromat and we walked, searching for a pay phone that wasn't overly visible. I was all tangled up about making the call. I didn't mind the walk—the nervous fist in my stomach took my mind off my pulsing ankle—and the farther I limped, the more I calmed down and was able to hear the truth in what the fat girl had said. Much as I wanted it, my mom wouldn't make everything better. She wouldn't sweep me into her protective embrace and fend off the nasty world. She would do exactly what she'd done before: turn me over to *people who know better* and hope that they would fix me, make me more like the child she'd always wanted, a person so different from who I'd always been.

And the more we walked, the harder I felt, like I was pulling the shell of Annabelle around me and tucking myself safely inside. By the time we found the phone booth, I wasn't even sure I had something to say anymore. But the fat girl gave me a little shove, so I stepped inside.

As soon as I closed the glass door my head began to throb. I dialed the number. The operator asked for money. I hung up and spun around. The fat girl crossed her arms and pointed a finger at me, so I turned back to the phone and dialed again. This time I dropped the coins in, slowly, one by one, but when it rang I hung up again. Change came whistling through the machine and clinked against the little metal door. I leaned forward and closed my eyes and rested my forehead against the shiny cool face of the phone.

I thought of the time Charlie had called to take me to the circus, how excited my mom had been to find a boy calling for me, something she could understand, and I'd done what I'd always done—I'd pushed her away.

My eyes welled up again. I wanted to rewind the last few weeks, the last few months, the last year. Oh, but it was dangerous to think like this. Dangerous and I couldn't afford it.

I still had almost five hundred dollars and a quarter jar of peanut butter. I still had my wits about me and a place I was headed. I was okay. Maybe that's all I needed to tell her: not to worry, everything would be okay.

I straightened up, threw my shoulders back, and dropped the coins in again. This time when the phone rang I didn't hang up.

But nobody answered.

~~~

The early bus to Macon was full of sleepy college students and no one tried to talk to me. I was wide awake and watched the highway carry us.

There was this world and it held me in its palm. I was skidding along, sliding up its hills and down into its valleys.

Everything had been so complicated and taken so long. And after all this time on the road with the fat girl, her suspicions about Charlie felt like jealousy, and I wanted none of that right now. I was ready to be somewhere already and not just heading somewhere.

The day was new and there were all sorts of ways that it might end. In that thin light, I dug deep inside and found the part of me that was glad my mom hadn't answered. I let it have its say all the way there.

NINE

WE finally found the Fartlesworth Circus set up in an old campgrounds outside of Mobile, Alabama.

I climbed down from the cab of a semi and thanked the driver for the blue cowboy hat he'd bought me for reminding him of his daughter. The fat girl had a hard time getting down but I didn't lend a hand. After all the days where it took everything in me to shut out the images of Gleryton and what I'd done, after every street corner that had held the possibility of getting caught and cuffed and dragged back, every donut shop that had hidden a cop who was waiting for me, I looked at that red-and-white tent flying its flags, at the spread of the midway, all the color and life of it separated from us by a chain-link fence, and couldn't help wishing I was alone.

I stopped to check my reflection in the dusty window of a blue sedan parked in the mud on the edge of the field. My short spiky hair stood up in uneven pale wisps all over my head, but dark roots were coming. I slapped the cowboy hat back on and groped around in my backpack for the blue eye shadow stick and touched up my eyes. I smoothed on some lipstick. I took off my jacket and tossed it on the ground with my backpack, then studied my reflection and untwisted my yellow sweater, yanked up the waist of my tights and down the hem of my jean skirt. I was ready to see Charlie.

~~~

We walked the circumference of the fence. The fat girl suggested climbing over, but I ignored her.

"Whatever, *Annabelle*," the fat girl said, sending soda cans and paper bags flying with a swift kick here or there. I didn't care if I got on her very last nerve right now, I only wanted to find Charlie and be told that there was a place for me. I wanted it so badly, it pulsed in my chest, making me edgy. The fat girl's mean fit didn't help, but neither was it going to get in my way.

We came to the entrance and I paid my four-dollar admission with a smile to the old lady in the ticket wagon, who told us the show wouldn't start for at least a few hours, that they'd just opened the midway. We walked through the gate and stood by the edge of the big striped tent. To our right, down a rusty hill, the midway was screaming for attention.

The whole place was nearly deserted, just a few people milling around, some couples with kids, a few teenagers. I recognized carnival games and sideshow signs. There were: AMOS RUBLE, TALLEST LIVING MAN IN THE EN-TIRE UNIVERSE! TINA AND TIM! WORLD'S SMALLEST TAP DANCING BROTHER AND SISTER! PROFESSOR CHARLES C. CHARLEY'S REVOLUTIONARY TRAINED FLEA EXTRAVAGANZA! GODZUKIA! HALF MAN/HALF MONSTER! and LILY VONGERT, THE WORLD'S ONLY THREE-LEGGED BEARDED LADY. We walked along the scrubby path and when we passed THE AMAZING RUBBERBOY! I couldn't help but think of Stretch, the contortionist who'd sold me the brochure. Had he had a trailer like this? A banner proclaiming his talents? There must have been a picture of him spelling his own name with his body and probably a talker to get the crowds in. Charlie had complained about Marco's talker, that he was some carny kid who didn't give a shit.

The fat girl stopped short. We had come to the end of the line. GER-MANIA LOUDON, THE FATTEST WOMAN ALIVE!

But no Digestivore.

I stood for a moment, not believing, and then I spun around and marched back up the line, past the sideshow trailers, past the carny games, all the way back up to the main tent, where I waited for a second, closed my eyes, and made a desperate wish.

Please, please, let them be there, please, and we missed them somehow, please.

Please.

I turned around and walked back down, forced myself to move slowly, not to run, not to panic yet, forced myself to walk one foot in front of the other, eyes open as wide as they could, *please, please.*

But I saw every inch of that strip, and Marco's trailer wasn't there.

At the end of the path, the fat girl waited where I'd left her.

"They're not here," I said, the words like rocks in my mouth. "Marco's trailer isn't here . . ." I sank down in the scrubby dirt.

"Get up!" she hissed.

I ignored her. Who cared anymore? What did it matter, any of it? What the hell had I been thinking coming here, all the way here, knowing nothing, thinking Charlie was going to take care of me? I'd been so certain, but there was no reason. Charlie's father hadn't said he'd run off with Fartlesworth, I just thought I knew him well enough. I thought I knew him well enough to know.

But I didn't.

"Get the fuck UP!"

This was not what I wanted. This was not what I'd been looking for.

"Do you think I'm PLAYING with YOU?! GET UP NOW!"

And this I didn't want either, a fight with the fat girl, but what did it matter if I stayed on the ground? If I drew attention to myself. What on earth did it matter, any of it? I was tired of running, tired of caring, tired of being lost.

But she cared. She was absolutely furious. She took my elbow and yanked me hard, up and over so that I fell and scrambled to stand as I was dragged with tremendous force over to a patch of grass near a small cotton candy stand.

A girl behind the counter looked up from her magazine as we passed and gave me the once-over, then went back to it. I didn't care.

The fat girl slapped me hard across the face. I was silent, just reached up to touch my burning cheek.

"Hello!" She hit me again, on the other side, and I raised my other hand. My face was hot. I looked down at my feet. Tears slid down my nose and fell in the dust, drop by drop.

The fat girl grabbed a handful of my hair and jerked my head back. She marched me backwards until we stood in the grass all the way to the side of the cotton candy stand, slightly out of view. She used her other palm to bat my hands away and grip my chin. Her soft moony face swam centimeters from mine. Her breath smelled like onions.

"You listen to me," she said softly, "you are not going to pieces here. You cannot go to pieces now. Understand? I will not have it. You will suck it up or I will punch and kick the shit out of you until you do." She jerked my head again and the roots of my hair stung. I closed my eyes.

"Faith," she said, and her voice came from deep inside me. "Ask yourself what you want to do, what you came this far to do. Did you come this

117

far to lie down? Did you come this far to dissolve in a pile on the ground like a blubbering baby?"

I didn't answer and I didn't open my eyes. I felt her let go of my chin, of my hair. My head floated free. And then, with a dull thud, her fist connected to my jaw.

I opened my eyes. The sky swam above me. I was flat on my back, and then the fat girl blocked my view. "Is this what you want?" She kicked me in the ribs and I curled up. Again she kicked me and again. Until finally something in me snapped and I turned on her in a fury slapping and kicking and biting back.

There was a long low sound from all sides and it was me, howling, me. A shadow fell over us.

"Ma'am," a voice said. "Lady? Can you hear me? Are you on drugs?"

I froze. I was on all fours. I had been straddling the fat girl, but she was no longer beneath me. I turned slowly and saw a pant leg, a belt. My purple backpack held out like a dirty thing.

I tried to stand, stumbled, swayed, and then managed a footing. I straightened my sweater and skirt and then turned around fully. It took me a blinking moment to figure out that I was facing the bearded Lily VonGert.

She looked as unsure of me as I was of her. I was still shaking, but I reached out and took my backpack and mumbled some thanks, some apology, none of which was decipherable.

Lily VonGert sized me up and down.

She was quite a bit taller than me and broad shouldered, with a long, silky brown mustache and beard. It was thin and similar in texture to her hair, which hung in wavy locks all around her face, framing big brown eyes. She had on pants and a V-neck sweater. I was eye level with her cleavage and knew she must feel me staring.

"What's your name?" she said, not unkindly.

"Annabelle." I hooked my backpack over one shoulder and tried to stand straighter, tried to summon the moxie of Annabelle, but I was still shaking.

"Annabelle, honey, are you an epileptic?"

I stared at her for a moment before I began to giggle, and once I'd started I couldn't stop. I shook my head, no, not epileptic, but even though I tried to squeeze the little giggles down they kept erupting. I was making awful noises.

"Are you high, honey?" She reached out and touched my arm, then my forehead. "Did you take something?"

I shook my head again, still spitting and giggling. I bit my lip so hard I tasted blood, but the sounds didn't stop until Lily VonGert put her arm around me and began to steer us behind the midway. Then I stopped. Maybe it was her strong, sour smell, or the sobriety of my situation, but I stopped freaking out and got quiet.

"I'm just disappointed," I said softly when we'd walked up a bit and were entering a cluster of trailers, but she appeared not to have heard me. She moved her arm down my back a little so that she could direct me with the pressure of her hand. I wondered where her third leg was.

When we came to a long silver trailer she stopped and so did I. There was a makeshift porch of sorts: plywood thrown down in front of the door, and a roof made of tarp hung from a nearby tree to a pole extending from the opposite corner of the trailer. On the plywood was a rocking chair and an upturned milk crate with an overflowing tin-can ashtray.

"Sit here for just a minute, Annabelle, okay?"

She didn't move until I'd nodded and settled myself in the chair. It was chilly there, in the shade, and the view wasn't spectacular: the backs of trailers, here and there small glimpses of the midway. Up the hill I could see the other side of the main tent. I thought I saw the makeshift door Charlie had used in Gleryton, but I couldn't be sure.

Soon, the fat girl appeared from the midway clutching an enormous pink fluff of cotton candy. She had to squeeze herself between two trailers with considerable effort, though they were a few feet apart. There were fingernail marks all down the right side of her face. She didn't look at me, but came and stood a little way off and stared at the tent, so the marks faced me. They were red and puffy and terrible, but I didn't apologize. I didn't say anything.

I just rocked back and forth, back and forth, cradling my backpack like a doll or a helpless child.

~~~

Lily VonGert was gone long enough that I drifted off to sleep. I woke, startled, to her fingers on my arm and her face near mine.

"Go in and talk to Mina," she said.

Or I thought she said. I moved my mouth but words didn't come out. It took a second to stand and then I said it.

"Mina the Ballerina of the Air?"

Lily shook her head at me, as if she were still unsure of what she was dealing with, and pushed me towards the door of the trailer.

I found myself facing a squat older woman with tufts of salt-and-pepper hair framing a pruney face. A cigarette dangled from the corner of her mouth. She had a handful of cash and sat, her chair tipped back, behind a table covered in plump white envelopes, some open, some sealed.

"Sit down," the woman said, gesturing with the money, and an ash the size of my pinkie trickled off the end of her cigarette, dusting her blue T-shirt. "Damn." She swiped at her ample chest with an envelope.

I realized I was staring dumbly. I sat on a bench against the wall across from her and put my backpack on the floor beside me. I sat up straight and tried to look presentable, but I was still sore and disoriented. Out the window, I saw trucks in the distance, rumbling down a highway flanked by brownish hills. One of those roads led to Gleryton. And then for a split second I pictured a line of police cars, lights flashing, sirens screaming, headed here to claim me and take me back. I swallowed.

The lady was watching, waiting expectantly. I blushed and stammered, "I . . . I . . ."

This seemed to annoy her. "I am Elaine Hachette and I run things around here. Now who the hell are you?"

"Annabelle."

"Annabelle what?"

I hesitated. No one had asked for Annabelle's last name before. I looked at the edge of the table, at the tiny cramped kitchen to my right. "Cabinet," I said.

"Annabelle *Cabinet*." She sighed and shook her head, causing more ash to crumble and fall. "Lord help us," she mumbled. She took a rubber band from the table, swiftly bound the money, and plunked it down on a mountain of envelopes.

"Okay, Annabelle. Are you epileptic?"

I shook my head.

"Prone to seizures?"

"No."

"Well, *Annabelle Cabinet*," she said, her voice dripping with sarcasm. "What the hell were you doing rolling around on the ground slapping yourself silly by the midway out there? We have families coming to the show today and we don't need that, don't need any kind of disruption. We've had enough of that this season."

I was sweating profusely by now, so hot I knew my face must be ten shades of red. She seemed to be waiting for an explanation, but I didn't have one. Nothing that would make any sense to anyone. By now I could only tell part of anything, anyway. And which part was the part to tell?

"I was hoping to get a job—" I began, but she hooted and took another long thin cigarette from the pack by her elbow.

"Good," she said, and tapped it against the table as if it offended her. "That's good. Great way to get a job. You come mess up sales by picking a fight with yourself, by pummeling yourself on the ground like you're having some kind of fit. That, my dear, is a *fantastic* way to impress a potential employer."

She stopped talking for a minute and looked at me. Her eyes were fierce and beady. Sweat rolled down my back.

She took a deep drag, and when she spoke again it was in a low conspiratorial voice. "So, Annabelle . . . how long you been on the road?" she said.

I half stood up, then sat again but didn't answer. I pulled my backpack into my arms, shielding myself with it, and held it tight to keep from panicking. *Breathe*, I told myself. *Breathe*. I swallowed again, hard. "What do you mean, exactly?"

"Ms. *Cabinet*," the woman said with exaggerated politeness. "If you want me to let you go without calling the cops—"

At this I stood again, heart pounding, but she raised her eyebrows until I sat back down.

"—we have to start with what you're up to. I have been in the world for sixty-two years and I know a runaway when I see one. You are dirty and confused and I'm guessing not a day past fifteen—"

"Sixteen," I mumbled.

"—and if you wish to reach an understanding with me then you better come clean immediately. Am I understood?"

I didn't know what else to do. I nodded.

And then I told her that I couldn't go back, just couldn't. That I was looking for Marco, for Charlie. That I would do anything she asked if she just let me stay.

Elaine looked at me hard. I felt her eyes take inventory not only of my words, but everything in my head. When I was done, silence settled on us like a fine mist and we stayed like that while she seemed to consider every disastrous ounce of trouble I could cause. But I met her gaze. I made myself. I could feel how important that was.

"Okay," she said, finally. "Here's the deal. You will pick up trash around the midway and in return I'll feed you, but that is it. You get two days with us and then you have to move on, because I don't need any more strays to look after, okay? I'm sorry it has to be this way. I ran away to join the circus when I was only a few years older than you. I know the tradition, but we can't afford it right now. Christmas is over. Can't be picking up extra mouths to feed just for nostalgia's sake. Not right now. Now, do you have a sleeping bag?"

I shook my head.

"Oh for Chrissake." She stubbed out her cigarette and crossed her arms. "What are you doing on the road without even a sleeping bag?"

She stopped like she was waiting for a response. My mouth had become unbearably dry. "I hadn't planned—"

"Hup!" She stopped me with a flat palm and a firm look. "Don't start telling me your sob story," she said. "I don't want to hear it. I'm not changing my mind. We can't afford it. Two days. That's all you get. Am I understood?"

"Yes," I said. But where are Charlie and Marco, I wanted to know. I held my tongue.

Elaine stood up and came around the table. She was plump and limped a little and there were streaks of ash all along her leg. "All right, Annabelle," she said, her voice kinder now. I stood too and she stuck her hand out to shake mine.

She limped ahead of me and opened the door, then waited for me to step outside before she locked it behind us and started off the makeshift porch. "I'm going to introduce you to my son, Sam," she called over her shoulder. "He'll show you what to do."

~~~

Behind one of the carny games a skinny guy with a thin mustache stood arguing with a dwarf clutching a clipboard. The back door of the game was open, and I could see some of it through the door. Knock-down ducks and water guns. But I was more interested in what lay beyond that. Even at our distance I could see the motion of the midway through the frame of cheap stuffed animals. And then I noticed that some of those stuffed animals looked familiar.

Stuffed chickens in various pastels.

A pink, a pale green, a light blue.

I shook my head and tried to focus.

"Hey!" Elaine called, limping slowly towards the arguing men. They both turned.

The man with the mustache ran his hands through his hair and smiled. "Yeah?" he said just as she walked up. She swatted him on the shoulder.

"Not you, Grouper," she said, smiling. "I wanted my son."

The dwarf looked completely annoyed. "I am busy," he said, and rolled his eyes.

"I need you to take care of something."

He sighed heavily and shook his head and began gesturing at the other guy with his clipboard. "Mother," he said with exaggerated patience, "I need a few more minutes with Grouper, here, and then I will come and I will find you, okay?"

Elaine patted him on the back. She seemed unfazed. "Thirty seconds," she said kindly, then turned and limped back to me.

I watched Sam's face get red and his eyes narrow. He said something low to Grouper, who nodded and then waited until Sam walked away to make a face at the back of his head. Grouper kicked the side of his game trailer before he passed through the door and shut it, sealing off my view of the midway.

Instead I watched Sam approach. His legs and arms were stumpy, but his torso was long. His head seemed large, out of place on his small body. He had short dark hair and a handsome face, beautiful even, with freckles and full pouty lips and Elaine's dark eyes, but he looked like he wanted to kill something.

"What?" He spit the word like it tasted bad.

"Charming," Elaine said. "Really, Sam."

He sighed—it was more like a hiss—but Elaine ignored him. "This is Annabelle," she said. "She's going to need a blanket or two. I told her we'd feed her if she picks up the trash. I want you to set her up."

She turned and limped away, leaving us alone.

"Great," Sam muttered. He glared at me. "That's just perfect." He marched off towards the big tent and I had to hurry to catch up with him.

~ ~ ~

He led me to the back of a large tractor-trailer and disappeared inside, returning to toss me a pile of thick black garbage bags and a pair of soiled work gloves. I caught the bags but dropped them to try and catch the gloves, which I dropped to catch a broom.

"Pick it up," Sam snapped. He climbed down from the truck and put his hands on his little hips and glared at me some more. Then he snatched back one of the gloves.

"You are going to put these on," he said, waving the glove as close to my face as he could reach, "and pick up every single nasty piece of garbage you see lying in the dirt or grass. Every cup or wrapper. Understand? Every newspaper or flyer. Every goddamn piece of gum or other disgusting crap you see. When this place is clean, you'll eat. Now come with me." He marched off again.

I collected everything as best I could and followed him. We continued back the way we'd come until he found a large green trailer, near the edge of the big tent again, almost back where we'd started. I wondered if he was trying to confuse me.

"Wilma! Open up," he said, thumping the door with both fists.

It opened. Wilma had straight black hair cut in bangs across her forehead and red, red lips. She wore blue rhinestoned granny glasses and a beaded white cardigan over a fiery orange dress from the fifties that was fitted through the waist and then flared out. When she moved, I heard crinolines. Her feet were buried in heavy black combat boots.

"What the hell do you want?" she said.

For the first time Sam seemed to balk in someone else's presence. "I need some blankets," he said, and glanced at my skirt and sweater. "And maybe some old pants, if you have any." He jabbed his thumb at me. "For this one."

"Did you just get hired?" Wilma said, smiling at me. I shook my head.

"No," Sam said. "Just get her some blankets."

She put her hands on her hips. "You watch that tone, Samuel."

Wilma disappeared into the trailer and Sam seemed to wilt. I shifted from one foot to the other. My ankle was killing me, but I didn't want to draw attention to it. And my stomach growled so loudly I didn't know how it was passing undetected.

Sam had his hands behind his back while he stared at the sky. A big blue vein in his forehead twitched and pulsed. The fat girl poked her head around the side of the trailer, but I pretended not to see her.

Wilma reemerged with two rough green army blankets, which she added to my overloaded arms. "So when did you run away?" she said.

I rolled my eyes and exhaled before I could stop myself, but it was so unfair. How come everyone here knew immediately that I'd run away?

"What makes you say that?" I said, but my voice caught and I had to clear my throat and say it again before I was understood. Then they both laughed at me.

"What?" Even I heard the humiliating whine in my voice.

"She's sweet, Sam," Wilma said. "I bet I can find her something to change into. Can we keep her?"

"That is not funny! That is not fucking funny and you know it!"

"Awwwww, I hit a little nerve there, huh Sammy?"

"I don't have to listen to this," Sam said. "Get her some clothes. She can sleep in the hay truck tonight. And she eats with the job-ins, so send her when the flag goes up. I have better things to take care of." He started to walk away, then stopped and turned back to me. "You better not 'lose' any of those blankets, Runaway," he said, miming quotation marks with his fingers. "And you better not have any kind of a drug thing going on. Either of those and I will tear you limb from limb. When you show up at the cookhouse I'm going to be there to inspect your work. I better not even find a fucking straw." He turned on a heel and marched off.

My face was really red now. I swallowed and stared at Wilma's big black feet and tried to shield myself with the garbage bags and broom.

I waited until I couldn't hear him anymore before turning to make sure he was really gone. When I glanced back at Wilma, she leaned against the doorway staring after him and she looked sad. It was a few moments before she remembered I was there.

Then she pointed out the cookhouse and gave me a pair of tattered navy work pants and a long gray shoelace to hold them up. Wilma told me to watch for the yellow flag. "I'm serious about that, Runaway. You miss that yellow flag and show up with the white one or the red or anything else and I promise you won't be eating tonight. Job-ins eat when the yellow goes up. We don't mix around here."

"It's Annabelle," I said. "My name is Annabelle."

She softened a bit. "Well," she said. "Listen, don't mind Sam. He's actually not a bad guy. He's just had his heart broken . . ."

She trailed off and I nodded, but after looking into Sam's eyes, I had no doubt that if I missed a gum wrapper I wouldn't get any dinner. He was the angriest man I'd ever met.

Wilma didn't invite me inside to change, so I walked around to the back of her trailer and checked furtively before taking off my skirt and pulling on the pants. I stuffed the skirt inside my backpack and stashed it under one wheel of the trailer, tossing some leaves around it for camouflage. I still didn't know where the hay truck was, but all I could think about was food and not pissing off Sam.

~~~

I worked diligently all afternoon filling every trash bag, and kept my eyes open for any sign of Marco or Charlie, but very little was familiar in this landscape. Apart from the layout, which seemed to be pretty much what it had been in Gleryton, I didn't recognize anyone or anything, so I let my mind melt into the hunt for trash. I picked up every scrap I saw, but still there was more. As soon as I thought an area was clean, I'd turn around to find that some guy had tossed his cotton candy on the ground. It amazed me how many people threw things *next* to the garbage can.

By the time the yellow flag went up, my ankle was white hot and I was exhausted. Sam wasn't at the entrance. I waited there for about ten minutes, the smell of warm food making my stomach growl, and then finally, after convincing myself that the flags were going to change soon and I was going to miss out, I went inside.

It looked like a tiny cafeteria, with the food along the far wall and a handful of long aluminum picnic tables. I took a tray and was given a big bowl of meaty chili, a roll, some cooked spinach, and a piece of yellow cake by a fat man in a hairnet, who seemed to be sizing me up. I collected a Styrofoam cup of lemonade and some utensils as quickly as I could and found a seat at the empty end of one of the tables.

It wasn't until then that I noticed that every other person in the room was a big man, and I mean *big*. The other end of the table was packed with them, and the table across the way. They were burly, rough guys of all ages, and every one of them looked scruffy and down on his luck.

I was scared, which made no sense. I mean, what were they going to do to me? But I was alone and felt like such a girl.

My hands shook. I spilled some of the chili. Where the hell was I? What had I gotten myself into? I'd given up everything familiar without any plan for the future. *Breathe*, I told myself. *Breathe*.

I managed to get some of the chili to my mouth. It was spicy and warm and good. I tried to focus on that, but my mind drifted to the boys at Homecoming. To the way they'd moved in packs down the halls.

"Hey!" I snapped to attention. It was Sam, his face all red. I stood up. "No, it's okay," he said. "That's fine. You sit and eat."

I sank back into my seat and felt all eyes on us. Sam climbed onto the bench opposite me. "You did a good job out there. I checked. Very thorough."

"Thanks."

"You can do it again tomorrow. Get someone to point out the hay truck. You can sleep there. Use the Porta Potties by the horses. We load out day after tomorrow. If you do a good job tomorrow, you can eat on Sunday too. Then you're on your own."

I swallowed. "Thank you," I said.

He ignored me and climbed down from the bench. "What the fuck are you looking at, Spencer?" he called to an enormous black man with long messy dreadlocks. "You want a piece of me?"

Spencer threw his head back and laughed. "Oh Lord," he said, wiping tears from his eyes. "Now that is some funny shit."

Sam gave him the finger and walked out.

Clang clang clang. The fat man from behind the counter knocked a big silver spoon against a metal serving bowl. "You folks got nine minutes," he said. "Then it's the red flag."

There were grumbles, but all the jostling and camaraderie stopped and people began to eat with fierce concentration, myself included. I felt some of them looking at me, but no one said anything. When I had inhaled as much as I was going to, I got a cup of water and drank it down and refilled it and drank it down.

"Where you from?" someone called. I didn't turn around or look up. I drank as much water as I could hold, then scraped my tray into the garbage, careful not to spill, and left the cookhouse.

Clang clang clang, I heard behind me. "You fools got two minutes."

~~~

The hay truck was near the elephant trucks, near the horse trailers, near the menagerie. A tall skinny guy with a British accent showed me where it was and how to open the latch. "Be sure to climb to the back," he said, and grinned. "Don't want to get hit with a pitchfork while you're sleeping."

It was a gruesome enough thought to petrify me, but even that couldn't keep me awake. My back ached and I couldn't wait to get my boots off and let my poor ankle rest. I climbed in with my backpack and the blankets. I hadn't expected the pitch blackness of it, but of course there were no windows, just some vents high up along the walls. I stumbled blindly towards the back of the truck enveloped by the rich, musty smell of hay. I heard creatures skitter beneath me. Mice? I shuddered and bundled myself in the blankets, using my backpack as a pillow, and disappeared into the dark abyss of sleep.

~~~

I lurched awake in the aftermath of a loud noise, listening with every pore of my body, blinking in the dark, my breathing so loud. And then it happened again. An elephant trumpeted and I heard running and shouting, all sorts of commotion.

I felt my way along the wall of the truck and fumbled with the latch. Lights had gone on in trailers all the way down the hill, but near the hay truck it was dark. It took me a minute to get my bearings. I could hear a crowd and as I came around towards the animal trucks, I saw people huddled together with flashlights, murmuring.

I couldn't hear what they were saying had happened and didn't want to draw attention to myself by asking. I crept towards the edge of the crowd. *Knew he was a pervert*, someone said. *Takes one to know one*, someone else answered, and there were a couple of appreciative snorts. *That's terrible*, a woman said. *You guys are terrible. He's dead. Don't you have any respect?* There was another response that prompted more twittering but I didn't hear it.

I heard sirens.

I couldn't have run faster if I'd expected them. One minute I was near the mass of people and the next I was tucked safely away in the hay, and even though I knew they'd probably come for the dead man, whoever he was, I couldn't help thinking that they might be for me.

"Go to sleep," I heard. It was the fat girl. She pulled me back to where my blankets were. I climbed back into them and lay there, my eyes wide open, hearing the slam of police car doors and trying not to breathe too loudly.

"Go to sleep," she said again. This time she smoothed the hair from my forehead and stretched out beside me.

"This was so stupid," I said. "I thought Charlie would know what to do . . ."

"Don't worry," she said. "We're here, aren't we?"

I curled up away from her. "We didn't have a plan," I said. "We didn't have any idea at all."

TEN

I BARELY slept, tossing and turning until well after I could see light through the high vents. Finally I drifted off, only to wake to the sound of scraping and a fresh breeze. I sat up and scared the bejeezus out of a tall man with a pitchfork. "Holy shit," he said. "Oh Holy Christ."

The night before seemed like a dream. "Do you know what time it is?"

"About ten," he said. "You missed the yellow flag if that's what you're wondering about, but they might give you coffee anyway if you ask nice."

I thanked him and pulled on my boots one by one. My tattoo was still tender and the other ankle still swollen. I left the blankets but collected my other things and climbed down from the truck. It was a fine bright morning but I was groggy and dense. I cracked my back and limped towards the cookhouse, purple backpack in tow.

I managed to get a cup of coffee, which did a little bit to clear my head. Soon enough I was deeply engrossed in filling my garbage bag with half-eaten candy bars and empty popcorn cartons.

Sometime before lunch Elaine sent for me. She was smoking on the makeshift porch in front of her silver trailer when I got there. "Come here," she said. "How'd you sleep? How's the Hotel Straw and Bale?" She gave a little laugh.

"It was fine," I said. "I slept okay. Though I guess I woke up in the middle of the night when—"

She stopped me with the palm of her hand and motioned me to follow her inside. She sat behind her desk and I took my spot on the bench. "So what'd the bigmouths around here tell you?"

"Nothing. No one told me—"

"All right," she said, using her stub of a cigarette to light another one. "Tell me this: how do you feel about animals?"

"Fine. I mean I like them, I guess."

Elaine blew smoke in a stream above my head. "Well, we have a problem. A very big problem. And it looks like you're our solution." She leaned back in her chair, crossed her feet on the desk, and studied me. "Remember the guy who showed you how to work the door to the hay truck?"

I nodded.

"That's Jim Brewer. He's our elephant trainer. Lovely man. Been with this show nine years. I guess you made a good impression, because he suggested you. Anyhow, I don't see as where we have much choice after what happened."

"What exactly . . . what did happen?"

"I'll level with you," she continued as though I hadn't spoken. "I'm not sure you're up to it. It's not easy work and this place is no kindergarten. But I can't lose another hand. I've got a sudden hole in the schedule that strands the show in this godawful town for three extra days. I was already down a costume assistant, a midway attraction, and a groom due to some previous unfortunate circumstances that the loose lips around here will probably tell you all about." She exhaled a thick column of smoke and I had to concentrate not to cough. "After last night, I'm down another. Anyway, you'll report to him today and we'll see how you do."

I swallowed. "I'll report to Jim?"

"To Jim," Elaine said. "That was his new groom we lost last night."

"Oh." I cleared my throat. "Can I ask what happened?"

"I do not want to get into the details of it," she said. "He was a job-in. Sam found him in Tennessee I think. If you must know, he molested one of the horses. We wouldn't have stood for that, but it doesn't matter because that horse kicked him in the head and killed him. Now let's move on."

She slapped her palm on the desk and sat up straight, then leaned towards me and punctuated her words with her cigarette. "You are a very lucky girl, arriving just in time to capitalize on our misfortune. If you do, in fact, turn out to be a sign from God that this tour isn't going to be a disaster, we will find that out. For now, you'll work extremely hard and in return you will have food and a decent place to stay for a few more days—something a little more luxurious than the Hotel Straw."

She smiled. "We'll see how you do with the tasks you're given. If you work hard, if you blend in with the Fartlesworth family, then when we move on, it is possible that you could come with us. If you continued to do well, then after a few months we would talk salary. Understand?"

I didn't know what to say. I realized I'd been holding my breath.

"Miss Cabinet?"

"Yes!" I said, and grinned so hard I thought my face might split in half. "Sure."

"Now let me ask you this, Miss Annabelle Cabinet." She squinted at me. "What exactly are you running from? You were seen ducking out of sight when the police came around last night. What are you afraid of?"

I swallowed. "What do you mean?"

"Don't play innocent with me, missy. If you want to stay here you will tell me your real name and who you've run away from. And if you give me any trouble while you're here, any reason not to trust you, any cause to worry about my people because of you, *anything at all*, then you'll be off with the cops faster than you can say shit."

"And, one more thing." She leaned in close and pointed the burning tip of the cigarette at me. "I don't like to be made a fool of. If you lie—if I find out you've lied to me—and I *always* find out, I'm very good at that— you'll have more than just the police to worry about. Am I understood?"

I nodded. "You are understood."

"Good. Now what is your name and where are you from?"

I took a deep breath. "Faith," I said. The word felt funny, tasted funny. "I'm Faith Duckle from Gleryton, North Carolina."

"And what, exactly, did you leave behind?"

"A mess," I said, finally. "And my mom."

"All right, Annabelle," she said, and stood up to shake my hand. "Welcome aboard, hon. This is how I came to this life. I ran away when I wasn't much older than you and made a go of it. We'll soon see what you're made of."

Elaine had me sit on the porch and wait for Sam. I could not believe the conversation that had just taken place, any of it. I could not believe that I might have a chance to go on with them. And I did not know what I would have done otherwise. I stood and smoothed my sweater.

Just then, Sam marched past me and knocked on the door. Elaine answered it. She indicated me with her cigarette. "Annabelle's going to groom for Jim and take over for what Yael was doing for Benny, okay? You can put her where Yael was—Wilma's trailer, right? Tell Wilma I'll take care of the money for now. Annabelle's with us on trial. Show her where she needs to go. I'll see you later."

She shut the door and Sam turned to me with a mixture of pity and disgust. "Come on," he said.

He led me back towards the hay truck, around to the other side of the big top where there were more vehicles. He rapped on the side of a brown Winnebago, but no one came out and he cursed under his breath.

I strode along beside him, into the big tent where an older man spreading sawdust waved at us, and then out again. Finally he told me what I was going to do.

I was to muck out Bluebell's and Olivia's stalls every day for Jim Brewer, the elephant trainer, and I was to make sure that they had fresh water and food. Every day. *Make an elephant unhappy and we'll all be unhappy*, I was told. I was to muck out the show horses' stalls and do whatever I was told by any of the animal trainers. And when I wasn't doing that, I was to help out in the costume trailer.

"If you handle those jobs," he said, looking past my elbow and into the distance somewhere, "and providing everyone doesn't hate you or think you're an annoying idiot, then you'll help with teardown when we move again."

"Teardown?"

He sighed with great exaggeration. "Take. This. Show. Down," he said like I was an annoying idiot. "We'll climb that mountain if we come to it. Come on."

~~~

Everything was happening so quickly, so easily that I worried it was going to backfire, that I was going to screw it up. My trusting Elaine with a big part of the truth meant only one thing: I had to be perfect and invisible all at once. Or else.

We found Jim Brewer a few hundred feet from the animal trucks with Bluebell and Olivia.

I'd never seen elephants in real life. They were both enormous, each a gray mountain with sharp white tusks and huge floppy ears. One stood by the truck, digging through a bale of hay, using her trunk to delicately sweep piles into her enormous mouth. The other watched us, her trunk swinging side to side. Standing beside her, Jim Brewer's head only reached the top of her leg. From there her shoulder was an enormous hill of leathery skin in many shades of gray. I had an urge to reach out and touch her. Just then there was a rumbling noise and the elephant shoved out several heaps of what my job would revolve around. Each was larger than my head and very fragrant. I looked at Jim and Sam and smiled as best I could.

". . . take her to Wilma's," Sam was saying. "She'll do whatever you need, but she's First of May, and how. You'll have to teach her. And I couldn't find Benny, so make introductions when you can."

Jim Brewer nodded. He was blond and tanned and had a sharp little goatee, which he tugged on now. "After the show, luv, I'll show you some basics and we'll see how you fare." His British accent was crisp and melodic.

They both stared at me until I realized they were waiting for some kind of response.

I cleared my throat, discombobulated. "Thank you," I said, and turned a foolish red.

Sam shook his head and we were off again, back to the green trailer under which I'd stashed my stuff the day before.

"This is Wilma's," he said, staring at the sky, so he didn't have to look at me. "You met her yesterday. This is where you'll sleep. It also happens to be the costume trailer for the show changes, which means you'd better not be in here during the show. You should be busy with other things anyway. So. Do what Wilma tells you and stay out of her way."

He took a deep breath and rapped on the door. Wilma answered. "Well, if it isn't the little runaway," she said.

"This is Annabelle," Sam almost mumbled. "She's taking over for Yael on a trial and Mom wants her living with you. She'll take care of the money. Um—"

"Hi, hon!" She turned to me, all sweetness and light. I felt myself blush. "Come on in."

"She has to—"

Wilma put her hand out. "You," she said firmly. "May leave."

He wilted, visibly, and I almost felt sorry for him. But as soon as he'd disappeared I exhaled and realized I'd been holding my breath.

~~~

Wilma motioned me inside. The trailer was different from any of the others I'd seen. It was larger, for one thing, and brighter. There were lights and mirrors everywhere, and costumes in pinks and reds and oranges and blues and greens—all shapes and sizes. Every inch of the trailer seemed to explode with glitter and rhinestones, shimmer and shine.

Instead of a kitchen, this trailer had wigs on stands lining an entire wall, like a decapitated chorus.

"Welcome, Annabelle." Wilma leaned against a rack of clothes and crossed her arms. "I'm glad to have company again. It's been a little lonely since Yael left." She considered me critically. "Pants aside, you look like you've been wearing the rest of that outfit for a while. Is it all you have?"

I nodded.

"Well, you don't want to muck in the only clothes you have, right?" She disappeared into the back. "Come here," she called, and I followed. Past all the trunks and racks, I saw bunk beds in the far right corner.

Wilma opened a trunk, then closed it and slid it off another with a bang. This she opened too, then considered its contents with her hands on her hips.

She turned and looked at me again and I felt her taking measurements. "Maybe this," she said, yanking out something pink, and then she shook her head and threw it back in favor of a blue work shirt, which she rejected for a dark green padded jacket. She pulled out a pair of jeans and two gray T-shirts and something red. A sweater? I couldn't be sure. And some long underwear, and a tank top and a pair of pale blue shorts.

"What size shoes?" she called over her shoulder and as I said eight, she mounted another trunk and dug around the shelves overhead, pulling down boxes and extracting boots. "Where did I put those socks?" she muttered.

She stopped and turned around.

"Hey," she said. "Why don't you take your coat off. Throw your bag on the top bunk there, huh? Stay awhile."

I did what I was told.

~~~

I liked Wilma, but I was quiet and careful, wary that I might do something to fuck it all up and thrust myself outside those gates again, searching and searching. I held up the clothes she'd found, and most of them seemed like they'd fit. The jeans were a little big but looked comfortable and I was excited to trade in my filthy tights and garbage-stained work pants. I asked Wilma if there was any clean underwear too, but she just laughed.

"Most of the folks around here don't wear it," she said. "So that would be a no."

I blushed deeply. Wilma showed me where to shower and told me that, despite Sam's admonition, I was welcome to hang out in the trailer during the matinee as long as I stayed on my bed out of the way.

"There are a lot of people in and out of here during a show," she said. "And believe me, you do *not* want to cross their paths."

When I was clean I pulled on the jeans and a gray T-shirt, climbed up on the top bunk, and immediately fell sound asleep.

~ ~ ~

I woke to the light touch of a hand on my arm. I opened my eyes to a metal ceiling, a metal wall. I turned towards the hand and blinked hard at Wilma before I remembered who she was.

"Annabelle," she said gently, and I realized she'd been calling me for some time now.

I nodded, struggling to emerge from a puddled dream world where people I knew—Jenny Sims, Missy Groski, and Mr. Feldman from school; Angelique and Marybeth from Clark's; Hilton and Cookie from Berrybrook—surrounded me shouting loud, indecipherable things.

"Hello," I managed, my voice creaky. "Are they coming in now?"

"Who?"

I had meant the matinee performers, but as I said it I looked beyond her shoulder and saw the dark sky outside the trailer. Had I missed reporting to Jim Brewer?! I sat up fast and conked my head on the ceiling.

"Ow!"

"Ow," Wilma said, touching her own head. "You have to be careful of that."

I scrambled down from the bed, hit the floor, and stumbled, my feet as prickly and strange as if they'd never been used. Wilma had exchanged her fiery dress for a tight black turtleneck that made her breasts look pointy, and a wide blue skirt with fuzzy sheep leaping across its bottom.

"What time is it?" I said.

"It's late," she said. "Happy New Year."

"Happy New Year?" I shook my head to try and clear it. "The people," I said, "I missed the people?"

"You missed some people, yes. Both shows and Victor and Mina hanging out after—they're on the trapeze. He catches."

She walked towards the front of the trailer while she spoke and I tripped after her.

"—I wouldn't have woken you, but I thought you should eat something so you don't wake up hungry later. I always wake up hungry when I haven't eaten, and you're in a strange place and wouldn't know where to find anything . . ."

We had come to the tiny table in the front. All the sewing debris on it had been pushed aside and in its wake was a paper plate overflowing with potato chips and an enormous sandwich, with a can of ginger ale at its helm.

"Jim Brewer," I said. "What about Jim Brewer? Sam told me to—"

Wilma stuck her hand out like a crossing guard. "Hey, I took care of it." She gave me a funny smile and then shook her head. "Jesus, either you're really conscientious or Elaine pumped you full of the fear of God. Just chill out. Don't worry. You report to Jim first thing in the morning."

I thanked her profusely and she gestured for me to sit down. I wouldn't have said I was hungry before, but in front of that sandwich my mouth flooded and my stomach moved angrily. I tried not to gulp.

Wilma settled herself across from me, stealing a chip now and then. She told me her full name was Wilmadine Esther Genersh, she was the second of six children—four boys and two girls—of the Genersh family, a clan of high-wire artists. She'd grown up in the Fartlesworth Circus, but never performed.

"Extreme vertigo," she said. "Deterred early on."

I asked about her family and she laughed, saying I'd meet them soon enough. "Dad coaches my brothers and sister now. He stopped performing when he fell four years ago, right after Mom died. But that's a long story." She dismissed it with a sigh. "You'll see the act, and everything, I'm sure. They're pretty great."

I wanted to say I already had. I remembered them from when Charlie snuck me into the show in Gleryton. They'd worn green-and-purple outfits with puffy sleeves. And they stood on each other's shoulders and juggled back and forth on the high wire. Their final high-wire pyramid had been made when a girl—her sister, I figured—was volleyed off the shoulders of one guy, tumbling and twisting through the air to land upright, with arms proudly outstretched, on the shoulders of another, who was perched on two more guys—all her brothers. Their act was energetic and exhausting to watch, my stomach clenched the whole time. I couldn't imagine what it had been like to grow up in such proximity, but grounded.

"What else?" she asked.

With a pang I thought of Charlie walking through the big top with that bounce in his step. I was afraid to ask. Instead I fished around for something else. "Did you ever wish you could do it, too?" I said, worrying immediately that it was too personal a question, but Wilma smiled wistfully and shook her head.

"I like what I do," she said. "I belong right here." And she pointed at the trailer floor, where pins glinted in the slim light.

She'd begun assisting in the costume trailer at the age of eight. Two years ago, almost eighty and nearly blind, the chief costumer had retired.

"I'd been doing most of the work for years, anyway," Wilma said. "I mean, not necessarily the design, but the fine work and the headdresses and all the repair. And it's been my life, so far. I like it, so it made sense to Elaine and Mitch—he was her husband, Mitch Fartlesworth—for me to take over." She leaned back against the edge of a cabinet and took her glasses off and rubbed her eyes. There were little red ridges to mark where they'd been. Without their dark shape, her face was pale and delicate. And in the evening light with her eyes closed, she looked much younger than I'd thought.

"How old are you?" I asked, and Wilma's eyes snapped open. The return of her direct gaze was startling without glasses to fence it off. "Twenty-three," she said. "You?"

I hesitated. Eighteen? Nineteen? But Elaine's voice rang in my head and I curbed the urge to lie.

"Sixteen," I said. I thought she looked disappointed, but I wasn't sure. She nodded.

"Oh!" she said, looking at my plate, and leapt up to open a small refrigerator under the wigs. I had finished the sandwich, chips, and ginger ale in record time and was still hungry, though my mouth was tired from eating so quickly.

"The pièce de résistance," Wilma announced, and extracted a pint of ice cream. She took two spoons from a cup by the sink and returned to sit opposite me.

I was prepared for Coffee Heath Bar Crunch and excessive coincidence, but it was Rocky Road. Wilma handed me a spoon and we both dug in. I was grateful Wilma hadn't asked anything more about me, although I wanted to believe I could have handled questions, produced a suitable background for Annabelle. But I reminded myself: no matter how much I liked folks, I had to watch out. I had to guard my secrets fiercely. I had to remember who I was and why I was there.

I dug in and the sweet creamy coldness was pure deliverance.

Wilma was quickly devouring the ice cream. With a large piece of chocolate dissolving on my tongue I felt like maybe it was an okay time to ask.

"Do you know Marco the Digestivore?" I said.

She stopped with her spoon in midair. "Yes."

I hesitated, but pushed ahead anyway. "Well, my friend, Charlie—" I started, but Wilma's closed eyes stopped me.

"You're a friend of Charlie Yates?" she said, as though it were blasphemous.

"Yes," I said, suddenly uneasy. I took another spoonful of the ice cream, its chill reassuring.

"Jesus. Does Elaine know that?"

I swallowed. "Yes," I said, wondering for a moment if that was true. But I had told her who I'd come to find, hadn't I?

"Well." This was somehow too much for Wilma. She seemed to forget I was there for a moment, and then it passed. "After all the mess, it's amazing that she hired you," she said, coldly.

"What mess?"

Wilma shook her head and pressed her lips together.

"Do you know where Charlie is?"

She looked up sharply. "Jail, I'd imagine."

I swallowed, unsure how to proceed. Charlie in jail? "What happened? Why is he in jail? Where is he in jail?"

Wilma shook her head. "I really don't want to talk about it. We left the three of them in Macon two weeks ago."

I drew a sharp breath. The three of them? I'd been in Macon a week ago, our last stop before Mobile. I could have done something. Charlie had been in trouble and I hadn't known it. I hadn't done anything to help.

I saw familiar movement out of the corner of my eye and turned, hoping to see a blue dress, an arm, the silhouette of the fat girl watching us, keeping track. But it was only the shadow of costumes hidden in the darkness, swinging gently from the structures that supported them.

~~~

Later I went back to bed. Wilma crawled into the bunk below, and I lay awake wondering if Charlie was okay and what he'd done. And wondering where the fat girl was. I wanted her now, a familiar face in this strange place. I thought how bizarre we must have appeared, fighting in the grass the day before. What that must have looked like. And they'd asked *Do you have epilepsy, are you on drugs?* I giggled and caught myself, put a hand over my mouth.

Below me Wilma snored lightly.

I had to be careful.

If I was to cry out in my sleep, spilling my secrets like beads so they littered the floor, all anyone had to do was notice them bumping underfoot. To pick one up and understand it, hear it, and make a phone call or two. They would come for me with sirens and straitjackets, with photo flashes and horror and disgust.

I shook my head and stared at the metal ceiling. It wasn't good to think of that, of any of it: his face bleeding, his tongue flying through the air. If I let my mind go there, it might all seep out of me when I least expected it. Better not to think of Gleryton, or what we'd fled.

I closed my eyes and concentrated on a field of flowers. There was a shape moving through the field, an enormous shape, blurry and indistinct, approaching slowly. I gave myself over to waiting patiently for it to approach, my mind relaxed and open. I fell asleep dreaming of Bluebell.

ELEVEN

I WAS up bright and early, the world full of light. I crept down from my bunk and pulled on the new jeans and work boots, a T-shirt. It was lovely to wake up clean, in a bed. To wake without the need to move on. I pulsed with energy.

Wilma was sound asleep.

I found coffee and the coffee maker, went out to the showers for water, and made us a pot. When it had brewed, I took a cup and sat in the open doorway watching the circus wake up.

That took a long time. Later I would come to know that mostly these were night people. Later I, too, would be a night person.

But today, after half a day and most of a night's sleep, I felt somewhere between wonderful and like I'd been run over by a Mack truck. My limbs tingled from so little use, my body cracked its way into place, and my head was filled with cotton, which the coffee dissolved, bit by bit.

I felt a hand on my back and turned expecting Wilma, but it was the fat girl, cross-legged on the floor behind me eating a cruller. "Hi," she said.

I didn't answer immediately, but smiled and took a long sip of coffee, then turned, leaning my head back against the doorjamb so I could see outside and inside. It was going to be a warmer day, you could tell, though right now it was chilly.

"How's your face?" I said finally, careful to keep my voice low, and indicated the scratches on her cheeks, which were still red and puffy.

"Fine," she said. "Why?"

AMANDA DAVIS

At that I wondered about my own face. I put the coffee down in the doorway and stepped over the fat girl, scanning the trailer for a mirror. I checked to see that Wilma's black hair still poked out from beneath a pile of blankets. She hadn't stirred.

Opposite the dress rack, there was a large mirror framed by little round lightbulbs. I almost didn't recognize the girl that stared out from it. Her face was bruised and swollen, her head crowned by wispy orange tufts with dull brown roots. She looked battered and wary, but tough. Her eyes guarded bottomless things.

I reached up and touched my cheek, the yellow, brown, and pale blue area around my eye. The skin was tender. Now I noticed that my jaw was tight, a little sore, though I hadn't really felt it the night before. I opened and closed my mouth. Besides the color of bruises, my face was ashy and gray.

"Morning."

Wilma shuffled behind me in lacy pink pajamas and blue bunny slippers. Without the accompanying makeup her granny glasses were harsh slices across her delicate face. I turned and saw the fat girl hold a finger to her lips, give a little wave, and tiptoe out the front door.

"Morning," I said. My voice creaked a little.

"You made coffee." Wilma sounded delighted.

I took a deep breath and rescued my own mug of coffee from the doorway, where I could see the fat girl ambling up the hill, her blue dress sharp and bright against the sleeping landscape. I took a sip, but the coffee had grown cold, so I tossed the remains of my cup out the door, where it splattered on the dull grass.

"Hey," Wilma said from behind me, the coffee bringing her to life once more. "You ready for a day in the circus?"

~~~

I was. Oh, I was! I reported to Jim Brewer, with a little cover-up on my bruised eye and my scratched cheek. Wilma had suggested it, without asking where the marks came from, though I felt the need to explain them.

"I fell down," I told her, and she gave me a knowing nod, which was fine. Let her believe whatever she wanted—it couldn't be any worse than their real origin.

Walking around towards the animal trailers I marveled at the bright morning, at where I was headed, at my good fortune in getting this chance at a job. I wished Charlie were here—I thought he'd get a kick out of it.

142

And then I thought about Charlie in jail and the whole of the late-night conversation and promised myself to be careful with questions. Lay low. Worry about Charlie later and for now just do what I was told.

And Jim Brewer had a lot for me to do.

I found him in the maze of animal trucks behind the big tent, sitting on a lawn chair between the two elephants, staring up at them when I got there.

I said, "Good morning."

He looked up at me. "How do you feel about animals?" His accent clipped his speech, making it sound like little drumbeats or the tapping of tiny nails.

"Good," I said. "I mean, they're cool, you know?" He motioned for me to sit beside him on another lawn chair and I did. From down here the elephants were even more enormous. Their trunks slithered and snaked through the air like enormous limber fingers with wet pink tips.

"Right, luv," Jim said. "That's a splendid beginning, but if you are going to properly learn to relate to Bluebell and Olivia then I need to know if I can trust you." He rose and stood between the elephants.

"This is Olivia," he said, patting the elephant to his right who was slightly bigger, a darker gray, and had one long tusk and one stumpy broken one. "And this wee one here is Bluebell, the baby. I'm mostly concerned with how you relate to Bluebell. Now don't get nervous—"

Could he tell that I was?

"—just answer truthfully. Take a look at Bluebell, here." He stroked her trunk, which she raised under his hand. "Look at her face and then close your eyes."

I did.

"Now, I want you to picture Bluebell's face, let it swim before you, and tell me the first impression you get of her, all right?"

I felt dorky with my eyes closed trying to envision Bluebell's face, but I took a deep breath and listened for an impression. What exactly did he mean?

"She's really huge," I said and giggled uncomfortably. How obvious. Duh, the elephant was large.

"Who is she, though?"

I felt stupid, but I tried to give myself over to it. I took a deep breath and concentrated and saw her large dark eyes in their heavy gray lids swim before me. "She's sensitive?" I said, "And strong? And really smart?"

Were those things true? No, I was talking about myself, what I hoped someone would say I was like. Still, I didn't have anything else to say. I sighed. "Can I open my eyes?"

"Oh," Jim said. "Yes. That was quite good." He stared at me with a penetrating gaze that made me wonder what he saw.

"Right," he said, after a minute. "Well, you should be okay, luv. We'll give you a try as my groom. Which means that you will do whatever I need you to do for the care of these animals. In addition, you will muck up after them and keep them in water—these bulls each drink about forty gallons a day, and pass nearly two hundred pounds of scat apiece, so this is no lean task—"

I guessed what scat was. There was a definite elephant smell, though not as strong or awful as the tigers had been in Gleryton.

"—and then I'll mostly want you to help me with dressing Bluebell for the show. There are several headpieces and they can be unwieldy. Olivia is a stubborn git, and very picky, and won't trust you for a while. But Bluebell's a real sweetheart, and you'll see that. Very smart, quite perceptive, and she has a wonderful sense of humor. She'll let you dress her, but she can get angry, like anyone. She follows Olivia. Follows her around like Olivia was her big sister. Olivia's forty-three, an Asian. I've had her for thirteen years. Bluebell's an African elephant, but born in captivity. She's only a kid, eleven—"

He rested his head against her leg and she reached her trunk around to fish through his pockets until she found an apple, which she delicately tossed into her mouth. When she opened it I saw her tongue. It was bigger than my whole arm.

"—and I've raised her. She likes company when we're on tour, likes someone around, or she gets lonely, and so that's a bit of your job when you're not busy."

I nodded. I was watching Bluebell watch us. She had finished the apple and stood, looming, her shoulders arcing into the enormous dark shadow of the elephant truck. Only a kid.

"Wow," I said.

Jim gave me a musty tan jumpsuit and showed me what to do. I watered and mucked—shoveled huge loaves of elephant poo into a wheelbarrow and then carted it off into the trees that lined the field.

"Excellent fertilizer," Jim told me, though I saw hay and orange peels in it, and in one pile a soda can and an empty cigarette pack. At some point Olivia lay down in the sun to nap and Bluebell soon followed. From the back, as I came up from the woods with the empty wheelbarrow, they looked like little mountains.

"Shhhh," Jim cautioned me like a protective parent. I tiptoed. My arms had really begun to ache. "Follow me," he said quietly, and led the way down the hill to meet Benny, the horse trainer.

When we reached the same brown Winnebago Sam had thumped unsuccessfully the day before, Jim stopped. "You're mostly to be with me," he said. "I'm your first responsibility, and you're *my* groom, but Benny may need a little help, as well."

He gave a quick knock and Benny Thomas stepped outside the trailer, followed by a posse of small black-and-white dogs. He was older than Jim, short and rumpled, with a pronounced overbite and a long jagged scar on his right cheek. His hair was jet black, shoe polish black, and shadows of black stained the tops of his ears. The five little dogs ran in enthusiastic circles, then settled themselves in a straight line and sat, mouths open, panting expectantly.

Jim introduced me and Benny nodded and said he could use my help now that Yael was gone.

Yael, Yael, Yael, I thought. Her shadow followed me everywhere I went.

"Hold on a minute," Benny told us, and he disappeared in the trailer. Jim laughed to himself and shook his head. When Benny returned he had five red balls, which he tossed one by one to the dogs. Then he motioned for me to follow him and bade Jim good-bye, with a gruff "I'll send her back later."

Jim waved to me and headed off towards the Midway. I trod back up the hill next to Benny, followed by the dogs. They were a funny sight behind us, following each other in single file—each with a red ball in his or her mouth.

"Stop," Benny called when we reached the paddock. "Preee-*sent!*"

Five red balls flew high in the air, and were caught in five tiny upturned mouths.

"Good little soldiers," Benny sang out, and the dogs dropped their balls and wagged their tails.

"Can I pet them?" I asked. Benny looked annoyed, but he nodded so I bent to nuzzle the dogs. They were squirming bundles of energy, so thrilled by my touch that it seemed they might wriggle right out of their skins with joy.

"What are their names?"

"That's not what you're here to learn," Benny snapped. I stood up slowly, my face hot, and shoved my hands in my pockets. *Deep breath,* I told myself. I kept quiet, followed Benny into the first stall, and paid attention. He spoke quickly and snorted a lot. And he had plenty for me to do.

He taught me to groom the three horses, Uno, Dos, and Billy, with broad firm strokes. To feed them, to check their hooves. He explained what tack was, how to put on a show saddle, then demonstrated how to trick Billy into her bridle and how to avoid getting kicked in the head by Uno. I was scared of that and there was a lot to remember. I concentrated so hard I thought my eyes might roll back into my head, but Benny turned out to be a nicer teacher than I'd thought. He even promised he'd teach me to ride if I "made good."

"Remember to ask if you don't know something," he said gruffly, as we were leaving the horses. "You'll be fine."

"Thanks."

"Indeed."

Benny called his dogs and they rallied around him, a wriggling mass of enthusiasm. They picked up their red balls and followed him back to the Winnebago.

~~~

I checked in with Jim, who sent me to Wilma. "After tonight you'll help us with the show," he said. "You'll help set up and you'll help us after. Tonight you'd just get in the way, so stay with Wilma, see what she needs. I'll see you tomorrow morning."

He gave me a mock salute, which I returned, grinning the stupid stiff smile I'd worn all day. As I walked away, my face ached from focus and good cheer, my body from all the lifting. I could barely raise my arms, and my shoulders were tight, my hands blistering and sore. I could tell it would all be worse by tomorrow.

Back at the trailer, Wilma squeezed her nose between two fingers and made me take off my jumpsuit and hang it up outside. She gave me a pair of slippers to replace the brown boots, which were also left outside the door. Then she offered me Band-Aids and dinner, and explained that I should stay on my bunk, out of the way, during the evening's show. "You just watch," she said. "I'm sure Jim and Benny exploited the hell out of you and you won't mind sitting still anyway. But try not to fall asleep. And don't get down, no matter what. There really isn't enough room."

I agreed, and gobbled the food gratefully. It felt wonderful just to sit and space out while Wilma spun around the place humming to herself and preparing for onslaught.

I jumped at a knock on the door and looked to Wilma, who stopped what she was doing and checked her watch. She made a curious face, and the person knocked again, louder this time. I stood up and she went to open it. It was Sam.

"Didn't you hear me knock?"

Wilma's easy mood disappeared instantly. She blocked the doorway with her arms crossed, looking like she might kick him in the face.

"What the hell do you want?" She spat the words like they were little knives, but they didn't seem to hit their mark. He gave her a slow dark smile and then pushed past her, through the doorway, and turned his attentions on me.

"You, Miss Annabelle Cabinet"—he pronounced it like it was French—"need to come with me."

I stood, my legs rubbery, and followed him outside.

It was dusk and the light was dim. The outline of Sam's tiny figure was illuminated by the big top ahead of us, until he turned off on a gravel path and led me to the campground picnic area, out of earshot of the trailers.

"Have a seat." Sam gestured with his clipboard.

I chose a picnic table and sat. When Sam hoisted himself up onto the bench across from me, we were almost eye level.

My mouth was dry. I swallowed. Sam didn't look at me but over my shoulder at something beyond me. He ran his stubby fingers through his dark tangle of hair.

"Annabelle," he said, finally. "Do you know what it means to make a promise?"

I nodded. I knew. I had made promises. I had kept them; I had broken them. I remembered Starling, remembered one moonless night with only her words in the dark.

Hey, she'd whispered. *Promise me you'll be all right.*

"Annabelle?" Sam waved his hand in front of my face. "Stay with me, here, okay?" He cleared his throat and offered me a cigarette. I took one and lit it.

The smoke came in sharp, delicious. I tried to clear the heaviness in my chest by shaking my head, but I felt myself floating. Drifting away.

Promise that from now on you'll tell me if something's wrong, my mother had whispered in the dark, late on the night that she'd delivered me from Berrybrook.

Promise you won't forget me, Starling had said.

I forced myself back to Sam, who didn't meet my gaze.

"I'm here."

"You didn't report to Jim yesterday. It was your first day and you didn't show up." His voice was tired. Behind him, the lights of the lot pulsed with energy. Voices drifted in and out of the trees.

"I fell asleep," I said. "When I woke, Wilma told me she'd spoken to Jim. I worked all day today." I offered up my blistered hands.

"I know," Sam said, and blew a stream of smoke from the side of his mouth. "Jim says you did a good job today, but I still have to give you a warning. My mother is watching you. I'm watching you. I haven't spoken to Benny yet, but we pull out the day after tomorrow. Keep your word."

I opened my mouth to protest, then thought better of it.

"Okay," I said. "Won't happen again."

This seemed to satisfy Sam. He exhaled. "Good. Now there's something else I wanted to talk to you about."

I settled myself attentively. Sam seemed to have a hard time finding the words. He scratched the back of his neck and sighed.

"It's Wilma," he said finally. "We can't go on like this." A pained expression crossed his face and he pursed his lips. "It's unacceptable."

Bit by bit he told me. Sam and Wilma had been good friends since they were kids. Yael and Wilma had become fast friends as soon as she'd joined the show. Sam fell hard for Yael but she wasn't interested in him. She began carrying on with someone else and Sam grew crazy with jealousy. "I loved her," he said. "You have to understand."

What I didn't understand was why he'd chosen to unburden himself to me, but I kept quiet and nodded and he continued.

Wilma got caught in the middle, he explained. Sam wanted to know who Yael was seeing, he knew it was someone, and Wilma tried to persuade Sam to let it go, but he wouldn't. Wilma told him it was a gamer named Frank and Sam forced Grouper, who ran the midway, to fire the guy. But Wilma had lied. It wasn't Frank that Yael was carrying on with. It was Marco Klieboski.

"Marco?"

Sam stopped his story and squinted at me. "You know Marco?"

I took a deep breath and smiled. "Sorry to interrupt."

"Anyway, Yael was having this thing with Marco and then this jerk, some friend of Marco's, shows up determined to do anything to travel with the show and Grouper convinces Mom to hire him. In two weeks Yael goes nuts. Bonkers. Knocks the friend out with an iron skillet and goes after Marco with a knife." He paused to light another cigarette and thrust the pack towards me, but this time I refused.

"She set his trailer on fire. We had to leave them all with the cops in Georgia."

He looked past me, and his eyes were bottomless and sad. "I'd like you to talk to Wilma. Tell her I'm sorry for everything, I really am. Tell her that you think she should give me a break. I know you've only known her a lit-tle bit but she might listen to you, and I'd really appreciate it."

I didn't know what to say. I swallowed and gave Sam a bewildered look.

"I would really *appreciate* it," he said again, and this time he met my gaze. "I'm sure the show would benefit from having someone with diplo-matic skills come along with us."

I understood.

~~~

When I got back to the trailer, Wilma was pulling wigs and arranging shoes in rows. She didn't ask about Sam's visit, but pointed and I crawled up onto my bunk.

I was unprepared for what followed, couldn't possibly have imagined the lunacy she'd warned me about. For the next two hours there was a near-constant flood of people in and out of the trailer. Each performer entered frantic and speedy, tossing off one costume in favor of a new one, reapply-ing makeup, trading off headdresses and wigs. It was very crowded, but they all seemed expert at dodging one another. I watched a woman bend over to tug on a new leotard, just missing the arm of a guy pulling on a sequined jacket. Centimeters closer and I was certain she'd have lost teeth.

Wilma couldn't hang anything up fast enough. Some things she dumped in a bin, with headdresses tossed on her bed, or, when that be-came a jumble, on mine. Some she draped over one arm and ignored, lug-ging them around until she was nearly buried by a mound of sparkly, colorful cloth. With her mouth full of pins, she made an exasperated face and tossed the costumes aside, continuing the whirlwind of dress, undress, and redress, stitch and fix, until the finale, when the trailer abruptly flooded—the height of the chaos—and emptied. There was a sudden si-lence, with me on my bunk, in awe, and Wilma spitting pins and exhaling.

"I cannot believe you do that every night," I said, finally.

"Twice when there's a matinee. Thank God the clowns have their own dress tent."

"Holy shit."

"I know," she said, and laughed. "One day off, one half-day of performances. That's the life I'm used to." She emptied the last of her load onto a trunk and reached below the wigs for two glasses, which she filled with whiskey. She offered me one. I hesitated.

"Oh, come on," she said, leaning against the mirror. "You've got to grow up sometime."

I smiled weakly, climbed down, and took the glass. The first sip made me wince, the taste was harsh and it burned going down, but then it warmed me, belly to fingertips. I sat across from her at the table.

"I can't believe I slept through that yesterday."

"Honey, you slept through that *twice*." We both laughed and then sat quietly for a while. I was exhausted, my whole body heavy and sore. I wondered how to bring up Sam.

"How'd you get those bruises?" Wilma said.

I smiled and rubbed my knee with the palm of my hand. "I walked into a door," I said. "I fell down."

Wilma swished her glass around, then refilled it.

"If you don't want to talk about it, just say so."

"I'm sorry."

"It's fine." But it didn't sound fine. My stomach began to tighten. The lie escaped before I had time to think of Elaine.

"This boyfriend . . . He's a long story that I'm glad is over."

This seemed to brighten her; she clucked her tongue and nodded. "Well, you're here now, where the creep won't find you."

I swallowed and tried to smile. Blue caught my eye. The fat girl stood in the doorway. "What a fucking mess," she said.

She was right: the trailer was a wreck. I looked around, but ignored her. I set my glass down and began to put stuff away, resigning Sam's problem to a later time. I had to ask Wilma where each gown or leotard or shiny, sequined top went, so it took the two of us almost an hour to return things to exactly where they belonged, preparing them for the grab of tomorrow's desperate hands. Wilma coached me the whole time. On a matinee day, she told me, the turnaround would be very quick and such straightening up was essential to a smooth run.

"If they can't find something, all hell breaks loose," she said, shaking out a pink sequined tailpiece and clipping it to a hanger. "And that, let me tell you, is a nightmare."

~~~

There are all kinds of nightmares. What about the one where you're on-stage in front of hundreds of people but you're not sure what play you're in or what the lines are and you look down to discover you're naked? Or there's the one I used to have after a busy night at Clark's: where an ever-spreading kudzu of tables demanded water, but each time I went to fetch it there were no clean glasses, or the glasses were hot and had to be rinsed before they could be used, and then once the water was presented there were twice as many dirty tables that needed to be cleared and twice as many again that needed water.

That night I had a new nightmare. I walked down the midway looking for Charlie, for Marco, but they weren't there, and when I turned to the big top it had disappeared. I began to run but when I reached the place where the tent had been, it wasn't there, replaced instead by an indoor flea market, a car show. When I turned back to the midway there was only an empty field, a parking lot.

I woke sweating, hands clenched, breathing a swift staccato.

If they left me I had nowhere to go.

"They won't leave you. Christ, you worry a lot." The fat girl stood by my bunk with a fist full of macaroons.

"What if I don't get Wilma to forgive Sam? How can you be sure?"

She talked with her mouth full, crumbs spitting every which way. "Because you're smarter than you think you are. And you've been playing your cards right." She extracted hay from my hair. "Plus you're working like a dog for no pay. Why leave you?"

TWELVE

B<small>Y</small> 9 A.M. we were standing by Bluebell. The fat girl wouldn't stop yawning. Jim and his lawn chairs were nowhere to be seen. Olivia sucked water from the trough and sprayed it into her mouth. I looked Bluebell in the eye, as best I could from far below it. "Hello, old girl," I said, then thought about how she was actually a little younger than me, and tried again. "Hey, Blue," I said. "How's it going?"

She swung her trunk around and combed some hay from the ground into a little pile. Then she swept it up in her trunk and deposited it in her huge mouth, keeping a watch on me the whole time. Her movements were smooth and nearly dainty, but her footprints were deep in the slightly damp ground.

"Hey, baby," the fat girl called suggestively. "Hey, good-looking!" I told her to cut it out and she told me that I was no fun. We'd left the trailer while Wilma slept, and I was grateful not to have to decide again whether or not to bring up Sam's request. I'd taken a muffin and eaten it while we walked towards the menagerie. Now I offered Bluebell what was left. She eyed me skeptically. I wondered if it was too small an offering of food, but soon her trunk swung towards me with its wet pink tip and swept the muffin away, dropping it into her cavernous mouth.

I looked around for more food. The fat girl pointed out a sack of potatoes near one of Jim's tires. I assumed it was for Bluebell and Olivia, but before I could do anything about it, Jim showed up with the lawn chairs under one arm. His hair was wet and he had dark circles under his eyes.

"Hi there," he said.

"Hi." I scrambled to find the shovel and wheelbarrow and began to go about the task of collecting both elephants' night deposits. Jim set up the chairs, greeted first Olivia and then Bluebell, rubbing each on the trunk and murmuring something. Then he crossed his arms and watched me. The fat girl sank into one of the chairs.

"I want to show you where the feed is," Jim called before disappearing into the truck. When he came back he had an enormous bag slung across his back, and I found myself watching the way the muscles of his arms bulged to hold it up. I swallowed. Olivia reached her trunk out towards Jim, and Bluebell shifted her weight excitedly, back and forth, back and forth.

He gave them the feed, then went to the hay truck for hay and spread some of that before them as well. I made a mental note to retrieve Wilma's army blankets.

"So, Annabelle," Jim said. "Where are you from?"

My blood froze. I leaned on the shovel. "Oh, around," I said, trying to sound casual, to keep my voice light. "You know, here and there." The fat girl rolled her eyes at me.

"Right," Jim said. "Well, that's surely got the ring of truth to it, eh, Blue?" He reached up and rubbed Bluebell's forehead while she scooped the hay into her mouth.

I continued my collection and kept quiet, my cheeks burning. When the wheelbarrow had a solid, hefty load I dropped the shovel in the grass and headed towards the trees. The fat girl followed.

"Hi," she said, her voice high and squeaky. "I'm from *around*. You ought to visit sometime!"

"Shut up and lick that," I said pointing at the vanilla soft serve dripping down her hand. I was in no mood for her mockery or her coaching.

"Spontaneity is not your strong suit," she said, tending to the drips. "Thought you'd appreciate a little lesson on lying while we're out of earshot of the elephant man." She took a step away and looked anxious. "I, uh . . ." she stuttered with an exaggerated look of sheer panic. "I ran into a door. I fell down."

"Give me a break," I said. "I wasn't ready. It's okay. Wilma didn't press it. I was just trying to be careful."

"Careful." She gave a snort. "Jesus. You're so careful that you're a danger to yourself. Now, come on. Where are you from?"

"Gleryton?"

"No, you idiot. Pick somewhere else. And make it somewhere you've actually been once or twice so you don't make an ass of yourself."

I thought about New York City. I'd been there once with my parents when I was a kid.

"You'll get caught in that one in about four minutes," she said, biting off the bottom of her cone with a snap. "Choose somewhere smaller and stay South for Chrissake, you don't sound like a Yankee."

"What about Charlotte?" I said. "Or Raleigh? Those are big places, but I've been there."

"You think those are big places but you were going to say you're from *New York*?" She giggled, shook her head, and sucked at the bottom of her cone. "How about Asheville," she said when she'd drained it dry. "Or Nashville? Somewhere you've actually been."

"I've been to Raleigh. And Chapel Hill."

She started to walk away, kicking up the brown grass. I watched her go, then dumped the wheelbarrow and shoved it ahead of me, leaping to catch up with her.

"What?" I was out of breath.

"You seem to think you have it all under control," she said, waving me away. "And I don't need to hang out where I'm not needed."

"Oh, come on," I said. "Don't go getting pouty . . ." But she put her hand up and strolled off like a diva.

~~~

When I got back, Jim was reclining in his lawn chair reading the paper. I wheeled back to the truck, only to find that more large smelly gifts from Bluebell and Olivia had been added to the pile. I shoveled and removed, shoveled and removed. My arms and shoulders ached, but I liked the senseless rhythm of it, the feeling of my muscles ripening, the world waking up.

And it was. All around, trailer and truck doors opened and slammed shut. Screen doors creaked and people shouted to one another.

In the field near Elaine's silver trailer, a bunch of men juggled steadily in groups of two, three, and four, and alone. They had clubs and balls, all sorts of things that caught light and flashed as they flew through the air. Every so often someone dropped a club or ball or fiery stick and the rhythm was interrupted only to resume again in a minute or so. They wove around and called things to one another, but I only heard their voices, not what they said.

Nearby, two red trailers with a painted banner—THE FAMILY GENERSH!—were parked in a V. Four big guys with black hair and no shirts on, whom I took for Wilma's brothers, were working out. Two did push-ups on the ground and two pulled chin-ups from their open door ways, then they switched places.

I dumped and shoveled, watered, shoveled and dumped, watching it all as I passed.

Soon Jim sent me to groom Uno, Billy, and Dos. The horse trailers were around the tent a little ways, and from that vantage point I could see a small figure hanging upside down from a trapeze rigged on a metal skeleton. Mina? There were others with her. Two men and another woman, all watching the figure spin.

Uno neighed and Billy stomped. Benny, the trainer, wasn't around, but I approached the horses, and starting with Dos I patted them one by one, stroking their enormous smooth faces and whispering my hello. They seemed almost tiny after standing between two elephants for so long, but I was careful not to stand behind them, because I couldn't remember who was the notorious kicker. All three seemed mild and agreeable for the most part, happy to let me groom them, feed them, and muck out their makeshift stalls.

By three o'clock I was finished. I passed by the red trailers again on my way to find Jim. The Genersh boys were stacked two people high now— two towers facing each other and juggling back and forth, one brother to the next. From far away they looked like awkward swaying trees playing a flawless complicated catch. On the ground nearby a young girl in a saggy blue leotard walked around upside down, balanced on her hands as firmly as if they were feet.

"Jenny, come inside and clean up right now!" The screen door to the closer trailer opened and a man in a wheelchair rolled down a small ramp and onto the ground near the girl. She walked towards him on her hands, all the blood in her body gathered in her head. Her face looked like a freckled tomato.

"Right side up," he snapped, and she obeyed, promptly and silently popping to her feet and brushing her black hair out of her face before scampering ahead of him into the trailer. Wilma's brothers didn't look down, just passed clubs with a steady thud, thud, thud of palm to prop, and circled each other like woozy giants.

When I found Jim a few minutes later, his newspaper was folded neatly on the lawn chair next to him and he had his eyes closed. I stood, not wanting to wake him, then carefully reached for the paper. I skimmed through the first section, looking for myself, but I didn't see anything.

There was an article about the state of the national economy, the decline of farming, but no inquiry into the disappearance of one wacko teenage girl from North Carolina.

It seemed so far away, all of it. Classes and visiting Andrea Dutton. Even Homecoming. They seemed like things that had happened to a whole other person.

"They did."

I didn't look up. I could feel her behind me.

"They happened to Faith Duckle. And you aren't her anymore."

I nodded. I had a lump in my throat. I was someone else. I was Annabelle and I had no past, no parents. Only a future.

"Don't think that means they aren't looking for you, though."

"I thought you didn't feel appreciated," I whispered.

Jim sat up and startled a giggle out of me. He stared like he wasn't sure who I was. "Whooo," he said finally. "That was some dream." I asked him what it was but he just shook his head and offered lunch.

He gave me a tuna sandwich from the cooler in the back of the truck and sat next to me on his lawn chair quietly eating his own. He didn't ask me any more questions about my place of origin.

"You know how to work a Polaroid?" he said, after a while, and I nodded.

"Good," he said. "Extra income. People can get their picture taken with Blue for four dollars. You can have fifty cents of every picture you take and I get the rest. When I get a new camera, you can do that." He looked over at Bluebell and shook his head. "She stepped on the last one."

I took a good long drink of ginger ale and watched the fat girl saunter away, the elephants step side to side as they ate.

"Tonight you should work the show," Jim said. "Get a taste of it. What do you think about that?"

"What?" I shook my head. "What did you say?"

"You work the show tonight, luv. Okay?"

"Absolutely!" I stood up, then sat down again. "Sure. Yes. Absolutely."

He smiled at my excitement and helped himself to the bag of chips by his feet. "You'll need a costume though. Tell Wilma to find you something cute. And don't worry, it'll be easy—you just do whatever I ask you. You'll help me lead 'em out, hand me the bull hook when I say. Like that. You've only got an hour and a half, so scat."

I chugged the rest of my soda and charged off toward the costume trailer. By the time I got there the sandwich was cramping my stomach and I was so out of breath it took me sitting and panting for a good few minutes before I could make myself understood by the confused Wilma.

"Costume," I finally managed. "Show. Jim. Elephants. Ring."

She rummaged around and found a worn green leotard with silver sparkles and pinkish-tan material down the center that gave the impression of a plunging neckline. It had a very threadbare part in the back.

"Used to belong to Leilana Lopez," Wilma said, digging around in a trunk for something. "She was taller than you, but it might work."

"What did she do?" I asked between gulps of water.

"Animals—balanced on Olivia's trunk and spun a ball in the air with her feet, and rode some trick ponies Benny used to have. Something with birds too—she had a lot of birds."

"What happened to her?"

"She got thrown." Wilma poked her head out from behind the dress rack. "I don't know why. I mean, riding she got thrown a lot, but it was Olivia who broke her back, which put her out of the show. Threw her across the ring for some reason—you'd have to ask Jim." She disappeared again. "That was years ago though. I heard she's with the Wallenda show now."

I nodded. It was a tiny, ratty old leotard but I held it in front of me like it was dangerous.

"Put it on," Wilma called, and then emerged from the back with a pair of fishnet stockings, some silver heels, and a pile of stiff blue-and-silver fabric.

I looked around for somewhere to change and Wilma rolled her eyes. "You've seen how many people are naked in here each show," she said. "Get over it."

"Yeah, get over it." The fat girl reclined at the table with popcorn and peanuts. "Let it all hang out, Faith."

I shot her a dirty look, but it had no effect on her icy smile. I took a deep breath and turned to the side, away from the fat girl, and pulled off my T-shirt, my jeans. I stepped one naked foot into the leotard and wiggled it on.

Wilma turned me around and surveyed the loose fit. "Take it off," she said, and when I did, she handed me the stockings. I pulled them on and tried the shoes. They fit. In them I was taller, but when I tried to walk I teetered. "Practice walking," Wilma called through a mouthful of pins. "Sawdust is a lot more difficult than the floor in here."

She ran the sewing machine a few times while I walked in circles around the room.

"Wow," said the fat girl, tossing kernels at me, then nuts. "If they could see you now."

And I looked up and saw myself, wobbling along in a bra and no panties, fishnet stockings and heels. Who the hell was I?

"Annabelle—"

Wilma handed me the leotard and this time it fit snugly, no sagging crotch, no limp shoulders. She fastened the blue-and-silver fabric around my waist with a hidden Velcro belt, so it formed a kind of peacock's tail.

"You just need makeup," she said. "And maybe a wig. Then you're all set."

I sat down and she fit a bobbed pink wig tightly over my scalp, tucking away wisps of my own bright hair. I tried not to blink while she glued long silver lashes to my lids and painted my face with a palette of bright colors and glitter. Her brushes were soft and her strokes tickled, but when I stood again and looked in the mirror I had disappeared. In my place stood a strange pale sparkly creature. And she was beautiful.

~~~

The fat girl walked me to the elephant truck tossing popcorn in my path to announce my arrival.

"Hear ye, hear ye," she hollered. "Step right up."

I ignored her as best I could. When we reached the elephants, Jim gave me an appreciative whistle and I blushed and made a clumsy curtsy.

"You look lovely, Annabelle. That Wilma," Jim said. "She does perform magic."

He looked pretty good himself. He wore a broad white top hat and a sequined light blue tuxedo that shimmered as he moved. His shirt was silver and ruffled, and even his shoes sparkled. But he smelled very strongly of sweat.

"Come on," he said. "We have plenty to do."

We dressed Olivia in a silver-and-white clown collar and Bluebell in a blue-and-white one. Then Jim urged them each down on their front knees and I helped him secure their headpieces—red diamond-shaped patches that were centered on each of their foreheads by thick, draping gold chains.

"Very elegant," Jim said when we were done. And then, "Up, girls."

"We have to crap them out now," he told me, and gave a signal. The elephants obediently stood on their hind legs. They were unbelievably huge. I asked what "crap them out" meant, though I thought knew: more work for me.

"Well, we don't want them to let loose in the ring, right? So gravity's going to give us a little hand right now. Down! Now let's take care of this little business. Luv, would you grab the shovel?"

I teetered over to the wheelbarrow in my heels, which were beginning to pinch. Jim led the elephants away from our entrance, one by one, and commanded each to stand on her back legs again for a count of ten.

"Now shit, Livvy, shit," he coaxed. "Come on, Olivia, honey, let it go, let it go . . ."

Behind him a colorful trio of clowns strolled by arguing about baseball.

"Come on, Blue, a big one for Papa, now, come on, girl . . ."

And so on, until each had released a huge heap of manure.

"Annabelle?" He gestured towards the pile and my heart sank a little to be shoveling shit in costume, but I smiled and got the wheelbarrow.

"Good girls," he said to the bulls, patting their trunks, and offered each an orange.

~~~

"We're nearly ready," Jim said a few minutes later, as he gathered a few props from the truck. He gave me a big red ball and a black bull hook to carry and took one of each himself. Then he told me to take Bluebell's lead and follow him.

I looked up at Bluebell and tried not to think about how easily she could crush me or kick me or pick me up in her enormous trunk and smash me repeatedly into the ground. Instead I thought about us walking calmly into a tent of strangers.

I am Annabelle, I thought. *I can do anything.* And I felt it, at that moment, more than I ever had.

Bluebell and I followed behind Jim and Olivia to the tent entrance, which was a flap in the side wall, a hidden door that had been tied off so you could see inside, through a wide aisle in the bleachers, and into the ring.

As we approached I heard the band playing something zippy and fun. The ringmaster's voice tumbled down from above: *"The fantastic frolicking Equine glories of the Thomasettes!"*

Out here in the night, it was hard to make out faces. Figures moved back and forth, their features hidden by costumes, by makeup, by darkness. A clip light attached to a post was aimed away from the entrance toward the ground to ensure that no one tripped, but it did nothing for identification.

In the ring, two glittering women rode in a circle standing on the backs of Uno and Billy with Dos close behind. They didn't hold on at all, these Thomasettes, just stood with their arms out as the horses rounded the ring. And then they flipped, both at the same time, so that the one who'd been on Uno, in the front, was now on Billy, and the one on Billy was now on Dos. The crowd loved it, but that was just the beginning, they did handstands, they leapt off and on the horses. At one point they cartwheeled back and forth, passing each other. Then one leapt off and the horses stopped running in a circle.

I turned to Jim, but he wasn't watching. He was whispering in Olivia's ear. We were surrounded by clowns in enormous shoes and white faces, their red noses held in their hands. Some were tall, some short. One was very short and looked suspiciously like Sam, but he was watching the show so I couldn't see his face.

Now, in the ring, one girl balanced on the shoulders of another. The horses circled again.

At the edge of the tent, I saw five shapes huddled together, four large, one small, and wondered if they were the Genershes. People looked ghostly, their faces disappearing into shadow unless the spill from the show caught a cheek, a chin, the curve of a forehead, the shine of a costume. I felt that I had plunged into the underbelly of a fantastic dream, and at the same time was more awake than I'd ever been before.

But I missed something. All at once the clowns pushed past, and from the darkness emerged a little car, which they chased into the ring. I hadn't seen the horse act finish and I hadn't seen where they'd gone, though I could hear their *clop clop clop* now, coming around the side of the tent.

"Annabelle, you do whatever I call out," Jim said softly. I turned to him and there were more performers walking behind the tent. Some I thought I recognized, some I couldn't make out.

"I mostly need you to stand by the edge of the ring and smile." He leaned under Bluebell's chin towards me. "I'll lead them through the show and then you'll let me pass with Olivia and you take Bluebell and we'll walk out to the right. The girls know the way, don't worry about that. I'll need you to hold the balls, the extra hook. Just stand there and look gorgeous, okay?"

I was glad he couldn't see me blush again. I nodded.

"Great."

Silence fell and the ringmaster instructed the audience to direct their attention upwards" . . . *Appreciate the danger being embraced for your benefit, ladies and gentlemen! At any moment she could plummet to her death, but she has a talent like no other! Ladies and gentlemen, the amazing Rapunzel Finelli hangs by her hair!"*

I stood on my toes, then crouched down to try and catch a glimpse of Rapunzel through the crowd, but Bluebell shifted and it occurred to me what a bad idea it was to crouch by an elephant.

Standing, I could make out hundreds of upturned faces.

"You ready?" Jim whispered, trading me the other red ball for the second bull hook. I told him I was.

We moved towards the opening, Jim and Olivia first, then Bluebell and me. Everyone parted to let us pass.

The aisle was dark, the ring was dark. The only light shone on a woman spinning and twirling from the ceiling by her long red hair. Beneath her there was nothing but sawdust and cement. She twisted her body into a series of shapes and smiled brightly, though the skin around her scalp was stretched taut.

Jim saw me wincing. "Looks like it hurts, doesn't it?" he whispered. "They start training for it when they're tots. By now they don't feel a thing. Step lively." He moved forward and smoothed his tuxedo. I took a deep breath and tugged at the seat of my leotard, moving aside the itchy blue tulle.

Jim looked back at me, then in moments we were moving again, through the thunder of applause.

" . . . *Ladies and gentlemen, in the center ring, the stylings of Professor Pachyderm, a man whose best friends weigh nearly six tons apiece!"*

It was loud inside. We stopped at the edge of the ring. In one graceful move, Olivia bent her head, Jim stepped up on her trunk, and she lifted him into the air, then began to walk again and Bluebell followed. I let go of her harness and stayed at the edge of the ring and did my best to smile, but I felt the heat of the lights and the people all around us, looking, their eyes like tiny hot bullets thumping me from all sides. I couldn't focus on anything, not even what Jim was doing. The sawdust made me want to sneeze, and trying not to made my eyes water. There was a strange soupiness to it all. My heart hammered away and everything sparkled. The band played tinny music so loud it seemed to echo in and out of every crevice, bouncing wildly around the enormous tent. I grinned until my jaw ached.

To my right the front row was visible. All along the ring sat a string of retarded adults in various poses of crippled excitement. One man's body seemed to twist without his control. Another drooped, held in a wheelchair by thick white straps. Several men and women with wide empty eyes stared at the ring without moving, their faces contorted but blank, or elastic with joy. Behind them rows of children and adults, children and adults, all riveted by us, by Bluebell and Olivia and Jim. By me.

And then, across from me, wearing a huge green-and-silver leotard and a matted pink wig, I saw the fat girl. She waved.

"Balls!" Jim called and I snapped to attention. He held his hand out as he came around, and I tossed him the first red ball, which he caught. My second throw wasn't as accurate and the ball rolled off to the side. People laughed. Hundreds and hundreds of people.

The fat girl shouted something I couldn't hear. She stepped to the side and her enormous body shook and rolled. I told myself not to look at her, to watch Jim and Olivia and Bluebell, but I couldn't stop. The fat girl offered popcorn to the front row, who were rapt with Jim's every move, with the elephants standing on tiny red platforms, with the shine of Jim's suit.

The fat girl pranced across the ring. Her whole body jiggled—she was cake batter, jelly, the rumble of water. Olivia and Jim whirled past and just missed stomping her. Bluebell came within inches, but the fat girl reached me unharmed.

"Look what I do for you," she said with a smile, and grabbed my arm, taking her place by my side, beaming, her eyes moist. "See how we belong together?"

~ ~ ~

After the show, I changed into jeans and a T-shirt and sat outside with Wilma, drinking whiskey and listening to the late-night sounds of the circus. The lights in the costume trailer were off and we were quiet. Wilma seemed sad and far away. At Berrybrook I'd been good at listening, but I'd never learned to ask questions or start conversations. If someone was upset, I didn't know what else to do besides be there quietly.

There were lights on in most trailers and in the distance someone strummed a guitar, someone sang. Every once in a while I heard laughter rise up from one direction or another.

I had an exhilarating pulse in my chest and, at the same time, a peaceful, floaty sense of calm. The unfamiliar understanding that I'd just been a part of something. Wilma shifted and refilled my glass. And then I remembered my promise to Sam.

I took a sip of the burning drink and when I felt it in my stomach I cleared my throat.

"You know the other day, when Sam asked to speak with me?"

"Shit," Wilma muttered, and poured herself another drink. She sighed. "Let me guess," she said. "He told you what good friends we were and how much he wants to make everything right again."

I nodded. "Sort of."

"Well, he can kiss my ass," she said, and stood. "Don't worry, Annabelle. I'm sure he threatened you or made all sorts of promises to you that he won't keep so that you felt you had to say something. You're only the fifth person who felt like they had to say something. He's such an ass."

She climbed a few steps and turned back.

"With him, everything is a dance," she said. "He's pulling you in, he's pushing you away. He's choreographing moves you're not even aware of. I'm sure his vision of what happened to Yael makes him sound like a saint. But believe me, he's not."

She tossed back the rest of her drink and opened the creaky door. It slammed behind her. In the darkness, with the whiskey and the laughter, her exit seemed to echo.

I sat still for a while and rubbed my arms to keep warm. I rewound the conversation we'd had and tried to find another way to have broached the subject, but I was pretty sure I'd done the best I could.

And then I thought about calling my mom again. It was late and she was probably asleep. I thought about the shine of her dark hair and the sweet way she smelled when she hugged me.

I wanted to tell her I was alive and okay. That I'd done something brave and new tonight, something I was proud of. That I missed her.

But then I remembered the ways I'd been a terrible disappointment and my throat caught.

The fat girl sat down beside me and put her arm over my shoulder. But I didn't want that. I didn't want her. I swallowed and pushed her away and we sat facing each other for a minute. Then I dried my tears on my sleeve, rose, and went to bed.

While I slept, Tony Giobambera took my hand and traced my heart line with his finger. He looked at me with unmistakable regret. I adjusted the skirt of my flouncy floor-length white gown. My pale blue sash matched his pale blue tuxedo.

He led me to the center of a crowded dance floor. All around us girls rocked slowly, their heads on the shoulders of their partners. Tony's hands slid along my back and he pulled me to him, so that I could rest my head like everyone else. The music thrummed, slow and gentle, but something cold was trickling down my back. I tried to step away a little, but Tony pulled me tightly, wrapping his arms around my waist and whispering things I couldn't quite make out. I heard the rush of water and as we turned I looked down at the floor and saw red, a puddle of red spreading across the black-and-white-checkered floor, creeping up the edge of my dress.

My mom stood behind him with her arms crossed.

I tried to yank myself back from Tony, but he had his arms under mine, his palms on my shoulders, his hands bleeding down my dress, pressing me firmly against him.

I sat up and banged my head.

Below me Wilma stirred, murmured something, then rolled over. I rubbed my tender forehead. Through the open windows I heard rain, a steady, thorough wash of rain. It was comforting, a soft blanket of noise, and soon, despite myself, I tumbled back into the dense embrace of sleep.

THIRTEEN

IN the morning I hiked through mud and made my way to the menagerie. Jim had left Bluebell and Olivia in the trucks all night to keep them dry. While we stood talking, they poked their trunks through the sliding vent doors, searching around like blind men feeling for a face.

"There are carrots in the cab," Jim said. He was flipping through his road atlas, an exercise that had started as a means for finding a route, but had devolved into a tour of circus memories, guided by his wandering finger. "Jesus," he called out as I fished around for the ten-pound bag of carrots. "I bloody remember Portland!"

I gave them each a carrot, then another, while Jim talked on and on about his first tour, his first elephant ("They're pregnant for a year and a half, you know"), how poorly he'd slept the night before ("Rain plagues me—I have such a fear of drowning").

"Hey!" Jim said, and shook the atlas at me. "I meant to tell you: Elaine stopped by on her way to breakfast to ask me if I could spare you for teardown. Isn't that terrific?"

I nodded. The bag was empty. There were no more carrots. I began to unwind the hose and then I stopped. "Wait a minute. Why is that terrific? What does that mean?"

"That," he said, "is her way of welcoming you."

His meaning took a few seconds to sink in. Then relief made me giddy. They were mine; it was mine, all of it! The show was pulling out, and I would be going with it.

"One time in Cincinnati," Jim said, "—I was on King Brothers then—

there was a kid who used to bring Olivia bagels every day and she loved him. Clever boy, maybe seven or eight years old—"

I could barely focus on what he was saying with all the joyful static in my head. I had a place to belong for at least the time being. I was Annabelle, a girl without a past, now a girl with a future. An elephant groom! I laughed out loud.

"—his name was. His parents were the wire act that season. What was their surname? Cabrini? Caputo? Something. Anyway, Olivia loved that little boy and he did something to upset his mum, I don't know what, but his mum was tearing him up and Olivia couldn't stand it. She was so upset. I knew something was wrong but I wasn't sure what it was, and then she pushed her way out—I didn't have her chained, mind you—pushed her way out into the stadium and grabbed that little boy with her trunk."

The elephants stopped moving, as though they also listened.

"Everybody's screaming and carrying on, but she didn't want to hurt him, just protect him. She pulled him away from his mother and put him under her like a baby elephant, so she could stand over him. It was the sweetest thing I ever saw."

Jim moved himself enough with this last story to scramble out of his chair, drop the atlas, and let the bulls out. Bluebell came first, then Olivia. Jim stood between them, alternately hugging each of them around the leg as they shifted in the mud. They touched his head with their trunks, one at a time.

I had hooked up the hose by now, but I dropped it and started to walk towards them. "Did you groom the horses yet?" Jim called, leaning his whole body into Bluebell's side and absently stroking her huge floppy ear.

I shook my head, but he wasn't watching. "No," I said.

"Right-o," he said without so much as a glance my way. I watched them stand in their cluster, a large family with only three members. Didn't I belong at least a little bit now?

I turned and made my way around to the horses. As I came to the horse trailer that marked the edge of their paddock, I heard agitated voices and then saw that Benny and Wilma were there. Benny stood to one side of Billy with his arms crossed while Wilma tried to coax the mare into a red-and-yellow headpiece with an enormous feathered plume. Billy tossed her head and gave a snort.

"It's too long," Benny said. He pointed to a piece that came to a point between Billy's nostrils.

"No, it's supposed to look like that—"

"She'll never stand for it."

"Benny, you have to give it a chance. She just has to get used to it."

"She doesn't have to get used to anything," he said, and ripped the headpiece off Billy, who whinnied to be free. Benny tossed it aside and a cascade of feathers tumbled off of the headpiece. Wilma looked like she'd been slapped. She gathered it all together and dumped it in a nearby carton.

"You're just a tired old man who's afraid of change," she said in a low voice that sounded close to tears. She picked up the box and turned, pushing past me in the direction of our trailer.

I stood awkwardly for a minute while Benny, his back to me, whispered to the horses and stroked their heads. I backed away quietly to walk the circumference of the grounds, to give Benny a moment to forget I'd been there, to give myself a moment alone.

I was signing on to all of this. To conflicts and allegiances I didn't know or understand. To a totally foreign world with its own rules that I had to learn, and fast.

Still, shit-shoveling or not, I couldn't imagine not going. What would I do instead? Go back to Gleryton and turn myself in?

No. No, I wasn't going to do that.

I passed the Genershes' trailer, which was quiet, and walked towards Amos Ruble, *Tallest Living Man in the Entire Universe!* He sat on a lawn chair in front of his trailer, whittling something, his long legs splayed before him like two fallen trees. As I passed, he lifted an arm to wave and I blushed and waved back. A few minutes later, when I came to Germania Loudon's trailer, I stopped. I was a few feet away, but from the back it looked like any other trailer.

"What do you think you're doing?" The fat girl stood there with a bag of chips. "Wanna go gawk at the fat lady, huh?"

I whirled around and stomped off.

"Don't forget your roots, honey!" she called after me. "There but for the grace of God . . ."

~~~

We loaded out that evening after the show. It took everyone doing his or her part and almost six hours to break the whole show down and pack it away. Labor united everyone except Sam, who seemed stressed out just carrying his clipboard and supervising.

I did my best to stay out of his way and avoid his gaze while simultaneously ignoring the fat girl, who trailed me, a lamb chop in one paw and a napkin in the other, prattling on about nothing. "Isn't this impressive," she kept saying. "Wow, will you look at that!"

I recognized lots of the job-ins from my yellow-flag meal. A posse of swarthy men who kept laughing among themselves were the fastest with the tent. I obeyed all instructions, but wasn't very good at most of the duties I was given and was soon told to go help Wilma. By then some of the performers had gone. Jim and Benny and the others with animal trucks had left first thing after the show because they were worried about weigh stations.

Wilma was almost done securing everything in the trailer by the time I got there. Her hair was pulled back in tiny black pigtails and she had an orange bandanna tied like a kerchief on her head. I blinked. She wore tight blue hot pants, a baseball T-shirt, and a small red golf jacket with her ever-present combat boots. It was the first time I'd ever seen her in anything but dresses and poodle skirts.

"My traveling garb," she said when I stood there staring.

I had changed after the show, but hadn't showered, so Wilma suggested I might *take this opportunity.* By the time I was done we were ready to go.

"Did your family leave already?" I asked, rubbing a towel through my hair. Wilma's mouth was pressed in a thin line and she stopped what she was doing for a second before she nodded. She looked like she might cry, but instead gave me a once-over and asked if I knew how to drive stick.

I considered lying, but thought better of it. The truth was that I had turned sixteen at Berrybrook and still hadn't gotten a license. "No," I said, and took a deep breath. "Actually, I don't know how to drive at all."

That did it. Wilma's face crumpled and she sank onto one of the trunks and sobbed. I didn't know what to do. I stood awkwardly for a minute, shifting back and forth, and then I went and sat next to her on the trunk, putting an arm around her shoulders and pulling her towards me. "It's okay," I murmured, though I wasn't sure it actually was. "It's okay."

She calmed down after a few minutes, hiccuped several times, then took a deep breath and slapped both palms on her thighs. "Well," she said firmly. "That's enough of that."

She dried her eyes with the sleeve of her jacket, and slammed out the door to get a pickup truck that had spent the better part of a week in the corner of the parking lot but would now haul us to the next town. When the door closed behind her it was very quiet. In the distance I heard the clanging and banging of the tent coming down, of people calling to one another, but inside the trailer nothing moved. The dresses had been tied back, the racks secured. Boards held the wigs in place and ropes held the trunks. The little table had been folded to the wall and the chairs were bungee-corded to its underside.

Even our pillows were secure.

But some things were missing, loose in the world. I walked over and sat on Wilma's bed. I listened for the fat girl, for the sound of chewing and swallowing, anything, but all I heard was the disassembly that came from outside.

Then I heard the truck. Wilma poked her head in and asked me to come outside so she could show me how to hitch up. I gave one last look around and followed her.

Soon we were ready to go. The truck was battered and blue, with an extra cab and a broken tape deck. "You're navigating," Wilma told me. "So you have to stay awake too. You're going to look for the arrows."

"What arrows?"

She strained to be patient. "There are arrows. We're going to follow them. The advance team laid them out. We'll stop on our way out and get coffee, something to eat."

That sounded wonderful. It was almost 1 A.M. and I was hungry. We climbed into the cab and closed our doors and Wilma shut her eyes before starting the engine. I saw her lips move and wondered if she was praying, and if so, what she asked for. Forgiveness? Guidance? The engine to turn over? I braced myself for scripture, but she just told me to put on my seat belt and pulled us around in a wide circle down the hill and through the campgrounds.

Most of the trailers we passed had their lights off. Many were hitched up to trucks of various sizes and shapes holding families preparing to go. The animal trucks were long gone. The midway had disappeared. By the time we pulled entirely around, the big top had dissolved into piles of things with men scrambling around them.

We drove towards the remnants of the tent and it looked more like preparation than dismemberment, the beginnings of something instead of the end. Everyone stopped what he or she was doing and waved to us, even Sam. My throat caught and I waved back, my grin nearly splitting my face apart. I felt connected, a part of the show, our truck and its contents the tissue of a larger muscle. I kept my face to the glass, so Wilma wouldn't see the tears that had sprung to my eyes, and watched it all until it was a spot in the distance that disappeared when we rounded the next bend.

And then we left it all behind and headed for the open road.

~~~

Soon there was nothing in the world besides us and the truck cab, the trailer and night and the dark stretch of highway. The tape deck didn't work, despite Wilma's fervent efforts to bring it back to life. "You just have to hit it," she kept saying, and pounding, until I worried that we were swerving and suggested maybe the tape deck just needed a little time to get used to moving again.

Wilma gave me an odd look, but stopped her banging and instead pointed to my side of the dashboard and instructed me to get a map. This was easier asked than accomplished. When I opened the glove compartment, an enormous pile of stuff tumbled into my lap and onto the floor. There were cigarettes and tampons, a pint of whiskey, a flashlight, one black leather glove with the fingers cut off, a wrench, a rag, a bandanna, part of a wax bag full of what looked like it had once been licorice, about thirty different keys, some nails, thumbtacks and safety pins, and a pack of condoms (French tickler, still in the box, which I quickly stuffed back into the glove compartment). At the bottom of it all, soft as a dishtowel, there was a faded, ratty map of the country.

"Who is the advance team?" I asked, as we spotted the first arrow telling us to take the on ramp to the highway. "Have I met them?"

"The twenty-four-hour man?" she said. "No. Used to be one guy who would ride ahead and book a place and arrange for all the advertising and everything. You know, take down the posters of whatever other show was coming to town, and hang up his own. Our advance team is a guy named Lou and his wife. He'll park us when we get there. I think she's always sleeping when we pull in. I've only met her a few times. Beginning-of-season picnics and stuff. You know, the Christmas party."

She snorted. "We used to have them—Christmas parties, I mean—before Elaine got this harebrained idea to tour all year. We used to close down after November and not start up until May, like everyone else. But it hasn't been like that since I was a kid."

~~~

We found a truck stop and pulled in to eat and fuel up. It had only been a week since I'd been in one, but somehow arriving with Wilma and our trailer—as a part of something instead of as a hitchhiker—the truck stop looked foreign. We walked through the trucker store first, admiring the boots and T-shirts, the strange selection of tapes, the water bottles and cowboy hats. They had one like the hat I'd been wearing when I arrived at Fartlesworth and Wilma put it on.

"Looks cute," I told her, but she shook her head and put it back on the rack. I wondered where mine was. In the trailer? I hadn't seen it in a while. I picked up the hat and put it on. Wilma was looking at key chains.

"What do you think?" I posed for her and she turned and saw me and smiled.

"Yikes," she said, but kindly. She came over and took the hat off and rumpled my hair. "I could cut it for you, if you want," she offered, running her fingers through with a critical eye. "Just even it out a little?"

"Sure."

"And we could even re-dye it, you know?"

I reached up and touched my hair. There was a mirror on the wall and I walked over and looked at myself. It was awful, she was right. It looked like someone had chewed the ends off, had chopped at it with no thought to shape or style. It looked like someone had cut it in the dirty bathroom of an abandoned gas station, didn't it?

"I'd like that," I said, and Wilma smiled.

"Good." She put her hands on my shoulders and steered me towards the restaurant. "When we get where we can sit for a few minutes in Shreveport, we'll see what we can do."

I felt self-conscious now, as we walked through the aisles of merchandise, past the stray truckers picking at gifts for their families or heading to the showers. We made our way to the restaurant and its familiarity was shocking after the foreignness of the store. I scanned the tables wondering if I would see anyone I knew, talkative Monty from Asheville or Willie who'd picked us up in Chattanooga, but there were only strangers, an array of men leaning against the walls of small booths with huge plates of finished or half-finished meat and potatoes on their tables, distractedly stirring their food with a fork, while talking on phones that protruded from the booth walls. It was almost 2 A.M. I saw something familiar in each face, something lonesome and tired. I focused instead on the back of Wilma's red jacket as the waitress led us to our own booth with its own phone.

Who should be waiting there, a triumphant look on her face and a blue cowboy hat on her head, but the fat girl.

Wilma slid into the booth and I slid in next to the fat girl, who tried to scoot over and make room but couldn't. I realized I was sitting on the edge of the booth and I wondered if Wilma would notice. The fat girl clamped a hand on my knee.

"We have a conversation pending," she said in the old chilly voice that meant something was wrong. "We have some things to sort out."

My cheeks burned but I didn't say anything. I read the menu. It was all meat. Big meat, bland meat, smothered meat, overcooked meat. I knew this food and it washed my hunger away, just the thought of it, the smell of it, which wafted all around us.

"I'm starving," Wilma said. I would have agreed with her only moments before but now I felt certain that anything solid would catch in my throat, prevented from going down as firmly as if there was a finger inside my neck pushing it back out. I tried to find something soft, something bland.

I ordered mashed potatoes.

"That's all you want?" Wilma said. She was more disturbed by my order than the waitress, who projected a very pure disinterest.

I nodded, asked for a hot tea also, and tried to make myself comfortable.

The fat girl's grip tightened. "I want to talk to you."

There was music playing and Wilma said something about the next show, about Shreveport, about performers. I had trouble listening.

"—and that will be different. But I'm sure it will all work out. It always does."

Maybe she could tell I wasn't listening. Maybe she'd been waiting to say it all along, I don't know. But quiet descended on our table, the mumbled conversations of the truckers all around us faded to a kind of white noise, and Wilma leaned towards me.

"If you want to call home, you can. I'm sure your family misses you."

I was too startled to reply. The fat girl jabbed me in the side and squeezed my knee again, which made me jump.

"I'll be right back," I said, indicating the direction of the rest rooms with my head. I extracted myself from the booth and made my way through the maze of tables, to the soothing familiarity of the generic public rest room. The fat girl followed close behind.

"What the hell are you doing?!" I shouted as soon as we were alone. "What is your fucking problem? I can't have a conversation with you in front of Wilma. What the hell were you up to out there?!"

She leaned against the wall between a condom machine and another machine that dispensed perfumes. I didn't want to look anymore, to look at her, at anything. I turned to face the wall I was near and pounded the button of the hand dryer nearest me. It came to life with a satisfying roar. I hit another, and another, until all five were on and the room sounded as though it had filled with a private audience of screaming fans.

"Are you done?"

I wasn't. I wasn't done. But I was defeated, the anger drained out of me so quickly that it took my breath with it. I doubled over and watched my feet, the cracked black toes of my cowboy boots.

"This can wait." Her voice was kind, all her evil swept away by my fit. I was too tired to do anything. Too tired to agree, too tired to argue.

Too tired to conceal how much I wanted her to leave.

"Fine," she said softly, and that was that. When I lifted my head she was gone. The door to the bathroom swung gently in her wake. I was all alone.

For some reason in the quiet I thought of Starling. Of Charlie coming to rescue her over and over again until he couldn't anymore. He had gotten me this far, even though he didn't know it. If it wasn't for him, where would I be?

I splashed water on my cheeks. It would be so nice to have Charlie around, I thought. To have someone around who knew the real me.

In the mirror I looked older than I once had. I looked like maybe I knew some things. I smiled. Maybe I did and maybe I didn't. Maybe it was best that he wasn't here, after all. Maybe I needed to do all this all on my own.

I dried my hands and took a deep breath and went out to face my mashed potatoes.

~~~

Wilma didn't bring it up again. We ate quietly and split a piece of apple pie. All around the room people leaned into their phones, talking to faraway folks. I tried to remember what my mother's voice sounded like, and it horrified me that I couldn't. The waitress came; we settled our check and made our way back to the truck.

Then we pulled back on the empty highway and fell into the rhythm of driving. I was dreamy with food, with the hum of the road and the dark secret shapes of the towns we passed. Wilma was focused and alert. She didn't seem to want to talk and I didn't have much to say. I scooted down in my seat and put my feet up on the dashboard. I adjusted to get comfortable and my boots made a few loud thumps. Suddenly the radio came on.

"Whoohoo!" Wilma fiddled with the dial until she found a crackling station playing a lonesome country song. The recording was old but catchy, and I found myself tapping along with it. I didn't know who it was, but Wilma did. She turned the volume way up and sang along and her voice was light and sweet.

> My heart is ever true
> I love no one but you
> My Dixie darling
> My Dixie queen

"Who is it?"

Wilma raised an eyebrow and cupped an ear towards me and I pointed at the radio. She was nodding in time to the music, tapping away on the steering wheel. "Carter Family," she said. "I love them." She reached down and began to dig around in a cubby near one of the gearshifts.

"I have one album. Where's the hell's that—*fuck!*"

She braked hard and we were both thrown back. Through the screech of wheels I saw something large lumber off into the dark. I pressed my face to the window again to try and see what it was but I couldn't.

We shuddered and stalled and came to a stop. In the silence my heart beat hard. "Maybe that was a moose," Wilma said. She exhaled and then turned the key and started the engine again. "Fuck, I'm full of adrenaline. Maybe it was a bear."

I didn't think Alabama was moose or bear country but didn't point that out.

"Well, it wasn't me, if that's what you were thinking."

At the sound of her voice, I flushed scarlet and tried not to be obvious about turning around, looking behind me into the tiny extra cab. I didn't have to turn far to see the fat girl and smell her cheese pizza. I glanced at Wilma but her eyes were on the road. I tried to communicate silently. I gave a small shake of the head to say No, *I hadn't thought it was you.*

"Bullshit," the fat girl said. "You always think it's me."

It didn't take long to find out what it really was. Almost immediately we saw the line of animal trucks pulled over to the side of the road.

"Oh fuck," Wilma said. In the spill of our headlights I could just make out the painted FARTLESWORTH CIRCUS! logo on the side of each truck before we pulled off in front of them and parked ourselves. I hadn't realized how much noise our truck made until Wilma turned off the motor. Then the silence seemed to roar around us.

Wilma sat with her hand on the keys for a minute before saying anything. I heard the fat girl chewing but forced myself to face front.

"Goddammit, I bet that was Bluebell again," Wilma said.

"Bluebell? You mean back there?"

Wilma nodded. "Do you remember where we were when that happened?"

"Kind of. It was right before that exit with the gas stations."

She nodded and sighed. "Come on," she said, and opened her door.

I followed her out. It was late and dewy. The moon was just past full or just getting there and lent a blue cast to everything. We walked back towards the idling animal trucks and their motors hummed like giant purring beasts. We heard their human passengers before we actually found everyone behind the last truck, which was Jim Brewer's.

"Look what the cat drug up," said a tall figure who I recognized as Creole Kevin, the tiger groom. He was leaning against the side of the truck alongside Steve, the tiger trainer, and Benny. Next to him, with his hands in his pockets, was a short brown guy I didn't know, and farther down, a pale lanky man with a drooping mustache.

"The cats are in the truck," Mustache said, but everyone ignored him.

"Where's Jim?" Wilma had her hands on her hips and her legs planted wide, a defiance in her stance that I didn't understand.

"Don't you worry about Jim," Benny snapped. "He's just fine without *your* help, little girl."

I couldn't see Wilma's face but I could feel her anger. She looked at her feet, and after a minute, she said quietly, "We saw her go." Then Wilma cleared her throat and raised her head and looked at each of the men, one at a time. "The bull. She crossed us on her way into the woods back by that last exit, about a mile or so ago."

"He'll find her," Benny said, and this time the tone of his voice was more gentle.

"Come on," Wilma said to me. "Let's go." She turned and marched off and I followed.

When we were back in the truck, she shook her head and started the engine. I couldn't tell what she was thinking. We pulled onto the highway again and Wilma told me to look on the map and see how far we had come. I waited a few minutes before I asked.

"What was that all about?"

"What?"

"Back there. I mean, does that happen a lot with Bluebell? And why did Benny want us out of there so bad?"

She looked at me, then back at the road before answering. When she did, it sounded as though the words were difficult to pronounce. "Jim and I were . . . *involved*. And it didn't work out," Wilma said. "Let's just say there's some fallout."

Involved sounded very grown-up.

"How much longer on Ninety-eight?" Wilma said without looking at me.

"Were you in love with him?"

She looked at me quickly, then back at the road. "Yes," she said. "But I don't want to talk about it."

I checked the soft map. "Another few miles," I said.

We spent them quietly, each lost in our own thoughts. I didn't know what Wilma was thinking, but I wondered how much a person could take. How many quiet things could fill you up before you overflowed with them. Or choked. And I was wondering how many secrets I could live with.

FOURTEEN

Bʏ the time we reached the fairgrounds in Shreveport it was full-on morning. Wilma didn't even unhitch the truck, just parked it where Lou said, got out, stretched, and headed for the trailer. I waited a moment before joining her.

We slept for a few hours and then put the show together. Jim had me scout out a place to dump the elephant dung—there was plenty of it from the night before and the morning. We weren't as close to a stand of trees this time, so my wheelbarrow rides were longer, my arms rattling as I hit ruts and rises. The air smelled like honeysuckle. Honeysuckle and elephant shit.

"Sometimes when we're traveling," Jim said, as I shoveled yet another load, "I scoop their mess into a Dumpster along the way. At night, though. Very late so no one will see."

I nodded. He'd been talking a blue streak all morning and I couldn't tell if it was his sleepless night tracking Bluebell—the animal trucks had rolled in nearly four hours after us and the big top couldn't go up without the elephants' help—or something else altogether. But I was too tired to care. Faced with my huge stinky task, I fell into the rhythm of removal. The shovel clanged against the metal wheelbarrow with each pass, the weight of it pulling me down to the trees. There was a heavy thump as it hit and then lightness up the hill towards the bulls.

"Once . . ." He chuckled, a sure sign that another reminiscence was on the way. "Outside Springfield, I think it was, Olivia turned over a Dumpster. *That* was a bloody mess, I tell you!"

I wiped the sweat off my face with the corner of a sleeve. Jim was sitting in his lawn chair with a Coke and the paper. It was beginning to bug me, his relaxing while I sweated. I kept having to remind myself how happy I was to be allowed to be there, to have a job with Fartlesworth.

"How did Bluebell get out of a moving truck?" I said.

Jim ignored me. "There are some towns where they'll come and get you," he said. "They'll even chase you down with the shit you dumped." He shook his head. "I hate that."

I went and deposited another load. When I returned Jim pointed to the back of the hauling truck and told me to scrub it down inside with soapy water. Then he leaned back, put his feet up on a bucket, and lit a cigarette.

"You know, I think I'm going to go do the horses first," I said. Jim raised his eyebrows but didn't object. It was the same job, but even changing the kind of poo I was to scoop seemed like a good idea.

I made my way over to the horse stalls and said hello to Billy and Dos and Uno. They were happy to see me and each in turn nuzzled my outstretched hand. Billy sniffed around to see if I'd smuggled him carrots, but I hadn't. I apologized and set about mucking stalls.

By the time I'd gotten around to grooming Dos, my irritation at Jim had worn off. It was just me and the horses, the sun, the sounds of people putting the show back together, calling to one another across the encampment. I forgot everything and focused on the feel of brush against hide, the smell of hay and manure. I'd just set to work on Uno when I heard a hello and turned to face two of the Genersh brothers. They stood just outside the paddock, sun on their faces, ruggedly handsome with freckles and pale skin framed by thick curly dark hair that stood out every which way. Both had big green eyes and except for their different-colored T-shirts, they looked very much alike.

"I'm Hugo," the one in red said. "He's Rod." Rod lifted his hand in a mock wave but didn't smile.

"I'm Annabelle."

"We've seen you around," Rod said, lifting his hand to cover his mouth, but not fast enough to hide his missing front teeth.

"Yeah, with the elephants and stuff," Hugo added, and smiled. His teeth were perfect and his eyes were warm. My stomach, all furry and light, abruptly shot into my throat.

"You've seen me around?"

Rod nodded and Hugo tilted his head and considered me at an angle.

"How come you're never at dinner?" Hugo said. "Is my stuck-up sister squirreling you away?"

"Dinner?"

"Dinner," Hugo said with a big grin. "You know, evening meal? You've heard of it, right? That food served around sunset?"

"Dinner." I was doomed to repeat everything, like a slow schoolgirl. I kept a hand on Uno, enjoying the feel of her warm solid body. I swallowed and ran my other hand through my choppy hair. They both had long lashes. I was sweaty and smelled like dung.

Rod pursed his lips and elbowed his twin. "Lay off, man, she's new. Maybe they don't eat where she's from."

I smiled. I wanted to turn and run but I was sure my legs wouldn't move even if I asked them to. "I ate in the cookhouse when I got here. With the job-ins. I guess I've just been eating in our trailer, you know, with Wilma." I ran my hand through my hair again and tried to look casual. "You don't eat in your trailer?"

Rod looked at me like I had antlers, but he answered without sarcasm. "Everyone eats together when their flag goes up," he said. "Stanley set up the pie car near the picnic grounds. Some cities we barbecue or eat in the parking lot, or if we aren't tenting, if it's like, an arena or something, sometimes we eat in the stands or whatever. But usually we eat together, you know. The show, I mean. My sister likes to eat by herself. She's a freak."

"So will we see you tonight?" Hugo said, and gave me that smile again.

I swallowed and nodded, sure my face was red as well as sweaty. "I'll be there," I said, and forced myself to turn and walk towards Billy and Dos.

But Hugo Genersh was like a sun, a star, a heavenly body. As I turned I could feel the heat of him behind me, illuminating my neck, my scalp, the backs of my knees. I didn't turn back to look but knew when they walked away, because I felt the world cool as Hugo took that light and directed it at someone else.

~~~

"My brothers are bad news," Wilma said later in the trailer. "Each in their own way. Oh, I guess that isn't fair. Rod means well, but he's only eighteen and he takes the world so literally and Dad hasn't been able to afford a bridge to replace the teeth he knocked out when he fell off the pyramid in practice. He's always a little lost in his books and stuff, I guess. Every year he gets a little weirder.

"James is completely self-involved and Luke is so flaky that sometimes it just feels like he isn't here. And Hugo . . ." She paused and looked out the window in the direction of her family's trailers. "Every girl who comes within fifty feet of Hugo falls in love with him and he knows it."

My heart sank at that. Of course he had that effect on everyone. Who was I to think I was special? I wasn't the girl who got chosen, the girl who got asked to dance. I was the girl who got red punch at Homecoming—

"Faith?"

I whipped around and caught sight of myself in the mirror, eyes enormous, red spots the size of quarters high on my cheeks. I could barely force the words out. "What did you call me?"

"Annabelle?" Wilma looked at me, bewildered. "What's wrong with you? Did you hear anything I said?" The fat girl stood behind me. Her reflection was wide and plain.

"I'm going to go lie down for a minute," I said.

"Are you okay?"

"I'm fine. I just want to lie down."

She shrugged, and continued to talk while I made my way to the bunk.

"My family's just fucked," she said. "I mean Jenny—you'd think the sun rose and set around Jenny the way everyone dotes on her. Some of that is just that she's the youngest I guess, and that she's *such* a part of the act—"

Her words overflowed with vinegar. "But they just revolve around her, my brothers, my father. So of course she's grown up spoiled. A spoiled brat. That's not really her fault, I guess."

I lay on my back and looked at the ceiling. Why did my body feel so heavy?

"You take it all too seriously," the fat girl said, inches from my face. She had a drumstick in one hand and a Twinkie in the other.

"You have to shut some of it off," she said. "Or you're going to go nuts."

"—I mean I never wanted to be a part of it, you know. I was always satisfied with my little world, the world that I found for myself—"

"You don't need anyone," the fat girl whispered. "You just need you."

"—because I knew that I was just as good as them, as people, I mean—"

"You just need you."

I put my hands over my ears and squeezed my face into a knot, my body into a ball.

"Are you okay?" I heard.

And then darkness.

~~~

Flu.

It got everyone eventually. It didn't start with me, but I was early in its tirade. I was feverish and achy and incredibly thirsty.

I tried to help clean up costumes after the show, but I was pretty useless and Wilma sent me back to bed. I tried not to sleep because I knew I had to go to Olivia and Bluebell, but I must have drifted off at some point.

I struggled from it, the blackness, the depths of the syrupy dream that had swallowed me, and made my way up the hill towards the animal trucks. There were wagons and wagons of shit, all of it belonging ultimately to me, my responsibility, mine to tow away and bury.

And then I woke in my bunk in a sweaty puddle of my own making and knew I hadn't made my way up the hill at all. I had been dreaming, hallucinating, and now was damp and clammy, but light as a new idea. I was back in my body, wobbly but no longer feverish.

I swung my legs down and fended off dizziness, landing and stumbling, steadied by the iron frame. It was late or very early, I couldn't tell which, and I felt that if I didn't hold on I might drift away, float up into the sky and evaporate like my fever.

Wilma sat by the window, her hands wrapped around a mug, her attention captured by something far away and sad. She hadn't heard me land, or didn't appear to, and I watched her for a moment before knocking on the side of a trunk to announce myself.

She shook her head, as if to scramble whatever unhappy thing had been there, and smiled at me, but her eyes were black and still far away and I wondered what she'd seen. I wanted all of it opened up, my secrets and her secrets, everything spilled out onto the floor in a festering mess for us to kick around, because I was tired and I'd had enough of all the weight.

I liked this feeling of lightness. It was what I imagined the world felt like from up on the trapeze, what Mina the Ballerina must know. It was what I imagined it felt like to fall when you saw the outstretched hands before you and knew you would come out of a spin and be caught. It was this lightness, this emptiness, this trust that you weren't about to plummet to an unforgiving surface, powered by the weight of yourself. No. You would spin and be caught, you would flip and fall and catch, and you would swing back to a platform at the end, arms in the air, high above the crowd, proud of your victory over what hadn't happened.

Wilma sipped from her mug. I was pretty sure it was whiskey. I didn't say anything, just crept towards her in my strange state and pulled out the other chair, drifting slowly into it like a feather.

She didn't say anything either. I took the mug from her and sipped without looking in. It was whiskey, whiskey mixed with tea, warm and fiery and sweet from sugar or honey. I could feel it rush through me, but Wilma took it back before I could drink again.

"You should eat something," she said. "You haven't eaten in days. I don't think a toddy is the best first meal." She examined her mug, then turned the handle carefully and drank from a place my lips hadn't touched.

"There's bread," she said. "You could toast some."

I nodded. But I wanted whiskey and tea, sweetness and warmth. I wanted nothing to fill me up or weigh me down. I wanted to feel the things that were creeping behind me, the slithering dark awful things I'd been dragging around for so long. I wanted to want to cry, but I didn't. Where was the fat girl? I looked around but she wasn't with us. She would have known what to do.

"You look so sad," I said. "What makes you so sad?"

Wilma took another sip of toddy before answering, and then it was slowly, with an angry quiver in the background. "Let's keep some things to ourselves," she said. "There's not a lot of privacy in this life. You need to mind your own business. Some things I don't want to share."

Who could argue with that? Certainly not me. I nodded and stood, unsteady as ever, and went off to find the bread, to make toast, reliable toast.

~ ~ ~

In the true morning, the circus woke up. I had reached some peace in that stretch between waking and morning, between dawn and now. I felt as if a tiny callus had formed, something rough and trustworthy covering what needed to be kept quiet and tucked away. I pictured it inside my body like a net or a web, keeping everything safe and possible. It was good. Firm. I could tend it and it might become impenetrable.

And I could feel the world all around me. This day would evolve until it was like all the others that stretched before me. I would scoop and shovel, brush and feed. We would perform, we would entertain. And at dusk I would gather with everyone else and eat a meal prepared for the circus. Hugo Genersh would be there, spreading his light. And Lily VonGert. And Mina and Victor and Elaine and Sam. Everyone would be there and we would feel like part of something larger than us. But we would each be alone inside our own skin.

The fat girl joined me on the step. Inside the trailer Wilma slept the hard uneasy sleep of one who dreams with whiskey. "We have a ways to go," the fat girl said. "But we've done all right so far."

I didn't answer, but I agreed. I didn't have to say anything. The fat girl knew it all, everything that happened and everything there was.

"You're going to leave someday," I said softly.

"We have a ways to go."

I nodded. In the distance Benny was trailed by five little figures, each with a red ball. We could hear the midway opening for business. Somewhere, I knew, people swung through the air, practicing for the evening show, for the spin and the plummet. For the act that would make the audience gasp.

I sipped my coffee, content to be alive. Content, for now, to be a part of something.

FIFTEEN

Aɴᴅ then days turned into weeks, which gathered into months, and I learned more about the world. I learned that in Springfield, Massachusetts, the land sloped gently. That in Montana the sky was enough to swallow you whole, but the people laughed with their heads thrown back and their mouths open, willing and grateful. In Iowa they were somewhat suspicious, but many saw the show twice. In St. Louis they didn't come at all, thrusting Elaine into the worst of spirits. We all felt her grim desperation in our bones. In Youngstown, Ohio, they came but they were drunk. In Morgantown, West Virginia, they circled us like prey, then entered the gates and were delighted.

I learned that in each town, each city, we were the same and they were different. Until the lights came up, until Ken Sparks, the ringmaster, began his trembling *Ladies and gentlemen!* Until the clowns tumbled out of their tiny car and the Genershes flipped from each other's shoulders high up on the wire. Until Roscoe Kryzyzewski flew from the cannon and Rapunzel Finelli spun from her hair. Until Bluebell and Olivia stood on their hind legs, one foot each balanced above delicate things—a china tea set, a balloon, a lone kitten—and didn't crush them.

But the final symbiosis belonged to Mina the Ballerina. When she ascended, fathers and mothers, sons and daughters, church groups and first dates, school classes, foster homes, and orphanages—the entire tent full of people breathed together and leaned forward in their seats. As Mina swooped and spun, whirled and then pretended to fall, catching herself with one hand or the tops of her feet, we moved as one. We gasped, we ooohed, we aahhhed as one. We clutched each other and covered our eyes, peeking through the slits our fingers made.

Her sister and brother-in-law warmed the crowd up, but nothing competed with that moment the net was removed, when the roustabouts scurried to the tune of the ringmaster's booming voice: *"Ladies and gentlemen, at the terrifying height of almost one hundred feet above the cold hard ground, Miss Mina the Balleriiiiiiiiiiiiiina of the Air will tempt fate and embrace destiny as she dances through the heavens for your entertainment!"*

We couldn't tear ourselves away.

~~~

And in each town there were policemen who stopped by to scan the crowd or were hired to manage the audience, to keep the peace. And in each place I was afraid of being recognized and careful to keep my distance. If anyone noticed, they didn't say anything. Circus people seemed especially able to let one another harbor things. I held it all close, certain that I could be undone quite quickly if I wasn't careful. But I became more and more comfortable with myself, as Annabelle. Gleryton began to feel like a movie I'd seen, a book I'd read. A sad story about some girl I'd barely known, some scared little girl who couldn't take care of herself. And I wasn't like that at all.

~~~

By then I had come to know everyone better. Even Wilma, still as secretive as ever. I came to know that she was complicated, fickle. That she was prone to fits of sleeplessness, that she resented the life as much as she clung to it. That she preferred to live far away, alone in her own mind.

Somewhere along the way she and Jim reconciled. One evening I came back to the trailer and he was there, his arms around her waist, their sudden silence a signal to grab what I came for and get out.

But the best thing, the most surprising thing, was that Rod Genersh and I became cautious friends. He liked to visit Bluebell and Olivia and the horses, and could explain things to me without making me feel foolish. He told me his mother had been a trick rider when she met his father and it was something that he missed, watching her gentle way with horses. She rarely rode once she'd learned the high wire, but in every show they'd been with she'd visited the horses and brought them apples, as he did now.

I enjoyed Rod's quiet company. I liked having him around and I'd begun to trust him. He didn't ask questions, he didn't invite the condemnation of the fat girl, and his presence was comfortable, easy. Hugo's light still lured me, but I'd quickly given up hope for any sort of heart-pounding attention from him.

I learned to live in the present, which meant shoveling shit and riding out the minidramas and scandals that were always erupting on a circus lot. It meant watching allegiances and working hard. And it meant keeping myself beyond scrutiny. I learned to keep Gleryton and all its secrets locked away.

Whatever vague notions I'd had about going to find Charlie, about trying to help him, dissipated slowly until they were gone. When I thought of him, it was as part of everything else I'd lost or left behind. It was as a piece of my former life. But I no longer thought of him often.

And then one day I was wheeling elephant shit down a hill towards a gully in rural Ohio, and the landscape was wide and clean and open and I felt, deep down, that things were about to be different.

I had this nagging feeling all day long; I couldn't put my finger on it, couldn't say exactly what I meant, just that I was sure. Change was coming. Or something was.

~~~

Once, in Phoenix, the fat girl suggested I introduce myself to the aerialists, but I was too shy to speak to them.

"Oh please," I'd said to her. "How am I going to do that?"

We were alone in the trailer in the early evening. It was a night off for everyone and the dry heat had left me sapped and too thirsty to do much of anything. I'd seen Wilma head for Jim's place. The fat girl had seized the opportunity to try on wigs.

"You just say hello, tell Mina you like her act." She flipped strands of long yellow hair over one shoulder. "How does this look?"

"I can't just say that. I can't just walk up to her and say that."

"I'm sure know who you are already. It's just a formality." She gave me a measured, pointed look. "I thought Annabelle could do anything."

But she couldn't—I hadn't been able to do it. I'd been with the show long enough to understand the circus hierarchy a little. As Benny had said one night: *The closer to God they are in the rafters, the more snobbish they are to us mere mortals.* Which seemed to be true of everyone but Rod.

I felt ridiculous, as though even talking to them, even saying hello to

Mina, would reveal everything about me. Instead I watched the aerialists stretching out near their trailer or securing their rigging in the big top, and tried to seem cool.

~~~

And then it was late spring and we were set up in a picnic grounds near Scranton, Pennsylvania. I still had the strange tingling sensation deep in my blood that something was afoot, but no idea why or what. I was bone tired from the months of climbing hills with my heavy wheelbarrow, but I was also stronger now. Sometimes, alone in the trailer, I looked at myself in the mirror and tried to understand how this new body, with its new shape, belonged to me. My arms and shoulders had grown ropey with shoveling and lifting. My face was angular, my waist narrow, my legs sinewy. In Tulsa, Wilma had cut all my hair so it was very short but would grow in evenly. We'd washed it blond again, banishing the orange, and though roots had returned more than once, I had come to appreciate this spiky light version of myself, had grown used to the reflection that found me in the mirror. Now, before the show, I put on my own makeup, applied long Mylar eyelashes, and liberally sprinkled glitter. All by myself, I transformed into that sparkly creature that danced in front of the crowds. I'd even begun to like her.

And the fat girl?

The fat girl was petulant, lonely, sad. She disappeared for whole days at a time and I fell completely into the rhythm of circus life, the monotonous drudgery of it, the familiar exhaustion. I never knew what to expect when she reappeared. Sometimes she was full of kind advice. Sometimes she was angry, or in a sour, bitter mood, and wanted to make sure I understood what danger I was in.

I had pushed it all away, and she knew that.

I had packed all images of Tony Giobambera and the others into a small room with a door, which I'd shut. And except for the occasional lightning bolt of memory, I didn't think of them, or of what we'd done, and the fat girl didn't like that at all.

But we were coming full circle, slowly and surely heading back to the mid-Atlantic, to Tennessee, North Carolina, the whole route refreshing itself. It would happen, the fat girl liked to remind me. Not tomorrow, but someday: we would play Gleryton. It was only a matter of time.

~~~

In Scranton, I left the elephants and walked past the aerial encampment on my way to our trailer to change for dinner. Victor and Mina ignored me, but the other half of their team—Victor's brother, Juan, and Juan's wife, Carla—sometimes said hello. I liked watching them use the trampoline, the way they flung themselves in the air, bouncing higher and higher and higher. I liked that before trying anything they hung upside down like enormous possums from bars they set up, and I liked the easy way they had with one another.

And after watching them, and the Genershes, for so many months, I'd taught myself to do a handstand by balancing against the side of the costume trailer. It had taken a little while. At first I'd seen stars, but as I did it more often—at least several times a day—my arms had grown stronger and the stars took longer to appear. By Pennsylvania I could do it easily, keeping steady with one foot touching the trailer and the rest of me extended into the air. Sometimes, for brief moments, I could balance without the wall of the trailer, but I wanted to be able to walk on my hands, like I'd seen Jenny Genersh do, as balanced and poised as if they were feet.

Scranton was wide and green, and everyone, the entire circus—performers, roustabouts, gamers, even Wilma—was gathering in the parking lot to eat together before the evening show. Rod Genersh caught me upside down when he came to get me for dinner.

"How long have you been at that?" Rod asked me.

I kicked down and stood. "A while."

"You look pretty good." He cracked his fingers and then his neck. He didn't cover his mouth around me anymore, so every sentence had a flash of gummy pink. "What made you start doing handstands?"

"I saw Mina and . . . it's stupid."

"No it's not."

I looked up to see if he was making fun, but he didn't seem to be. "I saw them do it. I don't know. I just think their act is amazing, you know?"

He nodded, solemn. "I know."

He watched me for a minute and then crossed his arms. "The next step is push-ups," he said. "You want to build strength and balance. Do a handstand and then do push-ups upside down so you're using your body weight. That's what the aerialists do. You ought to talk to Mina."

I glanced at him, grateful my face was already red. "You can talk to her," I said. "I'm just an elephant groom."

"So, I'll introduce you," Rod said. "All that status stuff. It's such bullshit anyway. I don't care." He squared his shoulders. "You just stick with me."

I didn't know how to say anything else without betraying how much it would mean to me, so I just watched my feet carve a circle in the dirt and shrugged.

"It's like this," Rod said and popped onto his hands. He didn't need a wall to balance. He looked completely comfortable upside down, and began to rise and fall, his arms rippling with the effort of it.

"Okay, already," I said. But I was watching.

~~~

"Get some food and then we'll find Mina," Rod said. He had already heaped his plate with potato salad and pickles. It was cool out and I wished I'd tied a jacket around my waist. Most people already had food and were sitting in small groups at picnic tables or on the grass. Across from us, Grouper and a skinny pale girl stole things from each other's plates and giggled. Wilma joined us in line. Her dark hair was twisted off her neck and her glasses hung from a chain around her throat. She was flushed and giddy.

"Hi," she said. "I haven't seen you in days."

It wasn't true, but Wilma seemed given to odd exaggeration lately, so I just smiled my reply. "Hi," I said.

"Your friend is back," she said, gesturing over her shoulder.

I glanced up expecting to see the fat girl strolling down the line the wrong way, snatching potato chips off people's plates. I looked at Wilma in confusion.

"The Digestivore," she said. "And that fucked-up boyfriend of his." Wilma put a hand on her hip. "They're joining up again," she said. "Go figure. Elaine rehired them."

~~~

What to do with that? When I was little and overwhelmed, there were songs to sing or my dad's lap in which to bury my face. In the picnic line of the circus there was nothing.

"Cool," I said. Inside I was trembling.

Charlie? I froze at the thought of him screaming my real name across the parking lot. I didn't realize I had dropped my plate until I felt something cold on my shin. I was standing in potato salad. It didn't matter. I had to find Charlie before he found me.

I stepped out of line and made my way across a stretch of blacktop. Had Elaine said anything to them? Or to Sam? Had Elaine told Sam my real name? I was stopped short by the weight of one dark shiny thought.

How on earth could they recognize me?

"They won't." The fat girl had caught up. "They couldn't and they won't. But you still need to find them first."

It was as though it was the first time I'd seen her in a while. The fat girl looked haggard. Her skin, usually so pink and round, hung off her in gray lumps and sags.

"You need to be very careful, hon." Her voice was soft. I felt sorry for ignoring her so much lately, for mocking her whenever I saw her. I had the urge to take her in my arms but instead I just stood there.

"I've never trusted him," she said. "Remember that. That's all I'm asking."

I nodded.

~~~

The big top had gone up early that morning, and the other trailers and trucks were arranged accordingly. The configuration was always as close to the same as possible. In the early afternoon only the skeleton of the show had been complete, but now the encampment seemed nearly ready.

We walked away from the picnickers. The fat girl hummed something and I felt strangely calm, all my anxiety located just behind us or beside us, not inside. Then, from halfway across the field behind the Midway, I saw a battered red pickup truck connected to Marco's trailer. DIGESTIVORE!

We reached the red truck. I touched the hood, and the cold metal was soothing. I ran my hand along the side, the rusty door. Through the window I saw a pack of cigarettes on the patched seat, a gray baseball cap.

All at once I thought of the chickens on my ankle, inked for all eternity, and everything in my head whirled into a dust storm then, all noise and clutter and confusion.

The fat girl coughed. I looked up from the window. Two men were approaching. Even from a distance I recognized them. One was definitely Marco. The other was a more illustrated Charlie, something colorful swirling out of his shirt and around the front of his neck.

As they ambled up, it was my voice that called to them, though it seemed to come from someone or somewhere else. "Hey there." I cleared my throat and tried again, louder this time. "Hi, guys," I said, and they stopped in the dirt beside the trailer. "It's been a long time."

There was a flicker in Marco's eyes, but Charlie just stared blankly, which caught me off guard. I stood for a second and then knelt and untied one of my mucking boots, flicked away the remnants of potato salad, and kicked it off.

"What are you doing?" one of them said. I peeled off my dirty brown sock so the chickens faced them.

"It's me," I said. "See? It's me."

Marco glanced at Charlie, who stared at my tattoo, a look of utter bewilderment compressing his features.

"Faith," I said, and had to lick my lips. "Faith Duckle."

So much for my fears of screeched recognition. My voice wavered and scrambled up an octave. "From the restaurant," I said. "Remember? Clark's. From Gleryton."

Then Charlie nodded slowly. "Right," he said. "Wow. Faith."

Marco shook his head. "I would never have recognized you," he said. "There was something familiar, but . . ."

Charlie still stared at the tattoo and abruptly I felt self-conscious. I pulled my sock back on and bent down to retie my boot. "What the hell are you doing here?" he said.

I took a deep breath and stood up. Where to begin? "Call me Annabelle," I said. "Let's start there."

~~~

It was a long way from that conversation back to the picnic grounds. The fat girl stood back and watched. She had a bag of popcorn and a nervous expression. I looked to her for guidance but she pretended not to notice. There was nothing but sky around us. Sky and stories and lies and truth. And the entire Fartlesworth Circus, and the rest of Pennsylvania.

We walked towards the picnickers and I was so nervous I didn't know what I might do: run screaming or laugh hysterically. My hands were shaking. I shoved them deep in my pockets.

"I'm a groom," I told them. "I've been on the road for months. First I was trying to find you, Charlie." At this he looked perplexed, so I breezed on to something else. I told them about the bus rides and the truck stops. I made it all sound funny and exciting. Inside I felt like every word was sandpaper rubbing me raw, while my head chanted what he'd almost said: *what do you mean you tried to find me?* He'd nearly said it. So what would have happened if I *had* gone after him?

"Ha, ha," I said. "And then there was this time in Atlanta . . ."

My mind raced and I kept talking, words tumbling over each other to keep them entertained. I didn't matter. I saw that. I didn't matter at all.

We reached the others, people clustered and seated. "I guess we're going to grab something," Charlie said, indicating the food table. "So . . ."

"Right," I said. "Right." My face was stiff, my eyes sore from not blinking. Charlie and Marco headed for the table of food. I followed, self-conscious, my face hot, my whole world a swirl of confusion. I felt a hand on my shoulder and pivoted. It was Rod Genersh.

"Hey," he said. "Where the hell did you go?"

"Wanted to say hello." I gestured over my shoulder with a lone thumb and fist. "I know them."

"Oh." Rod followed the direction of my gesture with his eyes and nodded. "They caused a lot of trouble back in Georgia last winter," he said. "Did they tell you why Elaine rehired them?"

I shrugged and swallowed, then shook my head. "Anyway, I was looking for you," Rod said. He took my arm and pulled me towards the trees. "Come on. It's time you were introduced."

He wove me past a group of clowns and a cluster of musicians to a blanket spread on nearby grass. It was the trapeze crowd, I could tell from a distance. I could also see the enormous back of someone I recognized.

"Mina," Rod said. "This is Annabelle."

All conversation stopped. Mina turned her tiny, pointed face in my direction. Close up she was older than I'd expected.

"Charmed," she said. Her voice had a warm musical accent. I shook her hand, then Victor's. He smiled with perfect white teeth and his grip was surprisingly gentle.

"This is Juan," Victor said. "And Carla. My brother and sister-in-law." Nods all around.

"And this is Germania."

I'd only ever seen her from a distance, but when the broad back turned to me I saw that Germania Loudon's face was soft and lovely, her features somehow enormous and delicate at the same time. She had full lips and heavy dramatic eyebrows. Her hair hung in long dark ringlets around her face. She looked nothing like I'd imagined.

"Hello," she said. I shook her hand too. It was like a small pillow.

"It's so nice to meet you all." I took a deep breath. "I'm a big fan."

"Show them your handstand," Rod said. I immediately turned crimson and shook my head.

A wave of disinterest passed over all faces at once. I had disappointed them. They were all performers and I was not. I was a groom. This was it,

I realized, the one and only chance to be accepted or recognized or appreciated by these people.

Victor turned back to Mina, who was reaching for the paper plates.

"No," I said. "I mean . . ." They all looked at me again. Only Germania smiled. "I need something to balance against," I hissed to Rod.

"Use my back," he said, and pivoted.

So I did, popping onto my hands with more precision than I ever had before. Every pore in my body was awake and striving to be perfect. Once upside down, I did a push-up like I'd seen Rod do, all the while keeping one foot lightly pressed against his back, the other in the air, toes pointed. And then I kicked down.

Through my stars and dizziness I heard them clapping.

"Very nice," Victor said, and smiled. Mina nodded.

I took a bow, feeling very brave indeed.

"What's all this?" The voice came from behind me and I turned to see Elaine limping towards us. Her face was flushed and she had a crumpled pack of cigarettes in one hand.

"Annabelle was showing off her handstand," Rod said.

Elaine gave me an assessing look. "Huh," she said, like it was the tip of so many other things. "Well . . ."

Then she turned her gaze on Germania. "I've been looking for you, Gerry," she said. "Could you come by the office after we shut down tonight?"

Germania nodded. Everyone else exchanged looks. Elaine patted me on the back, and then gave us all a little wave. "Toodaloo," she sang, and limped off.

There was silence for a moment, then Germania lumbered to her feet. "Holy hell," she said. "I am not looking forward to this."

Victor and Mina nodded knowingly. Juan stared at the ground and Carla looked away. Rod, scratching his arm, seemed oblivious to everything. I saw Charlie and Marco walking away, towards the Digestivore trailer, and thought that it was quite possible I might implode. Or explode. Either way.

Instead I went to find Jim and check in with Bluebell and Olivia before the show.

~ ~ ~

"Fuck him, that he doesn't recognize you," the fat girl said as we climbed the hill towards the big top.

"You said yourself that he wouldn't," I said. "And that's pretty valid. Don't you think I look different? I mean, look at me."

She wasn't listening though. She was huffing and puffing with a cheese sandwich clenched in one fist and potato chips tumbling from her stuffed pockets. She stopped every few feet to turn around.

"I just don't think he's who you think he is," she said.

I was exhausted by every single moment of the last hour and a half. Fighting with the fat girl was almost a comfort, but not quite.

"I think he's Starling's brother," I said.

"And you think that means he owes you something?"

I stopped at that. "Where are you going with this? What's your stupid point?"

"*What's your stupid point?*" she mimicked, a hand on each of her wide hips. "I'll tell you my stupid fucking point! You did something that some people won't want to forgive. And even if you *were* justified, those people may want to find you, Faith, they may want to know where the fuck you are. They may even think you're valuable to them."

I pushed past her and stomped up the hill.

"Think about it," she called after me, but I put my hands over my ears. I watched Bluebell's tail swing in the dusk and I slammed the shutters of my mind, closing out all the noise and mess and chaos. Only Olivia and Bluebell and their piles of shit remained. They were all I could handle right now.

But that didn't stop the other stuff from coming. That didn't stop the flood of memory that washed over me as I stroked Bluebell's trunk and whispered to her. That didn't stop the images that swelled and receded as I tossed Olivia an orange.

They were clear and harsh and I wasn't asleep to push them away.

Tony Giobambera's hand splayed on the rock. Each finger outlined by gray stone. The feel of the cleaver in my hand, warm and heavy, a satisfying weight. The approach, from behind, so he couldn't see me, wouldn't see me. But where was the fat girl? It was all slow motion and silence, even the roar of the crowd around the fighting students, silence. I saw their faces, distorted. Mouths open. *Get him*, a girl screamed. *Fight fight fight*, the chant, familiar and worn. It was in my blood, it pumped through my blood. *Fight fight fight* and those fingers splayed on the rock. Those lips parted, ready. Where was the fat girl? *Right here.* I felt her and she took the knife from me. It was she who held the cleaver and she who approached him. I was behind her. *Hold him down, Faith.* Her silent voice in my head. I grabbed his arm, felt him resist.

What the hell—and his words were coins, bright against the day, flipping out of his mouth to be carried by a powerful wind.

I held his wrist and she swung.

And the blood. And the sound. And his face. How had I forgotten? The slice of his face. His howl.

His bloody gaping face.

~~~

"What are you doing, luv?"

Jim found me sitting on a bucket in front of Bluebell. He was already dressed for the show and I hadn't heard him approach, hadn't heard anything but the roar of my own mind.

"You better hop to it," he said. He snapped his fingers. "Whoohoo? Annabelle?"

I shook my head and tried to clear it of all its mess, tried to shake out the screaming and the blood. It took nearly everything in me to push it away.

But I did.

"Hi there," I said. "Daydreaming. Sorry. I'll go change."

I felt tight inside, now. But empty. What had stayed with me was this: the fat girl took the knife. The fat girl did it, after all.

~~~

The show was only half full. "Slow night," a clown whispered dejectedly as we waited en masse for our entrances. I scratched my bottom where the tulle tail bit into me, and looked around. I didn't see Rod. I didn't see the aerialists.

Rapunzel Finelli stood to my left, cursing and shifting back and forth, her hair shining an irresistible copper as she moved. Bluebell swung her trunk towards Rapunzel's hair and Rapunzel shot me a look. "Keep the fucking bull away from me," she hissed.

Easier said than done. I tried to distract Bluebell, but she was having none of it.

"Use the hook," Jim whispered.

He meant the bull hook, which was sharp and cruel and awful, but I did. I prodded her with it and she left Rapunzel alone, shifting her enormous weight from one leg to the other and back. I felt seasick, as though everything threatened to spill over and drown me.

"Hold it together, Faith." The fat girl stood beside me in full sparkly getup, no food in her worried hands. "Hold it together, and we'll be okay."

But she'd been right: we were getting closer with each mile and each passing day. Closer to a place where people knew me. And if Charlie hadn't recognized me, that didn't mean my mom wouldn't. Or did it?

Hold it together. It was all I could do.

~~~

After the show I went back to the trailer and changed. I put on a pair of overalls Wilma had given me and a long-sleeved T-shirt. Since she'd begun sleeping at Jim's, we'd grown careful with each other. This was odd, but not unmanageable. After the first month and a half I'd gotten used to the costumes swinging in the dark and no longer woke to think they were a roomful of accusatory people.

I slipped into my cowboy boots, grabbed a cigarette from Wilma's stash, and tucked it behind my ear. "You mind?" I asked.

She shook her head.

I wrapped a jacket around my waist and walked out into the evening. The midway had been shut down, but light came from lots of the trailers. I made my way up the hill towards the Digestivore.

The night was empty and enormous. Voices bounced from one place to another. I was so wound inside myself that I didn't hear anything at first, and then heard everything at once, all the voices, the creaking, the tree whispers. All the late-night sounds of the circus, which I'd come to know so well. But tonight I was separated. Now that Charlie was here I could feel the shell of Annabelle, the seams where she left off and Faith lived. I had almost forgotten what it was like to be Faith. It fucking hurt.

I crunched across gravel and grass and came around the back of Marco's trailer. His lights were off. I didn't know quite what to do with myself or why I was there. I dug my hands into my pockets and jumped up and down several times. Then I sat on a stump a few feet back and lit the cigarette and smoked it down to its last embers, each breath standing in for the way I felt, so that when I pushed the blue smoke out it took some of me with it. The night pulsed with its uneven sounds and I wondered what I wanted.

At that moment, a light went on in the trailer. I froze, then crept slowly to the window. I saw the edge of a bed with someone curled asleep in it, and the legs of someone else sitting just out of sight with his feet propped on a trunk. Everything about the trailer was different than I'd remembered: the floor was a solid color; the bed was in a slightly different place. And then I remembered that Yael had burned the other one down. Or tried to.

I stood there for what seemed like a long time. Then the figure with his feet up moved towards a lamp. When his arm extended, I saw the brass ring tattoo. It was Marco in a gray T-shirt and red polka-dot boxers, with a thick book in his hand. He stretched, turned the lamp off, and the trailer plunged into darkness again. I blinked, willing my eyes to adjust. I could see—or I imagined I could see—a figure move towards the bed and climb in, curling around the other body. Around Charlie.

I backed away from the window and returned to my stump. The world melted into silence, all of it dissolving, the laughter, the voices, the movements of all these people. There, behind Marco's trailer, I felt it as deeply as I ever had: I was alone, all by myself out here in the world. Even Fartlesworth, for all its tolerance, was just a place I was. Alone.

"You've got me," the fat girl said, appearing suddenly in that way she had.

"No," I whispered, and watched her until she began to back away. Something in me was ripping slowly. I felt the jagged little tears in the fabric that held me together.

"I'm still here," she called, farther away now. "Just so you know."

But I ignored her, staying there in the night until I felt my legs go numb and was forced to revive them by walking back to my own trailer.

~ ~ ~

At Berrybrook, Dr. Ronnynole would say, *Faith, why don't you tell me about what happened. Something happened to make you feel that life was not worth living.*

No, I thought. It wasn't just one thing. It was a buildup of things, an accretion of emptiness and humiliation. It was a general sense of worthlessness that corroded me.

But I didn't trust him to understand that.

"I guess I just felt bad," I'd say. And shrug.

Starling loved me. And that had once been enough. It had been all I had.

But someday I was going to have to pay for this awful thing I'd done. Someday I was going to have to offer up my own blood for that tongue I'd sliced into the dirt.

Why hadn't I told anyone about Homecoming? That was the question slamming me again and again. Why hadn't I just said something? Then, at least, I'd have less explaining to do.

~~~

I had to talk to Charlie. I could barely push it away enough to fall asleep. But I managed, finally, tumbling into an uneasy darkness where I had a slow vivid dream.

It was late and I was in the big top looking up. The lights were off, but a gentle haze filtered in through the tent somehow, so that everything glowed a little. Fresh sawdust was down, a show was about to happen, but the whole place was peaceful and empty.

Except for me and the fat girl.

We sat cross-legged in the center ring, facing each other.

Tick tock, she said. *Tick tock*. And then something hit her face, a drop of something, and she looked up and I followed her gaze. Hanging by his feet from Rapunzel Finelli's rigging, a man in a straitjacket struggled to free himself, and blood rained down from the place where his hands should be.

I scrambled to the edge of the ring, wiping at my face. The whole place was suddenly dark and cold and the emptiness loomed.

What did you do? the fat girl hissed. She hadn't moved. Blood dripped down her enormous cheeks, and her face contorted. She held up a stained paper towel.

Look what you did—

I woke with a start. I was in the trailer, in the latest part of night, the earliest part of morning. And this time I was alone.

I climbed down from the bed and made my way through the maze of costumes to the small table by the window, where I looked out at the sloping landscape.

Was this what Wilma had seen all those nights she'd sat here sipping whiskey? Her life rolling away like the grass and the trees.

SIXTEEN

I FOUND Charlie midmorning. Actually, he found me. I'd shoveled Bluebell and Olivia's messes and moved on to the horses. Charlie appeared as
I was grooming Dos. I had spent the entire morning alone with animals,
and his voice caught me off guard.

"Hey there," he said.

"Ah," was the best I could manage. I coughed.

"I thought I'd just come say hello again," he said. "Heh, heh."

I focused on giving Dos's coat firm, even strokes. "So, how've you
been?" I didn't look directly at him.

"All right." He stood in front of Uno and reached out to touch her nose,
but I stopped him.

"She likes a carrot or something," I said, giving him half an apple from
the snack bucket. "If she doesn't know you, she won't want you touching
her face."

He nodded and thrust the apple towards her.

"Put it flat on your palm, like this."

He followed my example, flattening his palm and holding the apple out
like an offering. Uno took it, greedily devouring the whole thing in just a
few bites, and I rubbed her neck. Charlie reached out and scratched her
forehead, then cleared his throat. "Good girl," he murmured tentatively.
He cleared his throat again. "You sure are a long way from Gleryton, huh?"

I looked up and met his eyes for the first time. They were big and sad,
and I noticed the hollows of his cheeks, the sleeplessness. I turned back to
Dos. I felt weirdly private.

"We sure are," I said softly and had the urge to bury my face in Dos's neck, something I would have done without hesitation if I was alone, but I was self-conscious. I gave her a few pats and moved over to Billy.

"Sorry I didn't recognize you. But you sure have changed."

"Sure have." It came out snappier than I'd meant. I looked up and softened my words with a smile. Charlie still looked worried, loaded down. I was abruptly aware of something large looming around us, something in the shadows that he wanted to talk about.

"And yeah, we're a long way from home," I said. "It has been a long road here, you know?"

He nodded slowly, like I'd said something enormous and meaningful. I felt my muscles tightening, felt myself coil inside, ready to spring away if need be. *Deep breath*, I told myself. This was Charlie, after all, *Charlie*. What on earth was I worried about? I began to brush Billy, who tossed her tail at me and snorted.

"So you ran away, after all."

I swallowed. "Yeah."

"Well, you said you were going to."

"Yeah."

He was quiet. He'd sat himself on an empty bucket and now he rose and shook his leg as though it had fallen asleep. He brushed his hands back and forth on his jeans, to wipe away whatever he'd planned to confess. "Well, I'm glad you're okay," he said, and started to leave.

I couldn't stand it. "I was going to find you," I called after him.

He stopped. "What do you mean?"

"I mean . . ." I swallowed. I looked at his skinny legs, his hollow chest, anything but those haunted eyes. "I was looking for you. When I left town. I thought you'd know . . . I found the circus because I thought you'd be with them. Then I heard they'd left you in Macon. I didn't know what I could do."

I felt tears about to come and did my best to shove them down. He looked at something far away and I snuck a glance at his face. He seemed ten years older than when I'd last seen him.

"Well," he said finally.

"I'm sorry," I said.

"Oh, no. It's cool," he said, but I had the sense that he wasn't even there anymore, that he'd been launched into the sky by something I'd said.

"I figured I wouldn't be much help."

"Right. Well." He shook his head and gave a short laugh. "This is a good place. Glad they took you in. Glad you're okay and everything." He turned to go.

"Thanks," I called after him. But softly, and a few moments too late.

~~~

"See, you don't trust him after all," the fat girl said when Charlie had ambled away from the makeshift paddock and I had given Billy a good rubdown. "I've told you not to all along and it's even more true now."

I didn't answer her. I didn't have anything to say. I tried to tune her out, but the fat girl did her best to make some point without saying anything that made sense.

"At first, I thought his problems would touch you," she said. "Then they didn't. Now, I have a feeling that he thinks he's left them far behind, but he hasn't and he may never. Now everything matters and he doesn't know how he's going to get through the end of this day and into the next. And if he falls . . . he's going to fall hard."

Shut up, I thought, but didn't say it. I wanted her to stop talking. To stop talking, to stop eating, to stop plundering what was inside me, but I didn't say any of that either.

"He could take you down with him, Faith."

I turned sharply at that. "It's Annabelle," I said. "Annabelle."

"No it's not," she said, her voice like a knife. "It's Faith fucking Duckle."

I wanted to walk away, but everything erupted. It was all I could do not to scream. "*He* could take me down?! I don't trust *him*?" I said. "Look who's talking! Do you think he could possibly drag me down any goddamn farther than you?!"

There were pink spots high on her cheeks. "What are you saying?"

"You know what I'm saying."

"Oh, I don't think so. I think you need to spell this out for me."

That was fine with me. I spat it. "It was you! You are responsible for all of this: for why I can't go home, for why I'm pretending to be someone else. You are responsible for everything bad, do you know that? *Everything*. You think I don't know what you did? I know! I remember."

She was silent. Her brown eyes were big and bottomless. I swallowed. My hands were shaking.

"Think about that, Faith," she said softly. "Think about what happened and what you remember. What you really remember. Don't be afraid of what you're capable of. It got you this far."

I watched her leave. Anger pulsed inside of me, but there was something else too. Fear. I felt it at the back of my neck like a cool wind.

~~~

I was in costume waiting to go on when I heard the news: Germania Loudon would be singing during the show.

"Why?" I asked Rod. He smiled and the dim light flashed over his pink gums.

"She's always wanted to," he said. "She's been asking for it forever, but Elaine would never let her. Something mysterious went down last week— I don't know what—and now she's singing. Sam's in a sweat about it, so stay out of his way. He's taking it out on everyone."

I nodded. Sam didn't even look at me these days and I'd stopped worrying about the conversation I'd tried to have with Wilma on his behalf. Everyone seemed to ignore him, and I'd come to think of myself as part of everyone. *When in Rome*, I figured, and ignored him too.

Rod stepped aside to let the Thomasettes pass. One of them had the hiccups. "Goddammit, you stop that, Marie," her sister said.

"Besides, we're moving out tonight," Rod said. "So it doesn't really matter."

I knew he meant that Elaine would be onto worrying about making our nut at the next venue in the next town. Still, I felt surrounded by confusion and change. I thought about how the midway must look right now, packed with people milling about. What was Charlie doing, I wondered.

The clowns were leaving the ring and I leaned against Bluebell's leg. Jim turned and gave me the thumbs-up and I did it back to him. Bluebell shifted and put her trunk on my shoulder, but I stood and pushed it away. She had developed a habit of pulling off my wig at the last moment— she'd done it several times by now—and then carrying it around the ring with her, a candy-pink pom-pom. "Be good, Blue," I whispered, and patted my hair with one hand and my warning with the other.

Behind me someone whistled and then stopped. "See you after the show," Rod said, and just before he turned to join his brothers and sister, whose silhouettes were unmistakable against the tent, he leaned in and kissed me on the cheek.

I raised my hand to my face and watched him go, wondering if what I thought had just happened had actually just happened. Some clowns came around the side of the big top in their little car, and then there was a terrible sound, a swelling shriek, and the enormous wail of the audience:

Rapunzel Finelli had fallen to the unforgiving sawdust floor.

Jim rushed forward, leaving me with Olivia and Bluebell. *"Oh my God! Oh my God!"* It was my voice and the others around me. Through the canvas I saw Jim and Benny hoist Rapunzel to a standing position, her head lolling to the side.

"Somebody get Elaine," I heard from behind me. And then Sam said, "There's only one thing to do and we need to do it quick."

She was dead. I could see it. She was dead, dead, dead.

They walked her towards the bleachers. Benny made her hand wave to the crowd. The audience was silently hysterical and then the band started up, a rousing beat, and the lights changed and in came that little car again, packed to the gills with distraction. The clowns tumbled out one by one and the audience seemed to breathe a collective sigh of relief. Everything was okay, everything would be okay.

I stood there shaking, holding on to Bluebell and willing Olivia to stand still. Soon Jim came and patted me on the back.

"Holy Christ. Holy Christ." He muttered to himself, shaking his arms and legs and head. He closed his eyes and opened them, then turned to me and said gently: "Show goes on, luv. You okay? You ready?"

I nodded but couldn't stop trembling. The clowns tumbled and honked their horns. They juggled and jostled and ran around the ring making the audience howl with laughter. Somewhere, Rapunzel Finelli lay still.

Jim gave the nod and Bluebell and I followed him and Olivia into the ring. The ringmaster blew his whistle and hollered his familiar intro, but *stylings of Professor Pachyderm* sounded hollow and strange. I smiled until I thought my face might crack, and then it was over. I stumbled outside and left Bluebell to Jim. I made my way over to a tree behind the tent and sat breathing in the dark, waiting for the moment to pass and the awfulness of it all to disappear.

Much later, swirling red and blue lights crept silently towards the big top. There was no need to hurry, their intended passenger wasn't going anywhere. I stopped being able to breathe and stayed in the shadows opening and closing my mouth like a fish. The fat girl was right there by my side.

"You hadn't thought this far, had you, Faith?"

I couldn't get enough air to be angry at which name she'd used. "What do you know?" I gasped. She sat cross-legged beside me with a package of spring rolls in waxy paper.

"Do you see where we are?" She swept a spring roll across the scene. I saw a policeman talking to Hugo Genersh and scooted farther into the shadows.

"You got me here," I said slowly. "In some ways I'm grateful, but . . ."

"But what?"

"I know," I said. "I know what happened that day." I waited for movement, something, but she just watched me, eyes narrow.

"You did it," I said. "It wasn't me, it was you."

Her soft mouth trembled a little. She looked away and was quiet for a while before she shook her head and spoke. "You," she said quietly. "You are so messed up."

I waited for more but that was it. She lumbered to her feet, brushing imaginary dirt off her leotard, and walked away from the lights and the madness.

I watched her go until I couldn't make anything out anymore, and then I turned back to see the ambulance depart, lights off, moving stealthily in the cover of night.

I was so tired. Everything existed only in the immediate, in the present tense: our movement from town to town, the simple procession of days, my responsibilities, everything. Nothing survived from before.

Except Charlie. Except the fat girl. Except Faith.

She was in me, clacking around, banging up against the taut walls of Annabelle and wondering when she'd be allowed to breathe again.

You are so messed up.

The fat girl's words rattled in my head, marbles on a marble floor, around and around. All I could think was: I just want to sleep. But I remembered what that used to mean to me—I had wanted to die. That seemed like another world, a lifetime away, and in a sense it was.

And in a sense it wasn't.

Starling, whispering in the night: *My brother has never known who he is. He wants to save me, but that's not enough. He's never made sense of all the options there are. I think that's what's going to do him in: all the choices.*

What were my choices? Had I made the wrong choices?

You are so messed up.

That day, that last day. Walking through the halls, people jostling one another, lockers slamming, the bell ringing and its echo carrying for whole moments after it stopped. Pushing through the double doors, outside hit by a burst of cold air, and there he was. There he was on the rock where he always sat, his smug sitting smoking self letting us admire him if that's what we wanted. Expecting it. Expecting to be admired, when at his core was a dark bubbling thing that told him to hold my arms while they came at me, over and over. *Just hold her arms.* A black viscous thing that had let him talk to me as though nothing had happened.

Walking towards him, his face so sharp against the gray stone of the building, against the red brick of the low wall, against the dull noise of everything else.

And the warm heavy cleaver, the pleasantly warm weight of the cleaver in my hand.

"Hey."

It all dissolved, and I blinked up at Wilma, standing with feet spread, snapping her fingers. "Oh," I said. "Hi there."

She pulled her glasses off and polished them against her T-shirt. "We have to pack up," she said. "Tragedy—it's really fucking awful—but the show moves anyway and I need your help."

I nodded. My head still harbored the dull roar. I shook it hard to clear it. Wilma offered me a hand. "Thanks," I said, and struggled to my feet.

I looked around at the lights and the darkness. Wilma stretched and waved me to follow her and I did.

~ ~ ~

Elmira, New York. Then Buffalo. Then Lock Haven, Pennsylvania. Then Altoona.

Then Ohio. Kentucky. West Virginia. Working our way back. Delaware. Maryland. Virginia. Tennessee. North Carolina. Gleryton.

Working my way back.

Wilma talked as we drove. Talked about how amazing Rapunzel Finelli had been when she was younger, how terrible it was that she had fallen. Talked about how much Wilma's mother had loved to watch Rapunzel spin and spin. How that was the life they led, aerialists, depending for their very existence on the security of rigging, the hold of a single bolt.

"Religious," she said. "And superstitious, absolutely, about how to do it, about only doing their own. I mean everyone rigs for himself—fathers don't trust sons. It's like that, you know?"

I nodded. I was only half listening. Part of me was there, and part of me was walking across a huge map of the United States wondering who I would be by the time we reached Gleryton, all the while trying to suppress the dull throb of that day.

The warm weight of that cleaver in my hand.

"Hungry?"

Wilma was trying to tune in the radio, banging at it and twisting its knobs, while simultaneously watching the traffic in the rearview mirror. I shook my head. In front of us the night stretched in all directions and our road split it open. The sky was a dark, backlit blue. I felt hollow inside.

"I'm thinking we stop when we hit I-88." She looked over at me. "What's wrong? Annabelle, what is wrong?"

I was crying. I couldn't stop. Tears tumbled down my cheeks.

Wilma took a deep breath and reached over to pat my knee. "I know," she said softly. "Rapunzel was a real sweetheart." Her voice broke a little. "We will all miss her. They're talking about putting together some kind of memorial service for her tomorrow night. It's amazing how much ritual helps in times like these."

An enormous wave of exhaustion passed over me. I closed my eyes, but the blackness behind them pulsed with light and I was still crying. I willed my mind to empty, thing by thing, until all I saw was a clean white space, no windows or doors or people or knives. Just clean and empty and white.

Wilma woke me in Elmira. The day was breezy and the air smelled clean. The evening's performance had been canceled. There would be a memorial service instead.

After the show loaded in and I had mucked the bulls and horses, I went looking for Charlie. Instead I ran into Rod shuffling around with a mopey face outside the Genersh trailer. "What's wrong?" I asked.

Rod shrugged and swallowed, then shrugged again. He had his hands shoved deep in his pockets, and from the little spikes of kicked dirt around his feet, I gathered he'd been there awhile.

"What's going on?"

He shrugged again and kicked the ground. This was about the kiss on my cheek he'd given me. I knew it. I knew it and I couldn't possibly deal with it right now. If I had to drag it out of him, we weren't going to talk about it.

"Don't go," he said in a tiny voice.

"What?"

He cleared his throat. "Don't go."

I took a step forwards and waited, but he didn't seem to have anything to volunteer. It was going to be a lovely day and I was already tired of it.

"Rod?"

He sighed and turned his back to me, kicking at the ground again. "Fine, just go, then," he said. "I don't care. Go do whatever you have to do."

"What is going on with you?"

He didn't answer. Any other day I would have been able to talk to him, maybe even excited to, but not today. Today I couldn't do it. I was too folded in on myself. Too full of restless, dangerous energy.

"I'll see you later," I said. "I promise. At dinner. Or at Rapunzel's thing." I turned away from his disappointment and left him there.

~~~

I trudged along the row of trailers until I came to the midway. There they were, all the signs screaming invitations to people. SEE THE WORLD'S SMALLEST TAP DANCING BROTHER AND SISTER, TINA AND TIM! GODZUKIA! HALF MAN/HALF MONSTER! I walked down the dirt center of the midway, trying to read the signs as though for the first time. PROFESSOR CHARLES C. CHARLEY'S REVOLUTIONARY TRAINED FLEA EXTRAVAGANZA!

It wasn't so hard. These were the folks I didn't know so well, what with my world limited to scoop-and-dump, scoop-and-dump, and the costume trailer. I certainly didn't know them as well as the people I saw every day. I had never really noticed that before, had never given it a second thought. But now, as I walked between the games and show tents, I thought about what little I knew of each person inside his or her trailer. The midway folks didn't hang out as much, they kept to themselves.

Take THE WORLD'S SMALLEST TAP DANCING BROTHER AND SISTER, for example. I never saw them around, but I knew Tina and Tim were actually a married couple—midgets, both—who just pretended to be brother and sister, though Tim was black and Tina was Ukrainian. And I knew that Godzukia's real name was Bill, though I'd never even talked to him. I had seen Amos Ruble, TALLEST LIVING MAN IN THE ENTIRE UNIVERSE! lumbering across various fairgrounds. He was hard to miss because he was enormous, his hands the size of giant pumpkins—and just about as graceful. In Arizona, his cat had kittens and lots of people had taken one, including Jim. That was the last I remembered anyone mentioning him.

I knew firsthand that THE AMAZING RUBBERBOY was a brat. His name was Glen Block and he spent a lot of time tagging after Jenny Genersh. Rod couldn't stand him, and I found him irritating. His mother, Gina, was a shiny, voluptuous woman who always wore tight clothes and very high heels, no matter where we set up camp. She seemed to have a crush on Mr. Genersh. On more than one occasion I'd seen her hustling over to the Genersh trailer wearing fresh lipstick and carrying baked goods. Rod told me she'd grown up in the life—her father was a famous clown and her mother had run concessions for Clyde Beatty. Someone else must have been a contortionist—maybe Glen's dad, whoever he was. But in all the time I'd been with the show, I'd never seen Glen's act.

And beyond our odd introduction so many months and months before, I hadn't run into LILY VONGERT, THE WORLD'S ONLY THREE-LEGGED BEARDED LADY much at all. I'd never seen her mysterious third leg. Sometimes I saw her reading in a folding chair by her trailer.

And at the end, just before THE DIGESTIVORE, there was GERMANIA LOUDON, THE FATTEST WOMAN ALIVE! whose kind face I'd really only met that once, at the picnic grounds in Scranton.

From the little I'd seen of the outside of her trailer, Germania Loudon's living quarters seemed pretty normal—certainly not any bigger than anyone else's. I stopped walking, checked to make sure no one was watching, then ducked my head inside her show tent and looked around.

There were two billowy yellow curtains set up, and a large, bench-like folding chair. There didn't seem to be much else there. Just the chair. When Germania Loudon stepped out of her trailer and into that tent she was The Fat Lady, but what did she *do*? Just sit and let people look at her? Was that what a fat lady was—a spectacle? Something to be stared at?

Then it washed over me how much it must have meant to her to sing in the show. It must have meant everything. I wondered if that was what Elaine had summoned her away to discuss the day of the picnic, and whether she'd ever get a chance to do it again.

"Hey."

I jumped and turned, embarrassed to be caught gawking. But it was just Charlie.

"I thought it was you," he said.

"You scared me." I laughed. It seemed silly now, all my peeking at trailers, embarrassing. I walked towards Charlie, hoping he wouldn't ask, but he did.

"Were you going to visit Gerry?"

"No." I shook my head. "Just poking around, you know? I've been with the show this long and somehow I never come down here."

"That's pretty much the way it is. Most of the show performers don't deign to walk the midway, really. Or not often." He ran his hand through his coppery hair so that it stood up on one side. I put my hands in my pockets and rocked back and forth on my heels.

"How long have you been with the show by now, anyway?"

"Since right after Christmas," I said, and remembered what it had been like not to call my mom that day, how the fat girl had whispered me away from the idea.

"That must have been pretty lonely."

I looked away. I didn't want to have that conversation. "Whatever," I said. "I've been lonelier."

He leaned against a tree and cleared his throat. "So why'd you come here anyway?" he said, indicating the big top with his thumb. "You weren't really looking for me, were you?"

I licked my lips and exhaled. "Yeah," I said. "I was looking for you. I didn't know what else to do. I thought you might know."

"What would I know?"

"Well, I . . ." I looked around. We were entirely alone. "You said to . . . Look, I did something. Like we talked about. Only—" My hand flailed around, trying to find some way to put this all into words. "And I left. Just left. You said find you. You and Marco said why not run away with the circus and—"

"I never said—Marco didn't *mean* it! You can't lay this on me—"

"I'm not laying anything on you, I just—"

"I won't take responsibility, okay? I mean, you shouldn't have—I can barely . . ." His gray eyes were wide, and his chest heaved.

"God. Whatever." I rubbed my face and took a deep breath. "It doesn't matter, does it? For Chrissake, I can take care of myself. Obviously. Obviously I have."

"Stop it."

"What?"

"Stop it!"

"Stop *what*? God! After all that's happened, it doesn't matter, okay. I'm only telling you because you fucking asked!"

I crossed my arms. We were both quiet. In the distance I heard Sam yelling at someone and the sounds of a motor turning over. I shifted my weight from one foot to the other and watched my feet crush the grass.

He took a cigarette from his shirt pocket and lit it with shaky hands, tilting his head back and blowing smoke up into the air. "You're right," he said, after a minute. "I'm sorry. You're right."

"It's okay."

"No. You didn't ask me to take care of you." He picked a piece of tobacco from his tongue and flicked it into the grass. "You haven't asked for anything, really."

I nodded. The conversation felt so messy, so tangled up. I fished around for what was underneath it all, and came up with the thing I'd always meant to tell him. Might as well lay all the cards on the table.

"Listen," I said. "About Starling. You have to know it wasn't your fault."

"What?" He spit the word.

"Starling . . . what happened. I know it always worked out in the past, but I mean, I was there. There was nothing you could have done."

"I *know* that." He stuck a finger in my face and pointed. He had gone very white and his freckles stood out like punctuation marks. "*I* know that. That's not for *you* to tell *me*."

He turned and walked a few paces and stood with his back to me. He spat on the ground and I could see his hand shaking again.

I didn't want this, it wasn't what I wanted at all. None of it, not this conversation, not any of them.

Charlie blew smoke directly above him. "You're a good kid," he said, his jaw tight. "I know that . . ." He took another drag.

Nothing was supposed to turn out this way. I tried to swallow it down, but it swelled in me, this futility, this exhaustion. I felt my cracks giving, my seams splitting, my shell getting pushed from the inside and the out. What the hell was I to do? It swelled and then it spilled over, and I began to tremble as if I were freezing.

"Charlie," I said, and my teeth chattered. "I did something awful, Charlie."

He looked at me and some of the color returned to his face.

"I did something awful," I said, and I meant *she did something*, but how could I say that? Because I knew it, I knew it. The fat girl was me, she was part of me, wasn't she? We had done it together, this thing, this awful thing. We had done it together and it couldn't be undone.

I clattered and chattered and Charlie pulled me close and hugged me. He held me tight until I stopped shaking. I cried a little, then. And I felt better.

He slung one arm over my shoulder and walked me up the path a little ways. I was embarrassed at my red eyes, at my wet face, but I was also too weary to care. I was Faith and I was Annabelle all at once.

We walked towards the big top, Charlie holding me up. I saw Rod

Genersh slumped in a chair by his trailer and when he saw us he leapt up and sank down in one smooth, sad movement. At that moment I understood exactly what he'd wanted to tell me. It was a simple thing, a pure thing, and it was only mine. Rod Genersh loved me. It was like walking or breathing, I understood it without knowing why.

But Charlie led me past all the trailers and the animal trucks and the big top. He led me out of the fence, away from the fairgrounds, away from the circus. We walked along a treed road until we came to a path and could wander off into the woods, and that's what we did.

We didn't say much as we moved through the forest. He didn't ask me any more about what I'd done. He just let me be and we walked quietly until the light was coming from behind us and then we turned around and walked back.

The circus was right where we'd left it, busy and run down, and full of stories and allegiances. I walked through the gate after Charlie and when I did, I had a weird sense of coming home.

~~~

I left Charlie to grab a jacket from my trailer before Rapunzel's memorial service. Wilma was curled up asleep when I came in. I stood and watched her for a few moments. Her cheeks were flushed and her dark hair splayed across the pale pillow. She looked peaceful and vulnerable and much younger than usual.

I cleared my throat, but that had no effect, so I sat on the edge of the bed, ducking my head a little, and gave her shoulder a gentle shake. She blinked in confusion and reached for her glasses. "It's time for the service," I said. She nodded. Her eyes were red from crying.

We entered the big top together. Almost everyone was already sitting in the first two rows around the ring. We settled in near the clowns. When I looked to the right, I saw Rod and his brothers staring straight ahead.

It was quiet except for the sounds of chairs scraping wood or the creak of the bleachers themselves and some whispering. Then Elaine took the center ring and began to speak in a loud gravelly voice. "We have gathered today to remember one of our own, the lovely and talented Rapunzel Finelli."

She looked up. "I first met Rapunzel many years ago, when Mitch and I were just dating. She'd come off a season with Ringling and was thrilled to join us on the Press and Duncan show, was always telling us stories about how much better things were. She was incredibly generous to me—it was only my second season with a show, and she really took me under her wing.

And then later—" Elaine's voice broke. She stopped and put her head in her hand. There were sniffles to my left and right. Someone blew his nose.

Elaine began talking again but I couldn't focus. I saw the empty seats and heard the roar of the show, the sound of Rapunzel Finelli's body hitting the ground. I saw Jim shaking himself all over to remove what he'd just had to do: to carry a broken woman away. I saw Bluebell tossing her tail and swinging her trunk.

"Last year, when Mitch died, Rapunzel was more than just a shoulder to lean on," Elaine said. "And I was never able to thank her enough for that. She was one of the best hair hangers in the business and we were lucky to be graced by her." Elaine turned to Steve, the tiger trainer. His groom, Creole Kevin, sat stiffly by his side. "I am so sorry for our loss, Steve. Our prayers are with you."

Steve nodded. I turned to Wilma, who was studying her hands. "Were they dating?" I whispered. "Steve and Rapunzel?"

She blinked at me. "They're married," she said.

Mina and Victor took the ring, stopping to hug Elaine as she left, and spoke, looking up while they did. Then Mr. Genersh rolled his wheelchair out and talked about his wife's fall. Everyone was crying by now, or at least a little teary, the Genershes, Jim, everyone I could see.

Except Charlie. I spotted him next to Marco, dry eyed and wistful. I stared at him and tried to get his attention but he didn't look my way. When the service ended, Wilma hugged me, firm and quick, then moved off into the crowd.

I headed for Charlie, but the fat girl tapped me on the shoulder. I ignored her. We were surrounded by people. But then she was in front of me and I stopped. She pointed and I followed her back up the bleachers. We sat.

"You are driving me crazy," I said.

"*I'm* . . . I'm driving *you* crazy?! You listen to me," she said. "You wouldn't even be here if it weren't for me."

"Right," I said. "You've made that very clear. And you know what? You know what? I don't care. I. Don't. Care."

"Oh, you don't."

"No." I sighed. "I want you to leave me alone."

"Well, wouldn't that be convenient," she said. "Wouldn't that be easy. Then you could just drift along in your little dream world, right? And where would that get you?"

"I don't care," I said. "I'm serious. I don't."

"Well, you will, you ungrateful bitch," she said. "And if you think I'm just going to prance off into the sunset after all I've done for you, you've got another think coming."

"Oh, come on," I said, but I had never seen her quite this angry. Her whole body swelled. I tried to take some of it back by reaching out to touch her, but she jerked her hand away. "How soon they forget," she said, and disappeared.

I was way up in the nosebleed seats. I looked down and saw tiny groups of people clustered together on the sawdust floor talking and hugging. I rose to leave.

"I'm not leaving you," she said from somewhere behind me.

"Okay already," I said, and made my way down.

~ ~ ~

Later I found Charlie and we lay on the ground looking at the sky and passing a cigarette back and forth. We were quiet for a while and then I asked Charlie what I'd wanted to ask him for so long.

"Do you know why Starling wanted to die?"

He took a long drag and twirled the cigarette between his fingers. He exhaled in one long rush of filmy gray. It was quiet except for us and the occasional laugh from the trailers. There was a little wind and you could hear the tent creak every once in a while. He was silent so long that I thought he hadn't heard me.

"Why did you want to die?" he said finally.

I thought about that and hunted for the real answer, my mind clean and organized. I took the cigarette from his twirling fingers and twirled it in my own, watching the smoke zig and zag, clouding the stars.

"Because there was no more light," I said, and turned to see if he understood. "You know?"

He shook his head, stretched, and leaned back on his hands. I handed him the cigarette and he freed one arm to take it and rolled over on his side, facing me. "Not exactly," he said. "But I'm sure she did."

"But she knew how much you loved her," I said. Something deep down and raw crossed his face quickly and was gone. "She knew that."

He flopped onto his back and shrugged. "If there's no light, can you feel that?" he said. "And if you can't feel it, then how can you be sure?"

I considered that for a long time. I thought about the voice telling her over and over to end it all. And I thought about that darkness, its impenetrable density, and how Starling had let light in for me.

I closed my eyes and still I saw light. I was grateful for it. I told Charlie that.

He nodded. "Me too," he said.

I thought about the fat girl then, but I didn't say anything. I didn't even know what I would have said, just that I knew she was watching from somewhere.

"Do you know why Native Americans prefer round structures?" Charlie asked. His hands were tucked under his head now and he stared at the sky above us.

"What?" I sat up on one elbow. "What did you say?"

"Do you know why Indians prefer round structures, round buildings?"

"Why?"

"There are no shadows in a round room. No corners for the spirits to hide in."

I waited for something more, but it didn't come. He just watched the sky and then closed his eyes and was quiet long enough that I thought he'd fallen asleep.

"Live a round life," he said finally, softly, eyes closed. "Live a round life and you have no place to hide from yourself and nothing to run from."

His voice was hopeful and I thought about that. A round life. "I have corners," I said.

"Yeah," he said. "I know." He opened his eyes and sighed. Then he sat up, so he was looking down at me. "Listen, there's something you need to know."

"What?"

Charlie didn't answer. I sat up so that I faced him. He pulled his knees close and rested his chin on them. I saw the dark circles under his eyes.

He gave a long low whistle and smiled nervously. "I didn't realize this was going to be so hard."

"What is it?" I said, my voice barely a whisper. My heart had begun to pound.

"I suppose you know about what happened back in Georgia?"

"You mean with Yael and the fire?"

He was staring at his lap. He gave a short laugh and plucked a few blades of grass. "There are no secrets on a back lot," he said, opening his fingers so that the grass tumbled out. "Yeah."

"Well, only some of it." I was confused now. "I mean I heard a little bit."

"Well, we're clean now, you should know that. I should have told you right off. I meant to. I came to see you that day, to do it, but then I didn't." He paused. "I don't know . . . I couldn't. But. Well, after today . . . I mean, you have taken care of yourself. You seem to be in with people. So I figured maybe you could tell them, okay? That neither of us is using and we haven't in months."

I blinked. "Using what?"

He looked up. His face was more fragile than I'd noticed before. It felt like the first time he'd looked me in the eye since Gleryton.

He took a deep breath. "Smack," he said, after a minute. "Heroin. I'd gotten into it again in Gleryton, but I'm clean now. We're clean. New leaves all around, you know. No more stealing, no more lies. I'm a new man and so is Marco."

"Oh," I said. It was the only thing in my head. I stared at the tattoos on his hands, at the one that said PRINCE and the one that said FLAME.

"Was that why Yael burned down Marco's trailer?"

Charlie's face sprang into a tight, unhappy smile. "You know," he said. "I didn't really think about how hard it was going to be to come back here. It's the only place I've ever wanted to be, but somehow I forgot completely what it was like, you know? I mean how people talk and all the bullshit—" He was ripping out clumps of grass now, tossing them in a pile beside him.

He stopped himself, and sighed. "Sorry," he said, not looking at me. "I'm not mad at you, it's just—nothing is ever as easy as it should be, you know? I mean even the simplest things end up so complicated."

He seemed to deflate then. He pulled his knees to his chest again. He looked scared. I thought of the first time I'd visited Fartlesworth, of Charlie's electric, infectious joy in the big top. How grown-up I'd thought he was then. And how at Clark's I'd believed he was the only person in the world who could see me. How I'd listened to his every word, tried to smoke like him, to move like him. How I'd thought he had all the answers.

And then I remembered him nodding off by the Dumpster.

When I looked at him now, I saw what was left: a haggard, skinny shell of a guy. A broken kid not that much older than me.

~~~

"I told you," the fat girl said.

"You told me what?" I walked slowly towards the costume trailer, my head aching with so many things. I was calm. The world had turned over and I was still standing and each day was going to follow the next. It was as simple as that.

"I told you all along you couldn't trust him and now you understand how I was trying to protect you."

I didn't answer her. I didn't look at her.

"He's a loser. He always has been."

When I reached the trailer I stopped. "Go away and leave me alone," I said, and she turned and left.

I paused at the door and listened to the laughter coming from within. I thought about walking farther. Just walking and walking and never stopping. Instead I went in.

Wilma was sitting at the table with Grouper, a bottle of whiskey between them. Jim leaned against a stack of trunks, giggling. "Hi," I said, and they all stopped as though they hadn't noticed me come in.

A look passed from Wilma to Grouper to Jim and back to Grouper. "What?" I said. "Do you want me to go?"

"No," Grouper said, as Wilma nodded.

Jim smiled and reached for the whiskey. "Here, luv," he said. "I believe my ace groom deserves a drink!"

I took the bottle and sipped from it. The taste was fire but the warmth was nice.

"Can we trust her?" Grouper asked Wilma, who gave me an assessing look, then winked at me.

"Sure."

Jim made a grand sweeping gesture with his glass. "The distinguished Mr. Grouper, here, begs the hand of a certain lady."

I must have looked confused because Wilma laughed and used her elbow to turn Grouper towards me. "Grouper's going to ask Gerry to marry him!" she said. "And it's about damn time!"

"I was going to do it after she sang," Grouper confessed, all drunken smile. "But then she didn't sing. And after today . . ." He ran his hand through his thinning hair. "I don't want to wait, really." Then he fumbled in his pocket and pulled out a ring box and shook it as if to make some point. "I think I'm ready."

At this Jim and Wilma cracked up. It was all a little much for me; my mood of equanimity had ruptured into sleepiness and confusion. I hadn't even known Grouper was dating Gerry.

I must have said it aloud, because that made Wilma and Jim laugh even harder.

"Twelve years," Grouper said softly. "I haven't always been true, I admit it. But off and on it's been twelve years."

"Drink to that!" Jim said. And the bottle was passed around again.

~ ~ ~

Later, after I'd had enough whiskey to make me tipsy, Grouper stumbled home, and Jim and Wilma stumbled off to Jim's trailer. I lay awake in the dark and listened to my thoughts running this way and that, smashing into each other. Charlie with a needle in his arm. Starling listening to God. Me on the pay phone next to one of those guys. Who had no corners? I wondered.

The fat girl stood by the foot of my bed staring at me. She looked sad and furious. I turned over and faced the wall.

Charlie hadn't really seen me, I knew now. He'd been looking elsewhere.

And then I slept. In my sleep, I walked to my old house, walked up the driveway and onto the porch, paused to touch the stone wall of the place, then tried the front door.

It was locked.

SEVENTEEN

Summer came. The crowds were bigger, the nut was good, and Elaine was in a generous mood, smiling at anyone who passed her. Rod had stopped coming by since the day he'd wanted me to stay and talk to him and I had chosen to go find Charlie instead. Ever since then, he'd hung back, kept to himself, hadn't sought me out.

And even though part of me wanted nothing more in the whole world than to go find him and take his hands and look into his eyes and figure this whole thing out together, I hadn't. I'd left him alone. I don't know whether I was more afraid that he liked me or that he didn't. But I didn't know what to do about either of those things, so, like the brave soul that I was, I avoided him.

The fat girl and I were all angles with each other. We were on speaking terms, but just barely. She didn't understand why I wanted to be left alone. Why I wanted to pretend I had no past.

But, of course, if I had no past, then there was no fat girl. And she didn't like that one bit. Gleryton was close. One day the Fartlesworth Circus would pull into town and if I wasn't with the show, where would I be? I just wasn't quite able to let myself think about it, and it was all the fat girl had on her mind.

~~~

In West Virginia, we learned there might be a hole in the schedule, and everyone started talking about driving to the Delaware shore. Even though it was a few hours away, the beach seemed worth the trip, and the excitement was contagious. I heard Stanley and the other cooks talking about it in the pie car. I heard the canvas crew talking about it. Even Wilma, who'd been strange and dreamy since reuniting with Jim, seemed to buzz with energy at the idea of lying on a sandy beach.

"Do you tan?" she asked me.

I was sitting at the table of our trailer with my morning coffee. I nodded.

"I don't," she said. "But I have a wonderful hat. Look."

I turned and she posed in a gigantic straw sombrero. I gave her the thumbs-up sign, but in reality all the talk made me homesick for something I'd lost long ago.

I hadn't been to the ocean since the summer before my dad died, when we'd rented a cottage right on the shore. My mother spent the whole vacation lying on a towel in the sand reading thick paperbacks, her body carefully lathered and lotioned. My dad ran into the waves with me, swimming out far enough that my feet couldn't touch the sandy floor. We body-surfed, letting the waves break just over our heads and carry us in. We tried racing this way, riding them over and over until my lips were blue with cold even though the day and the water were so warm.

And then we ran up for lunch, me and my dad, our appetites enormous from all the activity, and, still in our wet sandy suits, we made huge sandwiches with every crazy thing we could find: peanut butter and tomato and hot sauce and sprouts and carrot slices and potato chips. Monster sandwiches, we called them: each one a towering monster of disgusting combinations, a joke just between us. And we sat out on the deck overlooking the sea and ate them, comparing notes on the strange incompatible mixture of flavors. It was my father's favorite ritual, these crazy sandwiches, and it drove my mother insane.

"*Disgusting*," she muttered under her breath, her mouth pressed in a thin angry line. She'd never approved of such ruckus, such extremes. It bothered her in some deep and exhausting way.

So it was our secret, our ritual, to do when we'd played hard and she still slept in the sun, on the sand. To enjoy before she caught us and was annoyed.

"You don't have to go."

Wilma's voice yanked me back to the morning. "Huh?" I said.

"If it's going to make you so moody, you don't have to go. Jim and I will go without you."

"No." I tucked it all away. "No, I think it will be fun."

~~~

Later that morning, I was sitting out in the open air with Bluebell and Olivia. Jim had gone into town to run errands, and I was taking a break from my duties and spending it tossing peanuts and watching the bulls try to catch them. Olivia swatted the nuts down, then flung her trunk out to retrieve them. Bluebell sometimes caught one or two, but only when Olivia batted a nut in her direction.

Someone approached from behind. I must have heard footsteps, but they didn't register, so when I was tapped on the shoulder I jumped, sending peanuts tumbling to the ground.

"Jesus fucking Christ," I said. My heart was pounding. The bulls began to scoop the nuts and I turned to find a startled, very toothy Rod. "You scared the hell out of me."

"Sorry." Rod's hand shot up to cover his mouth, then fluttered down to rest awkwardly on his hip. He was wearing a new pair of shorts, a new blue T-shirt—I could still see the creases. He smiled at me with a full set of teeth, but his expression was less one of joy than of pain, or great humiliation.

"Wow," I said. And it was surprising. With teeth, Rod looked more like Hugo, rugged and handsome, his features evened out and normalized by the addition of what had been missing. "When did you go get teeth? They look so great. Did they hurt?"

At this, his expression relaxed somewhat, though his smile still had a stressed-out quality, as though if his mouth were eyes, they'd be weeping from trying not to blink.

"Do you like them?" I said. "Do they feel strange?"

Rod's hand shot up and fluttered down again. His tongue ran itself along the surface of his new teeth and then he looked at the ground and began kicking it with his left sneaker. "Yeah," he said to his feet.

I took a deep breath. I was nervous. Part of me wanted to tell him I'd missed him. "How've you been?" I said.

He sighed and both hands came up to gesture in air circles, but he was still staring at the ground. He shifted his weight from one leg to the other. I didn't know what I was supposed to do, but I knew I'd said the wrong thing.

Just then Bluebell let loose a huge steamy load, which tumbled to the ground with a plop. I was grateful for something to do. I walked a few feet, patted Bluebell on the belly, then picked up my shovel.

"Aw Christ," Rod said, but it was more under his breath than to me. "Annabelle?"

"What is up with you?" I didn't stop filling the wheelbarrow. I knew what was up. All the things I'd been afraid of. And now, in a secret part of my stomach, I knew which one was right.

"I thought it would be different."

"What would be?"

"I thought you might . . . I thought I would . . . I thought everything would . . ." he trailed off in silence and I stopped scooping, put my shovel down, and improvised.

"Whatever you want to tell me," I said, "maybe it should wait. Or maybe you don't need to. It's okay. Or it will be. Everything works itself out, you know? Everything works itself out and what will be will be and you shouldn't worry about it." I was reaching now, I could feel it, but I didn't know what else to do. Instinctively I felt that if he finished any one of his sentences, I might take off running.

"Your new teeth look really terrific. You look terrific. I need to wheel this stuff down to the gully before it makes me pass out. Okay?"

He nodded, one slow, shameful jerk of the neck. Then he slowly raised his head and met my gaze. I was unprepared for what I saw then, for the seriousness, the intensity of what I saw, of what he wanted, and felt.

Me. He wanted me.

I swallowed and left him there, wheeling the poo away as fast as I could. All the time mouthing it: *Oh shit, oh man, oh shit.* Those words a mantra for the near hysteria bubbling up in me.

I stopped at the gully and emptied the wheelbarrow and stood there. I tried to imagine kissing Rod, but it just made me giggle nervously. If Hugo Genersh was a spotlight, swinging his beam from one place to the next, then Rod was a lantern, still and even and low.

Still, I liked him very much. I liked his quiet company, and the way he would appear by my side and look right at me. The way he included me in things, all the while making me feel like I was just some girl. A real girl, nothing freaky, nothing gross. My heart began to thump a little faster. *Oh shit. Oh man.* I wiped my brow with the sleeve of my T-shirt. It was hot. I got a whiff of my own smell and grimaced. What was Rod thinking?

Then I saw the fat girl approaching, a bucket of strawberries swinging from her wrist. She raked berries between her teeth and tossed their green tails behind her as she walked.

"Hey there," she said. "How are you?"

I blinked. "How am I?"

"Thought I'd ask," she said, biting into the red fruit. She had pink juice dribbling down her chins. I pointed at it, then poked around in my pocket for a tissue, but there wasn't one. She wiped it off with the back of a grubby blue sleeve.

"I'm fine," I said.

"Don't kiss him," she said. "If you want my advice, that is. I mean I wouldn't."

I rolled my eyes. "Thanks."

"Things happen, is all I'm saying. And feeling sorry for someone is never a good reason to touch them."

"I don't feel sorry for him," I said. What I felt, right then, was intruded upon.

"I mean it has all kinds of connotations. And it feels different for the one *kissing* for charity, than for the one *getting kissed*."

"I don't plan to kiss Rod for charity."

"I knew you wouldn't," she said. "After all, you know what that feels like, to be the one getting touched because someone feels sorry for you. Pretty awful when you realize it, right?"

She gave me a slow, pitying smile and I was Faith again in that instant. My whole body went hot. I swallowed. It burned where Tony Giobambera's hand had traced my cheek. He had felt sorry for me. After what he did.

"You're such a bitch," I said. "I don't want to talk about this anymore."

She narrowed her eyes. With a perfect, knowing smile she let it go. "Sure, honey," she said. "Whatever you want."

I covered my ears, and then grabbed my wheelbarrow, threw the shovel in with a clang, and started back for the animals as fast as I could go, her words like little ice cubes melting down my back. I didn't look, just hoped she wouldn't follow, and was grateful, when I returned to Bluebell and Olivia, to find the three of us alone.

~ ~ ~

But I couldn't shake the feeling that I was careening towards change and there was nothing I could do. For the rest of the afternoon I had a knot under my ribs worrying that Rod would come back and try to talk to me again. That he would try and tell me how he felt or what he wanted and I would have to respond one way or another. But he didn't.

And then in the twilight, by the show tent, I saw Rod walk by with his brother James and both were laughing and Rod tossed his head back and I felt my stomach flip over. In a good way.

I swallowed and tried to ignore it, to shove it away, but I knew it was there, this flutter. This way that Rod suddenly seemed different, was different. This way that I was.

I unfolded Olivia's glittery anklets and lay them across the lawn chair. I retrieved Bluebell's ruffled neckpiece and watched the performers making their way towards us, towards the tent. How could I ignore what I'd seen in his eyes? Wasn't that sort of what I'd wanted all along?

I had a show to put on, a routine to perform. I had responsibilities and they would not go away, even if my world was turning over. Benny waved as he walked by leading Uno and Dos in full dress. I waved back. His five little dogs trailed faithfully behind. I climbed up the stepladder and threw Bluebell's neckpiece over her shoulders, so that its ties hung down to where I could reach them from the ground. I climbed down and walked under her head, keeping one hand on her rough skin. It was so thick, and yet Jim had told me that she could feel the tiniest mosquito bite her.

"Blue, we're alike, you and me," I said, and tied the strings in a bow. "Because I'm not as tough as I should be either."

~~~

I woke to the same day there always was. I made coffee. I dressed and greeted the animals. I brushed Billy and Uno and Dos until they shone. And again I waited for Rod to show up and turn everything upside down, but he didn't.

"No day at the beach," Benny said, when I was oiling the horses' tack. "Did you hear? Elaine got the Shriners to sponsor another show, so no more hole. No hole, no beach."

He looked glum. "That's too bad," I said, though I was secretly relieved.

"Tell me about it. Those goddamn Shriner shows are always packed with animal freaks."

I nodded. Benny and Jim talked about the animal rights protesters a lot. I'd seen them a few times, standing with signs about mistreated elephants and stuff. But mostly the cops we hired kept them outside the gates where they couldn't bother anyone. At the last Shriner show, three motley, livid women dressed as bandaged elephants waved identical pictures of a scalded elephant. Jim did burn Bluebell's and Olivia's hair off with a blowtorch, I knew, and I didn't see why that was really necessary, what was wrong with their hair. Still, the elephants didn't seem to object very much. When they objected to something, there was no mistaking it.

"Why would I mistreat this creature?" Jim was always saying while he stroked one of the bulls. "She's my bread and butter!"

More disconcerting to me than the protesters were the stories I'd heard associated with them. A woman had been killed by one of Steve's tigers in Sarasota when she'd tried to "liberate" the cat by crawling in its cage. At another show, a guy had been mauled trying to pet a trained bear. He'd had to climb over fences and past warning signs to do it. Then he tried to sue the show. The general consensus seemed to be that they were crazy.

"Well, I bet there'll be a good turnout," I said. Benny snorted.

"When are we going to Virginia?" I said, but Benny wasn't listening anymore. He was watching Sam approach and muttering under his breath.

When he was within shouting distance, Sam squared his shoulders and looked at me. "Mother needs you in her trailer at four-thirty," he said. "Don't be late."

"Do you know what it's about?"

He gave a long sigh and shook his head. "Annabelle. If I did know, do you really think I'd tell you?"

"Never hurts to ask," I called after him as he strutted away. Benny didn't meet my gaze. "Never hurts to ask," I said to myself, but I had a bad feeling all of a sudden. I watered the horses, then headed to the costume trailer to consult with Wilma.

~~~

I took my boots off outside the door and found Wilma on her knees, pinning a complicated yellow feather-and-sequins number on one of the Thomasettes, who introduced herself as Marie.

"I've seen you around," she said. She had a sweetness in her voice that made her sound a little stupid. Up close her body was fascinating, entirely muscled and ropey, yet still smooth and feminine. "Ow," she said, and Wilma apologized, adjusting whatever had poked her.

"I love your act!" I said. "It's amazing how you leap on and off those horses. But won't that be hard to somersault in?"

"Thanks!" Marie looked down at the costume. "You think it'll be hard to somersault in?"

I felt Wilma's glare. "No," I said quickly. "I mean it *looks* that way, but that is the beauty of it, of all Wilma's costumes, you know? They *look* really complicated but they have this total ease of movement that is amazing . . ."

That seemed to do the trick. With relief, I drifted back to the bunk beds and climbed up on mine and waited.

"That girl," Wilma called to me as soon as the door had swung shut behind Marie, "is such a pain in the ass I can't even *tell* you."

"She seems sweet enough."

"Sure she does," Wilma threw the costume in a heap on a trunk in the corner, and sat beside it to unlace her high black combat boots. I propped myself up on one elbow to watch.

"But actually, that's her masterful trick. She's so sweet that you can't deny her anything, because you end up thinking it will destroy her, when actually she's made of granite—knows exactly what she wants and by golly she's going to have it! Doesn't budge an inch." Wilma sighed, rubbed her neck, then arched her back until it popped twice.

"I have remade that costume four times. FOUR! And we aren't talking about minor adjustments here either, I mean completely reimagined and reconstructed from scratch, an entire costume—and she isn't happy with it. Jesus!"

She crossed the room, turned off her work lights, and flopped on her bed. I leaned over the edge of the bunk and watched her eyes close.

"I'm just glad she left," Wilma said. "I thought I was going to have to kill you over that somersault comment."

"Sorry. I didn't know."

She threw a hand over her forehead and waved my apology away with the other. "I am so tired I could just cry," she said. Then she opened one eye and gave me a suspicious look. "What are you doing here, anyway?"

"Sam came by and told me to report to Elaine's trailer," I said. "Isn't that weird? I'm a little worried. Should I be worried?"

Something dark flashed across her face. She closed her eyes again and pinched her lips together. "How the hell should I know?"

"I don't know, I thought you might—that maybe you'd have an idea what it's about."

"No idea," she said.

"I hope it's nothing bad," I said. "I mean I hope I didn't do anything wrong."

Wilma didn't answer. I lay back on my own bunk. The trailer was cool and dark. In the distance I heard people's muted voices. How pleasant it would be to fall asleep. How incredibly delicious. But I had to go see Elaine at four-thirty. *Don't be late.*

"Have you and Sam ever worked that stuff out?" I asked.

"You ask too many questions," Wilma said. Her voice was firm and final. I waited a minute, then climbed down. She turned away from me and curled up.

I shut the door quietly behind me.

~ ~ ~

I returned to shoveling the elephantine mess with a strange balloon in my stomach. Why the hell did Elaine want to see me? When I could stand it no longer, I made my way to the stone benches by the outskirts of the aerial encampment, and there I smoked a cigarette and let my mind imagine the worst:

Elaine knows what I did and plans to turn me over to the police. She's seen a warrant for my arrest. She's been contacted by a private investigator hired by the Giobambera family and is turning me in for a handsome reward.

That's ridiculous, I told myself, but I had broken out in a thin sweat just thinking about it. What if they were there waiting for me at four-thirty? This could very well be it—I would be sent back to Gleryton in a police car.

I shook my head to expel the thought, but my hands had gone all clammy. For the first time it occurred to me that I was a *criminal.* I committed a crime. I had done something wrong, something really wrong. And even if I was justified, would the world care? Would the police care?

I am a wanted criminal.

I took a deep breath. Live a round life. How did I live a round life with secrets like these? How could anyone?

For just a moment, I let myself imagine how good it would feel to come clean, to confess it all. I felt sick to my stomach.

"I leave you alone for two minutes," the fat girl said, plopping down beside me. "And you fall apart. What are we going to do with you?"

"You," I said. "You are not helping." And then I noticed what was in her lap. A stained paper towel wrapped around something. Something small and long.

I swallowed. "Get rid of that."

She blinked at me, all wide-eyed innocence. "What do you think it is, Faith?"

"It's Annabelle," I said through gritted teeth. "Jesus Christ, I'm sick of this."

She didn't say anything. I held my breath and made myself look down. It was my whole other life wrapped up in that paper towel. It was Homecoming and Gleryton and Berrybrook. But it wasn't really Tony Giobambera's finger. I hadn't cut off his finger. I hadn't.

"Bury it," I said.

"Is that what you want? What you really want?"

I put my head in my hands and breathed the smell of dirt and of elephants and of horses and sweat. "I know what we did," I said. "I did it. I know." I exhaled and kept myself from running or screaming or trying to strangle her. "I want it fucking behind me, okay? I want to move forward. Bury it. Please? I want you to bury it."

I raised my head and looked at her then and I grew calm. Her eyes betrayed very little, but deep inside they protected sad things that I knew all about.

"I am not going to fall apart," I said. My words were sharp and true. "I'm scared, but I'm going to be fine. You should go away."

"You going to make me?" she said, shaking her Popsicle, but I stopped her with a hand on her wrist. Something in me had loosened.

"Maybe," I said. "I bet you we won't get to Gleryton together."

"Like you know anything."

"I know that," I said with all the conviction I could muster. I didn't know it exactly, especially as I couldn't even see myself getting to Gleryton, but I wanted to believe it so much I'd said it out loud to make it true.

"Everything's changing," I said. "I feel it."

She cocked her head. I wanted her gone, with every bone in me, but I put my arm around her shoulder and guided her head to rest on mine. "You go ahead and bury that," I said. "It doesn't change anything, I promise you."

She sighed. "We'll see," she said, but with so much affection it was almost a hug. "What would you ever do without me?"

~~~

When I left that bench I had more than an hour and lots of nervous energy. I headed for the midway, going out of my way to walk by the Genersh compound, but I didn't see Rod.

The midway was bustling. People drifted from tent to tent and in the bright afternoon the colors seemed as loud as the talkers beckoning traffic with their voices. First I peeked into Professor Charles C. Charley's tent, but there weren't many people yet and I didn't feel like waiting for the flea circus. I kept going until I came to Germania Loudon's trailer, but instead of going in, I went to finally see Marco's act.

I elbowed past a man with a toddler on his shoulders, and slipped by a guy and girl holding hands, pushing my way towards the Digestivore, following the sounds of his barker: *Ladies and gentlemen, the chance of a lifetime. Step in and see this creature swallow the most dangerous items imaginable! The Digestivore performs in just seven minutes!*

I waited on line with the others to pay my three dollars, but the blond boy playing barker recognized me and waved me in.

"Have you seen Charlie?"

He shook his head but was already making change for the man behind me, so I filed in with the others—men and women and children, a small crowd of us—and stood on the grassy floor of the tent waiting to see what Marco could swallow.

Tinny music filtered through from hidden speakers. Over and over again, the barker's disembodied voice proclaimed the feats we were about to see. *Ladies and gentlemen . . .* Part of me wanted to leave while I still could, but then the lights dimmed and a hush fell. Cymbals crashed from behind the curtain, which was slowly pulled back to reveal a large, shirtless man in dark red tights standing on a makeshift stage beside a lavishly decorated trunk. He had orange-and-black lightning bolts carved into his chest and his face was painted entirely red, except for his eyes and lips, which were ringed by sparkly blue.

Not Marco. This was *the Digestivore!*

The voice of the barker announced the Digestivore's talents and with a flourish the Digestivore brandished each item to be swallowed. I watched him consume six Ping-Pong balls, a rubber snake, a wristwatch belonging to someone in the crowd, and a lightbulb. Each item went down smoothly—you could see it travel down his throat—and returned unscathed. Then he whipped out a twenty-two-inch sword and slowly thrust it down his gullet. When that was inside him to the hilt, he bent over to show us the handle.

It was impressive and disgusting all at once. I felt like I didn't have quite enough air. When he picked up an umbrella, I'd had enough. I slipped outside and walked around back.

I spotted Charlie quickly. He was shirtless and his tattoos were bright against his pale skin and the dirty white trailer. He had his tongue in the barker boy's ear, his hand moving in the barker boy's pants.

When he saw me, he sat up and withdrew his hand. The barker continued to talk into a small microphone. I stared. I could hear the movements of the crowd and see the silhouette of Marco inside, but I could no longer remember what I was doing there or why I'd come to find Charlie. The guilty, slippery look on Charlie's face washed my mind clean.

He stood and brushed at his jeans, then glanced at the startled barker boy and approached me. I took a step back without meaning to.

A pained expression crossed Charlie's face. He shrugged his shoulders as if to say *what?* then stooped to pick up a white T-shirt, which he pulled on. He took my elbow and led me away from the trailers, down a hill out of sight. We trudged in silence through tall grass. The sun was still high overhead.

"That was nothing," he said finally. I stopped walking and he did too.

"Okay," I said. But I bit my lip. I was thinking, *Poor Marco.*

"It didn't mean anything."

I was uncomfortable and couldn't stand still. "Whatever."

"So I'm guessing you heard . . . ?"

"Heard what?" I waited for him to tell me that Marco had broken his heart, that the barker boy was only comforting him, something. But then I remembered being summoned to Elaine's and my stomach knotted itself again and again until it was a small solid mass underneath my ribs. I took a deep breath. "Heard what?" I said again.

Charlie squinted at me as though trying to see if I was lying and ran fingers through his spiky hair. I shook my head to try and clear it of the image of his hand in the talker's pants behind Marco's back, but it didn't work.

"Yael . . ." he began, then stopped and licked his lips. "Let's sit down."

He settled himself in the tall grass and motioned for me to do the same. We were surrounded then. Hidden. The world disappeared in a sea of stripey greens and browns.

"She's back."

"Yael's back?"

"That's what I heard," he said. "You didn't know?"

I shook my head. "Well, you're not going to like this, then," he said. "But I heard she's coming back to work with the bulls."

If it is possible to die for a second, to have every bodily function cease operation for a second, then that is what happened to me. "Annabelle?" Charlie said.

I gasped for air and blood began to flow through my body again, but I was cold all over. That was it. I knew it. I was getting canned, wasn't I? Cast out after so many months.

"Faith?"

I looked up. "Jesus," I said. "I'm fucked."

~~~

Elaine was waiting.

I walked slowly, relieved with each step that didn't reveal a string of flashing lights. At four-thirty exactly I stood outside the long silver trailer and tried to relax. There were no cop cars, no sirens or handcuffs in sight. Just the dilapidated makeshift porch that Elaine set up in each town, and the familiar mountain of half-smoked cigarettes in a can on an overturned milk crate by her rocking chair.

I smoothed my shirt. Knocked the hay off my jeans. If she was going to fire me I might as well look decent. I ran my fingers through my hair and then I knocked.

"Come on in," she called. She was sitting at her desk with a pen tucked behind one ear. The long delicate ash of a burning cigarette poked from between her fingers. "Ah, Annabelle," she said, like I was a cool breeze or an ice cream, and not a wanted criminal.

"Hi there." I took a deep breath and laughed nervously. "So what's up?"

Elaine smiled and motioned for me to sit. Something in me had hardened. I was frozen solid inside and out. *Go ahead and hit me with it*, I thought, as I sank onto that familiar bench. *Get it over with. Come on.*

"Let me tell you a story," Elaine said, and paused to light a cigarette. "Once upon a time there was a young girl in a whole lot of trouble who came to me and asked for work. She seemed to be made of good, solid, hardworking stuff and I liked her right off, so I hired her. I turned out to be right about her: she worked her ass off for me. She was faithful and determined, an all-around good egg.

"And I asked a lot of her. I asked her to work with animals she'd never been around. I asked her to help out a costume director who is a real piece of work, and at the same time stay out of her way. I asked her to be truthful and honest, even though I *knew* she was in trouble."

Elaine paused and swept ash off the desk and into her cupped palm, then delivered it into the trash can by her feet. My mouth had gone dry. I was beginning to sweat. I tried to smile. Elaine stretched and put both hands behind her head and continued.

"She didn't let me down, this girl: she did all of these things. But then something awful happened to her. She fell in love with a smooth character, a member of our sideshow."

I shook my head. "Listen," I said. "You've got it all wrong—"

But Elaine silenced me with a wave of her hand and continued. "She fell in love with a sideshow fellow who wasn't so bad—he was a sweet guy in some ways, I guess. But what nobody knew about this guy was that he also loved another guy. And that the particular man he loved also loved drugs.

"He wasn't a nasty fellow, and lord knows he wasn't the first or last member of this show to have interests in both sexes, so who can blame him for that? But he knew this young girl loved him. Yael. It's Yael I'm talking about. He knew Yael loved him and he seemed to care for her, but somehow it slipped his mind to tell her about this boyfriend of his, this damn junkie boyfriend. Then one day this junkie joined our show . . ."

"Charlie." I was cold inside.

Elaine took a cigarette and tapped it thoughtfully on the desk. "Yes," she said. "Charlie Yates. He showed up and he threw a wrench into the lives of these two people. He showed Marco the pleasures of heroin and he drove this poor girl so mad that she tried to burn him alive."

"But you hired them back."

"I hired them back." She inhaled deeply and blew four perfect rings in my direction. Her voice had taken on an edge I didn't recognize. She stubbed out her cigarette until it was crumpled flat in the ashtray and leaned towards me, punctuating with her index finger. "You know why? Because I believe in second chances. You might say I subscribe to them, second chances. I believe people can change and I believe that people deserve to redeem themselves. Because the opportunity was never properly extended to me, I religiously extend it to others. You see where I'm going with this?"

I shook my head.

"The boys have cleaned themselves up. I have their greatest assurances that they are no longer using drugs and they understand that a second chance is a final chance. Yael has had a lot of time to think about what she did. I understand love and I understand betrayal. Love is why I am with this show. I ran away with Mitch Fartlesworth when I was nineteen and believed the world was an elastic place. I was wrong—it betrayed me, see. But that's part of who I am."

She leaned back in her chair. "Yael was a member of the Fartlesworth family and would like to be again. She was an excellent groom, very good with the elephants. She's gotten herself together and wants to rejoin the show and I think she should."

She lit a new cigarette and studied me. So this was it. My services were no longer needed. The truth of that crashed in on me from all sides and I couldn't breathe. It was worse than if a police car or handcuffs had been waiting for me. At least then I would know where I was headed. Tears welled up and I tried unsuccessfully to blink them back.

If the circus didn't need me, where was I to go?

Elaine pounded the desk with a fist and I jumped. She narrowed her eyes. "A little birdie told me that you want to learn the trapeze. Is that true?"

I stared at her. I tried to swallow the enormous lump in my throat. From somewhere I found my voice. "Yes," I said softly.

"I see." She stared at me thoughtfully. "Well, you've proven yourself to me. You've been a real trouper and there's plenty of grunt work to go around. I think you've earned a chance to try what you want. I've talked to Victor. In return for you being their pack horse—you know, loading them in and out, and whatever else they need—he and Juan and Carla are willing to train you."

All I could do was blink my confusion and say the first thing that came into my head. "Not Mina?"

Elaine laughed. "Divas don't like disciples," she said. "You'll learn that soon enough."

I didn't understand but nodded as though I did. I didn't want to do anything to screw this up. "I'm excited," I told her, and I was. The world seemed to swell with possibility. "I am going to work so hard. So very, very hard."

"Oh, I'm sure of that," Elaine said, with a wink. "I wouldn't expect anything less of you."

She swiped at the ash that had just tumbled down her outstretched leg. "Now Wilma's asked to have Yael move back in, and I know Yael will want that. She's here, right now, but she's just visiting. She flew down to plead her case. So, you'll keep working for Jim a few more weeks, staying with Wilma. Yael may come a little earlier, but she joins up with us officially . . ." Elaine began to rifle all the papers on her desk until she found a black calendar. She used her finger to find her place. "Let's see, here . . . in Raleigh, North Carolina."

Elaine closed the book. "Isn't that your home state?"

I nodded. My throat had gone dry again. It was clear to me that soon I was going to have to deal with what I'd done.

"We're going early this year. Brand-new booking with a guarantee! I revamped the whole schedule." Elaine sounded proud of herself, but I was having trouble focusing. "What town are you from again? Lumberton?"

"Gleryton," I said.

"Right. Well, your last show with the bulls will be Raleigh. You'll go to Gleryton with the aerialists. Actually, from then on you'll travel with the aerialists. Okay?"

I opened my mouth. What could I possibly say?

"Sure." We shook on it.

~~~

I walked out of Elaine's trailer dizzy and light. I sat in the rocking chair for a minute to catch my breath. It looked like there was a storm coming. I rocked back and forth, back and forth. In the span of an afternoon the entire world had shifted.

The fat girl strolled up and tried to look casual.

"Go away," I said, and walked off the porch towards the animals.

She followed me. "You're going back to Gleryton."

"I said go away."

"And I said make me."

I whirled around and we held each other back with our eyes. What I needed right now was a friend, someone to talk to. Someone I could trust. Not this.

"You can trust me," the fat girl said, and smiled.

"You know what? I can't," I said. "I can't trust anyone. I can barely even trust myself."

I walked off towards the paddock. The sky had darkened and the wind was picking up. I buried my head in Billy's neck and stroked Dos on the nose. Then I left the horses and walked away from the paddock, past Olivia and Bluebell and away from the big top. I walked until I found a good tree and then I sat with my back to it and looked out at this small, intense world where I lived and let it all wash over me:

Charlie, Marco with needles in their arms.

Charlie fooling around with the barker boy.

Wilma rolling away from me because she knew. Of course she knew.

Who was what they seemed?

Even me. I lifted the hem of my pants and untied my boots so I could see my tattoo. How did it all add up?

I picked at a rock buried in the grass beside me and looked up at the leafy roof overhead. It smelled wonderful where I was. Fresh and alive. From far off I heard someone singing and thought of Starling.

She used to sing in her sleep. She sang in a thin voice, different from her waking voice, and I didn't know the songs, but the tunes were lilting, mournful. I knew, when I lay awake listening to Starling in the night, that this was how she must have sounded as a small child.

"Do you know you sing in your sleep?" I asked her once, and she was fascinated, though I think she believed I invented it. She listened attentively as I tried to re-create her songs, but my voice was too strong, my pitch was off, the melody escaped as soon as I tried to pin it down.

"I don't know any songs," Starling told me. "I've never been able to keep tunes in my head."

"You don't even know what you know," I'd told her.

And it was true of me as well. I didn't even know what I'd known in my bones: that the fat girl was right about Charlie in some ways, as she'd been right about Tony Giobambera. My bones had known what I could and couldn't trust Charlie with all along. That Wilma didn't want to be my friend. I'd understood instinctively not to show my hand, but I still felt betrayed by them.

The wind was whipping up. It looked like we were in for a rowdy summer storm.

I leaned my head back against the tree and closed my eyes. If I was honest with myself, the only person who hadn't yet turned out to be something other than he seemed was Rod.

"And me," the fat girl said.

I began to cry. "Goddammit," I said without opening my eyes. "Goddammit, you do not count!"

"Why?" she said.

I opened my eyes, but I was heaving now. Real heavy dry sobs, from way down where they'd been waiting. "Because," I said. "You are not real. No one can see you. You don't exist."

"I do," she said. "You see me. That's all I need."

~~~

I pushed open the door of the costume trailer, without knowing what I was going to say, and found Wilma sitting at the makeup mirror staring at herself. She didn't look up.

"You knew," I said.

Wilma traced a finger along her eyebrow and watched her reflection.

"It's always surprised me to see myself in a mirror," she said, and ran the same finger along the outline of her lips. "I look so much plainer than I feel."

I saw myself reflected behind her, but after so many months and so many miles, I was no longer surprised by how I looked. I just looked like me.

I climbed up on my bunk. Tucked into the tiny space by my bed I had taped a few Polaroids. Jim had taken some of me with Bluebell and Olivia. In one I was in costume, in another I was getting hay dumped on my head when Bluebell was fooling around. Another was of me dirty and surprised, dark streaks on my cheeks and a shovel full of poo in my hands. The last was of Rod, his head thrown back, laughing by the edge of the big top, its red stripe bold against his white shirt.

One by one I pulled each of them down. This was not my home. Wilma wanted me gone, would rather live with someone else.

And I had nothing left to say to Wilma, who had traded me in after all this time together. I climbed down and stepped out into the night and didn't say good-bye. The screen door slammed behind me.

~~~

Earlier in the day, I'd seen the canvas crew checking the tent stakes and now, as I walked towards the cookhouse, I saw Sam walking around and it looked like he was checking again. Circus people are so paranoid. For a while all people could talk about was that someone had been whistling right before Rapunzel Finelli fell, and whistling backstage was considered bad luck. On the other hand they were perversely relieved, because they believed bad things happened in threes. So after the fire fiasco with Yael, Marco, and Charlie and the death of the job-in who'd tried to give Uno a blow job, Rapunzel's death had capped off the season's disasters so everyone could relax. Except, judging from Sam's little kicks and the way he was squinting, he was not relaxed.

I ate quickly. Somehow amid all the chatter and camaraderie of the trainers and grooms, I managed to hear only the silence in my own head.

Outside the Genersh trailers, James was on Luke's shoulders and Rod was supporting Hugo. They juggled bowling pins back and forth in a complicated X, and seemed unfazed by the wind. Jenny Genersh sat at a card table with her father going over something in a workbook, and was using a big jar to hold down the stray pages she'd ripped out, which ruffled in the gusty air.

I missed him. It was as simple as that. And when Rod saw me, he flushed and dropped two consecutive pins.

"What the fuck?" Luke said, and called for them to stop.

"Sorry," Rod said. Hugo suggested they all take a break, then did a back flip off Rod's shoulders. "Ow!" Rod massaged his clavicle.

Hugo ruffled Rod's hair and winked at me. James and Luke had settled themselves in the shade facing me. "Is this a bad time?" I asked Rod. He shook his head. He was still pink.

I wanted to get away from all those Genersh eyes. "Can we go for a walk?"

Rod scratched his head and nodded. He followed me for a while, behind the row of trailers, towards the woods, lagging a step back. I didn't know where to begin, or even what exactly to say, only that I needed to do something. That I couldn't trust anyone but for some reason I trusted him.

I found a good tree to lean on and stopped. "So," I said. "Um . . ."

He was staring back at the tent. I took a deep breath. "You know what?" I said. "I miss you. You know, you not coming around and all."

He crossed his arms over his gray T-shirt and looked at his elbow, my feet. I had my back against that tree but still felt like I was falling. The sky was growing dark, and I thought I felt a drop of rain. I put my hand out, but it was dry.

"Some weather, huh?"

He glanced at me and looked down again. "Yep."

If I was waiting for some sign of what I'd seen before, there wasn't even a flicker. I started to feel stupid. Maybe he'd actually stopped coming by so that he didn't have to hang out with me anymore.

I licked my lips. "So . . ." I said. "I have to move out of your sister's place."

Rod nodded.

"I mean I'm real glad to be staying, you know? Did you hear Yael's coming back? Did you hear what I'm going to do?"

Rod sighed, then rolled his eyes. "*I'm* the one who told Elaine," he said. "*I'm* the one who got her to talk to Victor and those guys in the first place."

"Oh." My mouth had gone dry. "You sound angry. Are you angry at me?"

He didn't answer at first. Then he turned and started walking back towards his family.

"Rod? What the fuck? Rod!"

He stopped and faced me. "What do you want?"

"Can we please not shout this conversation?"

"Aaaagh!" he said. He kicked at the ground. "I AM NOT ANGRY!"

"Okay. Can I come talk to you? Don't you want to talk to me?" I took a step forward and he let me walk towards him. When I was about five feet away, he put up a hand to stop me.

"What the hell is your problem?" I said.

"You are my problem!" He squeezed his whole face together. "You don't get it, do you? You don't understand."

"I don't know," I said, taking a few more steps towards him. "I mean I thought that's what I came here about. Can't we be friends again?"

"Fuck," he said, and looked me right in the eyes. His were so clear and so sad that I took a step back.

"No, Annabelle, no! I don't want to be your friend," he said. "Fuck. I mean I want to be your friend, but I don't want to be your friend, you know? To just be your friend. Fuck! Hugo was so right. I am no good at this at all."

"You're fine," I said. "I'm the one who's no good at this."

There was definite rain now, big fat glops of it, and the wind was picking up, shaking the trees. "I don't know how to be," I said. "I have no idea how to talk about anything."

"What are you talking about? You're so cool. You're always so cool. You take everything in stride, I know you."

"No I'm not."

"Yes you are."

"No I'm not."

"You are too." We were shouting now, and the rain came down in sheets. "Nothing bothers you, you're just comfortable anywhere. I've watched you."

"For fuck's sake, Rod!" I shouted. "You have no idea what you're talking about. I am the hugest dork that was ever born."

He shook his head. And then he smiled. "You're the wettest dork that was ever born."

I smiled back. "You're pretty fucking wet yourself," I said. And then I leaned forward and took his hand.

As soon as I'd done it I froze, but he grinned at me, so I didn't let go. I tried to be calm but I was acutely aware of our bodies touching. More aware of that than the rain or the wind or anything else. I couldn't breathe, couldn't move, couldn't quite understand how we'd come to be like this.

Rod looked at our hands and at me and then he pulled me to him and into a hug. At first I was completely stiff, but he whispered, right in my ear, for me to relax and when I did, it was wet and warm and felt so totally normal that I started laughing, which started him laughing. He pulled back and looked at me, and then he leaned in to kiss me, but I panicked and turned my head so that his lips grazed my cheek. My heart was pounding, but I felt light all over, and incredibly warm. He put his arm around me and we started to run through the mud. After all, it was almost showtime and neither of us was in costume.

EIGHTEEN

THE next two weeks zipped by. Wilma and I were formal with each other. When we traveled, we navigated from town to town in silence, me pointing out arrows, her acknowledging them. Luckily our jumps weren't that long.

We moved around each other in the trailer like strangers, but it bothered me less and less. Now when she did things that bugged me, I told her instead of just taking it.

"You're snoring," I said, and leaned over to kick the bed frame when she woke me at 4 A.M. by sawing away. When I came in after the show and was ready to go to sleep, I asked her to move her things off my bed instead of just doing it for her.

Somehow knowing Wilma had no interest in being my friend made it much easier to live with her. And maybe she felt guilty, or maybe she was just counting the days until I moved out, but she acted like everything was the same as always, only more distant.

Meanwhile, I was busy kissing her brother. I was so giddy about the whole thing, I didn't know quite what to do with myself. Rod and I were both so silly and shy that it almost made it possible to talk about anything.

For Rod it seemed as though he'd suddenly been given license to say whatever came into his mind, and he did. He talked about his family a lot, and about his mom's death. He told me how he dreamed of going to college and living in the same town for four years. That seemed exotic to him. And he wanted to major in something practical so he could end up with a job and a house, all of which he saw as the normal life that he'd been deprived of by the circus.

I loved to listen to him. I loved the timbre of his voice when he said my name. I was terrified, each time I saw him, by all sorts of things, not the least of which was that he would want to touch me, and that I wouldn't know how to let him without thinking of all sorts of ways I'd already been touched that I didn't want to think about anymore. I worried that there were lots of things I couldn't say, wasn't sure I wanted to. I was afraid that if I talked about anything with him, matched his openness even a little bit, it might all come tumbling out.

But somehow, when we were actually together, it all seemed easy. It was just Rod, after all. And I knew him really well.

But we were almost back where I'd come from, and one way or another, I knew at some point I'd have some explaining to do.

~~~

When we finally got to North Carolina, something in my blood relaxed. The entire state smelled like home. The crowds began to look familiar, to feel familiar. There was something in the shape of people's faces, in the way they held themselves. It was exhilarating, and it was something I needed to be wary of. If I could recognize someone, I reminded myself, someone might possibly recognize me.

~~~

One morning I showered and dressed and made my way to the bulls.

And then I saw her.

I knew in my bones it was Yael. She had dark curly hair pulled back in a loose ponytail and she wore jeans and work boots and a faded gray T-shirt. I vaguely recognized her as the girl who'd slapped Charlie back in Gleryton. A lifetime ago.

I watched Yael rub Bluebell's leg, then whisper something into her giant ear. Bluebell tossed her head, with what seemed like delight. While she was greeting Olivia, I approached. I felt nervous.

"I'm Annabelle," I said. She turned, startled, but smiled. Her eyes were big and dark and brown. Her cheeks were freckled. She didn't look much older than me.

"You scared the fuck out of me," she said. "I'm Yael. I hear I'm booting you out of house and home."

"Not really," I said, and let myself relax a little. "Well, sort of."

We laughed. Olivia reached out her trunk and poked at Yael's pants to see if she had treats.

Yael pulled out a carrot and handed it over without looking.

"So you did this for a while? The groom thing?"

"Yes." I nodded. I felt awkward. "I'm going to miss them."

"Where are you going?" Yael made a face. "I thought you were staying?"

"I am, but I'm going to be busy. I'm going to work with the aerialists."

"Fuck," she said. "I'm afraid of heights. I could never do that. That's pretty intense."

I nodded. And then I thought about what Charlie had said, about how hard it was to be back. How everybody talked and how difficult it was to return to a life you loved when you wanted to start over, and I felt a surge of protectiveness towards this total stranger who was stealing my place. Bluebell let loose a mountain of poo.

I picked up the shovel, then smiled and handed it to Yael.

"Welcome back," I said.

~~~

I stayed with Yael for most of the morning. At first I was careful not to bring up Charlie or Marco or any of it. I helped her groom and muck the horses and hose down the elephants. And then, I asked where she'd been all this time, where she'd gone after Macon.

Her cheeks grew pink but her voice didn't falter. "I went home," she said. "I called my folks from the police station and my dad came to get me."

"Where do they live?"

"Pennsylvania," she said. "Outside Philly." She sat down in the shade and helped herself to a soda from Jim's cooler. "It was really rough," she said. "I mean being back there was weird. And there was all sorts of therapy and doctors. But as soon as they let me go, I came back here. I knew I wanted to come back, you know. I just knew it."

I nodded. I had not expected such a direct answer. Bluebell plucked a mound of hay and deposited it in her big pink mouth.

"You wanna know something amazing?" Yael said. "I mean this fucking blows my mind."

She pointed at the elephants. "They chain them when they're babies, right? Trainers put a chain around their ankle and drive a stake in the ground so the baby elephant won't wander off. Then this little animal, this little elephant grows up, very slowly, into a fucking huge creature. I mean, look at her! But she grew up with that chain—not the same one, they change it every year, or whatever—always there. Always around her ankle, see. So she still thinks she can't go anywhere, that she's held to the ground, trapped against her free will. When the truth is that she's big enough now to do whatever the fuck she wants." Yael took a long drink and laughed. "Blows my mind. And you know who told me that?" She waited for an answer.

"Who?"

"My fucking shrink. You believe that?"

"Huh," I said.

"I know." She abruptly stared off in the distance and I followed her gaze. Jim was coming towards us with a large sack.

"He's the same old coot," she said softly, and stood up. Jim dumped the bag in the back of the truck and swept Yael into his arms. "Yael, darling, how the hell are you?" he said. His voice twinkled with excitement.

"God, you look like shit, Jim. What nasty crap have you been drinking?"

He tossed his head back and laughed long and loud. "Oh, I missed you, doll. I bloody missed that filthy mouth of yours! Well, we have lots of catching up to do." He dragged the lawn chairs to face each other and sat down, motioning her to sit opposite him. I chose this moment to turn and go.

"Hey, Annabelle," she called after me. "Where you off to?"

"See you later," I said. I didn't know where I was off to, just that it was time to walk away.

~~~

I looked down as I walked, and thought about my own ankles. And then I went to find the aerialists.

Their trailers were at the other end of the lot, parked in a V near some trees. A rectangular trampoline was set up nearby with a harness outfitted overhead. I walked around the trampoline, past a trapeze rigged from a metal skeleton, and towards the vortex of the two trailers. It was very still and quiet. I didn't know which one was which, but I closed my eyes and picked, then knocked.

I heard movement behind me and then the other door opened. Victor stood there naked, except for a towel around his waist that he held closed.

"Annabelle?"

I nodded.

"Yes," he said. "This right now is not the best time. Perhaps you can come back?"

I nodded again and tried to keep my eyes on his face, but his body was beautiful. I heard movement behind him and then a voice called something in Spanish and he answered her.

"I'm sorry," I said. "I thought . . ."

"No. It is okay. Perhaps you go and then afterwards you come back. Perhaps tomorrow at three o'clock?"

"Yes. Right. Yes." I backed away from the door and he smiled, then closed it.

I was restless with this time on my hands. It was an unfamiliar feeling after so many months of constant purpose. I wandered up to the main tent and entered via the audience door, walking through the unmanned concession tent with its cheap gifts for sale. It was dim inside, but when I parted the curtain and passed into the big top, there was a show light on.

In the center of the ring, Steve had two of his tigers sitting on pedestals while a third followed the crack of his whip around the ring. His left arm was bandaged. Creole Kevin crouched nearby with props. Steve called commands and the tigers obeyed. I watched for a few moments but it felt like spying. I left as quietly as I'd entered.

I blinked at the brightness outside. The afternoon stretched before me. I figured I'd better get my things and make space for Yael.

~~~

After the evening show, I walked Bluebell back to the truck and told Jim I would miss her.

"She's not going anywhere, luv," he said. "And you'll be doing the show tomorrow. When you stop working with us, you can still come by and say hello. I'm sure she'll miss you too."

I nodded but felt funny. I wanted Jim to miss me also. And Olivia. I wanted them to notice I had gone, all of them, Benny, Billy, Uno, and Dos too. I wanted to believe that I was not so easily replaced.

~~~

Rod came to walk me to my new trailer. "This is silly," I said. "It's really not that much farther and the moon is full."

"You never know," Rod said. "I'm not going to risk it. There are dangerous creatures all over a circus lot." He made a werewolf face and I laughed.

"You just want to walk me home so you can take advantage of me your-self," I said.

He nodded. "It's as good a reason as any," he said, and took my hand to swing it back and forth.

"I told you I'm from around here," I said. "Right?"

"Annabelle," Rod said. "You rarely tell me anything."

"That's so not true." But I saw that he was serious. I stopped. "You're right," I said. "I'm sorry about that."

He shrugged. "You're a woman of mystery. I'm used to it."

We began walking again. "I'm from near here," I said. "And someday I'll tell you the whole damn story."

~~~

The light was on in the yellow trailer I was to share with Lola and Lauren Turner and Tammy-Ellen-Frances Fendenberger (whom everyone called Skip). When I'd dumped my stuff earlier in the afternoon, the trailer had been empty. It was clear which bed was mine—there was only one bare bunk—but not where my few things should go, so I'd left them all piled on my bed.

Now, when I entered, Lola and Lauren were drinking beers at a small fold-down table. They were fraternal twins but shared the same ash-blond hair and overbite. They dressed alike too: pale tight jeans and halter tops or huge pastel sweatshirts. They ran the concessions and their father, Rick, was the head canvas man. Skip wasn't there.

"Hey, lady!" Lola said. "How was the show?"

I felt shy. "Good," I said. "Full. How are you guys?"

"Great," Lola said. "Lauren put your stuff in the pink locker back there."

Lauren smiled and pointed.

"Oh." I saw that my bunk had been made up, and that my things were gone. I walked back past both sets of bunk beds to where four tall school lockers lined the rear wall. Inside the pink one, my clothes hung on hooks and my backpack squatted on the top shelf. My cowboy boots were neatly arranged on the locker floor.

"Thanks a lot," I said. "That was nice of you."

"No problem," Lola said. "Lauren likes things neat, so we let her straighten up for us."

"You're sharing a bunk with Skip," Lauren said, and coughed. "She snores but you get used to it."

"I already am," I said. "So does Wilma." I stood between the beds with a hand on my pillow, and let the strangeness of this new place wash over me. I stripped off my leotard and tail and changed into a T-shirt. I washed my face and climbed into bed. I was fast asleep in moments.

~~~

I woke to the feeling that I was being watched. I sat up in bed and stopped myself just before I hit my head. The fat girl stood at the end of my bed. She put her finger to her lips.

I heard movement and turned. Victor stood by my pillow, with another dark shape behind him. "Get dressed and come with me," he said softly. "Long pants. We'll be waiting outside."

I climbed down and scrambled into a pair of jeans and a T-shirt, checking to make sure everyone else was lost in sleep.

The fat girl followed me silently.

Victor was standing outside with Carla and Juan. "So you want to be with us," he said.

I nodded. Light was just beginning to creep over the horizon, making every solid thing seem as though it wavered. "I thought Elaine talked to you," I said.

"She did," Victor said. "But you cannot believe we would train you without knowing what you are made of? A handstand does not tell us enough about you." He smiled. "We must learn for ourselves what you are made of."

Juan crossed his arms. I started to feel uneasy.

"Even if you will only be carrying the heavy things for us for the next few years, if we are to trust you then we must know you. And in our family there is only one way to know you." Carla giggled.

Victor motioned. "You will please come with us."

I followed them into the big top. Juan disappeared and flicked a series of switches and all the tent lights came on, bright and sudden. I cringed, and blinked until my eyes had adjusted. Then I saw Victor looking up and followed his gaze. Through the mess of cables and wires I could see a trapeze tied off to a platform so high up that from where I stood it was the size of a postage stamp.

Juan and Carla returned dragging a huge canvas bag. They opened it and dumped its tangled contents on the ground.

It was the net.

I looked back up at that platform and down at the net. The three of them faced me, smiling.

"We can't just take your word for being brave," Victor said, and his smile no longer looked friendly to me. "We have to see what you are able to do."

"Oh my God." The words slipped out, and I felt myself begin to sweat.

"Don't worry," Victor said. "Carla and Juan will show you how to rig the net and how to fall. If you pay attention you will not get hurt. It is very easy." He uncrossed his arms and opened them to encompass the whole tent. "You did not think you could walk into the circus and be one of us, did you? You will prove yourself."

I watched his face for any trace of humor, but he meant what he said. Juan and Carla unrolled the net and stretched it out to its full size. They attached cables to it and tightened them until the net was firmly in place, stretched about eleven feet off the ground.

"He only means to scare you a little," Carla said when she was through. Her eyes were unmistakably kind. "We start with what is easiest first."

Juan locked his fingers together to create a step, then gave Carla a boost and she climbed onto the net. "You are going to land on your back," she said. "And then you will crawl or roll to the edge of the net like this, and then bend over," she said, demonstrating. She lay on her stomach on the net and crawled to its edge, then leaned over so that only her lower half was supported, grabbed a little of the net beneath her, and flipped around so that she hung from underneath the net, about five feet from the ground. She dropped lightly to the earth and raised her hands over her head, then took a bow.

"Now you try," she said.

I swallowed. I felt a hand at my back and a gentle pressure to step forward. I looked over my shoulder and the fat girl gave me the thumbs-up.

I took a deep breath and Juan boosted me to the net, just as he had Carla. I pulled myself on but had difficulty getting a footing. Then I tried to stand and fell over.

"Did you see Carla stand?!" Victor shouted. "No! You must do exactly as her. This is practice. The true test you must do exactly also. Pay attention."

I lay on my stomach. Eleven feet looked surprisingly high from up here. *This is nothing*, I told myself. *I can do this*. I scooted forward and hung down, then reached around and let my legs flip over my head until I was hanging. I dropped to my feet with a *thud*.

It wasn't so bad at all. It was easy, just as she'd said. "Hey, that was kind of fun," I said.

Carla smiled at me. "Good," Victor said. "Now you watch."

Above us Juan was halfway up the rigging, climbing towards a second platform, slightly lower. From where we stood, this one was the size of an index card.

"You watch what he does," Victor said. "This is like the high diving board. You stand and put your arms out and then you will fall and the air will catch you. You will fall slowly and you will turn over and land on your back. It is not hard. Just keep your head slightly tucked. You will land on your back and bounce a little bit, and then someday you will be able to train with us. Do you see?"

I nodded, but it was very high. Very far away from the earth, that platform. I made my hands into fists and thought of Mina spinning and spinning. Didn't I want that?

As Juan spread his arms and jumped forward, I wasn't so sure.

He fell, feet down, for a moment and then flattened, arcing beautifully in one simple, wide rotation. The net bounced him twice, and then he flipped himself free and came to stand beside Victor. Carla was already above us.

When she reached the platform, she raised an arm to signal Victor, then she jumped. I watched as hard as I could, memorizing the way she leaned forward ever so gently, falling with her arms straight out, tucking her head and landing, to be coughed back up by the net.

"Now it is your turn," Victor said. Carla climbed down and stood by him.

"Now?" I said. All three of them nodded. "I could get really hurt doing this, couldn't I?"

"Do not worry," Victor said. "Carla is going to attach a safety wire. If it looks like you might land terribly, Juan won't let you land."

I nodded. I felt very far away from everything. If it isn't so dangerous, I thought, as I followed Carla, then why did you drag me out of bed in the middle of the night to do it?

Carla fit me with a harness that looped snugly around my legs and waist. She braced herself against me and tightened the straps, then clipped me to a thick gray cable. I followed it all the way up until it disappeared into the glare of the lights.

"You can do this," the fat girl said. "Just don't look down."

I started to climb the ladder. It was a ropey material, but the rungs were hard. I climbed with my face aimed at the rigging high above. Maybe this is a dream, I thought. But the people below me got smaller and the fear inside me grew and I was pretty sure it was all happening for real.

About halfway up I grew tired. My hands were slippery with sweat. My whole body was suddenly so weak that I almost lost my grip. I rested for a moment, but then thought of falling off the ladder with no net below to catch me, and adrenaline powered me the rest of the way.

When I came to the platform I stopped. I didn't even know how to get off the ladder and climb around the tent pole and onto the platform's surface without falling, though somehow, blindly, I managed. It was the size of a kitchen table.

And then, holding myself very steady, clutching the cables around me, I allowed myself to look down.

I couldn't breathe. Below me the net was so small, I realized I could miss it. I could sail over it and crash to the ground. Or maybe be carried by a great wind and fly through the side walls and out over the compound. The people below me were tiny, I could barely see them, but I knew they were watching, waiting to see what I'd do.

There wasn't enough air. The lack of oxygen made me dizzy. *Oh my God.* I didn't want to fall, but I felt weak. What had made me think this was my calling? This? I was a fat girl. Fat girls belonged on the earth.

"You're not fat anymore," she said. She was standing beside me with a cupcake.

"You said once a fat girl, always a fat girl."

She peeled the paper down and took a bite. "I did," she said. "But I was wrong."

"I am not this brave."

"You are. Besides"—she licked her thumb—"how else do you think you're going to get down?"

I looked behind me at the stairs and knew with great certainty that there was no way I could climb down them backwards. Not all that way.

"This is easy," the fat girl said. "Just think about how far you've come. If you can do this, what can't you do?"

"Oh God," I said, and closed my eyes.

"Really," she said. "I think this is it."

"Oh God!" I said.

And jumped.

Falling.

Falling.

It felt slower than it should have but was easier than I'd thought. I was weightless and my descent was gradual. I remembered to tuck my head. At the last minute, Juan kept me from landing, tightening the safety cable so that I jerked, rolled, and then swung, back and forth, suspended above the net.

Juan let me down gently, and I flipped my way out of the net, though my hands were shaking so badly that I almost fell. I felt like I had snorted fifty cups of coffee, like there was lightning in my blood. I stood before them, my legs shaking, my hands jerking. My whole body trembled.

Victor said something, but I couldn't listen. I looked up and saw that platform again, empty now, and noted where the Genersh high wire was. My teeth began to chatter and Carla put her arm around me.

". . . it's okay," she was saying. "This happens to many people."

That was when I noticed that I'd wet my pants.

~~~

When I woke something was different. Something had changed and it wasn't just my trailer. I'd slept late, very late. Skip was at the kitchen table watching soaps on a small black-and-white television and eating a sandwich. "Hi," I said.

She looked up and smiled. "Annabelle, right? You slept late. Welcome to the flophouse." She went back to staring at the TV. "I hear you're joining with the aerialists."

"Yeah," I said, and shook my head at the rush of memories from the night before. "I . . . I start this afternoon."

"Well, I hope you still remember to talk to us little people."

I gave a short laugh. "Right. I'll try."

She looked up again. "I mean it," she said, and I could see she did. "The farther in the air they go . . ." She gestured with her potato chip. "The smaller we seem."

"I don't think that's exactly going to be a problem," I said. I dangled my legs off the side of the bed. I didn't think I liked her very much. "I've spent the last nine months shoveling elephant shit. I'm not going to turn into a snob all of a sudden."

"Sure," she said, and shook her head knowingly.

"What do *you* do?" It came out a little harsher than I'd meant.

"The books," she said. "And I coordinate some of the publicity stuff, but mostly I'm just the little numbers gal."

"Ah." I could tell that she didn't like me. either. She returned to her show and I went back to my locker and changed into a dirty T-shirt and shorts, making a mental note to retrieve my soiled jeans from the night before, which I'd rinsed and left out back to dry. I could see through the ruffled yellow curtains that it was bright out, and looked warm.

"See you," I said.

"Right," she said, and turned up the volume.

~~~

My legs felt stiff. In front of our trailer I stretched as best I could and then I went to the cookhouse and conned Stanley into giving me a cup of coffee.

"I hear you're going to give up the shit business," he said. "Good for you!"

It was muggy and hot. The air felt like a solid thing, and the coffee didn't help much, but it cleared my head and I could think. I found some shade near the ticket wagon and sat.

I had done something amazing in the middle of the night. It seemed like a dream, but it wasn't, I knew. The jeans had been there in the morning, just where I left them, and the glass of water I'd gotten before I went to sleep at the crack of seven or so.

I had done something I was proud of, something that made me feel strong.

And then I realized what was different, what was missing. Who was missing.

I scanned the horizon but I didn't see her. And I didn't feel her either. Was it possible? I didn't feel her. For the first time in forever I felt self-contained.

And I was able to make a little sense out of stuff. And I thought about how there was something I'd been wanting to do for so long now. Something I needed to do.

I picked up a hose near the tiger truck and sprayed myself and drank as much as I could. Then I headed to the blacktop, the parking lot. There was a pay phone there, I'd seen it, and I had a phone call to make.

Enough already, I figured. *Enough already*, I said to myself as I dialed the operator and had him place the call.

Someone answered. "Collect call from Faith," the operator said. "Will you accept?"

There was a pause and I held my breath. I watched the flags on the big top wave in the breeze.

A familiar voice said, "Yes."

Then: "Where are you?!" my mother said. "Honey, sweetheart, where are you?!"

"Mom," I said. "I'm fine. I miss you. I wanted you to know I'm fine."

"I've been so scared," she said. "But I just knew you would call today. I was thinking about you all day. Tell me where you are. Where are you, sweetheart?"

"I'm okay. Don't worry. Everything is going to be okay."

"Are you coming home? Please come home."

"Oh, Mom," I said. And swallowed. "I will. At some point."

There was silence.

"Mom?"

"How could you do this to me?" she said, angry now. "What have I ever done to deserve this?"

"No," I said. "Mom, I didn't want to hurt you—"

"You didn't want to hurt me?! You didn't want to hurt me?! Well, I guess you weren't thinking of me then, were you?"

"No, I—" I felt myself growing more lost by the second. "I just wanted you to know—"

"How could you, Faith? How could you do that to that poor boy?"

"Oh . . . poor boy! Mom, that poor boy . . ." I stopped. I ran my hand through my short hair. It was all I could do to remain standing. "It's a long story, Mom," I said, my voice quivering. "I just wanted to call."

"Faith, you come—"

"I love you, Mom," I said. "Take care."

I hung up the phone and sat down on the pavement. I was rattled but I didn't cry. I was done crying for right now.

I looked around, at this craziness that was passing for my life. For a minute when I picked up the phone I had thought about going to see her. I had thought that when we pulled into town, I could take a bus through Yander and just look. Just look at how everything was exactly as I left it so long ago. And maybe I'd just wind up at my house.

I put my chin on my knees. But I wasn't going to do that. Tomorrow the circus would load out and move to Gleryton and I would go with the show. And if someone managed to notice the strong blond girl lugging equipment for the aerialists, then so be it. Whatever was going to happen would happen, but I didn't want to be afraid anymore. Let them judge me for what I did. I could pick out every one of those boys, and turn them in. Every one.

~ ~ ~

I walked, dazed, back to my trailer. I showered and changed. At three o'clock I learned how to pack the rigging and unpack it. I learned how to roll the net, how to take apart the frame of the trampoline, the skeleton of the practice trapeze. I learned how to wrap things up and unwrap them. I learned where everything was stored.

"There will be more," Victor said. "Tomorrow you will show all of this to me. And you will do some push-ups, we will train you. It takes a long time. Many years. You will not be up high again for a long time. But you will see." He patted me on the back. "It was good last night."

I ran a hand through my hair. I was exhausted. Tired in my bones and blood. "I'm going to work hard, Victor. You'll see. I just want to learn."

He nodded. "Yes," he said. He looked sad.

~~~

It was that night, my last night with the bulls, that Gerry finally sang. We all gathered because we had a show to do, but there was a feeling in the air that everyone knew something special was about to happen, and that made me think Charlie had been wrong. It wasn't that the performers wouldn't deign to walk the midway, they just didn't get around to it. I mean, look how excited they were to hear Germania Loudon perform. They seemed thrilled.

I held Bluebell and tried to keep her calm. I felt the whole world unfolding in front of me, minute by minute, and I was ready for it. I could tell she sensed something was up because she kept shifting back and forth and tossing her trunk and Olivia was doing the same in front of us. I heard Jim murmuring to her and I whispered my own things to Bluebell.

It's going to be okay, I said. *You are so beautiful. Do you know that? You are such a big lovely sweetheart, Blue. You have such a good nature. Don't let them tell you different.*

She seemed to be listening, though maybe she just liked the sound of my voice. *Never you mind*, I told her. *I won't be too far away. I'll look in on you. I'll make sure you get enough carrots, that they're treating you right. I don't want you to forget me, okay?*

I pointed at the rigging, at Mina the Ballerina's trapeze, tied back and idle, waiting for her ascent.

I'm going to do that someday, I whispered, and rubbed her enormous flap of an ear. *I'm going to climb up there and fly.*

And I knew it was true, that my words were made of stones, that they would last and I would climb them.

I'm going to fly and flip and twist, I said. *And you know what? If I fall, someone is going to catch me.*

Bluebell tossed her head and shuffled her feet. I kept a calm hand on her neck, my tail shimmering behind me. In the dark, nearby, Grouper twisted his hands. Rod blew me a kiss. The clowns were still. Amos Ruble loomed above the Genersh boys. Even Lily VonGert was there, standing by Mr. Genersh's wheelchair, with Gina Block, the rubberboy's mom, beside them.

There was a moment of silence. Even the crickets were still. We held our breath and watched her round radiant face lift to the rafters, and then the world filled with the clear, sweet, and glorious voice of Germania Loudon.

An Afterword by Michael Chabon

Only dead writers get afterwords. Among all the hateful consequences of the early death of Amanda Davis on March 14, 2003, both to those who loved and miss her and to lovers of contemporary American fiction, this particular one—the words that you are now reading—is probably the most minor. I have spent the past five months or so hating every thing, and there have been so many that have come along, or popped up, or appeared in a magazine or the day's mail, to remind me that Amanda is dead. And now here I am, creating my own black-edged reminder. I guess that it's a cliché to write "it saddens me to have to write these words," but if so, the sentiment expressed is one that I have never truly experienced in my life before now. Every word that I string along here is bringing a cliché lump to my throat and a cliché tear to my eye. Every one of them is like each day that has passed since the fourteenth of March, a wedge driven into the crack that opened that afternoon, leaving Amanda forever on her side, back there, in the world that had Amanda Davis in it. There was no place, no need, in that world, for an afterword.

My wife, Ayelet Waldman, met her before I did—roped by Amanda and her golden lasso into a friendship that while heartbreakingly brief was one of the truest and fiercest I have ever stood next to and admired—and one of the first things she told me about Amanda is, I think, the most germane to my purpose here. "I just finished her book," Ayelet said, referring to the novel that you, too, have presumably just finished reading. "She's the real thing." Or maybe what she said was, "The girl can write." I'm not sure, anymore. It's only after your friend's airplane has crashed into a mountain in North Carolina—killing her, at the age of thirty-two, along with her mother and her father, who was flying the plane—that everything she ever said to you, and everything anyone ever said to you about her, takes on the weight and shadow, the damnable *significance*, of history.

At the time all that really registered, when I heard about Amanda from Ayelet, was the rare note of true enthusiasm in the voice of my wife, who reads almost everything, and in particular everything by youthful female novelists, and in particular those novels that treat in some way damaged girls with body-image problems, of which, God knows, there have been many, with doubtless many still to come. Some of these novelists, some of whose books she admired, she had also met, and liked, as she had instantly liked Amanda. Never had she pronounced this judgment on any of them. It was obvious to her that Amanda *had the goods*—maybe that was what she told me—and then, when I read Amanda's books, it was obvious to me, too. Her sentences had the quality of laws of nature, they were at once surprising and inevitable, as if Amanda had not written so much as discovered them. As the catcher Crash Davis said to his wild and talented young pitcher, Eppie LaLoosh, "God reached down from the sky and gave you a thunderbolt for a right arm." Amanda had that kind of great stuff.

It's unfair, as well as cruel, to try to assess the overall literary merit, not to mention the prospects for future greatness, of a young woman who managed to produce (while living a life replete as a Sabatini novel with scoundrels, circus performers, sterling friendships, true love, hairbreadth escapes, jobs at once menial and strange, and years of hard rowing in the galleys of the publishing world) a single short-story collection, the remarkable *Circling the Drain*, and a lone novel. I would give a good deal of money, blood, books, or years to be able to watch as Amanda, in a picture hat, looked back from the vantage of a long and productive career to reject her first published efforts as uneven, or "only halfway there," or worst of all, as *promising*; or to see her condescend to them, cuddle them almost, as mature writers sometimes do with their early books, the way we give our old stuffed pony or elephant, with its one missing shirt-button eye, a fond squeeze before returning it to the hatbox in the attic.

At bottom of this kind of behavior on the part of old, established writers is the undeniable way in which our young selves, and the books that issued from them, invariably seem to reproach us: with the fading of our fire, the diminishment of our porousness to the world and the people in it, the compromises made, the friendships abandoned, the opportunities squandered, the loss of velocity on our fastball. But Amanda never got to live long enough to sense the presence of her fine short stories and of this stirring, charming, beautifully written novel, as any kind of a threat or reproof. She was merely, justly, proud of them. On some level that was not buried very deeply, she *knew* that she was the real thing. This is, in fact, a characteristic of writers who are (alas it is often found, as well, among those who are not). After *Wonder When You'll Miss Me*, she was going to write a historical novel about early Jewish immigrants to the South, or a creepy modern gothic, and then after that she was going to try any one of a hundred other different kinds of novels, because she felt, rightly, that with her command of the English language, and her sharp, sharp mind, and her omnivorous interests, and her understanding of human emotion and, above all, with her unstoppable, inevitable, tormenting, at times even *unwelcome* compulsion to do the work, the hard and tedious work, she could have written just about any book she damn well wanted to.

And we will never get to read any of them. This and the story collection are all that we have, and the crack in the world falls farther and farther behind us. And Amanda's there, and we're here, and I've never yet written or read a book, with or without an afterword, that could do anything at all about that.

ACKNOWLEDGMENTS

I am grateful for the invaluable assistance of the Djerassi Resident Artists Foundation, the MacDowell Colony, the Tyrone Guthrie Center, and The Writers Room.

I wish to thank Stephanie Monseau and Keith Nelson for taking me along on the Bindlestiff Family Cirkus spring 1999 tour (and Scotty the Blue Bunny, without whom I would not have survived it), and also Eoin O'Brien and Mike Finn for sharing their stories with me.

For close readings of messy drafts, thank you to Judy Budnitz, Sheilah Coleman, Colin Dickerman, Dave Eggers, Susanna Einstein, Heidi Julavits, Katie McMenamin, Elissa Schappell, and Lucy Thurber.

Gigantic thanks to Colin Dickerman and Rob Weisbach for their early enthusiasm, and to my agent, Henry Dunow, and my editor, Krista Stroever, for all of their insight and energies.

And, finally, thank you to Anthony Schneider, whose unwavering belief, support, and love has made all the difference.

SOME CIRCUS BOOKS THE AUTHOR RECOMMENDS . . .

Ballentine, Bill. *Wild Tigers and Tame Fleas.* New York: Rinehart and Co. Inc., 1958.

Bradna, Fred, and Hartzell Spence. *The Big Top.* New York: Simon and Schuster, 1952.

Chalfoun, Michelle. *Roustabout.* New York: HarperCollins, 1995.

Chipperfield, Jimmy. *My Wild Life.* New York: G. P. Putnam's Sons, 1976.

Douglas-Hamilton, Iain and Oria. *Among the Elephants.* New York: Viking Press, 1975.

Drimmer, Fredrick. *Very Special People.* New York: Amjon Publishers Inc., 1973.

Durant, John and Alice. *Pictorial History of the American Circus.* New York: A. S. Barnes and Company, 1957.

Feiler, Bruce. *Under the Big Top: A Season with the Circus.* New York: Scribner, 1995.

Mannix, Daniel P. *Memoirs of a Sword Swallower.* San Francisco: V Search Publications, 1950.

McKennon, Joe. *Horse Dung Trail: Saga of American Circus.* Florida: Carnival Publishers of Sarasota, 1975.

Norwood, Edwin P. *The Circus Menagerie.* New York: Doubleday, Doran & Co., 1929.

O'Nan, Stewart. *The Circus Fire.* New York: Doubleday, 2000.

Sloan, Mark. *Hoaxes, Humbugs and Spectacle: Astonishing Photographs of Smelt Wrestlers, Human Projectiles, Giant Hailstones, Contortionists, Elephant Impersonators, and much, much, more!* New York: Villard Books, 1995.

Wilkins, Charles. *The Circus at the Edge of the Earth: Travels with the Great Wallenda Circus.* Toronto: McClelland and Stewart, Inc., 1998.

Wykes, Alan. *Circus: An Investigation into What Makes the Sawdust Fly.* London: Jupiter Books, 1977.

And any issue of the fantastic *James Taylor's SHOCKED and AMAZED: On and Off the Midway,* which is a high-quality 'zine published by Dolphin-Moon Press and Atomic Books of Baltimore, Maryland. www.atomicbooks.com.

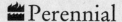 Perennial

Books by Amanda Davis:

CIRCLING THE DRAIN
Stories
ISBN 0-688-17909-6 (paperback)

Enter into the worlds of fifteen young women who, despite their vastly different circumstances, seem to negotiate an eerily similar and unavoidably dangerous emotional terrain. With a visceral bite or a surreal edge, each electrically charged story in *Circling the Drain* presents women trying to understand the nature of loss—of leaving or being left—and discovering that in the throes of feverish conflict, things are rarely what they seem.

"A well-guided tour of scarred souls who've witnessed terrible things, and surprisingly, found odd bits of beauty in them." —*New York Times Book Review*

WONDER WHEN YOU'LL MISS ME
A Novel
ISBN 0-06-053426-5 (paperback)

Follow sixteen-year-old Faith Duckle in this audacious and darkly funny tale as she moves through the difficult journey from the schoolyard to the harlequin world of the circus. *Wonder When You'll Miss Me* combines tender wit with page-turning energy and characters as original as they are memorable. By turns harrowing and poignant, lyrical and hilarious, it is a vibrant, compelling novel that explores the indelibility of high school and the smoke screens of perception and identity.

"Davis has made the modern psychological odyssey into a thrilling adventure."
—*Boston Globe*